BLASTOFF!

18 STAR-SPANNING STORIES

ROBERT JESCHONEK

Published by Blastoff Books, an imprint of Pie Press Publishing
411 Chancellor Street
Johnstown, Pennsylvania 15904
www.piepresspublishing.com

ALSO BY ROBERT JESCHONEK

WHERE NO FURRY HAS GONE BEFORE

C aptain Harmonious Curl the Big Brown Bear gazed in wonder and pity at the naked, hairless humanoid on the floor of the spacecraft's bridge, so lacking in the thick, lustrous fur that he and his team possessed.

Doctor Stripy Sinew, the Tiger of Much Hippocraticness, ran his silver handheld medical scanner over the form of the pink-skinned male on the floor. "I can tell you this much, Captain. The hairlessness is *not* a natural condition."

"Shaving, then?" said Curl. "*Forced* shaving, given all those *cuts* covering the body?"

Sinew kept watching the scanner with his big green eyes. "Something much more violent, I'm afraid. Those wounds are *bite marks* containing traces of toxic *venom*. And the other corpses we've found aboard this vessel were bitten in just the same way."

Curl shook his head. "What the hell *happened* here? There doesn't seem to be a lock of hair or patch of fur to be found *anywhere* on this ship!"

"Not to mention the 52 *dead people.*" Commander Bunny Hoppañero, big pink rabbit and first officer of Curl's crew, wasn't

1

afraid to keep the others grounded when she had to. "The *hair loss* is the *least* of it, don't you think?"

"In the distress message sent by these people, they appeared to have healthy *pelts* of fur," Curl said grimly. "By the *Cosmic Coiffure*, we *will* avenge this tragic loss of follicles."

"Loss of *life*, you mean," said Bunny.

Curl nodded forcefully. "That, too."

Bunny sighed and turned to Ensign Sipping Tenderly, a six-foot-tall sugar glider and engineering officer bent over a damaged control panel. "Any answers yet, Sip?"

"Nada." Sipping smacked the panel, which had been blasted into charred ruins by some kind of energy weapon. "Ship's logs are gone. Every log file you can think of is erased or hopelessly scrambled. I think some kind of EMP must have hit this vessel."

Just then, the team's Big Doggie, Frisky Delicato, broke in from the far side of the oblong-shaped bridge. "*Rrruff!* I think we might have *another* source of info, you furballs! Looky here!"

Curl and the others turned to see Frisky jumping up and down, panting and pointing at another naked, hairless male tucked into a compartment under a console. *This* body, however, had some *life* in it, groaning and twitching as they watched.

Sinew padded over and scanned Frisky's humanoid find without delay. "He's alive, all right, but unconscious and in shock. More of the bites, as well--and some *bigger* scars, too...possibly *self-inflicted.*" Immediately, he started medicating the man with a hypodermic from his kit. "We need to get him back to our ship ASAP to treat the shock and counteract the venom from the bites."

Curl looked around at what had once been the bright and busy nerve center of the ship. By the glow of emergency lamps, it looked like a dark and decimated ruin, scattered with hairless corpses. Every console and panel had been blasted and burned; some still sparked and smoldered. Every display screen had been shattered, and every control smashed. Then there was the blood spattered everywhere, decorating every surface with a film of crimson droplets.

What *had* happened aboard this ship? Curl shuddered as his imagination ran away with him, presenting one terrible scenario after another.

Especially the part about the involuntary pelt removal. He'd seen some awful things in his time among the stars as Captain of the *S.B.B. Furflier*, but he *never* got used to *that* kind of unnatural treatment.

Though, of course, the very fur that covered him was anything *but* natural--and the same went for every one of his shipmates.

Back aboard the *Furflier*--courtesy of the ship's quantum trebuchet telefurtation system--Curl ensured everything was in order, then retired to his quarters for a much-needed break.

He stood in front of the bathroom mirror for a moment, gazing into the dark eyes of his Big Brown Bear persona. Then, he tugged his left ear, and the bear's head split down the middle.

The two halves fell away on either side, revealing the face of the man inside the costume--pudgy and red-cheeked, with curly salt-and-pepper hair and a bushy mustache of the same extraction.

This, then, was the truth of Captain Curl and everyone aboard the *Furflier*. They were furries one and all, living their lives inside fur-covered animal costumes.

For each and every one of them, it was a *calling*. They honestly believed it was how they were meant to be--and thanks to the tech of their far-flung future era, they could *stay* that way as much as they chose to.

Gone were the discomforts and inconveniences that limited costumed furries of the past. The suits of the *Furflier*'s crew stayed the perfect temperature at all times, supplied all nutritional needs, disposed of biological waste, kept their bodies clean and sanitized, enabled their facial features and tails to move expressively, and provided excellent sensory inputs free of blind spots or other deficiencies. These suits actually bonded with the wearers at a neuro-muscular level, functioning as a kind of second skin. As for the rest of it...

Breaking character was *not* an option. As long as everyone stayed true to that edict, the suspension of disbelief was complete. Most of the time, it was like the suits were more real than the people *inside* them.

But sometimes, even a man who was *very* committed to his furry alter ego had to take off the suit for a moment.

Curl--a.k.a. Nathan Bailey, age 42--didn't often unmask. He even *slept* in the suit because he loved it so much. But after what he'd seen aboard the alien ship, he felt like he needed to catch his breath...remind himself there was someone inside the second skin.

Someone who might as well not even exist most of the time. Someone who felt himself slipping away these days, leaving not much more than a fur-covered shell.

But that was a *good* thing, wasn't it?

"They don't need *you*," he told his inner self in the mirror. "*Captain Curl* is the only one who can get them through this mission."

There wouldn't be a Captain Curl without me.

"Is that so, Nathan?" The face in the mirror was human, but the words were straight from Curl. "I wonder what they might say if they knew *who* you really were and *why* you're really *in* that suit? Would you still be a hero *then?*"

It doesn't matter. They'll never know.

"Because of the Code of Concealment? That no one on this ship is *ever* seen out of costume?" Curl chuckled. "You really think it's *impossible?*"

I've captained this ship for the past three years, and no one among my crew has ever been seen furless, least of all me.

Curl made a growling sound that turned into another cruel chuckle. "You better hope you're right, sport. Because the *instant* anyone sees you unmasked, your sorry-ass goose is *cooked.*"

Curl was back to normal when he swept out of the elevator and onto the bridge of the *Furflier*, as confident a brown-furred bear as he had ever been.

As always, the room was a hive of activity--and a showplace for the finest, furriest furnishings around. Every seat in the big, octagonal command center was lined with luxurious fur, mostly black with blond or silver highlights. Every console, control surface, wall, ceiling, and floor panel was similarly covered, though mostly in shimmering, brighter tints and animal prints.

As if it all wasn't captivating and luxurious enough, the bridge was equipped with a transformational randomizer that changed the fur's colors, patterns, and textures once every three hours. No one ever got bored on *that* bridge.

"Captain." Bunny approached, her big ears twitching as she gave him a perfunctory nod. "Still no luck with the derelict ship's records, and no additional survivors in the wreckage." She wiggled her cute little red nose. "However, we *have* found something."

How many times had Curl wondered what she looked like under her fur? "What is it? What have you found, Commander Hoppañero?"

Before Bunny could answer, Frisky bounded over between them and stole her thunder. "There's a trail! *Rrrruff!* Their nuclear pulse drive left a distinct *trail* we can follow!"

Bunny crossed her arms over her pink-furred chest and cocked her head in annoyance. "But there's no trace of the ship that attacked them, is there, Frisk?"

The Big Doggie wagged his tail vigorously. "That's right! But we can still follow the path of the *derelict* ship!"

Curl stared at the image of the wrecked ship on the big forward viewer. "So the origin point of those poor people--and, possibly, whoever or whatever tore the fur from them, is out there some-where, at the end of that path."

"Yessir yessir yessir!" Frisky spun in a circle, chasing his tail. "Probably!"

"Lieutenant Dressage!" Curl whirled and stormed over to the helmsman--a white-maned palomino with long, lustrous lashes--at her post behind the command chair.

Mariah Dressage whinnied and tossed her mane. "What'll it Captain, be?" Scrambled speech was just one of her many affectations.

"Lock onto the course of that derelict and follow it!" said Curl. "All best speed!"

"Aye, aye, sir!" Dressage smacked controls with her hoof-hands, which were covered in fine gray velvet. "All speed best, sir!"

"Excellent!" As the ship turned, and the view on the big screen spun from the derelict to a glittering, undisturbed starfield, Curl stormed toward the elevator. "Mister Bunny, you have the bridge! I need to check on the poor soul we pulled out of that hulk back there."

When the door of the Medical Center--the MedCent, for short--slid open, Curl was almost hit in the head by a flying tray of medical instruments.

As they crashed against the fur-covered wall of the hallway, Dr. Sinew's tiger roar followed (courtesy of his suit's audio modulator). Curl charged through the doorway on full alert, ready for any kind of fray.

What he saw in the room was Sinew and his panda-suited nurse, Bambooty Buddha, held at bay by the hairless survivor from the derelict. The man was wide awake now and more than a match for them, brandishing an I.V. pole like a spear from across a diagnostic bed.

But the expression on his face looked more like panic than rage to Curl.

6

"Hey!" Curl cleared his throat and stepped forward with his paws raised non-threateningly. "You're aboard the Star Braid Brotherhood Hairliner *Furflier*. I'm Harmonious Curl, captain of this ship. Whom do I have the honor of addressing?"

"Don't bother!" snapped Sinew. "He doesn't speak Fuzzish, and I couldn't get an *interpreclip* translator device on him before he flipped out on us!"

"Slowing down, Doc?" asked Curl.

"I didn't know he was coming around!" Sinew snarled in irritation, flexing the big whiskers that fanned out from his muzzle. "His vital signs just suddenly shot to waking levels, and he jumped off the bed and went berserk!"

"Knocked me against the wall." Bambooty always talked with her mouth full, perpetually chewing a bunch of mesh faux eucalyptus leaves. "Good thing MedCent's all fur-lined."

"You're just scared, aren't you?" Curl said to the patient in a calm voice. "I can't blame you, after what you've been through. Not a strand of fur left on you, you poor bare soul."

The man frowned and hesitated, then made a series of aggressive jabs with the pole, working his way around the bed.

Sinew roared again, standing his ground. "Nurse! Enough of this! Call Security!"

"Belay that!" Curl lunged forward and got hold of the pole. One good shove broke the hairless man's grip and pitched him backward, heaving him to the plush-furred floor.

In a flurry of motion, Sinew pounced tiger-style and pinned down the struggling man. "Give him 10 ccs Countsheepoxin, stat!"

Bambooty, as always, moved slowly, but eventually got the job done. Still chewing her leaves, she injected the patient in the upper arm with bright pink liquid from a hypodermic.

Curl watched as the two of them hauled the man up on the bed and strapped down his arms and legs. "How long will he be out?"

"About two hours," said Bambooty.

"And you'll set him up with an interpreclip in the meantime?"

"He'll have to be conscious for us to calibrate the syntax," said

Sinew. "Should take another three to five hours after he regains consciousness, depending on the complexity of his native tongue."

Curl nodded. "Maybe then we'll get to the bottom of the *hairtrocity* committed against the pelts of this poor devil and his crew."

"We could use some answers." Sinew pulled a scanner from the pocket of his white lab coat and played the controls with his velveteen claws. "Lab analysis indicates the bite marks resemble those left by the mandibles of an insect, but I can't be more specific at this time. The larger scars overlap those bites and resulted from repetitive self-administered jabbing and hacking motions from some kind of sharp instrument or object. As if..."

"As if he were trying to cut off whatever was biting him." Curl shook his head. "I hate to think of it."

Sinew put aside the scanner. "Did I hear we've changed course? That we're heading for wherever the derelict originated?"

"You heard correctly," said Curl.

Sinew turned his gaze to the man on the bed. "I wonder what *he* might say about that?"

"'Go faster'? 'Stop whatever did this before it hurts someone else'?"

"Would it hurt to wait and find out?" asked Sinew.

Curl snorted. "After what we saw on that derelict, I don't think we dare risk being late by even a hair."

Five years ago...

"Full stop, helmsman." Captain Nathan Bailey leaned forward in his command chair, thoughtfully stroking his jet-black mustache. A blue-green world enlarged on the viewer, gleaming in golden sunlight as it turned slowly among the stars.

"Welcome to Veridian Five." Dark-skinned and broad-shouldered, Science Officer Wade Robbins cut a towering figure in his bright yellow

8

uniform tunic and black pants. "Thriving colony of the Interstellar Entente, at least until the recent distress signal."

More like an Apocalypse signal, thought Nathan. He would never forget the screams in the background as the governor pleaded for help. "Hail the surface, Dom."

"No response, Captain," said Ensign Dominick DeGol, the communications officer of the startrotter I.E.S. Indefatigable. "Just the repeating distress call and a bunch of static."

"Life signs, Mr. Robbins?"

Wade's fingers rattled over keys as he checked the displays at his station. "Eleven thousand five hundred and twenty-seven sets of humanoid vitals, all weak--and fading."

"Then we'd better get down there." Nathan sprang from his chair and hurried for the door. "Dom, you have the bridge. Wade, you're with me. You, too, Score."

Head of Security Bethany Scorpio wheeled from her post, blonde pony-tail swinging, and fell in behind him. "Recommend every hair-trigger son of a bitch we've got for this detail, sir."

"You bring those big guns, Score," said Nathan as the door whooshed open before him. "God help us, I think we're going to need them."

It took only four hours for the *Furflier* to reach the end of the trail, all thanks to the ship's Dark Anti-Neutrino/Dark Energy Reactor (DANDER) drive. A gift from grateful aliens helped by the furries, the DANDER drive propelled the *Furflier* at amazing transluminal speeds, making the ship incredibly difficult to keep up with or track.

Not that the system was without its hitches. The dark anti-neutrinos and dark energy had some weird effects on the fur covering the crew and ship's interior. Sometimes, it made it stand on end and arc with flickering blue current; other times, it made it twist into geometric crop circles.

This time, as the ship dropped out of DANDER speed at its destination, all fur aboard her glowed and lengthened, swaying like fronds on a palm tree in a slow-motion breeze. Everyone looked around with wonder, taking in the scene with their cartoonish furry eyes--and a moment later, it all returned to normal.

Normal for a spaceship full of furries, that is.

"Tell me something." From his command chair, Curl watched the crimson orb of a red star glowing on the main viewer.

"We're in an uncharted star system," Dressage said from the helm with a toss of her white mane. "Star red, planets six, and orbital bodies various."

"Where exactly does the trail take us?"

Dressage whinnied. "Fifth from the star--a gas giant. One of its exact, to be moons."

"A moon of the gas giant, eh?" Curl had gotten so used to her scrambled speech that he instantly understood it perfectly. "The moon is habitable, then?"

Suddenly, Frisky leaped in front of him. "*Woof!* Negative, sir! All life signs are *under* the surface! Buried like *bones!*"

"And how many humanoid life signs are there?" asked Curl.

"One hundred and twenty-two!" As soon as Frisky said it, there was a loud ding from his post across the bridge. "One hundred and twenty-one!"

"So there *are* other survivors," said Curl.

"There are many *other* life signs, however," added Bunny, who was monitoring readouts from her first officer post alongside the command chair. "*Thousands* of them, all non-humanoid, distributed through a network of *tunnels* honeycombing the moon's interior."

"Put it onscreen." As soon as Curl asked, the viewer changed from a shot of the red star to the pale gray inhabited moon of the rainbow-striped gas giant. "I wonder if any of the survivors still have their hair."

"Or haven't been *mortally wounded?*" Bunny said with her usual exasperation.

Curl hit a button on the side of his chair, opening the intercom to the MedCent. "Hey, Doc. Is our friend ready to do some talking yet?"

There were angry shouts of gibberish in the background. "The interpreclip's taking longer than usual to establish a translation matrix!" said Sinew. "It doesn't seem to appreciate his syntax--and it doesn't help that *he* doesn't appreciate *our* efforts to communicate."

"Damn," said Curl. "We could sure use some tuned-in clips when we zap down to that moon. Talking to the locals would be a real plus."

"Best I can do is equip your team's clips with an incomplete translation matrix," said Sinew. "Then download an update once it's available."

"It'll have to do." Curl leaped from his chair and headed for the elevator door. "Dressage, you have the bridge. Bunny and Sipping, you're with me. Security Chief Rebound, assemble an armed detail and have them meet us in the telefurtation chamber. Doc Sinew, meet us there with the clips."

Five years ago...

"Dear God." Nathan's voice was hushed, his expression aghast as he gazed at the vast, sunbaked plain of Veridian Five. "There must be hundreds of them."

"Thousands." Wade stepped forward, holding his whirring, silver-skinned sci-probe device out in front of him. "Eleven thousand, five hundred and twenty-seven, to be exact."

"Every man, woman, and child in the colony." Nathan shook his head slowly. The team from the Indefatigable had arrived moments ago, and the shock was still setting in.

As far as the eye could see, the grassy ground was spread with humanoids, each shrouded in thick, strange fur. It was strange because it squirmed as they watched, and stranger still because...

"These people aren't supposed to have fur," said Wade.

"Yet they're covered in it," said Nathan. "From head to toe."

"Not just covered on the outside, either." Wade bent over a nearby body and adjusted his sci-probe, which whirred louder. "It's down their throats and throughout their pulmonary and digestive tracts, as well. They're infested with it."

Beth Scorpio kept both hands on her blaster rifle, setting a vigilant example for her six-person security detail. "If this doesn't have all the makings of a five-star shit-show, I don't know what does," she said.

"Are their vital signs still fading?" asked Nathan.

"Steadily." Wade crouched to get a closer scan of the body. "As if they're all falling toward a flatline."

"How long do they have?"

"Hard to say. Three hours, maybe." Wade was so focused on his sci-probe that he didn't see the hairy brown tendrils reaching toward him from the body.

Luckily, Scorpio did. Grabbing Wade by the shoulder, she yanked him back from the body just in time, leaving the hairs to flutter harmlessly.

"Thanks, Score." Wade nodded gratefully and resumed scanning as if nothing had happened.

"Can we help them, Wade?" asked Nathan. "Can they still be saved?"

"I don't think so," said Wade. "I think it's too late for them. Whatever these pelt-things are, they've become too deeply entangled with the colonists."

"We can't just abandon these people," said Nathan. "There must be something we can try."

"If the pelts are the problem, why not get rid of them?" said Scorpio.

"Get rid of them?" Nathan frowned.

"Shave them off," said Scorpio. "Why can't we just shave the damn things off?"

The chatter of projectile weapons fire was the first thing Curl heard after he was zapped into the big red-walled cavern under the surface of the moon. The weapons belonged to a line of seven humanoids who were arrayed inside the cave entrance, firing with abandon at some kind of menace churning in a cloud of dust and smoke there.

Thanks to the technician's scans and calculations aboard the *Furflier*, Curl and his team had materialized *behind* the line of fire instead of in front of it--but the danger was still great with all that ammo flying around.

As soon as Curl got a better look at the people shooting the guns, however, he felt better about his decision to rush into the situation. Every one of the seven men and women on the firing line was covered with a coat of fur.

"We're not too late," he said excitedly. "We can still make a difference for a lot of endangered fur."

"And people's *lives*," Bunny said with her usual edge.

Curl squinted into the clouds of smoke and dust kicked up by the hail of bullets. "But what the hell are they *shooting* at?"

"Can't tell from back here, mate." Rebound Bungee the Killa Kangaroo, gripping a blaster rifle (fur-covered, of course) in his white-gloved hands, took two hops closer to the action...then two more.

Curl slowly followed, and the rest of the team eased forward around him--Bunny, Sipping, and three of Rebound's security apes (one bright blue, one bright green, and one hot pink with fiery red highlights). Every member of the team kept a fur-swaddled blaster armed and held high.

Ahead of everyone, Rebound approached to within ten feet of the shooters and stopped. He peered into the smoke and dust for a moment--then turned to the rest of the team and shouted a single word.

"Bugs!"

As he said it, a foot-long silver insect leaped out of the smoke and landed on the shoulder of a dark-furred humanoid male in the middle of the firing line. Like a malevolent machine, the bug went to work with savage efficiency, tearing at the humanoid's fur with its poisonous claws and mandibles.

13

The other shooters kept up their fire, pounding the approaching enemy hidden in the dust and smoke. They didn't dare let up or risk being overwhelmed.

Without hesitation, Rebound leaped in to help the screaming man under attack. Flipping his rifle around, the kangaroo furry brought the butt crashing down on the bug. The creature reared up and flailed, jabbing its pincers at Rebound while keeping a firm grip on the humanoid's shoulder--and Curl finally had a clear shot at the thing. He cranked off a single bolt of blazing energy from his blaster, kicking the bug off the man and sending it screeching back into the smoke.

That was officially the end of holding back. Curl gave the word, and his people formed up behind the humanoids, adding their guns to the deadly barrage.

With the powerful blasters joining the fray, the furries and their new allies quickly made an impact. Bodily fluids and shards of bug legs, shells, and guts flew out of the cloud in every direction as the swarm was torn apart by the heavy fire.

Finally, then, a red-furred male humanoid shouted a single word, and his people stopped shooting. Curl followed that with an order of his own, and his team's guns fell silent as well.

There was no further sign or sound of bug activity as the smoke and dust cleared, exposing the debris-strewn battlefield.

"What *were* those things?" Sipping was panting a little from exertion as he finally lowered his blaster.

Curl watched as a humanoid female tended the injuries of the male who'd been attacked. Where the bug had gotten its claws and mandibles on him, the hair had been torn right out of his pale pink flesh.

"The same things that attacked that derelict vessel, no doubt," said Bunny.

"And left the sole survivor a hairless ruin," added Curl. "The devils."

Just then, the six uninjured humanoids clustered together, scowling at Curl and his furries and talking fast to each other. Curl strained to understand what they were saying, but his interpreclip with its incomplete matrix couldn't catch more than a few random words: *what...guns...and...know...shadows.*

Curl understood what happened next just fine, however, even without a fully-programmed interpreclip.

The six humanoids whirled, aimed their projectile rifles at the crew of the *Furflier*, and barked out threatening words that needed no translation.

Five years ago...

Even using laser-powered shaving kits, it took the whole crew of the Indefatigable *to rid the population of the Veridian Five colony of the squirming hair before three hours passed and they all died as Wade had warned. It didn't help that the crew had to double-team each colonist, with one crewman doing the shaving and internal removal and another blasting the pelts into oblivion. If the pelts weren't destroyed quickly enough, they aggressively tried to return to their former hosts or latch onto whoever was closest.*

As each colonist was set free, Dr. Dmitri Molotov and his team of medics roamed among the now-hairless host of patients, monitoring vitals and administering medications. They even sedated certain pelts that couldn't be easily restrained or removed, hitting them with a light mist of tranquilizer gas.

For three hours, the grassy plain was filled with the sounds of laser shavers and blasters and the inhuman screeches of parasitic, prehensile pelts. The men and women of the Indefatigable *raced against time with incredible focus, determined to free every living colonist before their vital signs zeroed out forever.*

One of his people, Wade Robbins, approached him when the three hours were almost up. "We did it, Captain. There's just one colonist left to clear."

"Great work, Wade." Smiling, Nathan clapped him on the shoulder. "I

think we saved a lot of lives here today."

That was the last time he smiled without a bear mask over his head for the next five years. It was the last time he felt good about himself as he was--Nathan Bailey--or thought of the man with that name without feeling crippling guilt.

And it all started with a single, shouted word from Dr. Molotov:
"Stop!!!"

"We are friends," Curl said calmly, hoping to relax the gun-pointing humanoids with his tone of voice alone. "Friends *help,* not *hurt.*"

The humanoids listened, but their expressions remained grim. The red-furred male in the middle, who seemed to be the leader, barked more words in a threatening way, jabbing his rifle at Curl.

"We can take 'em, Captain," said Rebound. "Wrap 'em up nice and pretty in a heartbeat."

"Stand by, Bungee." Curl bent down and placed his blaster on the ground, then straightened with his arms outstretched. "We *helped* you fight the bugs," he said to the humanoids. "We mean you *no* harm."

Again, the humanoid leader rattled off a string of what sounded like hostile gibberish to Curl.

Then, suddenly, there was a soft chime in Curl's left ear, and the leader's speech was gibberish no more. The download from Doc Sinew had come in, Curl realized, and the interpreclip's translation matrix for the language of the moon's inhabitants was complete. Finally, Curl could understand what they were saying and speak directly to them in their native tongue.

"For the last time, invaders, surrender your weapons!" That was what the humanoid leader was saying. "Hand them over or die!"

"Wait," Curl said in the local language. "We are only here to help you stop the bugs."

The leader looked surprised at hearing Curl use words he

understood. "Who are you? What do you call yourselves?"

"We call ourselves..." The next word gave the interpreclip some trouble before it came up with a translation. "...*furries.* And *I* am called Captain Harmonious Curl. What about *you?"*

"My name is Luo Oyo, and I am the commander of these people...what's *left* of them." Luo narrowed his eyes. "So how exactly did you *find* us?"

Curl pressed a button under his left ear, using a communication implant in the head of his costume to call the ship--Doc Sinew, in particular. "Hey Doc." He lowered his voice and reverted to the standard Fuzzish language. "Do we have a name for our patient yet?"

Sinew growled unhappily. "That's about *all* we have so far. He calls himself Azor. And one more thing." Sinew cleared his throat. "He says he doesn't want to be anywhere *near* this killer moon."

Curl pushed the button again, cutting off the channel. "Azor sent us," he told the humanoids. "He said you people could use some help."

The name-dropping (and outright lying to make Azor sound less negative) seemed to take the edge off the tension in the cave. The humanoids didn't put down their weapons, but they lowered them slightly and blinked at Curl with open curiosity.

"Tell us about your situation," Curl said in the local tongue. "Where are the rest of your people?"

Luo hesitated, then lowered his weapon to his side. "They're trapped in a chamber behind that rock-fall, which we created." He gestured at a pile of dust and debris spilling out of the right rear corner of the cave. "Aside from that cave-in, *we* are the last remaining defense between our survivors and the *hair-eaters.*"

"Seven of you against all those bugs?" asked Bunny.

"When we started, there were *two dozen* of us fighting them off," said Luo.

"They seem to have stopped," said Curl. "Together, we've held them off."

"For now." Luo looked over his shoulder at the mouth of the

tunnel where the bugs had encroached. "But they come in waves. They're relentless."

"You still have over a hundred survivors," said Curl.

"Out of *three hundred and fifty* in our original contingent," Luo said darkly.

"Which includes the 52 who left on the ship with Azor, correct?" asked Bunny.

"Yes," said Luo. "At least *they* escaped this nightmare."

"They didn't," said Bunny. "Azor is the only survivor."

All seven humanoids looked equally crestfallen. "What happened?" asked Luo.

"It looked like a bug attack, though we saw no bugs aboard the ship," explained Bunny. "And some kind of vessel struck, as well, breaching the hull and blowing out every system."

"Bastards!" snapped a female humanoid. "They couldn't let *anyone* escape."

"You sound like you know who did it," said Bunny.

"Our *masters* did it, of course," said the female. "We stole three ships and escaped the labor camp where they kept us imprisoned, and they tracked us to this moon. They destroyed two of the stolen ships, trapping most of us here, and now you tell us they got the *third*, too. They *murdered* our people."

"They and their *pets*," added a male. "The *hunter-killer bugs* they send to annihilate every *slave* who dares escape."

"But we didn't see anything *like* these bugs aboard Azor's ship," said Bunny. "Just the scars and venom left behind by their bites."

"They're fitted with self-destruct capsules," said Luo. "The Masters can annihilate them with the touch of a button, *after* they've slaughtered everyone in sight!"

Just as the words were spoken, the sounds of skittering and chittering started up again from beyond the entryway, swiftly getting louder.

"Here they come again!" Luo jammed a fresh clip of ammunition into his rifle and swung it around in the same smooth motion. "Don't let them take the freedom of our sisters and brothers!"

"Or their fur!" shouted Curl as he shouldered into the firing line and raised his blaster.

Five years ago...

"I said stop!" Dr. Molotov raced over and swatted the laser shaver out of the crewman's hand before he could go to work on the last unshaven colonist. "You were about to murder this woman!"

"What are you talking about, Doc?" Bailey, who'd been feeling so good a moment ago, scowled in confusion.

"It's already started." Red-faced, Molotov waved his scanner at the field of hairless bodies shaved by the crew. "Oh God, it's already begun."

As he said it, a nearby male body convulsed and collapsed on the ground. Seconds later, a distant female did the same, and then another.

And another.

It happened again and again across the plain, as one body after another went into spasms and then went limp. Over and over, Molotov's nurses and assistants called out the same verdict until it became so redundant that it no longer mattered.

By then, every member of the crew of the Indefatigable *knew exactly what was happening to the colonists spread out around them.*

"Every one of them is dying," said Molotov. "And it's our fault for not looking closer. *It we'd only probed deeper, we might have* seen *and* understood *the* truth."

"What truth is that?" asked Wade.

"That the pelt-things were keeping them alive, *not* killing *them," said Molotov. "The moment we started* shaving *them, we became the* true killers."

Bailey just stood and watched with dead eyes as the colonists he'd expected to save died in droves. A gulf of emptiness vaster than he'd ever thought possible opened up within him, pulling him toward it.

Medical personnel tried to stop the mass die-off, injecting drugs into the colonists in desperation. Other men and women of the crew tried to resuscitate the dead with equipment or simple techniques, to no avail.

"The pelts are sentient native lifeforms," explained Molotov. "And they're highly resistant to all forms of infection. The colonists' fading vital signs were due to a healing coma induced by the pelts as they fought off an epidemic killing the colony."

Bailey heard but didn't react. The sounds that were loudest to his ears were the grunts and cries of the dying colonists and the crewmen fighting in vain to save them.

Molotov shouted to his people, telling them to stop the heroic efforts-- but they ignored him. They kept fighting like the true heroes they'd always been, even in the face of the inevitable.

Even as their captain stood there, not lifting a finger or offering the slightest bit of leadership in their moment of greatest need.

The latest assault on the cave was much more intense than the previous one had been. Many more bugs poured into the entrance, scuttling over walls, floor, and ceiling alike. The foot-long silver insects seemed more aggressive than before, quicker to pounce and harder to kill.

Even with Curl's team adding their guns to the barrage, holding the line was almost impossible. One of the humanoids went down early and was dragged away screaming before anyone could free him. Another dropped soon after and was stripped hairless in seconds by the swarm, even as Rebound blasted off the bugs two and three at a time.

The crew of the *Furflier* suffered their first casualty, as well. Some of the bugs crossed the ceiling and came down behind the shooters, getting the drop on the bright blue security ape, Zil. In the space of a heartbeat, Zil was covered in bugs and hit the dirt floor, wailing and clawing at the swarm. Before anyone could assist, the creatures had torn through his fur suit and denuded his human form inside of every last vestige of hair. He died soon after from the biting and stinging, though the other apes turned in time to pick off the remaining infiltrators before they could slaughter anyone else.

It was enough to inspire the survivors to redouble their efforts. In a matter of moments, Curl and his team and the humanoids had forced the bugs into retreat. The sea of insects gave up the battle--for the moment--and rushed back down the hallway in a storm of legs, shells, and clacking mandibles.

Then it was time to tend to the dead. The humanoids had lost three, all told, and gently moved them to one side of the cave. Curl, meanwhile, said a few words over Zil and called for a moment of silence in his memory. When that was done, Curl called the ship and had Zil's body telefurted up. It was all he could do not to ask them to zap up the rest of the landing party at the same time, but there was still work to be done.

"So now we know," said Rebound. "Those things are just as hungry for *our* fur as the *slaves'*."

"They're bred and trained to be drawn to it," explained Luo. "It's a perfect system for the Masters, since they're born without a trace of hair on their bodies. The hair-eaters would never go after *them.*"

"So what happens if you shave it off?" asked Bunny. "Make yourselves as hairless as the Masters?"

"We don't know," said Luo.

"You mean you've never *tried* it?" asked Bunny.

Luo shook his head. "It goes against our faith. Only the furry can enter the kingdom of Next-Life."

"Makes sense," said Curl.

"Not if it means checking out of *this* life early," snapped Bunny.

"We believe strongly in preserving the fur," said Luo.

"Good for you," said Curl.

"But what about all those *people* of yours trapped in there?" Bunny gestured at the rock fall blocking the entrance to the chamber next-door. "What if removing their fur could *save* them?"

Curl frowned. "Zapping them up to the ship with the telefurter makes a lot more sense."

"No can do," said Sipping. "The walls in there are lined with deposits of electromagnetic ore that blocks our quantum trebuchet system."

"It blocks the Masters' scanners, too," said Luo. "That's why the bulk of our group holed up in there in the first place."

"But we zapped in *here* just fine," said Curl.

"Because the ore concentration is lighter." Sipping walked to a wall and ran his hand over it. "If we could get everyone in *here*, the *Furflier* could zap them aboard."

"*Or* the *bugs* might attack during the evacuation and turn it into a *bloodbath*," said Rebound.

"Unless we move really fast," said Curl.

"Or just *shave* everyone." Frustrated, Bunny stomped over to stand toe to toe with Luo. "It's the *logical* approach, don't you see? And it's only *temporary*. The fur will all *grow back.*"

"I understand," said Luo. "It's just, our *faith*..."

"...doesn't say anything about *sacrificing* yourselves without good *reason*, does it?"

Luo looked to his team, and no one volunteered an answer to the question.

"You and your people won't be the *only* ones going hairless," said Bunny. "*We'll* all have to strip down, too. We'll all be in this together."

"Maybe you're right," said Luo. "Maybe, in these extreme circumstances, it would still fall within the tenets of our faith if we..."

"No!" shouted Curl. "*Shaving* is *never* the answer!"

Three years ago...

"Hey, you're that guy, aren't you?" The bartender narrowed his dark

eyes and leaned over the bar, staring hard at Nathan. "The one who killed all those folks by shavin' 'em?"

Nathan tugged his fedora lower on his head, casting more of his face in shadow. "You've got the wrong man, pal."

"Yeah, sure! You're him, all right!" The bartender chuckled. "First drink's on the house, fella. I feel sorry for you, bein' court-martialed, kicked outta the service, and disgraced in every possible way like that."

"Forget it." Nathan turned and slouched away, pushing through the doors of the bar and out onto the streets of Bradbury, Mars before he raised further attention.

It was a scene that had played out often since that terrible day on Veridian Five. His disgrace had spread far and wide throughout the Interstellar Entente, turning him into a celebrity of the notorious type. Every time he let his guard down, someone spotted and called attention to him, always leading to an awkward, unpleasant scene. At various times, he'd been branded as incompetent, stupid, evil, sick, or just plain laughable-- and the worst of it was, he couldn't argue. He knew in his heart they were right, all of them; the deaths of all those people on Veridian Five had happened on his watch.

Slogging down the street in the rain, he tugged up the collar of his filthy, battered trench coat and thought about finding a place to sleep for the night. He'd finally exhausted his savings and didn't have a credit to his name, so his most likely sleeping place would be somewhere outdoors.

Just as he was seeking shelter, Nathan heard the sounds of a scuffle from a nearby alley. Against his better judgment, he took a peek on his way past--and was stunned.

Down that alley, a bulked-up goon was beating the hell out of what looked like a bear.

It shouldn't have been possible, since there were no bears on Mars as far as Nathan knew, but the fur-covered figure getting its ass kicked sure looked like a bear.

For some reason, seeing an innocent animal getting pounded like that struck a nerve. Nathan, who was usually too busy defending himself to stand up for anyone else, went charging down the alley, ready to fight.

"Captain," said Bunny. "May I have a word with you?" Guiding Curl by the elbow, she took him aside and lowered her voice. "Shaving *is* the answer this time, and you *know* it."

Curl shook his head emphatically. "It's *never* the answer. It's the biggest mistake you can *make.*"

Bunny leaned close and lowered her voice even more. "Now you listen to me, Curl. How often have I ever told you you're wrong?"

"You tell me that *all the time,*" said Curl.

"Okay, okay," said Bunny. "Well, I'm telling you again. *Shaving* is the best chance those people have for survival."

Curl kept shaking his head. "No! I can't let it *happen* again!"

Bunny grabbed him by the shoulders and gave him a rough shake. "Enough! Whatever the hell you went through in the past, I don't *care!* Whatever has you scared, get *over* it and do the right *thing!*"

"You don't understand!"

She shook him again, harder. "I understand you're *Captain Harmonious Curl* of the *S.B.B. Furflier.* As far as I'm concerned, that's *all* you've ever been and all that *matters!*"

Three years ago...

With surprise on his side, Nathan managed to get in a few good shots at the guy attacking the bear--but his advantage didn't last. As the thug turned, Nathan realized he'd been stabbing the bear with a knife and was ready to use it again.

The guy lunged, thrusting the knife at Nathan, but Nathan's military-honed reflexes kicked in. He jumped away at the last second, then lashed out with a kick that blew the knife out of the goon's hand, sending it clattering against the wall.

As the thug roared, Nathan dove for the knife and came up with it in his grip. He lashed out with it suddenly, slicing a red line along the guy's left bicep.

"Get out of here!" Years of pent-up frustration poured out of Nathan as he brandished the knife. "Get out of here or I swear I'll kill you!"

The thug made a quick feint, then ducked back as Nathan swept the blade at his throat. He feinted again, then backed away toward the mouth of the alley.

"Asshole!" he said. "Furry freaks deserve to be dead!"

Only after the thug had marched off into the night did Nathan take a closer look at the bear, which leaned heavily against the wall of the alley.

It was then that he realized it was actually someone in a bear costume.

With an agonized, deep-voiced moan, the man in the bear costume slumped to the floor of the alley, clutching his side. Tucking the knife in the pocket of his coat, Nathan crouched beside him.

"I'm dying." The bear-person's paws and side glistened with blood by the light of the Martian moon.

"Hang in there." Nathan got to his feet. "I'll call an ambulance or flag down a cop."

"Don't bother." The bear shook his head. "I can tell...I don't have much longer...to live. But one thing...you can *do...for me."*

Nathan frowned. "What's that?"

"Take my place," said the bear.

Nathan didn't understand what he was getting at. "Look, I'll find someone *to help. I promise I'll be right back."*

The bear reached up and tugged his left ear. The head of his costume split down the middle and fell away to either side, revealing a middle-aged, heavyset man with thinning black hair and a mustache and goatee of the same color.

"Stay...please," said the man in the costume. "I know...who you are."

"Okay, right." Nathan's heart sank. Was he doomed to be recognized everywhere, by *everyone? "Well, I really do have to go now, so..."*

"Wait!" The man grabbed hold of the hem of Nathan's overcoat. "Fate...brought us...together. You were a captain...and my ship will need a captain...without me. Please..."

Something in the man's voice held Nathan in place. "A ship? You have a ship?"

"It's called...the Furflier. *It is a refuge...a place where you can...reinvent yourself...or perhaps...be who you were always meant to be...and who you seemed to be before...will no longer matter." The man smiled, and there was a twinkle in his eye though the light of life was quickly fading from him. "Tell me...have you ever thought...about becoming a* furry?"

"I wouldn't even know where to begin," said Nathan.

"Easy," said the bear. "You take...my suit...and my name...and jump right in. No one...will know otherwise."

Nathan frowned. "What is your name, anyway?"

"Curl. Captain Harmonious Curl. And it is your *name from this day forward."*

"Captain Curl!" Sipping was watching the screen of his handheld scanner. "The bugs are massing in a space not far from here! There are hundreds of thousands, and the number keeps growing!"

"They reproduce rapidly," said Luo.

"They'll be headed here soon enough," said Rebound. "We're running out of time."

"Do we shave the survivors, or what?" asked Guana the hot pink security ape.

Curl's heart hammered in his chest inside the suit and sweat streamed down his back and sides. He felt like he was back on Veridian Five, about to order more than 11,000 beings to their deaths.

And yet he couldn't escape the feeling that Bunny was right. This time *was* different; perhaps the *wrong* choice on Veridian Five would be the *right* choice here.

"Will shaving hurt your people in any way?" he asked Luo. "Aside from breaking the rules of your faith?"

"Not that we know of," said Luo. "But none of my people ever shaves, so I can't say for sure."

"*But,*" said Bunny. "If you stay where you are, and the bugs come in force, how much longer will you survive?"

Luo sighed. "Not much longer."

"Well then." Bunny looked at Curl. "What do you think we should *do,* good Captain?"

Curl took a deep breath and let it out slowly. He thought of the original Captain Curl, his namesake, and wondered what *he* would do in this situation. He also thought of Captain Nathan Bailey of the *Indefatigable* and wondered what *he* would do.

"The bugs are continuing to mass," said Sipping.

"What do you say, Captain?" asked Rebound.

Curl nodded firmly. "I say start digging open that adjacent chamber so we can get those survivors out of there." He pressed a button under his left ear, opening a comm channel to the ship. "Frisky? Send down as many quantum shaving kits as you can, pronto! We've got over a hundred pelts to shave, and we don't have a moment to spare!"

Three years ago...

Nathan felt ridiculous at first. Putting on the dead man's bear suit felt like the absolute height of insanity.

What kind of people wore *those costumes, anyway? What the hell had to be* wrong *with them to make them want to dress up like make-believe cartoon animals?*

But after a while, he understood. He'd been longing for a safe place, for anonymity, and now he'd finally found *it.*

After cleaning up and repairing the dead man's costume and practicing how to operate it, he started to think the plan wasn't so crazy after all. In a short time, he felt right at home in that fur suit, inhabiting that character.

So by the time he set foot on the ship, the Furflier, *he only felt a little nervous. And when he met the crew for the first time, and saw they were all furries like he was, he knew he was among his own kind.*

Any worry he felt over getting found out as an imposter quickly faded. The crew instantly accepted him as their previous Captain Curl with no sign of concern or suspicion.

Couldn't they tell *there was a different man inside the suit? Didn't they* realize *his voice and mannerisms were different, and he lacked essential knowledge the previous Curl had possessed?*

Maybe it just didn't matter, just as it didn't matter to Nathan where exactly they'd gotten their ship, or who was funding their adventures. Maybe all that mattered was that a man in a big brown bear costume was in command, about to lead them back among the stars.

As he settled into the command chair on the bridge of the Furflier *for the first time, all he could think about was how great it felt to be back, to regain a captaincy--to be* useful *once more.*

He swore to himself that he would never give up that feeling. He would never take it for granted or make the kind of mistake that had led to his downfall once before.

And he would never let anyone see who was inside the suit, under any circumstances.

"We have to take off our suits," said Bunny. "It's the only way we can finish this job."

Curl's blood ran cold at the words, though they weren't unexpected. *Of course* they had to step out of their fur before the bugs arrived, if they didn't want to end up like poor Zil.

And they had to do it *now*. They'd shaved every refugee humanoid to a hairless state; now they had to escort them in groups out of the chamber lined with telefurter-blocking ore and get them zapped aboard the *Furflier*. They had to do it as fast as possible, in case the shaving alone wasn't enough to discourage the bugs.

To survive, every one of them had to be naked and hairless.

"The swarm is over a million strong, and it's headed this way!" said Sipping. "We have *seven minutes*, tops!"

"Then it's fur off, people! Let's go!" As she said it, Bunny tugged her left ear, and her costume split down the middle.

The others, except Curl, all did the same. In an instant, they stood revealed to each other as the people they'd always been.

For the first time, Curl saw that Bunny was a pudgy woman in her thirties with long, blonde hair. Sipping was an elderly Chinese man with gray hair and a short beard. Rebound was a black man in his forties with lots of tattoos. Guana the hot pink ape was a large, middle-aged woman with short brown hair, and Yego the bright green ape was a bald young man with a huge purple stain spread over his face.

Curl alone stood unrevealed, staring in stunned silence at the strange faces he'd never seen before, the faces of the people who'd become like family to him in other guises.

"All of you! Get shaving!" As she said it, Bunny grabbed a quantum shaver from a rock and used it on herself, vaporizing her lustrous blonde hair. The others did the same, burning off every last strand of hair on their bodies.

Except Curl.

"Five minutes!" shouted Sipping.

"Curl!" said Bunny. "Costume off! Do it now!"

But Curl couldn't do it. The instant the others saw who he really was, his life among them would be over. He'd rather die than lose everything again and have his life go back to the way it had been after Veridian Five.

At least, that was his thinking before the choice was taken out of his hands.

Without warning, Bunny leaped over and tugged his left ear to trigger the suit release. "I said get out of there!"

Curl's suit split open, peeling apart from head to toe. He

couldn't stop it from falling away, leaving him standing there before her for the first time.

She got a good look before he hid his face in his hands. All the furries did.

"No!" he howled. "Don't look at me, please!"

But Bunny just reached up and pulled his hands away. "You son of a bitch," she said, scowling.

"I know!" Curl felt tears well up in his eyes. "You all hate me, now that you know who I am!"

Bunny's eyes narrowed. "Fuck you."

"Just leave me here for the bugs! Just leave me to die!"

Bunny scowled a moment more, then pointed the quantum shaver at him and switched it on. "Why the hell would we do that?" Her scowl melted into a smile. "All I see is Captain Curl of the *S.B.B. Furflier*."

"What?" Curl looked around at his team and saw no hatred or rejection among them. Didn't they recognize him? Didn't they care what he'd done on Veridian Five?

The words of his predecessor, who'd died in that alley on Mars, came back to him: *It is a* refuge...*a place where you can...*reinvent *yourself...or perhaps...be who you were always* meant *to be...and who you* seemed *to be before...will no longer matter.*

"Less than two minutes!" shouted Sipping as he and the others hurried refugees out of the chamber.

"Get shaving!" Bunny pressed the shaver into Curl's hands and ran off to help the others.

The swarm roared in the distance, approaching fast. Projectile guns and blasters chattered and whined, picking off bugs. The *Furflier*'s telefurter zapped and crackled in the cave next-door.

And the quantum shaver hummed as Curl ran it over his head and body, choosing to survive.

One hundred and eighteen new furries roamed the decks of the *Furflier* that night, all former slaves, survivors of the carnage on the bug-infested moon.

The suits they wore belonged to the crew, who'd loaned them to help the refugees feel more at home. With all their hair shaved off, at least the ex-slaves could still observe the rules of their faith to some extent by being clad in *borrowed* fur. It would do in a pinch, they decided.

As for the crew, they were all too happy to make the gesture, awkward as it was for them at first. Some worried about what the others might think, but it turned out not to matter in the end. The names and personalities stayed the same; only the faces were different.

As Curl sat in his command chair, watching the furless crew (but not naked; they wore simple blue uniforms) interact, he felt better than he could have imagined given the circumstances. He felt more like his old self, like Nathan, but without the fear and self-loathing.

"Please sign this, Captain." Ensign Biggus Belfry of the engineering department handed over an e-clipboard with a report on the screen. He, like every member of the crew, treated Curl just the same as always; no one had made a single mention of who he was without the suit or what he'd done in the past, though surely *some* of them must have recognized him and known the whole story.

It was more than Curl could have expected, and much more than he thought he deserved. But perhaps, given this new chance, he might still do some good in the universe.

"Thank you, Ensign." Curl signed the report with his fingertip and handed the clipboard back to Belfry, who saluted and left.

Just then, the elevator door whooshed open, admitting Dr. Sinew to the bridge.

"Greetings, Harmonious." Without his tiger suit, Sinew was a tall, muscular man in his forties with short, black hair and a closely-trimmed beard. He was of Arab extraction, with deep, dark eyes and an olive complexion. "How fare you this fine day, good Captain?"

31

"Fairly well." Curl smiled. "And yourself? Still missing the stripes?"

Sinew chuckled. "My stripes are *always* with me, suit or no suit."

"What about the rest of the crew? Would you say they're adjusting equally well?"

"Some adjusted faster than others, as you'd expect," said Sinew. "But the general level of support has prevented any lingering difficulties. The power of fur is so strong, apparently, that its influence lingers even when the fur itself is gone."

"It might be gone a lot more, the way things are going." Just then, Bunny strolled over from the helm, where she'd been working with Dressage--a short, stocky woman with brown hair--to run a system diagnostic. "Some folks are talking about giving up their fur altogether or taking temporary breaks from it."

"Is that so?" said Curl.

"Do we have a problem with that?" asked Bunny.

Sinew shrugged. "Seems to me the Code of Concealment has already gone by the wayside thanks to our new friends' need for cover."

"In that case, I say the crew should go for it," said Curl. "It's up to the individual."

"A mixed crew on the *Furflier?*" Sinew let out a rumbling growl that was worthy of his tiger-striped alter ego. "Things could get *interesting.*"

"We can only hope," said Bunny.

The elevator door swished open again, and Sinew laughed. "We have company!"

Curl turned, and the hairs on the back of his neck jumped to attention. It was like seeing *himself* walking toward him, though he knew the man inside the Big Brown Bear suit was different now.

"Captain!" The bear--with Luo inside--waved as he strolled to the command chair. "Thanks again to you and all your crew for loaning my people the furs!"

"Anything to make you all feel better," said Curl. "Just let us know if there's anything else we can do."

"Actually, there is," said Luo the Bear. "I was wondering..."

"Yes?"

Luo cleared his throat. "Is there any way I could *keep* this fur? It's so *comfortable*. It makes me feel like a new *man...*er, *bear.*"

Curl felt a flicker of panic, but it passed. Strangely enough, he realized he didn't hate the idea. It felt pretty good to come out of hiding, as long as he was among friends. Maybe it was time he became his real self all the way.

"Maybe," he told Luo. "Let me think about it. After all, it's *vital* that the right *home* be found for *every* fur."

Bunny sighed with her usual irritation. "And every *person*, don't forget."

"Right." Curl grinned and nodded. "That, too."

THE STARS SO BLACK, THE SPACE SO WHITE

magine standing in the prow of a great sailing vessel, gazing out at the starry darkness as it folds around the nose of the ship. Now imagine the ship is in space.

And you are standing on an onyx gangplank, a sheer, black surface reflecting the starlight all around--creating the illusion that you are suspended without support in the void. Exposed to the nip and tug of so many rays and waves and streams and particles, yet somehow protected.

Watch as crackling suns and jewel-like worlds spin past. Wonder at the feathery, pastel tendrils of glowing nebulae. Grin with delight, because no matter how many times you see this, you can't help but marvel.

I can't help but marvel.

Welcome to my life. From Earthbound bartender savant to crewman on an alien spacecraft. From man of 20th century Earth to man of the cosmos.

You wish you were me. You *totally* wish you were me.

"I should have known." The voice behind me is high-pitched and piping with a fluttery vibrato. "I would find you here. Rudeee Tabernacle."

Turning, I smile at the dozens of multifaceted silver eyes staring my way, twisting on the ends of pale yellow tendrils. The tendrils are rooted in a glittering, creamy cloud, a misty blur of ever-shifting size and shape that hovers a meter above the onyx gang-plank. Who knew I could come to love and respect someone so alien?

Who knew I could come to see my *abductor* as my *friend*?

"You are not feeling. Worried, are you?" The voice emanates from somewhere in the cloud. It's the same voice I first heard fifty years ago, asking a question that changed my life forever and led me to this moment.

"Only hopeful." I bow, as is the custom in the fleet of the civiliza-tion whose name translates as The Rising. After fifty years among The Rising (though I look half as old as that, thanks to alien rejuve-nation techniques), I know all the right things to do and say...though I don't always do and say them. But that, too, is customary; it's part of my job, after all.

They call me a *Chancer*. An X-factor in a social hierarchy with too much order...and a need for controlled chaos in the face of a highly improvisational universe.

As for the alien, if you called him/her/it/them a captain/teacher/lama/inexplicable presence, you wouldn't be wrong. "We approach. The source of. The signal."

His/her/its/their actual name is unpronounceable for a human like me, so I go with a boiled-down nickname. "Most Eager, has the content of the signal changed?"

Most Eager hiss-cough-squeals in a way that equates to a human head-shake. "The signal continues. To repeat."

I know the message by heart by now. "*Black stars. White space. Forever screaming.*"

"We will be there. Soon, Rudeee. The..." He calls our giant vessel by the name its builders gave it, which translates like this (more or less): *Peacefaring Manyfold Transitory Translightenment Construct, Constant.* "...will arrive within. The hour."

I shorten the ship's name like always. "The *Transit*'s ready, Most

Eager. We'll do what we do best."

"Answer questions." Most Eager stiffens all his/her/its/their tendrils at once like stalks in a cornfield. It's a salute. "Save lives."

I answer with a salute of my own, holding both fists at shoulder height, opening them into flattened palms. "And set the stage for tomorrow."

Setting the stage is The Rising's truest mission, our reason for being among the stars in the first place. The galaxy is full of life-forms in varying degrees of evolution; we create mysteries that will draw them out here when the time is right to join the community of starfaring beings.

Speaking of mysteries, a ship like our own comes into view up ahead--a cluster of giant black shapeshifting objects, spherical at the moment like a bunch of grapes or a clutch of atoms in a molecule. The spheres, which normally blink with multicolored lights, are dark--and cut in half down the middle, wedged in a swirling halo of bright blue light.

"Do you think. They are still. Alive?" asks Most Eager.

I know he/she/it/they can tell if I'm lying, but I do it anyway. "Of course." After all, he/she/it/they has/have kin on that vessel.

More than kin. More like a protégé beloved above all others. And a *human*, like me.

Her name is Julie. And it is *her* voice--the voice of the trapped ship's first officer--repeating that message, over and over:

"Black stars. White space. Forever screaming."

Imagine a ship the size of a small moon, consisting of huge, interlinked objects--sometimes spherical, sometimes cubical, other times elliptical or dodecagonal or jagged as a giant virus with a billion points and peaks. A ship that shifts and changes depending on its task or environment.

Now imagine the *inside* of such a ship, which is equally as miraculous as the outside. Imagine diving through a sea of lights and colors, a jumble of bubbles and pockets and pods alive with sound and motion...some right-side-up, some upside-down, some sideways or inside-out or outways-upside-in...all rising and falling and bumping and merging and mingling...a harmonious bedlam fit to drive a sane man mad or a madman sane.

And all through it, imagine the *life* of a hundred-thousand worlds, from the brobdingnagian to the microscopic...all thronging in this vast and tumbling tumult. Imagine feathers, wings, scales, claws, beaks, fur, bone...skin, fluid, ooze, fumes, leaves, stems, crystals...chirps, howls, growls, chatters, barks, clicks, burbles...all of these and more.

Imagine all that, and you'll have some idea what the inside of the *Peacefaring Manyfold Transitory Translightenment Construct, Constant* is like. The *Transit*. My *home*.

And you'll know, at least a little, why I love it so. You'll know why the day they brought me here from Georgia was the best day of my life.

Diving down through the zero gravity "Flow" that exists between pockets and bubbles, I swoop past busy shipmates on their way to other destinations. A voice chimes in my head via Menta-com, the telepathic intercom that speaks in whatever language you understand best.

All crew to mystery stations. Approaching distressed vessel Impetuous Fractal Tracery Epicenter, Rarefied.

I see my own station below, a figure eight archipelago of chrome, glass, and superneuroconductive organo-ceramics sparking with current. As I drop toward it, localized gravity rises, reeling me in until I land lightly on the polished floor.

"Rudy!" One of my colleagues, a being I call Paraffino, waves his sixteen waxy arms. "Take a look at the data from our scans of the *Fractal Tracery*."

I hurry over and lean in beside him, taking in the flurry of multicolored holographic text dancing in midair around us.

"No life signs." I can't keep the disappointment out of my voice. "And no power."

"Except the battery backup that is powering the distress beacon." says Paraffino.

"Here's a question," says a tiny voice in my left ear, the whine of an insect. "Why does the *FracTrace* appear to be cut in half, yet it bends space-time as if it were *one thousand times* its recorded size?"

I scowl. "Some kind of sensor mirage?"

"Considered and discounted." The tiny voice's owner flits in front of my face--a silver mosquito-like creature half the length of my little finger. I call him KeeZee McGee. "Diagnostics reveal zero chance of impaired functionality in our sensor arrays."

"What about *psychic* mirages?" I raise an eyebrow. "Maybe the sensor data only *looks* hinky because our *minds* are being warped."

"Unlikely." Another voice speaks up across the archipelago-- make that *five hundred* voices, a chorus of every pitch and timbre singing as one. "The Mindset system confirms no perceptual defects in any member of our crew." The chorus belongs to a toothy shark-bunny thing I call Adorakilla.

"We need to send in a probe," says another colleague--a kind of half-rock/half-bush I call Stick-n-Stone. Her voice sounds like crackling gravel mixed with rustling leaves. "If anyone from the *FracTrace* is still alive, they must be on the other side of that phenomenon."

"Whatever it is," says Paraffino.

Some of us are about to find out. Just then, the Mentacom announces a mission to the derelict vessel, leaving in five minutes. Guess who's part of the Go Team?

Stick-n-Stone, for one. "Better go grab my gear." She rolls over the edge of the archipelago, where the Flow spins her off into the heights.

"Wish me luck." I smile and salute the others with flattened palms. "If I don't make it back, give my Zeppelin collection to Gassy Rictus."

I laugh as I leap up into the Flow. I've come up with so many nicknames, they can't always tell the real ones from the fake anymore.

Our little silver scout disk spins on its vertical axis like a coin, flashing from the *Transit* at a rate of speed that would blow your mind.

Inside, the six members of the Go Team stay glued to our psych-feeds, images of our destination beamed continuously into our brains. Even Most Eager--commander of this mission--closes the eyes on his/her/its/their yellow tendrils and looks inward at the mind-cast images.

"Five hundred units from *Fractal Tracery* and closing." Walking Reef, a creature who looks exactly as his nickname suggests, is piloting our disk.

Just then, something pings, and one of the holographic displays around Reef's head (a cluster of multicolored non-aquatic coral) flashes red-gold-red. "This is interesting. The sensor mirage seems to be intensifying. The part of the *Fractal Trace* on the other side of the phenomenon now appears to be *one hundred thousand times* the size of the original vessel."

"Makes no sense," rumbles our science officer, Stick-n-Stone, from her cradle in the floor. "Some kind of quantum magnification effect?"

"But why would it change as we get closer?" asks Ever Luminous, the slow-motion firework in the shape of a humanoid biped. He's the team's medical officer, as well as its lightshow-in-chief. "To such an extent, I mean?"

"Two hundred units and closing," says Reef.

We all stir, adjusting our gear--environmental suits, packs, lights, weapons. Any minute now, our scout craft will dock with *Fractal,* and we'll have our chance to learn the truth.

The sixth member of our team, security specialist Twelvefold Sinner, is first out of the airlock after we dock. Imagine someone who has twelve distinct selves sharing the same coordinates in space-time, each one a drastically different species with a different personality, language, and power set. That's our Sinner.

This time, he's wearing a form that's a mountain of muscle on three legs, with a face on the black-feathered chest and no head on the shoulders. He doesn't even need an environmental suit in that form; he's impervious to the airless cold inside the depressurized ship.

I walk out after him in my slimline gold foil environmental suit...and gasp. The interior of a Rising vessel without power is a sight to behold.

The world inside the giant ship is frozen in place. The pods and pockets and bubbles hang suspended, held aloft by passive magnetic failsafes...but no equipment is running. There's none of the tumult I've come to expect from an operational ship.

And none of the usual lights, either. It's only because of the glow from the swirling blue disk cutting through the middle of the sphere that I can see the frozen enormity of the *Fractal Tracery* sprawling before me.

As the rest of the Go Team files out of the scout, I gaze into that blue glow. "What did they stumble into here?"

"We couldn't have fashioned a better mystery ourselves," says Walking Reef, lumbering up beside me.

"Yet we need to. Stay on task." Most Eager drifts up ahead of us in the shimmery bubble that's his/her/its/their version of an environmental suit. "What does the data. Look like from here?"

"This is odd." Stick-n-Stone rolls up in what looks like a gold foil bowling ball bag, studying holographic readouts floating around her. "Sensor data is fluctuating wildly. One minute, the missing half of the *Fractal Tracery* reads as being 500,000 times larger than it should be...and then, it's a million times *smaller*."

Most Eager hardens his cloud into a pearly pointer aimed at the blue disk. "What else is on. The other side. Of that anomaly?"

"The only thing I've detected so far is the other half of the *Frac-Trace*," says Stick-n-Stone.

"Send in. A probe," says Most Eager.

Reef's mottled gray pseudopod arms weave through the air, bringing a set of hovering holo-controls into view around his head. Seconds later, a blinking black sphere the size of a soccer ball shoots past us from the scout ship and rockets toward the anomaly. It dives into the center of the disk without causing a single ripple of blue light.

Nothing changes for long moments after that. The blue light swirls silently like always, revealing no trace of the device.

"What does telemetry. Look like?" asks Most Eager.

Walking Reef's starfish eyes remain fixed on his holo-readouts. "Gibberish. The data coming through makes no sense."

"What if it's scrambled or encrypted?" asks Ever Luminous.

"Wait!" Reef's pseudopods whip through the readouts. "I'm *getting* something. Some kind of static...and it's building in intensity."

As soon as the words leave his twenty-five mouths, the anomaly flares, washing us all in blinding white light. The deck vibrates under my feet.

Before any of us can react, a powerful suction starts dragging us toward the anomaly.

Twelvefold Sinner is the first to go. Despite his great size and powerful musculature, the suction wrenches him off his feet like an untethered balloon and spins him into the center of the disk.

The rest of us follow, one by one--lifting off and hurtling into the anomaly. I'm the last to go, dropping all my gear and clinging to a Flow antenna mounted on the floor with my legs in the air...and then the antenna snaps. I bolt feet-first through the ship, narrowly missing most of the obstacles along the way.

Then I punch through the anomaly, and I black out.

The first thing I see when I open my eyes is a field of white flecked with black. Gazing into it, I wonder if it's a leftover effect of the anomaly's blinding flare.

Instinctively, I reach up to rub my eyes. As I'm massaging them, I realize something.

There should be a helmet between my eyes and my hand.

Terrified, I yank my hand away and gulp for breath, filling my lungs...which shouldn't be possible if the other side of the anomaly is as airless as the ship and space on the entry side.

Heart racing, I thrash myself to a seated position and look around. Where are my people?

The members of the Go Team are scattered over the ebony deck, alive and stirring in spite of the bumpy ride through the anomaly. Most Eager is closest, twenty meters away--though the distance, as I watch, seems to grow. Some kind of optical illusion? Or is it related to the size-distorted data we were picking up earlier from outside the anomaly?

The same applies to other reference points in my surroundings. The familiar habitats and equipment that fill this half of the *Fractal Tracery* float above us, changing as I stare--sometimes appearing closer, sometimes farther away.

But the distance dilation effect isn't the strangest thing about this side of the ship. As I take in my surroundings, another realization slams into my brain.

The spotted white field is outside *the ship. I am seeing it through gaping holes in the hull.*

The hull is stretched so far, it seems to have more holes than substance--and as I watch, it stretches farther, to the point of almost disappearing in the black-flecked whiteness.

Then, without warning, it springs back. The sight is disorienting enough to make me dizzy.

Shake it off. Whatever's happening here, I need to Take Steps. Figure It Out. Find What I Came Here For. The missing crew of the *Fractal Tracery*, in other words.

Then one of them finds me first.

"Hello, Rudy!" Julie's voice booms from all around me. "Thank you for coming!"

She coalesces from all directions, pieces fading into view and sliding together. And the pieces are *enormous.* As she gathers like metal dust accreting on a magnet, she seems to me to be *thirty meters tall* or more. She *towers* over me, a behemoth in a silver foil jumpsuit, beaming with teeth like skyscrapers, throwing out gusts of wind with each toss of her long, glossy, black hair.

"I missed you, Rudy!" As Julie says it, her body compresses, flowing down to stand before me at normal human size, just under two meters tall and slender as always. "I never thought I'd see *any* of you again!" She reaches out, takes my hand, and helps me to my feet.

"Tell me what you know." Disoriented, I wobble when I get up. "Where are we? Where's the rest of the crew?"

"So many questions." She smiles and squeezes my hand. "Same old Rudy."

Impatient, I pull my hand from her grip and grab her shoulders. "Is your *crew* still *alive*?"

"Define 'alive.'" She giggles when she says it.

I frown. The Julie I know is a serious person, a real Type-A. We've been colleagues and friends for 25 years, ever since she was abducted/recruited by The Rising, and I don't think I've ever heard her giggle before. "You think this is *funny?*"

"It's just..." She tilts her head to one side. "Things are *different* over here."

Most Eager's quivery voice pipes up behind us. "Different. In what ways?"

Julie shrugs off my grip and turns, bending over to smile at his/her/its/their weaving yellow eye-stalks. "Isn't it obvious? The *stars* are *black* here. And *space* is *white*."

No one from the Go Team has an intact environmental suit. I realize this when the others gather around us. Even Most Eager's protective bubble is nowhere to be seen.

Not that it seems to be a problem. We're all breathing and functioning normally, though as far as I can tell, the *Fractal Tracery* has been breached to what passes for open space over here, and none of the ship's systems are online.

Are we dead? Delusional? Transformed? Mysteries abound.

And *deepen*, the more answers we get.

"Think of this place as *Heaven*." Julie seems to slide farther away, then pops back to the middle of our little group. "Think of it as *paradise*. The first and best universe in existence. The prototype, the template, for all the universes that came after."

"Which makes *our* universe. What, exactly?" asks Most Eager.

"A *mistake*." Julie smirks and shrugs. "Or so I'm told."

"Told by whom?" growls Twelvefold Sinner.

Another shrug from Julie. "Someone who knows."

"Is this *someone* sustaining us somehow?" asks Stick-n-Stone. "Providing life support in the hard vacuum of space?"

Julie shakes her head. "There's no hard vacuum in space here. So, technically, we shouldn't even call it 'space,' I suppose. It's not *empty*."

"The rest of the crew. Is where?" Most Eager's every silvery eye is fixed on Julie.

"Aren't you going to ask me how we got here?" Julie grows to five times her normal height. "Don't you want to know how we crossed over?"

"If it reveals. The fate of the crew."

"We were improvising." Julie stretches further, then compresses.

"And it wasn't the *first* time, either." Back to normal size, she winks devilishly.

"What *kind* of improvising?" asks Ever Luminous, the lights inside him growing dim.

"Instead of just signaling *inward*, to developing species within our universe," explains Julie, "we were signaling *outward*. To other, *higher* levels."

"But that is not. The mission. Of The Rising," says Most Eager.

"'The Rising?'" Julie folds her arms over her chest. "You haven't *risen* in a long time, have you?"

"The mission. Is to inspire. Other species. To rise." Most Eager sounds indignant. "In so doing. We *all* rise."

"You've stalled out, and you know it," says Julie. "*Everyone* in The Rising knows it. And some of us decided to act on it. We've been sending signals beyond the boundaries of our local space-time for a while now--and we finally got an *answer*. An *invitation*." She spreads her arms wide. "This ship, the *Fractal Tracery*, was closest to the coordinates for the rendezvous."

"What kind of invitation?" asks Reef.

"The same one you're about to get." Julie smiles warmly. "They're throwing you a line."

"A line?" snarls Twelvefold Sinner.

"A *lifeline*." Julie nods slowly.

"What the hell are you talking about?" I ask.

"The end of the universe." Julie grins and claps her hands. "*Your* universe. It's coming any *minute* now."

As we stand there, trying to take in what Julie has told us, she points at the biggest gap in the hull. "See that?"

As she says it, I glimpse movement in the milk-white field beyond the ship. A shape coalesces in the firmament--a lumpy gray patch growing larger as I watch. It unfolds rapidly, taking on contour and color, expanding to blot out the black stars and fill the view through the ship's porous skin.

"That's where we're going." Julie waves for us to follow. "Abandon ship!"

Moving away from our entry point doesn't seem like a good idea. But I might not have a choice. As I stare at the drifting mass outside the hull--now a gleaming island of crystal structures and a rainbow riot of vegetation--I'm pulled toward it.

"Let go," says Julie. "Focus on our destination. Focus on what you want to have happen. That's how it works over here." Her feet leave the floor, and she drifts toward the hole in the hull.

I try the opposite, focusing on staying put...and it works. As the rest of the Go Team lifts off, sailing toward the island, I stay behind.

But I don't hold back for long. The pull intensifies, overcoming my resistance, and I rise from the deck, turning in a lazy spiral.

Against my will, I rise through the hull, into the whiteness, drifting toward the island shining with light from some source I cannot see.

I remember another time, fifty years ago, when I was also caught in the grip of an alien force. Not knowing if I would ever see my home again.

It was a beam of light that night, an amber shaft dropping from the starry Georgia sky to lift me in its warm, shivering nimbus. It picked me up when I was walking home from the bar I was tending.

I still remember how terrified I was when I glimpsed the outline of the spherical ship above me, silhouetted against the Moon. Was I heading for an alien dissection table?

Anything was possible that night. As smart as I was (self-taught, no money for school), as young (23) and restless as I was, I still feared what was coming.

Then, after I crossed the threshold into that marvelous craft, and beheld Most Eager for the first time, and heard his question, his incredible offer, I seized my new destiny with both hands and all my heart.

As we approach the island suspended in white-space, I make out more details: glittering crystal spires amid a sea of multicolored plant life (or something alien that resembles vegetation from a distance); clouds the color of violets and goldenrod, some raining downward, others up; pulsing obsidian mountain peaks smoking like volcanos...and the smoke is neon green and moves like it's alive.

We sail in over the treetops and swoop toward the highest spire. Then, as so often happens in the Whiteverse (as I've just now nick-named the place), the distance changes, suddenly tripling. Julie laughs, and the gap quickly closes, flinging us up to the spire so fast, I think we're going to crash into it.

Instead, we all touch down lightly on the ground in front of it.

"Here we are." Julie gestures at the spire. Big crystal doors swing open, their multitudes of facets twinkling. "Go on in."

"Is the crew. Of the *Fractal Tracery*. In there?" asks Most Eager.

"What about the supposed end of our universe?" says Reef. "Will we find out how to stop it?"

"All I can say is, this will be the most important meeting of your life." Julie bows and waves us toward the doors.

Swallowing hard, I follow Most Eager through the doorway. The rest of the Go Team files in behind us.

We enter a huge, circular chamber with crystal walls that sweep up like the sides of a funnel into the towering spire above. Every-where, we are surrounded by spots of light reflected from the crys-tal, thousands of sparkling flecks hanging like frozen confetti on every surface.

"Who's coming to this meeting, other than us?" I ask. "And when will they be gracing us with their presence?"

"Think of them as saviors," says Julie. "And they've been here all along."

She claps, and three figures suddenly unfold from what looked until now like empty space in the middle of the room.

Though "unfold" isn't quite the right word for it. It's more like the figures are perfectly two-dimensional, practically invisible when viewed on edge--and they *turn* so their flat sides face us.

Only then do we see that they look like white paper cutouts in the shape of blocky, humanoid monoliths. The one in the middle is tallest (over three meters), with the most squared-off head; the one on the left is shorter, with a more angular, back-sloped skull; and the one on the right is even shorter and more rounded than either of them.

When they speak, their voices sound like layer upon layer of static blending together. It's only after the first few words that I realize the static is familiar. I've heard it before, many times.

It's identical to the cosmic microwave background radiation, the soundtrack of the Big Bang that started our universe.

"Welcome, blessed guests," says Middle Cutout.

"Your new life starts here and now," says Left Cutout. *"Infinite white heavens await your exploration."*

Stick-n-Stone rolls up beside me. "What if we aren't done exploring our *old* heavens?"

"Forget them," says Right Cutout. *"They will be gone soon."*

A tiny object rises from behind Middle Cutout, a glowing golden orb the size of a golf ball. It hovers above his head, turning and pulsing with dazzling white light.

"All the matter and energy of a new universe resides in this Seed," explains Middle Cutout. *"We send it now into your universe, where it will replace that misbegotten atrocity with something superior in every way."*

I can believe that Seed is loaded with the contents of a new universe. I can feel its awesome *power*, its *weight*, from across the room.

"Why destroy. Our universe?" asks Most Eager.

"It was a mistake," says Right Cutout. *"A defective copy."*

"Based on this *template of perfection."* Willowy paper arms emerge from Middle Cutout's flattened body and spread wide. *"The copy should have been destroyed long ago."*

"Yet it survived, hidden, until now," says Left Cutout. *"Draining the life from our original cosmos through a secret link left over from the birth process."*

"The parasitic universe devours our Wonderverse to feed its own growth," says Left Cutout. *"Its contents are corrupt."*

"Including its *inhabitants*?" I gesture at myself and my ship-mates. "Then why bring us here before you destroy it?"

"Because we believe some are worth saving," says Right Cutout.

"And she *has convinced us you are among that number,"* says Middle Cutout.

I turn my gaze to Julie. "We're here because of you?"

"You're my friends." She salutes Most Eager with palms upraised. "My *mentor*. I wanted to save you."

"At what cost?" asks Most Eager.

"We ask only that you help us to seek other lifeforms worth saving from other doomed universes," says Right Cutout.

"Just go on doing what The Rising has *been* doing, in other words," says Julie. "Recruiting the best and the brightest."

A picture takes shape in my mind. "These other universes. Why exactly are they doomed?"

The Cutouts are silent for a moment. Then the one in the middle finally confirms what I've been thinking.

"Like your universe, they are inferior copies," he says. *"And para-sites. They must be destroyed for our universe to survive and thrive."*

"And how many of these doomed universes are there?" I ask.

Again, hesitation. *"All of them. All but the first and best, our Wonderverse."*

"Ah." I look at Julie. "And the crew of the *Fractal Tracery?* Were they made this same offer, by any chance?"

Julie nods.

"And did they accept it?"

"They weren't interested." The look in her eyes speaks volumes.

"But you are?" I ask her.

"Let's just say I was given a second chance to consider the offer," says Julie. "And I saw the light."

Reading between the lines, I understand the truth about why she wanted us here. Her crew is gone, presumably eliminated for refusing to support the Cutouts' program of mass universe extermination. She is the sole survivor, preserved by the Cutouts to aid their dark plans--probably controlled by them to some extent--and she needs our help to resist them and save our home universe.

Though how exactly we can provide that help remains to be seen. Already, the Seed is gliding across the chamber, chiming softly. How long until it makes a beeline for the anomaly and our universe on the other side?

Chancer that I am, I hear the call of X-factor craziness loud and clear. The only question that matters now is, how do we stop the Seed from destroying our universe?

An idea comes to me in a flash. Catching Most Eager's eye (dozens of them), I give him/her/it/them a sign--moving my hands together and apart with thumbs and forefingers pinched as if I'm stretching something. I need him/her/it/them to fill some time.

He/she/it/they understand the signal and set out to keep the Cutouts talking. "So what happened to. The crew of the. *Fractal Tracery.* If they were not. Interested in the offer?"

Even as the Cutouts answer the question, I turn to Twelvefold Sinner. "I need your other selves," I tell him quietly. "All at once."

Sinner scowls. "You know that's impossible. Only one self at a time can occupy my body's coordinates."

"Have you ever *tried* to manifest all twelve at once?"

50

"The physical laws of the universe prevent it," Sinner says darkly.

I pat him on the shoulder. "But we aren't *in* our universe anymore."

Sinner's scowl lightens.

"You heard Julie." I wink. "'Focus on what you want to have happen. That's how it works over here.'"

"But what if it works?" asks Sinner. "Then what?"

"Stop that Seed," I tell him. "Or *detonate* it."

Looking up, I see the Seed is almost overhead. Time to set the rest of the plan in motion.

"Ever Luminous!" I don't bother keeping my voice down anymore. "Give us a lightshow! Make it a big one!"

Ever Luminous doesn't question me; he just cuts loose with a burst of red and white fireworks projected outside his body.

"Reef! Go bowling with Stone!" I point at the Cutouts. "Knock down the pins!"

I don't have to tell them twice. Reef scoops up Stick-n-Stone and hefts her like a bowling ball. Good thing I taught them how to bowl back on the *Transit*.

Meanwhile, Julie's yelling. "Whatever you're doing, stop it!" Maybe she's fooling the Cutouts, but it doesn't sound to me like her heart is in it.

Not that it matters either way with our universe on the line. "Sinner! Do it!" I shout.

Sinner shuts his eyes and clenches his chest-face, concentrating with all his might. He shudders the way he always does before switching selves, only harder.

While that's happening, Luminous throws off more fireworks, filling the chamber with flares and sparks. Reef hurls Stick-n-Stone over the crystal floor like a bowling ball--but *this* ball hoots and hollers as she hurtles toward the Cutouts.

And the Seed keeps gliding toward the doors.

Just then, Sinner howls and explodes in a burst of blinding white light. When the light fades, I see the experiment was a success. Where once there was a single Sinner, twelve very different versions of the same being now stand.

"Stop that Seed!" Even as I shout the words, all twelve Sinners leap into action at once, scrambling toward the Seed.

Unfortunately, the Cutouts take action as well. The three figures quickly fold themselves into new forms--what look like an origami bird of prey, an origami dragon, and a giant origami spider.

They're on the twelve Sinners in a heartbeat, springing across the chamber with the usual distance-warping magic of the Wonderverse. Somehow, though they look like origami paper sculptures, they go through the Sinners like threshers through crops on an agriplanet.

Who would have thought an origami spider could take down a metal-plated commando version of Sinner with built-in organic cannons in his face, chest, and belly? Who would have thought an origami dragon could thrash a purple-skinned, musclebound berserker Sinner into cutlets? And who would ever have imagined an origami bird of prey taking down not only a giant warrior plant Sinner, but ice-monster and speed demon Sinners as well?

All that's happening, and more. The Cutouts, whatever they are, possess immense power. At the rate they're going, the twelve Sinners will be minus-twelve before long.

If I want their sacrifice to mean anything, I'd better act fast.

As two more Sinners crash and burn, I whip around and fix my eyes on the prize: the shimmering, airborne Seed. Then, I focus my will on zooming across the chamber to intercept it.

Yet I go nowhere.

Come on! Any other time, things jump around randomly in this so-called Wonderverse, leaping closer and farther away with ridiculous ease. Why not *now?*

The Seed accelerates toward the door, and I break into a run. Then, suddenly, someone leaps in front of me, blocking the way. It's Julie, grown to three meters tall and scowling as she reaches for me.

I try to dodge her grasp, but I can't. She scoops me up so fast, it knocks the breath right out of me.

She squeezes me so tightly, I think she's going to crush me. Have the Cutouts intensified their control over her?

But her scowl quickly becomes a smile as he swings me up close and plants a kiss on my forehead. "Thank you," she says warmly. "I knew I called in the right people for the job."

Then, she whips around and throws me like a football at the Seed.

Even so, the Seed keeps gaining speed; there's no way I'll catch up with it. My universe is doomed. The biggest mission of my life is about to end in failure.

And then it isn't. Suddenly, an invisible force swoops in and wraps around me. As it lifts me off the floor and carries me toward the Seed, I hear a thousand screaming voices in my head.

As I reel from the unexpected blast of input, I remember the content of the signal that brought us to the *Fractal Tracery* in the first place: *Black stars. White space. Forever screaming.*

This, I realize, is the rest of the mystery. The puzzle beyond the anomaly ends here.

The screaming coalesces into words, telling a story that answers vital questions. It is then that I recognize the voices.

They belong to the crew of the *Fractal Tracery*.

The crew--every last one of them--refused to help the Cutouts harvest survivors from universes they planned to destroy. In return for their refusal, they were murdered, converted to this stream of unified souls even as Julie was shielded and put to use. The souls continued to try to stop the Cutouts, but in their insubstantial state, they failed.

Now, together, *we* are going to *succeed*.

The stream of souls whisks me across the chamber to intercept the Seed. Without thinking, I clamp both hands around it, feeling the pain of its surging power and potential.

It ought to burn a hole right through me and zoom out the door anyway--but the soulstream, grounded and focused by my physical form, restrains it. Cocoons it.

And then, offers to trigger it.

The souls give me a choice. The only way to stop the Seed from obliterating our universe is to set it off now. If we do that, *this* universe and every living thing in it will be destroyed, making way for a *new* universe born from the Seed. But *our* universe--*my* universe, my *home*--will be preserved.

Am I willing to make that trade?

I smile. The souls know the answer before I can say it aloud.

Together, we focus our wills on the Seed. It grows unbearably hot in my hands, and I feel a strange euphoria rippling through me.

Followed by an explosion that tears me apart in every way imaginable for what feels like an eternity of agony.

When I awaken, the Whiteverse/Wonderverse is gone. A new universe has been created in its place.

And *my* home universe, somewhere beyond the boundaries of this one, is intact. I know this, I *sense* it...though I don't know how to get back there. I am trapped in the new universe that sprang from the Seed before it could destroy the universe of my birth.

Frankly, that's okay with me. *This* is my home now. I am linked to it in ways I never imagined before, playing a role I never expected in this vast and amazing creation.

Perhaps because I was at the epicenter of the new Big Bang, I am a part of it all. Somehow, my consciousness remains intact, for I possess an awareness of this universe in all its immense entirety.

And let me just say, this is one *magnificent* universe. The physical laws here are eccentric and unpredictable. What would have been impossible back home is not only possible, but *likely*, over here. The result is a place of such beauty, surprise, and diversity that, trust me, it would blow your mind like a Big Bang seed if you ever came here.

The stars are much larger and more colorful here, not limited to spherical shapes. They orbit planets instead of vice versa, and are inhabited by sentient fission reactions building cities from stable solar prominences.

Space itself is mostly filled with a glittering golden medium that's a combination of dark anti-matter and time in a gaseous state.

And the *lifeforms* exist in such staggering abundance, variety, complexity, and hardiness that they put my home universe and the Cutouts of the Wonderverse to shame.

Do you like the sound of all that? Good; I'm quite proud of it. After all, I helped make it what it is today, and I'm helping influence what it becomes next.

Somehow, I have influence over this place. That's why, for example, evolution here is based on cooperation, not conflict. It's why there's no death or decay, no sickness or pain or sorrow. Because that's the way I think it *should* be.

It's also why there's a constellation of mega-stars inhabited by the souls of the crew of the *Fractal Tracery*. It's why entire worlds are dedicated to the recreated selves of my shipmates from the *Transit*, plus a resurrected, Cutout-free Julie.

What inspired me to use my influence the way I have, to shape this universe into what it's becoming? On some level, I guess I'm still carrying out my mission from my days with The Rising, planting mysteries to draw out species who might one day become spacefarers.

But on another level, some creations have meaning for me alone. Like the blue-green planet in a distant quadrant, the one that forever looks, sounds, and smells like a Georgia night fifty years before the latest Big Bang. The one where a bartender who looks a lot like me walks down a country lane in the moonlight, only to be caught in a shaft of amber light from above.

And a creature that looks like a cloud with dozens of silver eyes on dozens of squirming yellow tendrils asks him a question that changes his life forever. A question that is more prophetic than perhaps even he/she/it/they realizes as the historic words are spoken:

"Would you like. To experience. A universe?"

FOOD CHAINS

Only as I devour the flesh of Manny's finger for what must be the hundredth--and final--time do I finally realize that I love him back.

It truly blows my mind. It's one thing for Rations to fall in love with those who feed on them--it's not uncommon at all--but who ever heard of a woman falling for her food?

This just might be a first.

Too bad no one will likely ever know. Too bad both of us will die before long.

Manny will die from being eaten alive, and I will die of starvation when there's no more Manny left to eat.

"Have some more, Lupe." He has one finger left, a right thumb, and he presses it toward me. He has a smile on his sugar-white face with its tutti-frutti swirls like he's a child offering me candy.

I shake my head. "I'll be okay." My voice is hoarse. "Save it for later."

Manny frowns and opens his mouth like he's going to argue. Then, he smiles sadly and pulls back the thumb. "Maybe you're right."

"Double damn skippy I'm right." I force on a smirk of my own for his benefit. The truth is, my stomach's still rumbling something fierce, but my Ration's got to stretch.

There's always been plenty of Manny to go around, but not anymore. These days, he can't replace what I eat.

This time, when he's gone, he's gone for good.

Two months ago, when I first met Manny, I couldn't have imagined feeling sorry about running out of him. He was nothing but food to me then...food I wouldn't eat, at that.

It wasn't the taste of him that I hated, since I hadn't actually tasted him back then. It was just that I hated all his kind.

In fact, I just about shot him on sight the first time I saw him. Just about shot my lover and hired gun, Guapo Vasquez, in the bargain.

Guapo *knew* how I felt about Rations...and yet, there he was, strolling up the gangway of my spaceship, the *Puerco*, with one of those tutti-frutti naked little bastards right behind him.

Yet another rule broken by damn Guapo. For someone I let screw me as much as he did, the guy spent an awful lot of time screwing *with* me.

The pistol was in my hand about a heartbeat after I saw them. "*Mierda!*" I said, catching the Ration in my sights and flicking the gun's settings to maximum everything.

Better believe the tutti-frutti hairless bastard stopped walking...though he didn't stop smiling. Right at me.

That was a mistake on his part. His wide-eyed, sparkle-toothed, never-ending smile reminded me so much of someone I'd once known that it nearly got him killed.

"What the flap *is* this, Guapo?" The gun in my hand didn't twitch.

Guapo whistled a tune and walked toward me like nothing out of the ordinary was happening. He combed one hand through his oily, black hair and used the other hand to scratch his private parts. "You drunk, *dulcita*? This is a *Ration*. Got 'im *cheap*, too."

"I *know* what he is!" I wanted to swing the gun around to Guapo, but I couldn't bring myself to let the Ration's tutti-frutti bald head out of the sights. "What's he *doing* here?"

Guapo stopped in front of me and pointed at his mouth. "He's gonna *feed* us, babe. That's what Rations *do*."

"Damnit!" I shot a glare at Guapo. "I've got, what? *One* lousy *rule*? *One rule*, and you can't *follow* it?" I whipped the gun around and shook it at Guapo. "*No Rations*, remember?"

Guapo stared down at me with his dark, half-lidded eyes. He reached out and tucked my long, brown hair behind my ears. "Cold storage on the *Puerco*'s down, *novia*. We got no way to keep fresh food."

"We'll have plenty of cash after the job on Polvo," I said. "The bounty for killing that man-eater's gonna be enough to rehab half the ship."

"Yeah," said Guapo. "And in the meantime, we gotta eat *something*. Something that doesn't have to be *refrigerated*."

I tossed my head, shaking the hair from behind my ears, then swung the gun back to aim at the Ration. He hadn't moved an inch. "I won't eat *that*. I'll *never* eat that."

"My name is Manna," said the Ration. The multicolored swirls on his sugar-white skin twisted and changed as he spoke. "You can call me Manny."

Guapo stomped over and clapped a hand on Manny's shoulder. "Got him for a song, babe. Next to nothin'. He's used, but he's strictly Grade A."

"That's right." Manny nodded and patted his hairless chest with both hands. "Zero defects. My last owner only sold me because he was strapped for cash." Manny cupped his hand, shook it, and pretended to fling dice out of it. "Gambling, y'know."

"Out!" I took a step toward Manny. "Get the flap *out*!"

Just then, Guapo looked past me and grinned. "Hey, Frogface!"

He jammed two fingers in his mouth and whistled loud. "C'mere and try some'a this!"

Frogface, my pilot and engineer, had just entered the cargo bay. At Guapo's whistle, he waddled out from behind me and headed straight for Guapo and Manny.

Frogface was in such a hurry that he literally dropped what he was doing, letting a power drill bang the deckplates in his wake. "Great! I'm starvin', Guap!"

Still smiling, Manny extended his arms toward Guapo and Frogface. "If I may make a suggestion, gentlemen," he said. "The biceps are especially tender today. I'm roasting them up as we speak."

Frogface, whose given name was Felix Suerte, rubbed his hands together. He looked more like a duck than a frog, with lips curled like a beak and a broad, flat nose--which, of course, was the joke behind his nickname. "I like the sound a' that." He reached for Manny's right arm. "Think I'll try some."

Guapo leaned in and sank his teeth into Manny's left bicep. He came away with a mouthful of meat and chewed it slowly. "Top quality," he said when he could manage to speak. "Compliments to the chef."

"Why thank you, sir." Manny took a little bow.

As Frogface took a bite, and Guapo took another, my stomach churned. I wanted to look away, but that would have meant letting Manny out of my sights.

I grimaced and clenched my teeth. I couldn't stand watching people eat those things.

Rations were genetically engineered to be delicious and nutritious. They could use body chemistry to cook and season their flesh to taste, infuse it with a seemingly limitless number of flavors...then regenerate and replace every bite taken out. They were happy to do it, too.

But every time I saw someone eating a Ration, it still looked like a nightmare to me.

"Hey, Lupe, come on." Guapo swallowed his latest mouthful. "Try some a' this. You won't *believe* how tender."

"Get off the ship." I took another step toward Manny. "Either you *walk* off, or I *shoot* you and throw out your dead body."

"Lupe!" Frogface looked up from the forearm he'd been gnawing. "Quit scaring my dinner!"

"Yeah, Lupe." Guapo patted Manny's bald head. "You wanna eat powdered cactus and spiderwebs all the way to Polvo, that's your business. Froggy and me want fresh food."

"Forget it!" I took another step toward Manny, then another.

"Let me put it this way," said Guapo. "If Manny leaves, Froggy and me leave, too."

So that was the end of it, right there, and I knew it. No way I was taking on the mission to Polvo without Guapo and Frogface. I stopped moving toward Manny, though I kept him in my sights an extra minute for effect.

Then, I lowered the gun.

"That's a girl." Guapo winked and hiked a thumb at Manny's chest. "Now have a bite, huh? You'll feel better."

I shot Guapo the kind of glare that let him know he wasn't getting any from me for a long time. I turned the glare on Manny, too, but it didn't seem to faze him.

He knew better than to say a word to me at that moment, but the sparkly smile never left his face.

Typical Ration. Always look as friendly and appetizing as possible, no matter how annoying you might turn out to be.

But that wasn't why I hated him.

Guapo and Frogface might have won the battle, but I didn't let them enjoy it. We spent three more days planetside on Saguaro getting ready for the trip, and I worked them like dogs. Didn't say more than the bare minimum to either of them the whole time, either.

And Guapo sure as flap didn't get anywhere near my bed. Not that he didn't try.

Manny, at least, kept his distance from me. While the *Puerco* was on the ground, I saw him only a handful of times, and he hardly said a word to me. Never offered me a bite, either, which was smart on his part.

In fact, the closest we came to a conversation was the time we walked down a narrow corridor from different directions at the same moment. Instead of moving to opposite sides, we both kept moving to the same side of the corridor. We did it three times before Manny finally laughed and pressed himself against the wall.

"After you," he said, gesturing for me to pass. "Great minds think alike, I guess."

"Flap you, food." I leaned my shoulder into him as I pushed past. "Stay in the *maldecido* commisary where you belong, eh?"

I hated that tutti-frutti little bastard so much it hurt. I'm talking physical pain in my gut and my heart.

I'm talking the kind of hate that's so huge it just about replaces you. It works on you day after day for a lifetime, eating away at you.

And it starts when you're little more than a baby. That's the best time for it.

I was eight years old when my three brothers and I caught Cornucopia. This was twenty-four years ago, and we were all starving to death during the famine on Polvo, our homeworld.

We sneaked over the wall of the estate where Cornucopia lived, and then we threw a net over her and hauled her to a shack out in Barrio Sucio.

We cheered and laughed as we tied her up, because we were heroes. We were too late to save poor dead Mama and Papa, but we'd saved ourselves and our friends. Maybe we'd even saved the whole barrio.

It had been so long since we'd eaten well, we'd forgotten what real food tasted like. Now, we had a living, breathing Ration all to ourselves. If we took good enough care of her, we might never go hungry again, no matter how long the famine lasted on our world.

At least that was the plan.

"You remember me, don't you?" As the boys tightened the ropes around Cornucopia's shoulders and torso, I patted the top of her smooth, bald head.

Cornucopia nodded. That same old sparkly Ration smile was pasted onto her pudgy face. "The little beggar girl. Always begging for a bite of me." Her voice tinkled like tiny bells when she spoke.

"And you never said 'yes.' Not once." I pinched the meat of her shoulder, thinking about sinking my teeth into her. "But I guess you can't say 'no' anymore."

"Actually, I can," said Cornucopia. The iridescent swirls on her face flowed and changed color. "Nothing has changed."

"Like flap!" My oldest brother, Roto, took a deep whiff at the back of her neck. "You're *ours* now! You have to *feed* us!"

"No," said Cornucopia. "I don't."

"And why is that?" I made a face at her. I wasn't taking her seriously.

"I'm still someone else's property." Cornucopia nodded. "Señor Gustavo still owns me, and I can't feed anyone unless he tells me."

Roto's wild, frizzy puff of black hair bounced as he laughed. "We aren't going to ask your permission, y'know."

"Yeah," said my other brother, Miguel. "Don't look like you can stop us, either."

"You're right, I can't." Cornucopia's angelic smile drifted from Roto to Miguel to my third brother, Oswaldo.

"Didn't think so." Miguel grinned and drove his teeth into her tricep. He tore off a hunk of meat and chewed it with his eyes closed, an expression of perfect bliss on his face.

62

I understood why he hadn't been able to wait. None of us had eaten anything but bugs and rotten garbage for weeks. My stomach growled just from watching him.

"That's good," said Miguel. "Oh God, that's good."

Oswaldo, just a year older than I, was the next to pounce. He bit into the flesh of Cornucopia's right thigh and came away with a mouthful dripping with rainbow blood.

Miguel laughed. "Thank God," he said. "Oh, thank God." Then he hugged Oswaldo.

I was just about to go in for a bite of my own when Cornucopia spoke up. "You were right when you said I couldn't stop you."

"Tell me about it." Oswaldo bit off another hunk of her thigh.

"I can do something else, though." Cornucopia's smile never wavered. "I can kill you."

Roto smirked. "Good one. Kill us how?"

Cornucopia looked a little embarrassed. The swirls on her face shifted from blue-green and gold to red and deep pink. "Poison," she said. "If my owner hasn't programmed your genetic code into my glands, one bite of my flesh will poison you."

Oswaldo stopped chewing his food. So did Miguel.

"She's bluffing," said Roto. "The *perra's* trying to scare us into letting her go."

I glared at the Ration. I had a horrible feeling she wasn't bluffing at all. "Why didn't you say something till now?"

Cornucopia shrugged. "Would you have believed me?"

Miguel groaned. Oswaldo coughed.

"Don't listen to her," said Roto. "She just wants to escape."

"That's not an issue." Cornucopia shook her head slowly, still smiling. "The *policia* are almost here. They followed a tracking tag in my bloodstream."

Automatically, I looked toward the door. Then, when Miguel and Oswaldo started vomiting, I looked at them instead.

"What's the cure?" I shouted.

"There is no cure," said Cornucopia. "They'll be dead in minutes."

I heard sirens outside the shack, and I went to my suffering brothers. As they collapsed--first Oswaldo, then Miguel--I dropped to my knees with them. I felt as if my own guts were being torn out by rough hands.

For many years, death had been my constant companion on Polvo...but this was different. These brothers were all I held precious in the world, all that had kept me alive in the darkest of times.

And the worst of it was, their deaths could have been prevented so easily.

As they released their dying breaths, I glared at Cornucopia. Even then, that damned sparkle-toothed smile never left her face.

Is it any wonder that twenty-four years later, I didn't join in the Ration lovefest rolling through the *Puerco* all the way from Saguaro to Polvo?

During the trip through space, Guapo and Frogface palled around with Manny like he was their long-lost childhood friend. They were inseparable.

They were always together in the cockpit or the break room or the tool room. Guapo and Frogface were always nibbling on some hunk of Manny--a meaty haunch or a crispy ear or a candy-coated fingernail--and Manny was always telling jokes or stories about the many people who'd eaten him before. They invited me to join them again and again, but I never did, and I hated them for being such flapholes. I hated them for bringing Manny onboard, and I hated them for having so much fun with him right in front of me.

The truth was, my bad mood wasn't just because of Manny, though. I was also full of dread at the thought of returning to my homeworld. Good old Polvo, dust bowl of the galaxy, final resting place of two of my brothers.

And now, maybe my third brother as well.

It was the real reason we were going to that craphole planet, though Guapo and Frogface didn't know it.

We were going to look for my brother, Roto, who had disappeared a month ago on Polvo, at the height of a rash of attacks by a man-eating alien monster.

Guapo and Frogface thought we'd been hired to kill that man-eater, but no one had hired us. I was taking us to Polvo to find Roto, though I'd gladly gun down any man-eater that came between me and my brother.

A week after leaving Saguaro, we landed on Polvo. My heart pounded as we got ready to leave the ship.

As I got ready to see home for the first time in over two decades.

"Remember." Guapo grabbed an ultraviolet rifle off the rack on the cargo bay wall. "If you see yourself coming, shoot to kill." He wrapped one black-gloved hand around the barrel of the rifle and curled the other around the grip.

"That's kind of a no-brainer, isn't it?" Frogface snickered. "You see yourself, you're either lookin' at a mirror or one of these *reflejo* creatures."

"It's harder than you think, killing your identical twin," said Guapo. "Why do you think so few people have managed to do it?"

"It's the perfect camouflage." I finished braiding my long, brown hair in a ponytail and flipped it over my shoulder. "At the very least, seeing your perfect mirror image can rattle you just long enough for a *reflejo* to pounce."

"And sink its teeth into you." Guapo snarled and gnashed his teeth like a wolf, then laughed. "Not that anyone knows what *reflejos* use for teeth or what they really look like in the first place."

I smacked a red button on a panel on the wall, and the cargo bay door rolled up into the ceiling. Before the door had finished opening, a swirl of gray dust lashed in from outside, followed by a flying black spider-bug as big as my fist.

Welcome back to Polvo.

Guapo swung his rifle around and picked off the *araña volando* with one quick flash of purple light. The creature screamed as it died, and Guapo hooted.

"I shot your dinner, *dulcita*!" Guapo sneered at me. "Since you won't eat the Ration, you can fry that up with some butter and salt!"

"You shot it, you eat it," I told him. "I'll stick with my jerky and fruit leather." While Guapo and Frogface yukked it up, I slid extra weapons charges and a hunting knife into my belt loops.

When I was done and looked up, I noticed Manny watching me. He smiled at first, but then his sparkly smile quivered and faded.

"What's *your* problem, flap-off?" I snapped at him.

Manny shrugged. "I, uh...I have a bad feeling about this place."

"Since when does *food* have *feelings*?" I sneered as I pulled on my goggles.

"Maybe this'll make you feel better," said Guapo. Smiling, he strolled over and handed Manny a rifle.

"Oh, for God's sake." For the umpteenth time, I wondered what I'd ever seen in Guapo. "You're giving the *food* a *gun*?"

"Why the hell not?" Guapo slapped Manny on the back. "I sure don't want no *reflejo* chowing down on him."

"Actually," said Manny, "any unauthorized parties who eat me will die."

"But who knows with these crazy *reflejos*, eh?" said Guapo.

"If the *reflejos* are at all organic in nature," said Manny, "the toxins generated by my anti-theft system will..."

I cut him off right there. I knew all about the Rations' anti-theft system.

So did Miguel and Oswaldo.

"Shut up, all of you." I armed my rifle and stalked toward the open cargo bay door. "Let's get this damn show on the road. We've gotta go kill us a man-eater."

"Thank you for coming," said the governor of Pesadilla province. "Your help means more to the people of planet Polvo in this time of crisis than you will ever know. I only regret that I found it necessary to relocate before your arrival."

"Found it necessary to run away like the cowardly *gatito* you are, you mean!" said Guapo, aiming his ultraviolet rifle dead-on at the governor's face on the video screen. "Die, flapper!"

Guapo squeezed the trigger, and a bolt of purple energy sizzled across the governor's office and pierced the video screen. Smoke and shards of layered crystal circuitry erupted from the impact point, and the image of the governor's face flickered off the screen.

But her voice kept talking from the undamaged audio speakers.

"Very sorry I can't greet you in person," she said, "but my staff and I thought it best if we moved off-world for the duration. Please contact us at the following frequency when you've eliminated the threat."

Guapo whipped his rifle toward one of the speakers, but I swatted his arm before he could fire. "We need to hear this," I told him.

Guapo lowered the rifle but kept a tight grip on it.

"Here's what we know," said the governor's recorded voice. "The man-eater has ranged across Pesadilla, Grito, and Rasgón provinces. However, we believe it has a refuge in the Cambio region of southwest Pesadilla."

Guapo shot me a look, and I nodded. After growing up on that craphole planet, I knew plenty about the Cambio.

"This is the first case we've encountered of a *reflejo* turning man-eater," said the governor. "Given the abilities and native intelligence of these creatures, we believe we are fortunate that the death toll to date has not risen above 257."

"257?" Frogface whistled through his duck-bill lips.

"Nothin' left but hair and gristle," said Guapo.

"Madre de Dios." Frogface made a hasty sign of the cross over his forehead, chest, and shoulders.

Guapo puffed out his breath. "What'd you expect for the kind'a paycheck we're gettin'? Fish in a flappin' barrel?"

The governor was still talking. "Best of luck on your mission. We salute you and your unit, and we promise that your selfless courage will never be forgotten. Thank you, men of the..."

Before she could say another syllable, I swept my rifle around and fried the speakers.

"Yeah!" Guapo fired off another purple bolt from his own rifle, plowing a charred furrow in the ceiling. "*There's* the *chica* I love! Good riddance to that stuck-up *reflejo perra* who's been takin' your place lately."

I didn't dignify his remarks with an answer or even a look. Instead, I turned and charged past everyone, right out the office door into the blazing sunlight of midday Polvo.

The truth was, the *perra*--the bitch--was still in charge of me. I'd shot out the speakers not for fun or out of anger, but because if Guapo and Frogface had heard the rest of the governor's recording, it would have been a dead giveaway.

The governor had already saluted our "unit," and had started to thank "the men of the..."

As in "the men of the 24th Spaceborne Division of Mexifleet," who were the ones who were supposed to do the job we'd come to do. They'd be on Polvo in three days.

I'd brought us there three days early to try to save my brother, Roto, before the Mexifleet Marines came in with guns blazing. Brute force, not precision, was Mexifleet's style. If there was still anything left of Roto to save, and he was anywhere near the man-eating *reflejo* when the Marines caught up with it, there wouldn't be anything left of Roto for long.

In other words, no one was paying us to do this job.

The only possible reward would be getting Roto out alive. My crew's cut of the pay would be zero percent of nothing.

As well as I got along with Guapo and Frogface, that's the kind of information that can get a girl like me keelhauled out here in the ol' rough and tumble.

We flew out to the Cambio and parked the *Puerco* on a ridge about a mile and a half back from the border. Frogface whined about having to walk the extra distance, but Guapo explained how we needed to sneak up on the *reflejo's* turf.

The real reason I made sure we parked that far away was this: the borders of the Cambio are always changing, just like everything out there, and you do *not* want your spacecraft ending up inside those borders.

Trust me on that one.

"Should we bring a cart?" Frogface said as we straggled out of the *Puerco's* cargo bay. "For Manny, I mean?"

I wanted to slap his face tomato-red, but I settled for shooting him a serious stink-eye. "No, we are *not* hauling Manny in a cart." I adjusted the straps of my backpack, which was heavy with jerky, fruit leather, and tubes of nutri-paste. "The whole *point* of Rations is that you don't have to store, preserve, or *carry* them."

Manny smiled at Frogface and nodded. "Like livestock, Froggy. Right? It was easier for ancient travelers when their food did the walking."

"Shut up, flap." As usual, I wasn't in the mood for the tutti-frutti little bastard. "Shut up and play with your rifle. Feel free to point it at yourself and pull the trigger."

"I'd probably just grow back," said Manny. "I can regenerate, remember?"

"And I can reload," I said, glaring at him as I stalked past. "Again and again and again."

You can't see the border of the Cambio, but you always know when you've stepped across it.

It starts as a chill flickering up your spine, and then it spreads out. Your arms and legs tremble, and sometimes you drop what you're carrying. Then, there's a mighty squeeze in the pit of your stomach, and a flare of heartburn pushing up through your throat.

Then, suddenly, there's a fizzy, weightless dizziness, like the top of your head has floated off and your brain is turning and sizzling like butter in a skillet.

After that, it's smooth sailing. If you don't give up and cross back over the border, the storm of feelings settles down. It never quite goes away till you leave the Cambio, but at least you can stand it.

It's a hell of a place, the Cambio. I guess I should've warned my men what to expect...but if I had, they wouldn't've gone in with me.

In which case, they'd still be alive today.

"What the *flap*?" Frogface almost fell as he stumbled over the border.

Guapo marched across okay, but then he threw himself down on a boulder and held his head. "*Dios!* Feels like I'm turnin' inside out!"

I'd been back and forth over the border often enough in my life that at least I could mask its effects. "Come on," I said, stomping ahead through the gray sand. "Walk it off, you *gatitos*."

To my surprise, Manny strolled up alongside me, seemingly unaffected by the border. Smiling, he extended two fingers toward me.

"You oughtta try the tips," he said. "I hear they're excellent."

"Go flap yourself." I hated that tutti-frutti little hairless bastard even more for not getting zapped at the border like everyone else.

"They tell me the wine's even better," said Manny. "Want a taste?"

"I don't even wanna *know* where *that* comes from, you flappin' freak," I said, walking faster to get away from him.

When I was a little girl, my friends and I used to run through the Cambio on a dare, dodging the shifting landscape and trying not to get killed. We only ever lost one of us--Ernesto Chiapas, who disappeared down a sudden sinkhole in the middle of a run.

Maybe I was going to see ol' Ernesto again after all those years. The terrain of the Cambio was just as unpredictable and dangerous as before.

As Guapo, Frogface, Manny, and I walked onward, following a faint human blood trail with Guapo's sniffer glove, the land was in constant upheaval around us. Geysers and steam vents erupted without warning, spraying us with water and heat. Landslides rumbled down hillsides, and tremors shook the ground. Spines and humps and shelves of rock thrust up suddenly alongside or in front of us...and in one case, underneath us. We tumbled ass over teakettle down the rising slope, barely missing a jagged, deep crevasse as it opened below us.

To me, it was just a typical day in the Cambio...but Guapo and Frogface weren't as easygoing about it.

"What the *hell*, Lupe?" said Guapo after a flying, head-sized rock almost took off his head. "This place is *loco*."

"No one knows for sure what causes the instability." As I said it, a stream of bubbling red lava ran out of the side of a nearby mesa that hadn't been there five minutes ago. "Some say it's the nexus of powerful cosmic energies, focused by an immense celestial convergence. Some say it's the intersection point of multiple dimensional rifts, moving in and out of phase with our reality. Others say it's Mother Polvo's rectum, and she's got a thousand-year case of Montezuma's revenge."

"It's beautiful," said Manny. The multicolored swirls on his skin shifted from mostly green and yellow to a peach and purple scheme. "It's violent and terrifying and beautiful."

"You're flappin' cracked." Frogface grabbed Manny's left arm

71

and bit into the tricep. Rainbow blood ran down his duckbill lips and chin as he chewed the mouthful of meat. "Thanks, bro."

Manny smiled and nodded. "*De nada, Ranito.*"

"How can you eat at a time like this?" said Guapo.

"I always eat when I'm nervous." Frogface leaned in for another bite. "Oh, is this good." He kept chewing as he talked. "Tastes like chicken marsala."

Guapo watched a flume of steam burst out of the ground twenty yards away. "What the hell." He slung his ultraviolet rifle over his shoulder and headed for Manny. "Save me some a' that."

As usual, I turned up my nose and turned away.

Two weeks later, when Guapo and Frogface were long dead, and I hadn't eaten in over a week, I stopped turning up my nose at Manny.

The jerky, fruit leather, and nutri-paste from my backpack were long gone. I had collapsed from hunger and exhaustion during another of our endless marches under the blazing sun of the Cambio.

Manny held my head in his lap and lowered a finger to my lips. He was smiling, and the sun cast a halo around him.

"Go ahead," he said softly. "It's all right."

I was so weak with hunger and fever that I could barely shake my head. "I...won't."

"Just have a bite," said Manny. "I won't tell anyone. Nobody will know what a flappin' *hipócrita* you are."

I remember thinking at that moment how much I hated myself...first, for smiling at the tutti-frutti bastard's joke, and second, for wanting him.

For wanting more than anything in the universe to eat his flesh.

But what really amazed me was how little I cared when I finally bit into him. When he slid the tip of his index finger between my teeth, and I nipped off one tender bite and chewed.

I remember there were tears in my eyes. The flesh was sweet and soft as lobster, and it tasted faintly of drawn butter and paprika.

He pushed the finger further into my mouth. "Have some more." There was no trace of gloating or sarcasm in his voice, just concern. "I've added meds for the fever."

I nipped at him again, and this time the bite was bigger. It tasted even better than the first, and I closed my eyes as the flavor surged through me.

"More." Manny pushed the finger deeper.

I bit down again and pulled more meat from the bone. Again, the latest bite tasted better than the one before.

"D-does it hurt you?" I swallowed and licked my lips. "When someone...eats you?"

"Yes," said Manny, and then he pressed another finger toward me. "Now have some more."

Two weeks before, on my first day in the Cambio with Guapo, Frogface, and Manny, I couldn't imagine that the time would come when I would taste a Ration. I honestly thought I'd let myself die first.

Our quarry seemed to feel the same way. His first target, when he came after us, was not the Ration.

It happened that first night, after we'd made camp. Thanks to the marker beacons planted long ago by explorers of the Cambio, we'd found a *bolsillo sólido*--a solid pocket, a rare area of limited geologic change...compared to the rest of the Cambio, anyway.

We were sitting around the campfire in the *bolsillo*, winding down. As usual, Frogface was nibbling on a hunk of Manny, and Guapo was trying to get a taste of me.

If I'd just given Guapo a little love instead of pushing him away, he might still be alive today. Instead, he stomped off to take a whiz...and it turned out to be the kind of whiz you don't come back from.

My last words to the man who, as much as he annoyed me, I had never been able not to love for long? "Go flap yourself, flap-face."

Two hours later, we found him by flashlight, fifty yards from camp. And fifty-five yards. And seventy-five, seventy-eight, eighty-two, and eighty-six yards.

Guapo had been ripped into little-bitty pieces and scattered all over the landscape. Most of the pieces didn't have much meat left on them, either.

"It was the man-eater," Frogface said in a horrified whisper.

"Ya think so?" Even as I pushed around pieces of Guapo with a stick, recognizing the occasional beauty mark or shred of clothing, I couldn't believe this was all that was left of him. I couldn't believe that such a big, forceful presence was gone from the world.

Most of all, I couldn't believe that none of us had heard a single sound when such a noisy sonofabitch had been torn apart and devoured.

I think Frogface knew he'd be the next to go.

The morning after Guapo's death, Frogface begged me to take him back to the *Puerco*. He was almost in tears when I told him he'd have to walk out himself.

"I'll never make it," he said. "If the *reflejo* doesn't get me, the Cambio will."

I slung Guapo's rifle over my back and nodded in Manny's direction. "I'm sure your little chew toy will watch your back."

Frogface brightened. "That's true." He grinned at Manny. "He's got a gun."

That was when the tutti-frutti bastard surprised me. "No can do, Froggy," he said. "Don't you think Guapo would've wanted us to finish our mission?"

"No," said Frogface, but the look in his eyes told me he knew better. "He'd say the flap with it."

Smiling like always, Manny walked over and stood beside me. "Somebody has to stop the man-eater, right?"

Frogface looked back in the direction of the border, then looked at us. Finally, he sighed and shook his head.

"There oughtta be a fresh trail after last night." He drew a sniffer glove from his belt pouch and pulled the glove onto his hand. "We'll get a bead on that thing for sure."

I glanced over at Manny, who was still standing beside me. To his credit, he didn't say a word...just met my gaze, then broke eye contact.

I, on the other hand, opened my big mouth. "Kiss my *nalgas* all you want, you good-for-nothing flap-head." I spit in the gray sand at his feet. "I still got your number."

Manny just smiled. "Someday," he said, "you'll have to tell me why you love me so much."

Cornucopia pointed a color-swirled finger at my brother, Roto, who sat in the prisoner cage at the front of the courtroom.

"That's him," said Cornucopia. "That's one of the boys who stole me from Señor Gustavo."

I was eight years old, and Roto was twelve. It was the day after we were caught holding Cornucopia the Ration captive in our shack in Barrio Sucio.

The day after Miguel and Oswaldo died from eating the Ration's poisoned flesh.

The prosecutor waved his cigar toward Roto. "What role, if any, did he play in the group that stole you?"

75

"He was the leader." Cornucopia nodded. "He gave the orders."

"Thank you." The prosecutor ran a hand over his wavy silver hair. "You may step down."

"In the matter of the province of Pesadilla versus Roto Calderon," said the jury foreman, "we find the accused guilty."

"Roto Calderon," said the judge. "I sentence you to ten years of hard labor at the Campo Esclavo maximum security facility. Take him away."

As they led Roto from the courtroom in shackles, I was free to go. Roto had taken all the blame, lied that I'd been trying to stop him...and Cornucopia had backed his story.

Why she did it, I'll never know. Did she feel guilty and think she'd ruined my life enough? Or did she think I would suffer more this way?

Through it all, the sparkly little smile never left her tutti-frutti face. The whole time that she was helping send away the only person I had left in the world now that she'd killed my other brothers, she smiled.

As her owner bit into her shoulder, and I was turned out, starving, into the street, she smiled.

Twenty-four years later, I felt Manny's hand touch my shoulder, and I didn't brush it away.

"That's enough," he said. "Don't keep watching."

But I had to. The man in the video flickering on the wall of the bone-strewn, bone-white cave was Roto. My brother.

And he was a changed man.

We had watched it happen, Manny and I. We had followed the trail of poor, dead Frogface's body parts to the cave, where we had found the video diary. We had switched on the blood-smeared projector and watched the whole horrible story of my brother's transformation, as urgent and immediate as if it were not recorded but happening live right there in front of us.

In the early entries, Roto had been bitter but hopeful. Prison had scarred but not broken him. He had come to the Cambio to live among the *reflejos* and learn their secrets. He had recorded his observations in the video diary and planned to use it as the raw material for a documentary.

In later entries of the diary, Roto had become more and more excited. His frizzy brown puff of hair had bounced as he talked about how he had been hungry all his life, but feeding the *reflejos* had changed all that.

"I was wrong," he had said. "I always thought the most important part of life was to *eat*...but it's more important to *be eaten*."

Shortly after that, Roto had started singing in a language I'd never heard before. He had stopped wearing clothes and had shaved all the hair from his body. Mysterious wounds had appeared on his flesh. He had started crawling around on all fours and making animal noises.

Then, there had been one last coherent entry.

"Must feed others now," Roto had said. "Feed *humans*, not *reflejos*. Become like a *Ration*...but how? I can't feed others my flesh like a Ration."

Roto had paced back and forth in the video, mumbling and striking his forehead with the heels of his hands. Then, he had stopped. "Wait!" His eyes had flared with mad inspiration. "I know what to do! Rations *kill*! I will *kill* like a Ration."

The next time we saw him...

"No more, Lupe." Manny tried to turn me away from the video. "Please."

But I couldn't look away.

Until that moment, I had thought that a man-eating *reflejo* had killed all those people on Polvo. I had thought that a *reflejo* had torn apart Guapo and Frogface and captured Roto.

But a *reflejo* was not to blame.

In the video flickering on the cave wall, Roto used a hunting knife to kill a man. Then, he...

"Don't look, Lupe," said Manny, tugging on my shoulder.

Then, Roto fed pieces of the dead man to another man chained to the floor. The man wailed and spit out the human flesh, but Roto forced in more, and the man started to choke.

"He thinks he's a Ration." My voice was a whisper.

"The *reflejos* did something to him," said Manny. "Or the Cambio changed him. Or both. He lost his mind."

"No!" The voice of my brother, Roto, echoed in the cave. "I *am* a Ration!"

My heart hammered in my chest. Roto's voice was not coming from the video.

All of a sudden, he sprang up in front of me, between the projector and the cave wall. "*Hermaaana,*" he said. "You're just in time for *dinner.*"

Naked, hairless, and blood-smeared, Roto gaped at me with wild, red eyes. In his left hand, he clutched Frogface's half-eaten arm; I recognized the sniffer glove that Frogface had been wearing when he'd disappeared.

"Luuupe." Roto held out Frogface's arm. "I am a *Ration*. Let me *feed* you."

Video of Roto stuffing more human meat into the choking man's mouth flickered over his body. He smiled at me with blood-stained teeth.

Behind me, I heard Manny cock his rifle.

"Close your eyes, Lupe," he said, and this time I did what he told me.

And then he pulled the trigger.

Here's the thing about the Cambio: more than the land changes here.

Sometimes, people cross the border because they *want* to change. The Cambio is unpredictable, so people have no idea what changes it might bring...but *anything* would be better than the way things are now, right?

Only one thing's for certain: the Cambio will change you. People who walk out might not even be recognizable as the same people who walked in.

Just look at poor Roto. Would he have become a murderous cannibal freak if he'd stayed out of the Cambio?

Then there's Manny and me. What about the changes *we're* going through?

Once again, Manny offers me the last finger he has left, a right thumb. This time, I take it.

Not long ago, it would have grown back, but not anymore. I'll never taste that thumb again, or any part of him that I eat.

He's been this way for a month. One day, he just stopped being able to regenerate. I guess the Cambio screwed him.

The Cambio's screwed us both another way, too. We're lost.

We've been wandering through the shifting landscape ever since we left Roto's cave. Our high tech equipment has been just as useless as our sense of direction.

And it's starting to look like we won't make it out of here alive.

"Have some more." Manny pushes his fingerless left hand at me. "There's still meat in the palm and forearm."

Gently, I touch his arm. I'm so hungry, I could eat everything that's left...but looking at what's left makes me sad.

The tutti-frutti flesh is pitted and gouged from all the bites I've taken. Very little skin remains. In places, I can see clear to the bone.

His right arm is even more damaged. From shoulder to wrist, the meat's all gone, except what I couldn't suck from between the bones.

The rest of him isn't much better. I've been rationing him, trying to make him last, but I've been eating him for a month with him not being able to regenerate. Even losing just a little bit every day for that long will make a man disappear.

"How much longer?" I reach up and stroke his cheek, which is intact. "How much longer can you keep going?"

Manny shrugs. "I won't know until I get there. This has never happened to me before."

"We'll be all right." As I gaze into his eyes, my heart pounds and my stomach growls at the same time. God help me, even as I try to comfort him, I want to eat what's left of him. "Maybe you'll regenerate when we make it out of here."

"Maybe." How can he keep smiling? He's literally full of holes, staggering lost through a parched, shifting wasteland, and he still has a smile on his face. "Either way, I want you to promise me something."

"What?" I trace a swirl of red and yellow as it slowly twists through the sugar-white skin of his forehead. Now that's he's half-eaten and can't regrow, the swirls don't move and change as much as they once did.

"No guilt." Manny reaches up to touch my face, then looks at his fingerless stump and changes his mind. "This is what I was born to do. To feed the hungry."

A tear rolls down my cheek. I make the promise, but I know I won't keep it.

Not unless a miracle can keep us both alive.

"No guilt," says Manny. A whisper is all he can manage.

His head is in my lap. His ears and nose are gone. So are bits of his cheeks and chin.

And still, he is smiling.

"Hold on," I tell him. "Please, Manny." My back is to the sun, to shield him from its blinding rays.

He can barely move. I've made him last almost two more weeks, but I think I've taken one bite too many.

And we're still lost in the Cambio. It's as if this place is a living thing, using its ever-changing terrain to turn us in circles and keep us always from finding our way out.

My stomach growls.

"Go ahead," he says. "Dig in."

I wish I could, because I'm starving...but he's literally down to bare bones. I've left the bare minimum for survival--internal organs, veins and arteries, enough strips of muscle to move--and even that isn't enough to keep him alive anymore.

Whatever I eat next will paralyze him...and what I eat after that will kill him.

"I wish there was something I could do." I stroke his face and try to ignore the signs of my hunger--the heaviness, the aches, the slackness of my muscles.

He has given everything to me. The least I can do is give him what little I have to offer. What comfort I can muster.

"Now I know what it's like," he says.

"What's that?"

"Hunger." Manny nods. "Not being able...to fill the void inside you."

The ground rumbles, and I ignore it. "Rations don't feel hunger?"

"We could...but what we eat...is plentiful." He takes a deep, shaky breath and lets it back out.

It occurs to me that I've never seen a Ration eat. "What is it? What do you eat?"

"Your breath." Manny's eyes meet mine. "The microscopic airborne life...you breathe out. The organic molecules. The carbon dioxide and water vapor.

"I recycle it. I give it back to you...in a form that will sustain you.

"At least...I used to."

I never knew. "We feed *you*?"

He nods. "And we...feed *you*...in return."

I never cared. After Cornucopia...until Manny...I wanted to know as little about Rations as possible. I never knew we were *connected*.

I never knew the feeding worked *both ways*.

Tears run down my emaciated cheeks and off the tip of my chin. "I wish I could still do it," I say. "I wish I could feed you now."

Manny coughs. His head twitches in my lap. "Lupe." His voice grows weaker. "I don't think...I can keep going."

"Just rest," I tell him. "Rest now, darling."

I hear a landslide in the distance. I hear the Cambio groan and creak and crack beneath us.

"You know...what you have to do now," says Manny. "Time...for the feast. *El banquete del muerte.*"

I wipe away tears and shake my head. I don't want to listen.

"Eat as much of me...as you can hold. Stuff yourself. What's left...will rot."

"No." How did I come to love him so much? I don't understand. How did I get to this place?

"Do it, Lupe. You need the energy."

"No!" He's right, and I hate him for it. I love him and I hate him for what he's telling me to do.

"It's my last request." His smile is fading. The tutti-frutti swirls have stopped moving. "Don't let me...go to waste."

That's when I do it.

I'm in a daze. I hardly realize that I'm pushing my index finger toward his mouth. Toward his half-eaten lips.

"Lupe, no." His whisper trails off, and he closes his eyes.

When the tip of my finger touches his lower lip, I stop. I know what a futile gesture I am making, but I also know it doesn't matter that I make it. No one will know but him, and he will understand.

So I push onward.

My fingertip passes between his lips. I feel the ridges of his teeth scrape the skin.

I push the finger in past the first knuckle, and then I tell him to eat. "I love you." I want him to live, and I wish with all my heart

The Cambio jumps. A new geyser hisses to life.

I wish with all my heart that I could bring him back. At least I want him to know that I would do this for him, I would do it if I could.

Far away, there is a thunderclap. The bubbling of lava.

"Please, Manny." I hold his chin with my free hand and push it up, as if that will make him take a bite. His teeth press into the flesh of my finger.

The ground beneath us trembles and rises. We ride the newborn mesa toward the sky.

Suddenly, Manny's teeth clench.

I start to cry out as he bites into my fingertip...and then I catch myself. "Good, Manny." He bites down with surprising force, and I shut my eyes against the pain. "Take what you need."

I feel him nip the meat from the bone. This is it, I realize.

This is how he feels.

I slide out my finger, the tip ragged and red. I suck away the oozing blood, which tastes strangely sweet, like vanilla.

And Manny chews.

When I lower the finger from my lips, it has stopped bleeding. The tiny wound is no longer red at all, in fact. It is pink and smooth.

And as I watch...

"Lupe?" His voice is a whisper, but no weaker than before.

As I watch, the smooth, pink flesh rises like bread dough. Tiny grooves etch the surface, perfectly matching the surrounding fingerprint.

The finger heals. Right before my eyes, it heals.

Within seconds, I can't tell where the edges of the wound once were.

Something has happened to me. I am only beginning to understand.

One thing's for certain: the Cambio will change you.

"Lupe?" Manny's eyes flutter open. His smile dimly flickers back into view. "What did you...give me?"

I push the same finger toward his lips. Warmth and light surge through my body, filling my belly, my chest, my throat.

My heart.

Tears of joy pour down my face like spring rain. They taste like wine.

"Eat up, my love," I tell him. "There's more where that came from."

LUMINARIA

As I ride the space elevator up the Skywire and out of Earth's atmosphere, I think of a helium balloon that my little boy, Rally, let go of in the park one day. The balloon ran away from him, shooting up into the sky, never to return.

I feel like that balloon.

What I shall find at the top of the Skywire, I do not know. What has become of humanity's other half, no one can say.

I am on my way to find out. I only hope that in the process, before my illness claims me, I will discover what became of Rally...and his mother, my wife.

"It seems to be running fine, doesn't it, Gabe?" says the man next to me, an engineer named Arlo Stripe. "I'm impressed, considering how long it's been out of service."

Fifty years ago, on a day we call The Silencing, a hauler loaded with freight and passengers climbed this elevator into space. Instead of descending the elevator wire twenty-eight hours later, as scheduled, the hauler did not come back down for five decades.

Today, one week after the hauler returned to Earth, I ride it back up with Arlo and three others. We are the first humans to reach space in fifty years...not counting the fifty-four million Spacesiders whom no one Earthside has heard from since the elevator's last trip.

"Now at twenty-thousand feet and rising," says the pilot, Wayne DuBois. He turns and winks one bright green eye. "No worries." His neck is thick, his hair shaved to black stubble--military all the way.

"My heart is pounding," says communications specialist Norrie Lomax, who sits behind me. She tucks her long, brown hair behind her ears and gazes out the porthole at the darkening sky rushing past. "Will we find Heaven or Hell? Life...or death?" As usual, she narrates aloud for the benefit of the flake mic stuck to her lower lip. "Will we ever see our homes and loved ones again?" Her words are transmitted back to the rest of humanity on the ground, who wait breathlessly to find out what happened to the Missing.

"Slow going, huh?" says Arlo, who seems to enjoy baiting me. "Too bad that brane drive of yours didn't work out. It sure would get us there faster."

I don't answer. The brane drive was supposed to be the fasted propulsion system ever designed for space travel. It made me king of the scientific world--for about five minutes.

Then, it melted down...and I lost everything else that mattered on the very same day.

Arlo doesn't stop trying to get a rise out of me. "Will your friends be glad to see us?"

I run my bony fingers through my thin, white hair and chuckle. "I sure hope so," I say, refusing to take the bait. The fact remains, though, and looms large in my mind: I am the only person who was asked for by name. The message found seared in the hauler's hull asked for a

return-trip crew consisting of an unnamed pilot, engineer, communications specialist--and me, Gabriel Shard.

Why this is, I have no idea. I am not the only space scientist on the planet, and I have no special connection to the Skywire project. As far as I can tell, my only distinctive characteristic is the aggressive tumor turning my brain into goo.

Still, I cannot say that I regret being chosen for the trip. Being among the first to return to the stars is quite an honor.

Not that I care about honor. Not that I really care about anything other than finding out what became of my wife and child.

They were on their way to Mars when the Silencing hit. According to what I've been able to piece together, they should have been riding down the Martian elevator on their way to the surface when all communications ceased.

If, by some miracle, I find her alive, my wife, Sharon, will be seventy-three years old. My son, Rally, who was seven on Silencing Day, will be fifty-seven.

As for me, I am eighty-two and change.

The whole time that we are inside Fulcrum, the deserted station that is our first stop along the Skywire, every one of us feels like we are being watched. We are so spooked that we agree unanimously not to split up, though it will take us an extra day to explore the whole place that way.

The worst of it is that we find no message telling us where everyone went...and we see no sign of death, destruction, or evacuation to explain their disappearance.

"There are no bodies," Norrie tells the folks at home. "There is not a drop of blood."

Engineer Arlo says that the equipment still functions flawlessly. The station holds steady in geostationary orbit, 35,000 kilometers above sea level.

Life support is at optimal levels, though none of us removes his environment suit. We are able to operate the computers, though they give up no clue to what happened here fifty years ago.

Hundreds of people were aboard this station, and then they were gone. It might as well have been magic that made them disappear.

"It's as if they were taken," Norrie says for the home audience. "Swept away suddenly and all at once by a great wind, without warning."

More like balloons, I think. Helium balloons let go by children, left to shoot off into the glittering blackness and out of sight forever.

If I ever see Sharon and Rally again, I will apologize for leaving them.

Fifty years ago, I was restless and vain and irresponsible. I was a rising star in my field, the inventor of the amazing brane-drive (which hadn't failed yet). I was blinded by ego and greed...and I abandoned my wife and child. That was why Sharon and Rally were on the way to Mars; they were going to live with Sharon's sister, because I'd left them.

And then they left me.

In fifty years, I have not passed a single hour without regretting what I lost.

Our next stop is the asteroid, Cruithne.

When we reach Cruithne, I am struck by an agonizing headache. I throw up twice and black out for what I am told is nearly three minutes. I feel much better after increasing the rate of my onboard morphine drip.

It's nice that I can always rely on Arlo for an encouraging word. "Maybe the cancer's a good thing," he says. "Maybe you won't taste so good to whatever's out here swallowing people up."

I salute him with an obscene gesture and look out the window of the hauler as we glide into the asteroid.

The tunnel through the heart of Cruithne is well-lit, but like empty Fulcrum far below it, the asteroid shows no signs of life. No one inside responds to signals from the hauler.

The asteroid maintains its orbit at 45,000 kilometers above sea level--almost at the end of the Skywire. It serves as a counter-weight, balancing the wire against the centripetal force of Earth's rotation.

I wonder if it's here that we'll encounter the other forces at work on the Skywire.

Wayne docks the hauler inside Cruithne, and we debark.

Fifty years ago, I could not have imagined it would come to this. Not until that one awful day.

It was the day of the last big test of the brane drive. Every other test had gone magnificently, sending probes and test animals dozens and hundreds of light years across space in an instant. Now it was time for a man to take the trip.

Frank Cardoza made a crazy face as he climbed into the octagonal capsule. Anything for a laugh, that guy.

We never saw him again.

Instead of hopping into the continuum between our universe's membrane and the next, then skipping across thousands of light years in minutes, Cardoza's capsule imploded. There was a surge of radiation, and he was gone.

The air inside Cruithne station is dark and still as Wayne and Arlo walk out of the airlock. It quickly changes, though, flashing to shimmering, golden life in a mist of fine, flickering sparks.

It happens as soon as my spacesuited feet come down on the station's deckplates.

"What the hell?" Wayne flicks his gloved hand through the sparks, scattering them like gold dust in a stream.

Arlo stirs the air with a sensor wand and watches readouts on his spacesuit's sleeve. "Ionized particles suspended in a magnetic field." He takes a step forward, pointing the blinking wand ahead of him. "The field intensifies in that direction."

"It's beautiful," says Norrie as we walk single file down the corridor. "Like a dream."

At the end of the corridor, the glitter in the air brightens. Wayne turns right through a double doorway, then stops suddenly.

Arlo crowds up behind him. "What is it?"

"Home." Wayne starts forward again, and Arlo follows.

I turn the corner next and see what they see. My eyes widen as the faceplate of my helmet dims against the rising light.

In the middle of the big room on the other side of the doorway, a glowing replica of the solar system hangs in midair, tipped so the plane of the ecliptic is at a 45-degree angle. The planets spin and revolve slowly around the sun, coasting like marbles through the flickering froth.

Then, all at once, the whole thing shoots away like a child's balloon. The sun, the planets, the moons, and the asteroids all zoom off as one unified body.

And they leave behind scattered points of winking radiance. Hundreds, thousands...millions of them, bobbing on the cosmic current like shipwreck survivors on the surface of the sea.

The twinkling points drift and fade, sinking into darkness. Then, they flare brightly and swirl together, swimming with purpose instead of aimlessly drifting. They coalesce in a single sphere of surging, golden light.

The sphere turns slowly, pulsing with energy. It spins and

bounces, gradually becoming more agitated...and then, it begins to shed blips of light. The blips pulse out of the sphere one at a time and leap away, always in exactly the same direction.

"Just look at this." Norrie widens her left eye--the one with the camera lens built in--and fixes it on the glowing, spinning sphere. "A message...but what does it mean?"

I realize she's right. Someone left this or sent this for us to see.

I walk all the way around it, stopping to let the pulsing blips of light dissolve against my chest. "What do you think, Arlo?"

"Impressive holography." Arlo waves the sensor wand through the glowing sphere without causing a ripple.

"I meant the message." Another blip melts into the front of my silver spacesuit.

"You tell me, Mr. Space Scientist," says Arlo.

Wayne the pilot cuts in. "It's a story," he says. "*Their* story."

"The Missing," I say. "They began in our solar system..."

"And then they were stolen away." Norrie's voice has the melodramatic tone of a bad actor in a bad movie. "Kidnapped beyond the stars."

I've had mixed feelings about the Silencing. On the one hand, I lost my wife and son that day.

On the other hand, whatever happened, whatever took them, it distracted the world from my failure. The destruction of the brane drive capsule and the loss of its pilot would have led the world's newscasts on any other day.

It took the Silencing to move my awful story to the back burner.

The brane drive disaster became a sidebar, just like every other story that happened the same day as the Silencing.

In that one small thing, I've always thought, I was lucky.

"Look behind you," says Wayne. "At the lights."

I turn from the glowing sphere and look back as he says. For the first time, I realize that the blips of light emitted by the sphere do not stop when they pass through my chest. They keep going.

The blips cross the room and continue through the double doors into the corridor. They form a single-file column, like the dashed yellow line down the middle of a highway.

And they keep going further than that. The line of blips passes right through the wall on the far side of the corridor.

I look at Wayne and Arlo and Norrie, but I don't need to. We've all had the same idea at once.

Wayne takes the lead, following the blips out of the room. The rest of us follow.

"What's on the other side of this?" Wayne thumps the corridor wall with his fist.

Arlo taps the wall with the sensor wand and watches the readout on his glove. "Couple hundred feet of storage and passages. Then vacuum."

"We need to see what's on the other end of these," says Wayne, pointing at the dashed line of glowing blips.

Arlo watches his readout, then nods and starts down the corridor. "This way."

Minutes later, we reach an outside wall with a window...and I catch my breath.

"Oh my God," says Norrie.

The blips don't stop at the wall. They continue beyond it, pointing into space...a dashed line running perfectly parallel to the Skywire.

"Looks like an arrow to me," says Arlo.

"Gee," says Wayne. "Whatcha think we should do next?"

We follow the line of blips from Cruithne, moving slowly. Being careful. After Cruithne, we have fewer than 2,000 kilometers of wire left to traverse.

"We're at 46,200 kilometers," says Wayne. "Running out of wire."

Norrie's voice is hushed for the home audience. "We will have to turn back soon. Will we find the answers we seek before it's too late?"

The hauler continues to crawl forward, and the kilometers tick away. Ahead, we can see the line of blips push further into the darkness, running parallel to the wire; in fact, the dashed line runs right through the hauler as we drift onward.

"46,500," Wayne says before long.

"See anything out there?" says Arlo.

"Nothing," I say, squinting at the window in the nose of the hauler. "Just Terminus."

The round, silver pad of Terminus looms in the distance, capping the end of the Skywire at 47,000 kilometers out. I've never seen it up close before; the sight of it makes my heart pound.

Terminus means you've gone too far. Instead of boarding a ship at Fulcrum or Cruithne, you've reached the end of the line.

If the hauler jumps the wire at Terminus, we're gone for good; the hauler's emergency thrusters could never get us all the way back to Earth.

"46,700," says Wayne.

"Still nothing," says Arlo. "Just us and the blips."

Nothing changes by 46,900 kilometers, except Wayne slows the hauler even more.

I wonder what's out there. Who's out there.

The hauler bumps to a stop at Terminus, nose resting against the silver foil pad.

"47,000 kilometers," says Wayne. "Last stop."

I left my wife and son on a beautiful summer night in Chautauqua, New York. Rally and I had one last twilight game of catch in the park. Sharon and I made love one last time by candlelight.

Then, while they both slept, I left a letter on the bedstand and let myself out. Without looking back, I ambled out of the inn and down the dirt path toward the gate.

Katydids whirred in the trees around me. Fireflies danced back and forth across the path. The air smelled warm and sweet and made me think of summer nights in my boyhood.

The path was lit by luminaria placed along both sides, candles flickering in frosted glass jars at my feet. Rows of lights to mark my passage from one life to the next, as if there was something noble about what I was doing.

As miserable as I've been ever since, I have never forgotten the beauty of that night.

"What was that?" Norrie jumps, and her voice rises with sudden panic.

I follow her gaze out the side window of the hauler. "What was what?"

"Oh my God!" She doesn't sound like she's performing for the home audience anymore. "Didn't you...there it is again!"

A blinding flash swoops out of nowhere and hurtles toward us. Before anyone can react constructively, the flash collides with the hauler...and the hauler pitches to one side.

Something else hits us after that, and the hauler rolls. We're all buckled in, but I still manage to whack my head against the window.

"What hit us?" says Arlo, but no one answers his question.

The hauler keeps rolling. I know what Wayne's going to tell us before he even says a word.

"We've broken free." His voice is too calm. "We're off the Skywire."

Space spins past my window as the hauler continues its roll through the vacuum. Terminus swings past again and again, its silver pad intersected by the line of blips that started all the way back at Cruithne.

Blips that I now can see, from my new vantage point, continue well beyond Terminus.

"Firing thrusters," says Wayne. "Let's see if we can get her straightened out."

As soon as he says it, the hauler catches in mid-roll with a jolt and heaves back in the other direction. There's another jolt, and another after that, and we finally stop spinning.

"Heading back for the wire," says Wayne.

"Spacewalk time." Arlo already has a helmet in his hand. "Good thing you've got an engineer aboard."

Something new catches my eye then, and my heart races. "Wait! Hold position!"

"What? Why?" says Wayne.

"Incoming!" I point at the forward window, at the ball of light surging in the distance.

The light lunges toward us, then swoops down and stops. At first, I don't realize the significance of where it parks.

Then, as the hauler drifts up to a different angle, I see it. I get it.

The ball of light rests directly in the path of the line of blips, as if this is what they were pointing at from the start.

I barely remember putting on my helmet and sealing my spacesuit. I hardly remember the call coming in over the hauler's radio:

"Send out Gabriel Shard."

But here I am, floating in space, connected to the hauler by what seems like the thinnest of tethers.

And I'm face-to-face with the ball of light, transfixed by the bright colors swirling over its opalescent surface.

I wonder if it's going to kill me.

"Your radio...is off. This is...between us." The voice in my ear is the same one that called me from the hauler. It's made of static, a crackling whisper that I can barely make out. The fact that my pulse is pounding in my ears doesn't help.

All I know for sure is that the voice sounds vaguely human...and male. The voice of a grown man.

"Who are you?" I try to say it fearlessly.

"I am...the last signpost," says the voice. "Number fifty-four million."

"Signpost?" I say. "Marking what?"

The voice dissolves in a surge of crackling hiss, followed by silence. Then, it returns, clearer than before. "You left us."

As I stare at the ball of light, its surface takes on a reddish cast. "What do you mean?"

"Fifty-four million spaceside biologicals," says the voice. "Left behind by your drive."

I frown behind my shaded faceplate. "The brane drive?"

"Left us all behind," says the voice.

I'm still not sure where this is going. "But the brane drive failed."

"It succeeded more than you knew," says the voice. "Instead of moving one man through space, it moved the entire galaxy."

I listen, but I don't believe him. It isn't possible.

"When you left," says the voice. "You took the whole galaxy with you."

"Who are you?" I stare harder into the sphere, looking for some trace of human features...finding nothing.

"The last signpost," says the voice. "The end of the road."

"What road?"

"That one." The ball of light drifts to one side. Its surface shifts from red to bright white.

In the distance, I see another ball of light flare to life. Another ignites beyond that...and another.

And another. All in a line.

They stretch off into the darkness like streetlamps along a street. Reflectors along a highway.

Or candlelit luminaria along a wooded path on a summer's night.

"Fifty-four million souls," says the voice. "Spanning the space between this galaxy and where it once was. Where we were left behind."

More luminaria ignite in the distance, extending the line. "Wait." I point to the glowing road. "Do you mean to say that they...that you...are connected with the missing Spacesiders?"

"We *are* the Spacesiders." The ball of light pulses, colors shifting between white and yellow.

My head swims. "I don't understand. If you were left behind when the galaxy jumped away, how could you have survived? You would have been left in open space."

"We changed," says the light.

"Changed how?"

"We died," says the light.

My frown deepens. "You're trying to tell me you're ghosts?"

"Souls." The light flares to twice its size. "Human souls have always gone into space after death. This is our true Heaven after all."

As I stare into the sphere, swirling colors gather and shift,

97

suggesting moving images behind a curtain...never quite clear, never quite solid.

"What you're telling me," I say, "is that I'm responsible for The Silencing?"

"Yes," says the light.

"And that I killed fifty-four million people?" I swallow hard. "Is that why you asked for me? Out of all the people on Earth?"

"No," says the light. "We want you to be the first to travel the golden road. To see the home we've made."

"Then why?" I spread my arms as wide as the bulky spacesuit will let me. "Why me?"

Finally, the shifting colors coalesce into shapes...blurred and jumpy, but recognizable.

A human face, glimpsed through incandescent mist. The face of a child.

A boy, about seven years old.

"Because you're my father." The light's voice changes to that of a little boy.

The face and voice leave no room for error. I have seen and heard them nightly for fifty years, in my dreams.

"Rally?"

"Yes Dad." The face in the light smiles. I see freckles and missing front teeth. "We came back for you."

Mystified, I reach out...then pull back my hand. "Oh my God." My heart flutters in my chest, fighting to break free. "Is that really you?"

The sphere compresses and reshapes itself in the form of a seven-year-old boy. Glowing with pure white light, he reaches behind me and unclips the tether that links me to the hauler. Then, he grabs my gloved hand with both his own and holds it tight.

"Come on, Dad," says Rally. "This way."

With that, the two of us start toward the Golden Road. Luminous signpost souls shine in the darkness as far as I can see, aligned in a straight shot from Terminus like a continuation of the Skywire itself.

Rally pulls us along under his own power, shedding streams of glitter from his fingers and toes. Looking back, I watch our trail swirl and twinkle in the night...and something else catches my eye.

A spacesuited figure stands in the open airlock of the hauler, reeling in the disconnected tether. He or she does not look my way or offer any sign of recognition.

But that's all right. I find a sign elsewhere.

Another spacesuited form floats across my field of vision. This one drifts loose in the void, slowly gliding away from Terminus. The body inside is limp, the arms frozen in an upraised position, gloved hands spread wide.

As if waving goodbye.

I give him a wave of my own and turn back to the road. The radiant luminaria stretch out ahead, shining like stars or fireflies, pointing the way to another new life.

LENIN OF THE STARS

As we sit on the terrace in the oppressive jungle heat, I slide a shot of crystal clear vodka across the glass table. The man who was once Senator Joseph McCarthy taps the rim with one index finger and chuckles.

"Come on now." He shakes his head, smirking. "You know I don't touch *that* stuff, Vladimir."

I shrug and throw back my own shot. Feel the burn rolling down my throat like a slow-motion solar flare. "I've had lots of names," I say as I pour another. "Why do you insist on calling me by *that* one?"

"Vladimir Ilyich Ulyanov." McCarthy says it with grand sarcasm. "You'll always be Lenin to me."

"Ha." I down the second shot and clap the glass on the table. "And you'll always be an incompetent fear-mongering bastard to me."

"You talk like I didn't just kill your hand-picked Red Guard." He gestures at the twelve charred corpses strewn about the terrace. Five are still smoking in the blazing mid-morning sun. "Like it isn't just you and me here now."

I smile and raise the vodka bottle. The rays of the sun play through it on my face, refracted by the uneven crystal. "How 'bout if I drink you for it?" I shake the bottle. "I'll drink you for the revolution."

Something screeches in the treetops (bird, cat, monkey?) and McCarthy stops smirking. "You've led your last revolution, Lenin. End of story." He spreads his hands, exposing the octagonal barrels of the fusion guns mounted in his palms.

"And what if I'm not done here?" This time, I drink my shot straight from the bottle.

"Don't you think you've done enough to screw up this planet? And *ours*?" McCarthy aims his fusion guns at my head. "You're done, all right. Just as soon as we clear up some unfinished business."

I watch a flock of flamingos drift up into the turquoise sky. The scene reminds me of our homeworld, thousands of light years away. "What might that be?"

"I need to know where she is," says McCarthy. "Where is Irina?"

I laugh and shake my head, unwilling to tell him the truth. Because the truth is, I don't know where the love of my life has gone.

The first time I met Irina, I was blown away by how beautiful she was. The purple-and-green-tinted crystalline clusters of her body glittered in the auditorium's ever-flowing fireworks. Two of her six multifaceted eyes were silver, and four were gold, a mark of great passion and intelligence. Even her parasites had a special look about them as they danced around her body, multicolored tongues of flame weaving in and out of her vent slits.

I was never the same after that first glimpse of her. I had never seen anyone so beautiful in all my life.

"I believe we can help the humans." Those were the first words I heard her say. "I believe our way of life can change their world for the better and make them civilized enough to be welcomed into the community of worlds."

This was one of our pre-mission briefings on the homeworld. Sixty-five of us in one room, getting ready to take another crack at the problem children of the galaxy--human beings. Other species had tried and failed to help humanity get its act together, but we honestly believed we'd be different.

To tell you the truth, just watching and listening to Irina was enough to make me believe with all my hearts.

"It's not their fault, you know." Irina (her name wasn't Irina then, it was unpronounceably alien) glided around the stage as images of human violence flickered in the air above her. "They've evolved in a hyper-competitive ecosphere. 'Eat or be eaten' is written deep in their genetic code."

"And it's up to us to teach them how the rest of the galaxy lives." As I spoke, I hoped she wouldn't pick up on the nervous quaver in my voice.

"Share and share alike, yes." Irina smiled. "No more 'dog eat dog,' as the humans say."

"What about 'kill or be killed?'" This time, it was the one who later became Joseph McCarthy who spoke--all ice blue crystals swirling with pink tongues of flame. Even then, he was a contrarian. "What if the humans kill us all as part of their 'ecosphere?'"

"As you know," said Irina, "they won't see us as beings from another world. We'll be altered to look like them."

McCarthy made a disparaging sound like pebbles clacking together in a glass vase. "And you don't think that will *increase* our chances of being killed?"

"Not for we brilliant few." Irina's voice was full of conviction. Her green and purple clusters pulsed with an electric neon tinge. "Not for those of us with all that's right and just on our side. Not for the denizens of the galactic *workers' paradise*."

With that, sixty-four of us went wild in the auditorium, singing and clattering with inspired elation. Passing silvery gellid packets of pure, noble emotion back and forth. At least in my case, inspired by pure and growing love.

Only McCarthy stood apart and pouted, a clear sign he should have been drummed out of the mission. But Irina always said we crystal saviors needed all facets to catch the light.

Though the truth is, a single cracked facet can ruin the view completely.

It was the happiest day of my life.

A massive movement of people swelled the streets of Petrograd, Russia, flowing down every byway in an irresistible human tide. The roar of cheers and song filled the cold October air, the sound of change rising amid the ancient onion-domed towers.

Change that we had brought into being.

Irina's hands slid up over my shoulders. "We've done it," she said. "We've begun the world revolution."

I turned from the window and swept her into my arms. "Yes, *milaya moya.*" I called her that for the first time, called her *my sweet.* And then I did something else for the first time, too. "*Ya tebya lyublyu.*" *I love you,* I said, and then I kissed her.

She did not push me away.

The moment washed over me, and I reveled in it. My makeshift pseudo-human heart thundered in time with the marching feet outside my window.

I had traveled thousands of light-years from my homeworld to get to this moment. I had toiled five decades on Earth in a myriad of human identities to make this happen, as had all of us. Now here I was, in the Earth year 1917, playing the role of a human named Lenin, calling history's shots from my headquarters in the Smolny Institute in Petrograd.

Kissing the greatest love I'd ever known outside my service to humanity and the universe.

"*Laskovaya moya.*" Irina said it in a whisper. She kissed me again, then leaned back to gaze at me with dancing green eyes. "Your timing is auspicious, my darling. Our greatest work is yet to come."

I caressed the side of her face. "Together, we cannot *help* but succeed."

"Come on." Eyes twinkling, she backed away, pulling me with her. "Let's drink it in. Let's go outside."

Changing our features so we wouldn't be recognized, we slipped out a back door of the Institute. Merging with the vast crowd in front of the building, where people were cheering my name, we laughed and held each other close.

"Don't let it go to your head," said Irina.

"Of course not!" I said it with a grin.

"Not that you'll get the chance." Irina shrugged. "You'll be somebody new in a couple of years, and so will I."

As the crowd continued to cheer and sing around us, I stared at her face. Even disguised, it couldn't conceal her radiance, her passion, her certainty. As ever, she held me mesmerized.

"Who will we be in five years, Irina?" I said. "In ten years? Do you know?"

She tipped her head and smiled. "The plan is fluid, of course, but yes. I have some idea."

"Will we be together?" I took a deep breath. "Can you tell me that much, at least?"

She looked at me for a long moment as the crowd continued to cheer my name. The currents of history roiled around us like white-water, churning and seething, overflowing their banks. Thanks to us, the mass of humanity was thrashing closer to a glorious communal destiny among the proletariat of the stars.

"We will not always be together." Irina wrapped her arms around me. "But we will not always be apart."

It wasn't the answer I'd had in mind, but I let it pass as she drew me against her. As she pressed her full lips against mine, and we kissed in the pulsating heart of the revolution.

Both of us knowing we were breaking a fundamental rule of our mission. Not because we were falling in love.

But because we were being selfish.

The next time I saw Irina was nearly four decades later, standing over the dead body of Josef Stalin.

Stalin lay on the floor of his private quarters in Kuntsevo, sprawled at Irina's feet. She stood with her hands on her hips, shaking her head as she looked down at him.

"I'm starting to notice a pattern here." She said it without looking up when I entered the room. She knew it was me, after all; she'd summoned me here from China. "Human gets power. Human abuses power. Human subverts the cause of the workers' revolution."

I crouched beside Stalin's body, letting the mask of my current prime identity--Mao Zhedong, President of the People's Republic of China--melt back into the face I'd worn so long ago as Vladimir Lenin. "I thought he was a great choice, too, Irina. Just like everyone else did."

"Maybe that's the problem." Irina sounded tired. "We make lousy choices."

Placing my hand over Stalin's face, I slid his eyelids shut. "Or it's just going to take longer than we thought, dragging these people into the age of communal civilization."

"There's another possibility, as well," said Irina. "Perhaps we need to modify our strategy."

I got to my feet and shrugged. "That's always a possibility when dealing with complex sentient beings." Face to face with Irina, I gazed into her eyes. They were darker than I remembered and no longer sparkling. "Sentient beings can be highly unpredictable." *Like you*, I thought.

As I watched her stare into space, I wondered why she'd shut me out for forty years. I wondered if she still felt anything for me at all.

"I've been thinking." She turned away and paced across the room. "I've been working on a new approach."

"Tell me," I said. Anything to keep her talking, to spend more time with her.

"I've developed a new identity over the past decades." She stopped pacing and changed shape over Stalin. Until that moment, she'd worn the form of a young woman with long, brown hair. Before my eyes, she became a middle-aged man in a dark suit, stocky and bald. "Meet Nikita Krushchev. I'll be taking the reins now that Stalin is dead."

I folded my arms over my chest. I'd known she was Krushchev, though I hadn't heard it directly from her. I hadn't heard *anything* from her in forty years.

Irina tapped her chin with a forefinger. "Meet the new face of the revolution. The harbinger of a bold new era."

"So you're following in my footsteps?" I shifted my face to look like my past identity of Vladimir Lenin. "Doing the driving *yourself* instead of trusting a flawed human?"

Irina the bald middle-aged man nodded. "The USSR has been turned inward against itself for too long. Why punish and purge the very workers we need to advance the revolution? Better to secure their allegiance with incentives while working to weaken the outside institutions that seek to oppose the proletariat."

I looked down at the body of Stalin and frowned. "You're talking about reversing the policies of the past thirty-one years."

"I call it De-Stalinization," said Irina. "Let up the pressure at home, increase the pressure abroad. Speed up the timetable of the worldwide revolution."

I listened and nodded. Even in the body of a middle-aged

human male, she could sway me. Even after forty years apart, my feelings for her hadn't changed.

"China is coming along nicely." I switched my face back to Chairman Mao's, pear-shaped and heavy-jowled, with a dark fringe of hair around the back and sides of my head. "I think Earth will reach a tipping point soon, and the international proletariat will unify."

"All the more reason to press forward strategically," said Irina.

Reaching over Stalin's body on the floor, I clapped a hand on Irina's shoulder. "Tell me what you need me to do." I gave her shoulder a squeeze and gazed deep into her eyes. "You know I will stand by your side."

Irina held my gaze for a long moment, then laid her hand on my forearm. "Stay the course. That's all."

"I'll have one of the others take my place as Mao," I said. "You'll need my help to consolidate power here."

"I need your help most in China right now," said Irina. "The People's Republic is at a formative, vulnerable stage."

Instead of giving up and letting go, I took hold of her other shoulder. "No." It was the first time I'd ever said that to her. "I'm staying with you."

"That's sweet." Irina lightly touched my face. "But no. You have your orders."

"Orders?" I pulled away from her. "I don't understand. Why did you call me here if you didn't want my help?"

"To warn you," said Irina. "Our own people are working against us."

I was stunned to hear it. "Who?"

"Senator Joe McCarthy, for one. Our U.S. operations are in a shambles thanks to him." Irina sighed. "And there are others. I don't know who yet."

"Unbelievable." I shook my head in amazement. "How could *any* of us turn against the revolution?"

Irina moved closer, shifting back to the form she'd worn earlier, that of a brown-haired woman. Taking hold of my arms, she gazed into my eyes with blazing intensity. "*You* would never betray me, would you?"

I met her gaze with unshakeable steadiness. "Of course not." Her fingers dug painfully into my arms, but I refused to flinch. "How could you even *ask* me that?"

Irina held me a moment longer, then leaned forward and kissed me softly on the lips. "*That* is why I summoned you." Her voice was a whisper in my ear. "Because I had to be sure."

The scent of her mesmerized me. I could barely think straight. "That's it?"

"For now." When she drew away from me, she was Krushchev again.

Standing there, I felt shaky and disoriented. I'd been so *close* to her for the first time in forty years, and now she was moving out of reach again. She'd kissed me, but the kiss had felt empty, intended only as a guarantee of my loyalty.

There was so much I wanted to say to her, so much I *should* have said...but all I managed was this: "When will I see you again?"

"Every time you open a newspaper," said Irina/Krushchev. "I'm going to take the world by storm."

Nine years later, in October 1962, Irina/Krushchev leaped up from behind her desk as I burst into her office in the Kremlin. She came up with revolver in hand, leveled right at me.

Irina got off two shots without a word. They both missed as I bolted across the office.

Dropping as another shot exploded from the gun, I rolled over the floor and stopped behind a chair with fat red cushions. "Irina! Don't shoot!" I thought hearing that name might make her hold her fire.

But no. She cracked off another shot, straight through the chair, barely missing me.

Taking a breath, I prepared to charge. I'd known this would be the hardest part of my mission. That was really saying something, considering how many times I'd had to change shape and use force to get through security in the heavily fortified inner sanctum of the Kremlin.

But it had to be done. Irina was on the verge of making a horrible mistake, and I had to stop her.

I had to stop her from destroying humanity.

Crouching, I hoisted the chair off the floor and heaved it at her. As it crashed down on her desk, I darted after it.

Irina sidestepped, firing wide. As I dove across the desk at her, though, she got off one more shot.

This time, the bullet struck its target. I caught the lead in the meat of my shoulder, and my body flared with sudden pain.

But I wasn't about to let it stop me. My hands connected, throwing her over backward, sending the gun flying from her grip. We hurtled to the floor, pulling a desktop TV set down with us.

The TV burst to smithereens on the hardwood, spraying us with glass shrapnel. Irina flailed underneath me, using all the mass of her Krushchev disguise to try to throw me.

But I would not be dislodged. I shifted my own form again, changing from an athletic young man to an obese middle-aged one, pressing her down with my greater weight.

"Irina!" Holding her down, I shifted the flesh of my shoulder. Out popped the bullet, ending my pain. "Stop and listen to me!"

She kept thrashing, fighting to break free. "Get off! Let go!"

"You are subverting the cause of the interstellar revolution!" I said. "The community of worlds will not condone your actions!"

Irina bucked and squirmed, scowling with rage. "The situation is under control!"

"You're wrong!" I said. "U.S. forces are at DEFCON 2. Kennedy's about to attack."

"He's bluffing!" said Irina.

"If you don't pull your missiles out of Cuba, there will be worldwide nuclear war tomorrow." I locked eyes with her, dead serious. "Humanity will be exterminated or close to it within days."

Irina shook her head. "You don't understand. We've been negotiating with the Americans through back channels. We're close to a breakthrough!"

"Listen to yourself!" I said. "You're willing to risk the *extinction* of all *humankind*. You'd sacrifice the very proletariat we've come to set free!"

"It won't come to that," said Irina.

"But it *could*. Taking the world to the *brink* like this makes it *possible*."

"It's *always* possible on this throwback planet," said Irina. "We're working to make it *less* possible."

"So it won't bother you?" I said. "Being responsible for the annihilation of an entire *species?*"

"*You* should *talk*. How many millions of humans have you condemned to death in the name of the People's Republic of China?"

"There's a big difference between *purging* and *extinction*."

"Which won't *matter*, because the Americans are about to *capitulate*," said Irina.

Just then, heavy footsteps marched into the room. "Premier Krushchev!" A thickly built silver-haired man in an olive drab and red uniform gaped in alarm at the wreckage.

Hastily, I took on the shape of an official I'd knocked out on my way to Irina's office. "The Premier tripped and fell," I said as I helped Irina to her feet. "Are you all right now, sir?" said the uniformed man.

"Yes, I'm fine, Boris." Irina dusted herself off. "You're here because of the noise, I suppose?"

"No, sir," said Boris. "I have a message from Intelligence." He stopped talking and stared at me.

"Go ahead." Irina waved dismissively in my direction. "Comrade Sergei is cleared to hear such information."

"Yes, sir." Boris glanced my way once more, then focused on Irina. "Our forces in Cuba have shot down an American U-2 spy plane."

"Oh?" Irina leaned forward on the desk. "The pilot?"

"Dead," said Boris. "And the Americans have shut down the back channel talks."

Irina took a breath and slowly released it. Her whole body stiffened. "Permanently?" she said.

"Unknown at this time," said Boris. "However, Intelligence confirms that the U.S. is about to launch an attack."

"On Cuba," said Irina.

"And the motherland," said Boris. "War is imminent."

"I see." Irina closed her eyes and rubbed her temples.

"Premier." Boris took off his cap and took a step forward. "The defense ministers agree it is time to exercise the preemptive strike option."

"I understand." Irina cleared her throat. She shot me a look, then sat down on the edge of the desk.

"The ministers await your orders," said Boris.

"Soon enough." Irina waved him off. "I wish to weigh the options first, General."

Boris hung there for a moment, expectant, then saluted. "I'll be just outside, Premier Krushchev."

"Thank you," said Irina.

With that, Boris spun and headed for the door...only to stop midway and turn. "We *will* bury them, sir," he said. "Just as you once promised." Then, he snapped back around and marched out of the office.

When he'd pulled the doors shut behind him, Irina slumped and shook her head. Without a second thought, I put my arm around her shoulders.

"What happened to me?" Her voice was slow and distant. "How did I get like this?"

"We've been away from home a long time," I said. "Maybe we've started to think like the humans."

Irina was silent for a long moment, staring at the shattered TV set on the floor. I wanted to comfort her, make everything better, but I was also acutely aware that time was running out.

"What next?" I said.

She sighed and slid off the edge of the desk. "Try to stop this, if we still can. Give the Americans what they want and hope for the best."

Irina walked around the desk, straightening her jacket and tie, and I followed. "Let me help," I said.

"You can't," said Irina. "I have to undo my own mistakes."

I headed her off at the door. "Then come with me when it's over." Reaching out, I took her hand. "We'll get away from all this."

"Thank you." Irina squeezed my hand and gazed sadly into my eyes. "But I have more to do now than I ever imagined." With that, she pulled her hand from my grip and reached past me for the door handle.

"You deserve some time away," I said. "You've already done so much."

"Yes." Irina smiled ruefully. Her dark eyes held no trace of happiness. "And I'm starting to think that every last bit of it was wrong."

As soon as the spy slipped me the microfilm, he gasped and crumpled to the sidewalk. A pool of dark crimson spread out around him, radiating from his head.

I didn't wait around to look for the bullethole. Leaping into action, I charged across the street and down an alley, stuffing the microfilm in my pants pocket on the fly. Footsteps clattered on the cobblestones behind me as I ducked into the cheering crowd up ahead.

Heart hammering, I fought my way through the mass of spectators watching the street. No one paid me much attention; all eyes were focused on the men and bulls stampeding down the main drag in the searing July heat.

One thought swirled in my mind as I struggled through the crowd: who had leaked the rendezvous details to the West? Who had known I'd be receiving the microfilm in Pamplona, Spain during the Running of the Bulls?

At least I had a chance of getting away with it. There were plenty of ways to use the crowds and chaos against my pursuer.

Also ways for my pursuer to use them against me. As I plowed forward, a bullet punched through the head of a man in front of me. He dropped dead in my path, knocking me back into a crush of spectators.

As I disentangled myself, another shot whistled past my head and blasted into a woman's chest. People screamed and ducked, giving me my first clear look at the shooter.

And I gasped. The face was unfamiliar--a young woman with long, black hair--but the scent was unmistakable. It was *her*...changed yet again, facing me once more in the heat of the Cold War. In the five years since her defection after the Cuban Missile Crisis, I'd battled her dozens of times in one way or another. She'd gone from communist leader to hands-on field operative fighting for the cause of capitalism and the red, white, and blue. From lover to arch-enemy.

Irina.

With an icy stare locked on her face, she swung up her gun and pulled the trigger twice. I leaped away before the shots could connect and sprinted into the street, joining the rush of runners and bulls.

No time to stop and reason with her; I'd tried that before. Since nearly triggering the annihilation of humanity as leader of the Soviet Union, she'd been steadfast in her new cause. I knew she'd stop at nothing to snatch the microfilm and strike another blow against communism.

As I raced down the street, a dark-haired young man in white t-shirt and pants hurtled past me. Glancing back, I saw why he was running so fast: a monstrous black bull barrelled up behind me, huge horns gleaming white in the afternoon sun.

The bull seemed to decide I was a better target, because it followed me when I veered. Whichever way I went, it galloped after me, heaving and snorting.

As if I didn't have enough trouble to deal with, Irina fired more shots in my direction. A nearby runner cried out and dropped, head bouncing off the cobblestones.

Dashing through the mayhem, I caught up with another bull up ahead. Clapping my hands on its haunches, I vaulted up onto its back and held tight, waiting for impact.

Seconds later, the first bull rammed the second full force from behind. My mount stumbled around and went down hard; I barely sprang off in time to avoid being crushed.

I still made a bad landing, though, twisting my ankle when I hit. Forcing back the flash of pain, I staggered into the crowd on the sidewalk.

I managed to make it into an alley and braced myself against a wall. It took a few seconds to shapeshift away the damage to my ankle.

Which was just enough time for Irina to get me.

"Hello, Comrade." I heard her voice at the same instant I felt the gun barrel touch my left temple.

"Irina." Turning my head, I gazed into the bright green eyes of her latest face.

For a moment, I felt like we were back in Moscow again, fifty years ago, in 1917. I imagined our love was new and true once more, playing sweetly over the strains of the people's revolution.

Then, she punched me in the stomach. "You have something that belongs to me." Her voice was cold.

"I do," I said. "My heart."

She punched me again, harder. "That microfilm could bring down America. I won't let that happen."

"Stop fighting for the capitalists," I said. "Remember why we came here. Remember the galactic workers' paradise."

"The corrupt communist system drove humanity to the brink of annihilation." Irina punched me again. "We thought a capitalist ideology was aggressive and self-destructive, but *communism* was the more ruthless and ravenous aggressor!"

I shook my head against the barrel of her gun. "What about the interstellar revolution?"

"There's a *new* one." Irina smiled. "An interstellar *counter-revolution*."

"What?" I frowned. "What are you talking about?"

"It's just gotten started," said Irina. "You'll see."

"What kind of counter-revolution?"

"Join us." Irina leaned closer. "Help us change the galaxy for the better. Help *me* change the galaxy, my darling."

I had no idea what she was talking about. I had no reason to believe she felt any kind of affection for me at all.

But as I stared at her, so close, so familiar, I longed to do what she asked. To do *anything* she asked of me, however insane or impossible it might be.

Because I had *never* lost my love for her, and I never would. No matter how much she hurt me, I knew I could never give up on her.

"Please." She leaned even closer. "We can be together like before. Blazing beacons shining light in the darkness." She drifted closer then, and her lips touched mine. For the first time in fifty years, she kissed me.

In that moment, I nearly went with her. I almost joined the counter-revolution without knowing a thing about it.

But something sparked within my good socialist soul, and I held back. "I cannot oppose the proletariat," I told her. "I am a servant of interstellar communism."

Irina sighed. "Poor thing." She leaned forward once more and whispered in my ear. "Soon, there will *be* no interstellar communism for you to *serve*."

With that, she shot me in the head.

She dug the microfilm from my pocket and left me for dead. Which to our kind, is only dead for a little while. Even as she disappeared in the chaos of Pamplona, I began to reassemble the scattered bits of my human disguise. My shattered mind and senses began to reassert themselves.

But the pain of what she'd done would last much longer than that.

Thirty-seven years later, in the Earth year 2004, I was in the pilot seat of a fighter spacecraft, soaring through the bright blue sky over the Indian Ocean.

Morning sunlight gleamed off my topaz crystalline clusters and multifaceted eyes. I'd reverted to my native form; it was the only way to handle the complex controls of the fighter, which was from my homeworld.

And flying that fighter was the only way I could help win an interstellar war.

Checking the holographic displays in the cockpit, I spotted my target down below. I manipulated controls, and the fighter dropped through the cloud deck.

Emerging from the woolly clouds, I stared in stunned amazement at the tableau before me. Two huge vessels hung in the sky, vast starfaring warships from many light years away. As I watched, they fired enormous cannons, blasting each other with monstrous beams of fiery golden energy.

Tiny fighter craft like my own swarmed all around the warships, spinning and swooping and shooting. One exploded in a burst of orange light, then another; a third tumbled out of control and cracked up against the side of one of the warships.

So this was how civil war looked among the peoples of the interstellar workers' paradise. It was so much different from the hordes of humans hacking each other to bits in the mud with primitive weapons.

And yet, it was so much the same.

The war had been part of my life for years, of course. I'd seen plenty of action on Earth...but this was the first battle of this scope I'd been part of. I'd never seen anything like it in space, either, before coming to Earth. There hadn't been an interstellar war in millions of years, thanks to the lasting peace of the galactic revolution and workers' paradise.

But that was before the counter-revolution. That was before the twisted ideas of Earth had infected the interstellar community.

Suddenly, a flash of light seared across my forward shields, and I knew it was time to take action. Spinning my fighter counter-clockwise, I saw a gunboat coasting toward me like a big silver needle, artillery blazing.

I let loose a few rounds from my fusion guns, then whipped around and hightailed it toward one of the giant warships. The gunboat stayed in pursuit part of the way, until a shockwave picked it up like a toy and hurled it off my tail.

Finessing the controls, I closed in on the warship. I knew it was the enemy from its colors (red and black) and the symbols etched into its hull. It was a ship of the Capitalist Alliance, believers in the wealth of the few at the expense of the many...staunch enemies of the communists of the Interstellar Proletariat.

They were my enemies, though they were no different in appearance than me. I'd come to kill them, though we'd originated from the same homeworld, maybe even the same city or street.

Such was the legacy of the counter-revolution I'd first learned of thirty-seven years ago in Pamplona.

Not that the reasons for the fight much mattered anymore. My mind was focused completely on reaching my goal and doing as much damage as possible to it.

Flying forward, I threaded the maze of enemy fighters with weapons blazing. I banked and dove and twirled, eluding one opponent after another, leaving a trail of smoking and sputtering warcraft in my wake.

Soon, the Capitalist Alliance warship loomed before me, gun batteries blasting in every direction but mine. For that moment, I had a clear path to a gash in the hull amidships, the perfect place to inject a fusion torpedo.

Bearing down, I raced for the gash, calibrating a torpedo firing solution en route. Before I could release the payload, though, the enemy warship suddenly buckled and rolled in my direction.

I pulled up as fast as I could, speeding out of the listing ship's shadow. Just as I cleared the crash zone, the mighty vessel keeled over, barely missing me.

Then, with a series of massive explosions, it split in two. The fore and aft sections scissored apart...and the prow of the Proletariat warship plowed between them. The battered Proletariat ship had brought the capitalists down by ramming them.

But now both warships were heading for the sea.

Instantly grasping the implications, I climbed for the cloud bank as fast as I could. It was time to gain some altitude, time to put as much distance as possible between my fighter and the impending splashdown.

That was when the signal came in over my radio. A familiar voice broke through my furious focus.

It was a distress call. "I'm going down! Help!" It was *her* call, the one call I couldn't refuse. Even after everything that had happened between us, I could never turn my back on her. "My escape pod won't eject! Please help me!"

It was Irina.

Zeroing in on her signal, I whipped around and shot seaward again. Even as the warships plunged toward what I knew would be a catastrophic impact, I dove down after them.

Within seconds, I saw Irina's fighter spinning out of control, spewing plumes of black smoke. The engines were blown to hell, and the nose was mangled, which probably explained the problem with the escape pod.

I had scant seconds to dislodge that pod. Even then, we'd both be doomed if we didn't instantly blast away at maximum speed.

The enormous warships would hit the water soon, throwing out waves of titanic proportions. If we were really unlucky, the impact combined with the battle damage the ships had suffered would blow up one or both of their fusion reactor power plants.

In which case, all bets were off.

Swooping around Irina's fighter, I shot off the nose with an energy pulse from my guns. Then, swinging around, I blew off the tail behind her. The severed pieces of her fighter fell away, leaving the cockpit escape pod in its translucent housing cube.

Just as the cube started to drop, the housing snapped away, blown free from inside by Irina. The propellant ring on the base of her ovoid pod flared to life, burning white hot, and the pod shot suddenly upward with Irina inside.

I rocketed after her without looking back. Over the whine of my fighter's engines, I heard the thundering roar of the warships splashing down.

Irina's pod leaped into the cloud deck, and I followed. We didn't dare slow down on the other side, in the open sky. Our survival depended on gaining as much altitude as possible.

Shockwaves bucked our craft as we punched ever higher. My fighter shook with rising intensity, battling the waves and the g-forces trying to tear it apart.

Irina's pod shivered and spun, then fell away.

My mind swirled with sudden grief. Going back for her would be certain death.

But I was seized by the impulse to try.

The last time she'd truly seemed to love me had been almost a century ago. Since then, she'd used and abused me, betrayed and undermined me, fought and killed me again and again. How could I still feel any love for her?

Or was that what love was about? Pain, upheaval, destruction, the end of the world?

I cut the fighter's acceleration and scanned the skies below me. I made ready to dive down and retrieve her...or accompany her into annihilation.

My scanners were all static. That meant at least one of the warships' fusion drives had ruptured. The Indian Ocean had become ground zero of a nuclear detonation.

But I had to go back for her.

Steeling myself, I toggled controls, ready to swing the fighter around. Ready for anything.

And that was when her glittering crystalline pod came streaking up past me like a shooting star in reverse.

When we'd reached a safe altitude, we stopped climbing. We hung in the stratosphere and looked down at the distant ocean, watching the devastation as it spread.

The battle itself had been cloaked from human technology, unseen by the world, but its effects would be felt by millions. When the warships sank and the fusion drives erupted, the ocean floor heaved from the force of the blast. A monstrous quake wrenched the crust of the Earth, slamming out colossal waves in all directions.

As we watched like satellites from far above, a monumental tsunami crashed down over islands and coastlines, obliterating anything in its path. Snuffing out hundreds of thousands of lives in Indonesia, Sri Lanka, Thailand, India.

We opened a radio channel between our craft, but neither of us said a word for a long time. We just watched as destruction swept that part of the world, destruction that we had helped bring about.

"I only wanted to help," said Irina. "I thought I was doing the right thing."

I didn't say a word. Far below, another tsunami was surging up from the sea, lashing toward shores that had already been laid waste by the first brutal onslaught.

"I wanted to free our people," said Irina. "I wanted to end the oppression of communist totalitarianism."

Still, I said nothing. I wondered how the people in the path of the cataclysm felt, gazing up in horror at the sky-high mountain of water hurtling toward them. Would they care which ideology had done the most to set that mountain in motion? Would any of them agree that the sacrifice would be worth it?

"I'm finished," said Irina. "All my efforts have brought nothing but death and disaster wherever I've gone." She sighed. "No more."

Yet another tsunami cut loose in the Indian Ocean. More people died screaming thousands of feet below us.

"Maybe I should just let myself fall," said Irina. "Drop down in the middle of that nightmare and die. I deserve it."

Finally, I spoke. "Shut up, Irina."

I saw her gape at me from her crystalline escape pod. All six of her multifaceted eyes--two silver, four gold--fixed on me in shocked amazement.

"I've been thinking," I told her. "And I've realized something. I couldn't see it before, because I loved you, but now I see it."

"Because you don't love me anymore?" said Irina.

The sun shone through her green and purple clusters of crystals, glittering within the intricate web of facets. Her fiery parasites zipped around her like schools of flaming fish, weaving in and out of her vent slits.

The sunlight and firelight danced when she moved, and I felt again the way I'd felt so long ago, watching her during the pre-mission briefings in the auditorium on our homeworld. For better and worse, it had been the one constant in my life.

Even now, after everything. Even now.

"I will always love you," I told her.

She gave me a look I couldn't fathom. "What did you realize?"

"You need me. You always have," I said. "And the galaxy needs a new Lenin."

Five years later, I'm on the terrace of a villa in the heart of the Colombian jungle, sitting across from a fellow extraterrestrial who looks like Senator Joseph McCarthy. He's killed twelve of my men, whose bodies still smolder in the hot sun around us, and now he wants to know where Irina is.

The truth, which I'm not about to tell him, is that I don't know exactly where she is at this moment...but I *do* know she's on her way.

I down another swig of vodka and look at McCarthy through the cut crystal bottle. He's still so blind, so backward, so limited by his all-consuming sociopolitical ideology. I feel like I'm watching a primitive lifeform as it struggles in the mud, wholly unable to comprehend the full potential of the complex landscape around it.

"Where is she, Lenin?" McCarthy's voice is a snarl. "Where's your commie she-devil mistress?"

"She's not a communist anymore," I tell him. "And she's not my mistress. Keep up, Joe."

With an angry roar, McCarthy flips over the glass table, which shatters on the cobblestone terrace. I barely manage to save the vodka bottle, which I was just about to set down on the table's blue-tinted surface.

"No more beating around the bush!" McCarthy springs from his rattan chair and swats the bottle from my grip. It smashes to bits against a wrought iron light post. "You'll *beg* to tell me by the time I'm done with you!"

I smile as McCarthy lunges forward and wraps his thick hands around my throat. "Wait! I'm prepared to make you an offer!"

He lets up the pressure but doesn't let go. "That was fast." He shrugs. "I would've guessed you had more tolerance for torture, you pinko bastard."

"Join us." I lock eyes with McCarthy, trying to draw him in with sheer force of will. "Forget capitalism. Forget communism. Forget all that."

"A new sales pitch." McCarthy sneers. "How original."

"Help us end the wars on Earth and the war in space," I tell him. "Help us move beyond the hidebound systems of the past. Help us spread a revolutionary new philosophy conceived by a radical new Lenin."

"Would this new Lenin happen to be *you*, comrade?" says McCarthy.

When I look over his shoulder, I smile. "And *her*." My makeshift heart beats faster. She has arrived not a moment too soon, machete in hand.

The love of my life. My guiding light in smooth times and rough. My true partner now, reborn after the battle of the Indian Ocean tsunami, committed to a life of change from a new point of view.

McCarthy starts to turn. Irina draws back and swings the machete, lopping off his head with the graceful elegance of a ballerina.

I leap from my chair and sweep her into my arms. The machete clatters to the cobblestones as we kiss. As the two halves of the new Lenin bind themselves one to the other once more.

This is the formula that eluded her for so long, the one that was staring her in the face from the start. Again and again, she turned me away, when what she should have done was embrace me. Accept me as an equal and consult me for balance. Go forth driven by love instead of self-righteousness.

Now see what revolution has hatched from this union. We bear a new gospel born not of conflict, but compassion: harmony among peoples by way of shapeshifting. Empathic metamorphosis. Truly love your neighbor as yourself by *becoming* your neighbor. Literally walk a mile in his shoes...and feet, and body, and life.

Yes, human beings can learn this, and we've been teaching it for the past five years. Using shapeshifting as a bridge to understanding instead of a weapon. It's really gone viral, and the movement's about to reach critical mass. Next stop, we take the show back home and end the galactic civil war.

All because of one simple secret it took us a century to figure out.

"Welcome home, darling." Smiling, I touch the side of her face. I run my fingers through her soft red hair.

"I love you." Irina says it with tears in her eyes.

The secret is this: *We are nothing without each other.*

ROBBING THEM DOUBLE-BLIND

issuda of the Heelee:

S When the door of the great silver orb slid open in the steaming purple jungle that morning, my people and I were mesmerized. As we slithered in for a closer look, we couldn't take our eyes off the upright, two-legged beings in identical black clothing, so different from any species on our world.

It was one of the greatest moments in our *lives*, in the history of our *world*, enough to make our forked tongues flicker and our fur stand on end. Finally, we were on the cusp; things were about to change for us in magnificent ways...even if we didn't understand a single word the three aliens said when they stepped out of their orb.

We hissed back at them in our own language, the height of futility--at least until the female with the long, dark hair raised a black box the size of her hand and pointed it at us. As we hissed, the box flashed and beeped...and when it stopped, and the female spoke, we *understood* her. It was a *miracle*...further proof that our momentous occasion was infused with true *magic*.

"Greetings." The voice from the box was similar to the female's, only stiffer, and the sounds didn't match the movements of her mouth. There was a delay as she spoke and the box translated her gibberish into words we could understand.

My people and I drew back in surprise, then pressed closer than ever, enthralled by the sight and sound of a completely alien creature speaking our language.

"We are called *humans*, and we come in peace." The female's red lips curled up at the corners, and she showed her gleaming white teeth, giving her pale pink face a look that I assumed, based on her calm tone of voice, was meant to appear non-threatening. It was a facial expression I soon came to realize was the human equivalent of a *smile*, which is *very* different among *my* people. "I am President Limi Tintinabula of the Humanish Connectorat, and I bring you the *sweetest* tidings of friendship and cosmic creaturehood."

"Presssident? What isss that?" As I spoke, I heard the human's talk box chatter with words from her language, presumably translating what I said so she could understand it.

"A *leader*. And these men are leaders, too." Limi gestured at the blond-haired male to the right of her, who had a strip of the same-colored hair above his upper lip. "This is Vice President Mannik Coopernecium. And this..." She gestured at the big, bald female to her left. "...is Secretary General Quayn Vesper."

"And what isss a *Connectorat*?" I asked.

"A group of worlds joined together to pursue common interests." Limi nodded her head. "And one of those interests is exploration and reaching out to peoples and planets we have not yet encountered. Which is why we are here." Her mouth curled and widened more to show more teeth. "To get to know you and your world. To see if you are worthy of membership in our grand interplanetary organization."

"*Membership?*" I was thrilled by her words. "Interplanetary organization?"

"So where do we start the tour?" asked Mannik. "When visitors come to your world, what do you show them first?"

"We have never had visssitorsss like you."

"Like *humans*, you mean?" asked Quayn.

126

"Like *anyone*."

"Well then, even better." Limi bowed at the midsection. "It is our very great honor to be the first visitors to your world."

"Thank you," I told her. "You and your companionsss are mossst welcome, Presssident Tintinabula."

Limi straightened. "And what do they call *you*, my friend? What do your *people* call themselves?"

"My people are the *Heelee*." When I said it, as is our custom, the assembled crowd shook the chiming rattles on the tips of their tails in unison. "As for *me*, my name isss *Sissuda*."

"Excellent, Sissuda," said Limi. "Now show us the wonders of your world, so we may fully appreciate all that the Heelee have to offer."

Limi Tintinabula (Not a President):

How does it feel, being surrounded by giant, fur-covered alien snakes who could *easily* crush the life out of you, and instead having them offer you the keys to their kingdom? *Awesome!*

That's exactly how it went when the boys and I emerged from our spaceship, the *Anne Bonny*, in the jungle on planet Kaleidos that day and spooned out our usual line of B.S. The furry snakes--sorry, the *Heelee*--were so damn naïve, they bought in without any coercion or artistry whatsoever on our part. Communicating via our linguafilter translation device, we lied like crazy, from the part about my being a president to the part about us considering them for membership in the Humanish Connectorat, and they gobbled it up. Almost made me feel sorry for them.

Almost.

But the truth is, as Sissuda (the head spokes-snake) showed us around, I felt less and less sorry and more and more greedy. Because for a bunch of furry snakes, these Heelee sure knew how to keep up a treasure trove.

"Would you look at *that!*" My first mate, Mannik, practically slobbered in my ear when he caught sight of the giant golden egg in the middle of Slithertown (or whatever the Heelee called their little jungle settlement). "And it's *solid gold!*" He held up his scanner so I could see the readings on the egg. "That *alone* makes this our biggest haul *yet.*"

He was so right, it made my heart skip a beat. And it only got better from there.

"I'm glad you enjoyed ssseeing the *Olon*. Now come right thisss way, Presssident Limi." Sissuda led us down a winding path, his brown-furred body with its white polka dots sliding between purple-leafed bushes and yellow-trunked trees with shrouds of indigo flowers reaching all the way to the ground. "I will show you one of our holiest relics."

Jutting from a clearing surrounded by those indigo shroud-trees was a huge crystalline spike glinting with sunlight. It was jagged as a lightning bolt stuck in the ground and a meter higher than Quayn, the tallest among us.

And that wasn't all that was special about it.

"Solid *diamond*," whispered Mannik, sounding like he was about to have a coronary. "And there's another *two meters* of it wedged underground!"

"Wow." Coming from our woman of few words, Lieutenant Quayn, it was a mouthful and a half.

I felt a slight sweat on my upper lip and dabbed it away, struggling to conceal my own greedy excitement from our hosts.

"Thisss isss the *Obeliqua Fundimensis.*" Sissuda wound the length of his body around the giant crystal. "It isss where we come to worship the glory of our creatorsss, the *Drossa Ominosia*, and pray for delivery from their legendary demonic enemiesss, the Insidix."

"I must say, it's astonishingly beautiful," I told him, even as I worked to calculate the object's value on the open market. "Your people are lucky to have such a remarkable holy icon."

"It hasss kept us sssafe and in harmony for many thousssandsss of agesss," said Sissuda. "Ssso long asss it ssstandsss, nothing can diminish usss. Our prosssperity isss guaranteed."

Might not want to bet the farm on that. "Your gods and relics are powerful indeed," I told him. "How else have they smiled upon the Heelee?"

"Yeah," said Mannik. "What other goodies did they give you?"

"Come with me, and you will sssee." Unwinding from the crystal, Sissuda glided along a twisted path, and we followed. What other wonders might await us at our next destination?

The best yet, it turned out. Sissuda led us into a cave carpeted with furred snakes in a state of constant agitation. After he cleared a path to a darkened alcove, he flicked his tail against a switch on the wall, and the alcove brightened with patches of bioluminescent moss.

Bathed in that white light, an octagonal gemstone the size of a basketball turned slowly on a rotating metal stand. As it turned, I could see it contained many colors, from red to blue to yellow to green. I could *hear* it, too, ringing with high, jingling tones like a choir of bells.

"A *song stone!*" Mannik could hardly contain himself. "Only a *handful* have ever been found *anywhere* in the galaxy!"

As he gushed, the Heelee around us all raised their heads and hummed along with the stone, matching its tune perfectly. Their humming echoed in the cave, and the stone's song grew louder, too, as if feeding on their sympathetic vibrations.

"That's so *beautiful.*" I wasn't lying when I said it. The swelling song in the cave was probably the loveliest thing I'd ever heard in my life, aside from the singing sky-fish of Califraja. It made me think of growing up there, on planet Califraja, spending endless days and nights on bright green beaches by rolling scarlet seas. Now that I'd gotten away from there and traveled the stars with my crew of lowlifes, I sometimes wanted to go back there and forget all the bad shit I'd done.

"We call it the *Talimax.*" Sissuda stopped singing, though no one else did. "It isss sssaid the evil Insidix firssst entered our world by passsing through it. There are thossse who believe the only way to keep them at bay isss by joining our voicesss with that of the ssstone to interfere with their dark musssic."

"Well, it's remarkable," I told him through the linguafilter. "I've never heard anything like it."

"You sssee?" Sissuda flickered his tongue and tail in a way I've come to realize is the equivalent of a smile among his people. "We *do* have much to offer your Connectorat."

"You sure do!" Mannik chuckled. "I like what I see so far!"

"Impressive," said Quayn.

"And that's not even *all* of it. There's *so* much more to see!" With one last run of hums in tune with the stone, Sissuda looped around and slithered back the way we'd come.

As we all fell in step behind him, I couldn't help wondering how any intelligent being could be so utterly trusting. The snake had never seen us before that day; he knew nothing about us except what we'd told him. Was it possible such creatures existed, with no concept of suspicion? And further, that they'd look like *snakes*, of all things?

Not that I was complaining, mind you. Fleecing a pushover species would be a nice change of pace, after some of the slippery scoundrels we'd come up against recently.

"Gonna be a busy night, ain't it, boss?" said Mannik as we followed the snake through the jungle.

"How right you are," I said softly. "Good thing we've got plenty of laser diggers and antigravity lifters."

"Probably don't even need *stealth mode* for these trusting little snakes, though, huh?" said Mannik.

"Maybe not," I told him. "But *they're* not the only ones we need to worry about, are they? So let's not be *stupid* about it."

Sissuda of the Heelee:

At first, I didn't realize the next morning would be the most terrible I'd ever known. I never would have expected it, coming after our remarkable first encounter with intelligent life from beyond the stars.

The night before, we'd had a celebratory feast in honor of President Limi and her companions, which had left me exhausted. The rest of my people had likewise worn themselves out and were all still asleep when I awoke.

When I slid out of my burrow in Heeleetown Prime that morning, the sun was already shining brightly, and the air was warm. The breeze carried the smell of breakfast--rodents on the move not far away.

The breeze also carried another scent, which I recognized as the sweat of the humans. Slithering down a path, I found them walking my way through the purple vines, clad this time in red-colored clothing instead of black.

"Sissuda!" President Limi waved energetically. Her two companions were both waving, too--even the bald female who rarely spoke or made a friendly gesture.

I reared up and flickered my tongue in response. "Greetingsss, Presssident."

"How are you this fine morning?" As before, Limi carried the blinking black talk box that let me understand the speech of her and her fellow humans and vice versa.

"I'm well, thank you," I told her. "And what of yourssselvesss?"

"Never been better!" Mannik's mouth with its upturned corners opened wider than ever. It was an expression that I now knew indicated great joy. "Must be something *special* about this planet of yours!"

"Wonderful to hear you sssay that," I said. "You enjoyed the feassst lassst night, I take it?"

"*Did* we!" Quayn's eyes widened, and she rubbed her belly.

"So where are you off to?" Limi asked me. "What do you typically do first thing in the morning?"

"Yeah," said Mannik. "And where can you get a good cup of coffee around here?"

"Coffee?"

"Never mind," said Limi. "But what *do* you do as part of your morning ritual?"

"Ah, ritual." I darted down a path through a copse of indigo shroud trees. "Thisss way."

"This way to what?" asked Limi as she and the others followed.

"My morning prayersss." A speckled rodent with four eyes and six furry legs scampered in front of me and froze. I resisted the temptation to gulp him down and instead scared him off with a nasty hiss and baring of fangs.

"Prayers?" said Limi. "To your gods? To ask for what?"

"We asssk for nothing," I told her. "We have all that we could ever need or want. Only good thingsss happen here. We pray only to thank the godsss for our paradissse of pure--"

Suddenly, I froze. What I saw up ahead was not right. I had come to the right place, I could *smell* it, but something about it was terribly wrong.

"No!" I shot away from the indigo shroud trees and crossed the clearing in a desperate flash. Sure enough, what I'd expected to see there was gone, leaving nothing in its place but a hole in the ground.

"What is it?" Limi sounded concerned. "What happened, Sissuda?"

I was in a blind panic, crawling around and around the empty hole. "The *Obeliqua Fundimensssisss* is *gone*! It hasss *disssappeared!*"

"You mean the giant crystal?" asked Limi. "The one you said was one of your holiest relics?"

"It hasss been here all of my *life!*" I stopped circling and went down into the hole, searching for some sign of the missing relic. "It *can't* be gone."

"Gee, little guy," said Mannik. "That's just *terrible*. That was one beautiful *diamond*, all right."

"Sure was," agreed Quayn.

"Where *isss* it? I don't *underssstand!*"

"Sissuda, calm down," said Limi. "Is it possible it *sank*? Are there fissures or sinkholes around here?"

"None!" I combed the fresh dirt for remnants or clues but found nothing. The Obeliqua was gone without a trace. "The Drossa Ominosia who created it would *never* have placed it on fractured or weakened ground."

"Well, this is gonna sound kind'a crazy," said Mannik. "But is it possible someone might have *stolen* it?"

"Ssstolen?" I stopped squirming in the dirt and looked up at him. "What doesss *that* mean?"

"To *steal* something means to *take* what doesn't *belong* to you without permission," explained Mannik. "It's what *thieves* do. Surely, you must have *thieves* on your planet."

"Why would we need to *take* what doesssn't belong to usss if we already have everything we *need?*"

"You snake people crack me up," said Mannik, and then Limi gave him a dark look and he stopped talking.

Meanwhile, my heart felt like it would explode from all the sorrow. Raising my head, I cried to the sky, letting out a high-pitched wail of pure anguish. *Eee-lee, lee, lee. Eee-lee, lee, lee.*

"Sissuda?" Limi crouched at the edge of the hole, her features pinched in what I came to realize was an expression of great worry. "What can we do? Let us help."

But there was nothing they could do, so I kept singing...at least until I heard someone else singing from another place, not far away.

Springing out of the hole, I sped through the brush toward that song, focused only on reaching it. Because the one thing I knew at that moment was this: whoever was doing that singing had nothing to do with *my* song or the Obeliqua.

When at last I reached the singer and saw where she was, I wished I hadn't. Because seeing her there, at the mouth of that cave, and hearing the agony in every note of her keening song, meant the day was getting much worse.

I didn't stop to talk to her about it. Better, I thought, to get it over with and see for myself.

Racing inside the cave, I spotted the alcove instantly, bathed in the pale moss-light--and *empty.* Another precious artifact was gone.

"The *Talimax,* too?" Limi, who'd followed with her fellow humans all the way from the Obeliqua's clearing, sounded shocked at the mouth of the cave. "It's *gone?"*

I reared up, bobbing my head in dismay. "Gone." Then, I let out another howl of anguish, raising my voice to the heavens.

Only to hear yet *another* cry in the distance.

This time, following the wailing song took me back to the middle of Heeleetown Prime. Here, a dozen Heelee joined in anguished song, with more chiming in every minute.

Because the *Olon,* the great golden egg that always towered there, gleaming in sunlight, was gone as well.

"I can't believe thisss." As a crowd continued to grow, voices joined in mourning the inconceivable loss, I went limp at Limi's feet. "It'sss like the end of the world."

"Poor Sissuda," said Limi. "I'm so sorry this happened to you and your people."

"You can say that again," said Mannik. "It's a real tragedy."

As I glanced up, I wondered at the look on his face. He, unlike Limi, was smiling.

"Total tragedy." Quayn was also smiling. "Just the worst."

Was it possible? Did humans sometimes *smile* at times of great sadness? Because both Mannik and Quayn were smiling as they watched my people cry and thrash before them, mourning the loss of something so precious, its value could never truly be calculated.

Limi Tintinabula (Still Not a President):

Does feeling sorry for a bunch of hairy alien snakes make me a bad thief? If so, then maybe I am, because I *did* feel sorry for the Heelee after we took their precious shit.

We'd worked hard to get it the night before, using every high-tech trick in the book to keep quiet while hauling it all right out from under their noses. We'd busted our humps, no doubt about it--but now that the treasures were stowed away aboard our ship, I couldn't stop feeling guilty for what we'd done to the snakes.

They were just so *distraught*, shrieking in anguish because their holy relics were gone. Every single *one* of them was howling at once with so much heartfelt pain, it seemed like it would *never* stop.

Meanwhile, my partners and I just stood there and let it wash over us. Though I felt a pang of regret for the poor snakes, Mannik and Quayn were tickled pink that we were getting away with the crime. It was all I could do to keep them from giggling out loud about the whole thing.

And why *shouldn't* they have been laughing? After all, we'd done *much* worse in the past and gotten away with it. So what if these snakes were the biggest bunch of rubes we'd ever encountered? So what if they were so dumb, they took the challenge right out of it for us?

The money we'd make from selling the things we'd taken would spend just as well, wouldn't it? All we had to do now was get off Snakeworld and cash in the goodies for a new life.

Though *that* might not be so simple if certain *complications* came into play, which we'd learned by now to expect in our line of work.

So being nervous made sense and came with the territory. "I think it's time to go." I looked around for the best exit lane through the mob of Heelee howling around us. There was no clear route, though I noticed the snakes were slightly sparser in one direction.

"But it's just gettin' good." Mannik was on the verge of bursting into laughter. "It's the whole reason we stuck around after last night, remember? To enjoy the reaction?"

"Well, I'm sorry I let you talk me into it," I said. "We should've left as soon as we were done."

"Lighten up, 'Prez.'" Mannik clapped me on the back. "They're freakin' *snakes.*"

"With *fur,*" added Quayn, sneering.

"I know," I told them. "But maybe wallowing in their sadness is over the top. Haven't we done enough, stealing their holiest artifacts?"

"If you feel that bad about it," said Mannik, "we can always leave 'em some of our holy *turds* to worship."

Just then, Sissuda stopped howling and slithered over to us. I had to elbow both Mannik and Quayn in the side to stop them from snickering.

"Presssident Limi?" Sissuda lifted his head and upper body to me and raised his voice to make himself heard over the Heelee's howling. "Isss there anything you can do to help usss get our missssing thingsss back?"

"If only we could." I had to crank up the volume on the linguafilter so he could hear the translation. "We don't know *what* happened to them, do we?" I asked Mannik.

"We don't have a clue." Mannik pulled out his handheld scanner device and tapped the controls, watching the readout on the screen. "Not a trace of suspicious activity on our ship's sensors last night or this morning."

"Sissuda, do you or your people have any ideas?" I asked. "What about the Insidix you've mentioned? Didn't you say they emerged from the Talimax?"

"Yeah, the *Insidix,*" said Mannik. "You said they're shadowy, right?"

"But they have never *taken* from usss before," said Sissuda. "They have never been so *brazen.*"

"It *had* to be them," insisted Mannik. "They're *messing* with you poor, innocent folks."

"But that would mean our creators, the Drossa Ominosia, have *forsssaken* us. That we have fallen from their favor. Otherwise, they would have intervened and stopped the Insidix." Sissuda slowly lowered his head to the ground. "Perhapsss it isss a sssign."

Sissuda fell silent, even as the crying of the hundreds of other Heelee around us grew louder. Their mourning seemed to be reaching a peak; the piercing shrieks were hurting my ears.

"We should be going." The linguafilter was barely audible over the shrieking. "Thank you for the hospitality, but we need to leave."

"Wait!" Sissuda popped up straight again. "Can't you ssstay one more night? We have ssso many other treasuresss yet to show you!"

"Treasures?" That got Quayn's attention.

"Hidden in other placesss," said Sissuda. "I can take you to sssee them tomorrow, if you can wait."

"Hell yes, we can wait!" Mannik grinned. "See you in the morning, snake buddy!"

"We need to leave, though." I gave him a meaningful glare. "We have to get to our *next stop*, remember?"

"Shame on you, President Limi." Mannik shook his head in apparent disgust. "Don't you think spending one more night here is the *least* we can do for these poor snake people?"

"Yeah," agreed Quayn.

Feeling Sissuda's expectant eyes upon me, I finally nodded. "All right. One more night."

"Thank you, my friendsss," said Sissuda. "I will show you many more wondersss, I promissse. Perhapsss you will show me sssome as well."

"Such as?" said Mannik.

"Perhapsss your magical ship might yet find sssome trace of the Insssidix and help usss retrieve our holy relicsss." With that, Sissuda flipped around and resumed singing with his people, adding his high-pitched cries to the chorus of keening howls from the Heelee around him.

Sissuda of the Heelee:

That terrible day of loss was followed by a terrible night. The singing of my people went on until long after dark; it never really let up until the Heelee started dropping into exhausted, restless slumber.

Even then, Heeleetown Prime was filled with anguished whimpers and moans. With our best-loved relics gone, none of us felt right anymore; we felt sick and exposed, unable to directly connect to our gods or resist the will of the shadowy Insidix.

It was hard to consider an existence without those things that had given our lives meaning. I couldn't imagine any of it feeling any less terrible, no matter how long we lived and got used to it.

But I was wrong. Things got much better after all, and soon.

The next morning, I expected to be greeted by a resumption of agonized singing. As emotional as my people are, I assumed their mourning would go on for some time to come.

Instead, I woke to a completely different sound--the chirping and whistling of *Heelee happiness*, coming from all around me.

At first, I thought I was hearing things. Happiness? So soon after pure *agony*? It made no *sense*.

But then, when I crawled out of my burrow and saw what was happening in Heeleetown Prime, I realized the world had changed again. What I heard was *no* hallucination.

Everywhere I looked among the mounds and nests and burrows, my fellow Heelee whistled and chirped with delight. Heads up and swaying, they danced with joy in the bright jungle sunlight, fur rippling in the gentle morning breeze. And every one of them was looking in the same direction, at the cause of their delight.

They were all looking at the giant golden egg towering over the middle of town.

Gazing up at its glittering skin, I marveled at the miracle of its presence. The Olon, which had been gone just a day ago, had *returned*.

Drawing closer, I puzzled at this turn of events. That it had been moved once before was hard enough to believe. That it had come back was *impossible* to accept.

Yet also *wonderful* beyond imagining. Like my fellow Heelee, I lifted my head off the ground and swayed with glee.

Then someone told me the Obeliqua Fundimensis and the Talimax had come back, too, and I whistled and chirped myself into a state of perfect ecstasy.

Limi Tintinabula (Not a President and Never Will Be):

"Limi! Lock and load!" That was what Mannik said when he woke me from a sound sleep that morning, turning on the lights in my quarters and tossing a rifle on my bed. "We've got us some *snakes* to kill!"

"What the *hell?*" I leaped out of bed in my black nightshirt, ratcheting into a state of instant readiness. "Are we under *attack?*"

"We need to *show* those damn reptiles!" Mannik was waving his own rifle around, livid. "We've gotta *teach* 'em!"

With that, he charged out of the room. I followed down the hall, not knowing *what* to expect. Had the Heelee invaded our ship? Were they trying to force their way aboard? Had we underestimated their suspiciousness and potential for violence *that* much?

"Here!" Mannik ran up to the door of the cargo bay and slapped the big red control button mounted on the wall beside it. "Just *look* what they've done!"

The door slid open from right to left. The lights flashed on automatically, revealing our cargo bay spread out before us. The cargo bay that should have been *full*.

But which instead was incredibly *empty*.

"Oh my God." I stepped inside and looked around. "What happened to the *relics*?"

"The damn *worms* must've gotten them somehow!" Enraged, Mannik cracked the butt of his rifle against the wall. "All their shit is *gone*."

"But how is that *possible?*"

139

"Don't ask *me!* They couldn't have gotten *in* here, let alone brought in the heavy equipment they'd need to *lug* that shit with their primitive level of technology."

I looked at the surveillance cameras in the corners of the ceiling. "What about the ship's records? Anything on video?"

"Nothing! The haul was *here*, and then it was just *gone!*"

I shook my head. "So where *is* it? If the haul isn't *here*, where *is* it?" I did my best to sound baffled, though in truth I had a hunch about what might have happened. It was important, given the forces that might be at work here, for us to act our parts perfectly in this drama. If we weren't convincing, there was no way my plan could succeed.

Just then, Quayn broke in over the intercom. "Time for a walk, folks. You won't *believe* what I'm seeing on the spycams we planted in Snaketown."

Sissuda of the Heelee:

I was still caught up in the celebration for the return of our relics when President Limi and her companions returned to Heeleetown Prime. I darted over immediately, excited to see them in the midst of our happy occasion.

But the expressions on their faces surprised me. None of them was smiling. All three of them had the creased-brow look that I'd learned was the human version of a frown.

"Greetingsss to you all!" I lifted my head high and swayed before them. "Come and cccelebrate with usss! There'sss been a miracle!"

Limi spoke into her talk box. "What kind of miracle?"

"Our greatesssst, holiesssst relicsss have been *returned* to usss!" I told her. "Which makesss them even *holier!*"

"Is that so?" said Mannik. "And who exactly returned them to you?"

"Nobody knowsss!" I said joyfully. "And *it doesssn't matter.* All that mattersss is that the Olon, the Obeliqua Fundimensssisss and the Talimax have all come back to usss!"

I danced and cheered, hoping the President and her companions might join me, but they didn't. They just continued to stare with creased brows at the spot in the middle of town where the Olon now stood once more.

"No one saw anything unusual?" asked Limi. "There were no witnesses to the miracle?"

"It happened while we were all asssleep," I told her. "When we woke, all our relicsss had been returned to usss!"

"But doesn't it make you wonder?" asked Limi.

"Wonder about what?"

"Why were they taken in the first place? And why were they brought back?" Limi narrowed her eyes and walked through the swaying, whistling crowd toward the Olon.

I trailed after her, ahead of her friends. "What are you doing?"

"Making sure." Limi nudged her way through a cluster of jubilant Heelee.

"Sure of what?" I asked.

"The miracle." As Limi approached the egg, which was almost as tall as she was, she reached out to touch it. "Mannik, take a reading," she said over her shoulder.

Mannik slouched over, pulling out his scanner device. The scanner blinked and beeped as he ran it over the Olon's surface, watching the little screen closely.

"I don't undersssstand," I said as the beeping got louder.

"Do you *know* this is your original Olon?" asked Limi. "Do you know it for a *fact?"*

"Well of coursssse it is," I said. "What elsssse would it be?"

"A counterfeit," said Limi. "It happens all the time."

"Counterfeit?"

"Someone steals something valuable, makes a copy, and puts back the copy. Then they sell the original for a fortune." Limi nodded. "Many times, the original owners don't even know their treasure was replaced."

I thought about it, staring at the glittering golden Olon. The multitude of sparkling flecks in its surface seemed the same to me as they had ever been. "It sssoundsss terrible, but it didn't happen here," I said. "That is the sssame Olon I've known for my entire life."

"How can you be *sure*?" said Limi.

"He's right." Mannik shrugged his shoulders as he pulled the scanner away from the Olon. "Go figure."

"Okay then." Limi turned and headed back through the crowd. "We ought to check the other ones as well."

"Why can't you just accept the miracle?" I shouted as she walked away from me. "Why can't you *believe?*"

She stopped and spun to face me. "I believe *something* happened here, but it might not be what you *think*."

"Yeah!" said Quayn.

"What elssse *could* have happened?" I asked.

"You said the Insidix might have taken your relics," said Limi. "What if they did it for a *reason?* What if they *tampered* with them in ways we can't *detect?* And if they *did* all that, you should *ask* yourself *why* they did it. How might it affect your *people?*"

I stared at her, processing what she'd said. Try as I might, I couldn't dismiss the possibilities and questions. *Someone* had stolen our relics for *some* reason.

"I'm just saying." Limi shrugged. "Maybe asking a few questions wouldn't be a bad thing."

Limi Tintinabula (Not Even Remotely Presidential):

"We should just *kill* all the snakes and take their shit again! I'll bet *then* it won't miraculously disappear from our cargo hold!"

That was what Mannik said when we got back to the *Anne Bonny*...and before that, en route to the *Bonny*, as well. As usual, he was ruled by a one-track mind--and this time, that mind was set on murder.

"Listen, calm down," I told him. "The *snakes* didn't take our haul, and you know it. We *all* do."

Mannik's rage shifted. I could tell from the look in his eyes that he knew what I was talking about. When I glanced over at Quayn, I could see that she understood, too...finally. By now, it wasn't something I should have needed to remind them about, but they weren't always quick on the uptake.

This truth they both recognized was not something to talk about openly. It could only be referred to indirectly, obliquely, in code.

Now more than ever, we had to play it just right.

As we continued down the corridor, I cleared my throat. "We're back on the same page, then?"

Quayn gripped my shoulder and whispered in my ear. "It's one of *those* deals again? We're on *their* radar?"

I rolled my eyes at her and shook off her hand. After all we'd been through over the years, she knew better than to ask those questions out loud.

"Now listen." I stopped and spun to face the two of them. I've got this figured out, okay?"

Mannik didn't look convinced. "But what about...?"

I shushed him with a sweep of my hand. "We won't go home *empty-handed*, and we won't need to *kill* the snakes, either. This is all going to work out fine."

"So we *are* going to take it back?" asked Mannik. "Steal all the goodies and get off this shitball planet before *we* get *robbed* again?"

"Sort of." I headed for the cargo bay with the other two close behind. "We're going to take *one* of the goodies."

"Just one?" Quayn sounded incredulous.

"Just one," I told her.

"Which one?" asked Quayn.

"And *why*?" asked Mannik.

"You'll see." I opened the cargo bag door and marched inside.

"Now somebody give me a hand with the antigravity lifters, would you?"

Sissuda of the Heelee:

Though President Limi had gone back to her ship, I couldn't stop thinking about what she had said. Was it possible that the Insidix had tampered with our relics? If so, might it affect my people somehow?

It was scary to consider, especially because it made some sense. Why else would the relics disappear and reappear spontaneously, with no intervention from the Heelee or humans?

And it raised a question for which I had no good answer: How could I find out the truth about what was done to the relics and how it might impact the Heelee?

I went to sleep that night thinking I would never know the answers. Perhaps I would wonder about them for the rest of my life, always looking in vain for some sign of the truth behind what had happened. Always wondering if something dark had changed my people in ways I might not realize until it was too late.

Though the way things turned out, I *did* get another chance to seek the truth.

The next morning, when I woke and slid out of my burrow, I heard fresh cries of grief through the jungle. I followed them, racing through the purple brush in a state of fevered intensity, wondering what new distress had befallen my fellow Heelee.

When I reached the source, however, I found that the cause was not new at all. The cries of sorrow led me into a cave I knew all too well, the home of our holy relic, the Talimax.

Which was *gone. Again.*

Somehow, it had disappeared again in the night, vanished without a trace as it had two nights before.

And its disappearance could be explained no better this time than the first. No clues remained of whatever force or agent had taken it. Asking around among the mourners, I discovered there were no witnesses to the theft, either. The incident was just as inexplicable as the one that had preceded it; it was identical.

Except for one thing. This time, the Talimax was the only relic that had been taken.

I went from one site to the other and saw the proof with my own eyes. Though the Talimax was gone, the Obeliqua Fundimensis and the Olon were right where they were supposed to be.

Why this was, I had no idea. It made no sense, just as it had made no sense when all three relics had been taken the first time.

And it made me wonder what exactly would happen next. Would the other two relics be taken, so all three were gone again? Would one disappear each day, as another was returned? Would we go on like this indefinitely, with relics disappearing and reappearing in unpredictable patterns for reasons we could not fathom?

It would be enough to drive me crazy and take the rest of the Heelee with me. Or was that the purpose all along, from the beginning?

Perhaps, I thought, there might be a way to seek the answers I wanted after all.

The night after the three relics had disappeared all at once, we had not posted any kind of guard. What good would it have done? Our most priceless treasures had already been taken.

Perhaps, if we *had* put guards in place, they might have seen the truth behind the vanishings. They might have gotten actual *answers*.

And it might work that way *now* if we didn't make the same mistake twice. If someone waited at the vacant site tonight, and the Talimax was returned, he might get to see *who* or *what* returned it. He might get to solve the mystery and stop the cycle of disappearance and reappearance for good.

That was exactly my plan for that night, after the rest of the Heelee went off to sleep. That was why I alone reentered the vacant cave of the Talimax and hid myself in a crack in the base of the wall, waiting for something to happen. Waiting for an opportunity that might never arrive.

That was why I fought the urge to fall asleep with all my strength. Because I had to *see*. I had to *ask*.

I had to *know*. And, perhaps, I had to find a way to *end* this madness.

Limi Tintinabula (Homo Sapiens Non-Presidentus):

"Shouldn't we be *guarding* this thing?" Mannik smacked the side of the Talimax, which was back on display in the *Anne Bonny's* cargo bay.

"Absolutely not," I told him. We'd re-stolen the giant, singing gemstone from the Heelee and returned it to the cargo bay, where we'd kept it the *first* time we'd stolen it. But making the treasure harder for someone else to steal away from us was the *last* thing I wanted to do. Leaving the Talimax ripe for the taking was a vital part of my plan.

"I still think we should just take off and get paid for what we have." Mannik still had his grouch on about the whole situation, no matter how many times I'd laid it out for him. He and Quayn both had a tendency to argue against agreed-upon plans in the heat of the moment. "A bird in the cargo hold is worth three in the bush."

"This is how it has to be," I said firmly. "Trust me. It will all work out for the best."

Quayn grunted. "Define 'best.'"

"Let's go, guys." I hit the light switch on the wall by the door, and the bay darkened. "Nighty night, now."

"But I..." Quayn looked around with a scowl. "What if some-one...shows up?"

"We can only hope." I took her arm and guided her into the corridor. "That's what you call a best-case scenario."

Sissuda of the Heelee:

It was deep in the heart of the night when the elliptical blue glow began to flash in the middle of the cave. It was bright enough to wake me, thank the Drossa, though I'd fallen asleep in spite of my best efforts not to.

Inching my nose out of the crack where I'd holed up, I watched as the glow grew brighter. Part of it broke away, forming a second, smaller body of light that spun around the first a few times before zipping across the cave.

The smaller glow landed in the niche in the wall that the Talimax had once occupied, where it bounced around and flashed energetically. After a moment or two of that, it settled down, resting in the middle of the niche. Its glow gradually faded, revealing the stolen Talimax back in its rightful place, on display.

Meanwhile, the larger blue glow in the middle of the cave got brighter instead of dimming. Its flashing began to accelerate, which worried me. What if it was getting ready to disappear?

I lunged out of my crack in the wall and raced toward it breathlessly. Had I hesitated too long to approach it? Was I losing my opportunity?

"Wait!" I swooped to a stop and flung up my head, flicking my tongue at the blue glow. "I need to talk to you!"

The glow backed away, and I followed. I didn't care if it was dangerous or not; I wanted answers.

"Just *talk* to me! Pleassse!" I rose up higher from the floor of the cave, demanding to be seen. "Tell me why you're *doing* thisss! Why do you keep *taking* our relicsss, then bringing them *back?*"

This time, the glow didn't move away from me. It just hovered there silently, flashing as I faced it.

"Tell me!" I said. "What doesss it all *mean?*"

After a moment, the central area of the glow took on a more solid shape, coalescing into what looked like a loosely coiled spiral studded with unblinking alien eyes of many colors, all directed at me. In the middle of the coils, a red-lipped mouth bobbed on a crimson stalk, finally opening to reveal copious white fangs with jagged tips.

"Why do we *do* this?" Though the coiled thing had no visible talk box, I understood its words instantly. Somehow, its rumbling, deep voice spoke perfect Heelee from the start. "We do it to clean up the *mess* left behind by the troublesome *humans.*"

"Messss? Humansss?" Confusion wracked me. "I don't undersssstand."

"The humans are reckless," said the thing. "We protect the rest of the galaxy from their thoughtless and wicked behavior."

I shook my head hard as if that might clear it--but it didn't. "Who *are* you, anyway?"

"You may call us the *Vizigog*," said the coiled spiral thing. "You may think of us as humanity's *chaperones* and the galaxy's last *defense*."

I continued to stare at the thing as it turned slowly within its elliptical cloud of blue glow. It seemed to warp and distend as I watched, as if I were seeing it move through a flawed lens or the rippling surface of water.

"I sssstill don't understand," I told it. "What doesss taking and bringing back our relicsss again and again have to do with the humansss?"

"*We*, the Vizigog, only *brought them back*. The *humans* are the ones who *took* them."

Wrapping my head around what I'd heard took some doing. "You mean Presssident Limi and her people?"

"Yes," said the Vizigog. "Though the one known as Limi is no president."

"But she sssaid she wasss, and..."

"She is a liar. A teller of untruths. It is a thing that humans do."

I thought about this for a moment. "How do I know *you* are not a liar?"

"You don't," said the Vizigog. "But I am not. If you are uncertain whom to trust, however, ask yourself which of us *brought back* the things your people treasure."

Again, I had to think. "What about the Insssidix?"

"They do not exist. Have you ever *seen* one? Has anyone you've ever *met* seen one?"

"But *why?*" I asked. "Why would the humansss *take* our thingsss and *lie* about it?"

"Because of *greed*," said the Vizigog. "The most powerful force motivating human behavior."

"Greed?"

"The desire to possess as much as possible," said the Vizigog. "To *take* what others have and get away with it. To exalt oneself over fellow beings by owning the greater share of resources."

"And thisss isss a bad thing?" I asked.

"The humans don't see it that way, but yes. Their greed has driven them to make terrible mistakes, forcing us to intercede again and again to prevent greater harm to other species of the cosmos."

"Which isss why you're here now, bringing back our Talimax."

"Yes," said the Vizigog. "To prevent harm to the Heelee. To give you back your rightful heritage."

"I sssee." This time, I was the one who backed away as I wrestled with all he had told me. If what he'd said was true, the humans had lied and taken our things because they were greedy. I knew I should be angry with them because of what they'd done.

But I couldn't. Try as I might, I couldn't hate Limi, Mannik, and Quayn. If anything, I realized I *admired* them.

Using only words, they had gotten away with stealing the most precious relics from my people. If not for the Vizigog's intervention, we never even would have *known* the humans were responsible.

"I sstill can't believe humansss can do thisss," I said. "That they can lie and get away with it."

"Not just humans, unfortunately," said the Vizigog. "*Anyone* can do it."

"Anyone?"

"But the humans are very good at it." The Vizigog's blue glow

149

dimmed. "They have fooled many beings and caused many problems, which is why they need chaperones. If not for us following
them around, cleaning up their biggest messes, they might have
destroyed *half the galaxy* by now...or *been* destroyed themselves."

"Half the galaxy?" How could simple, fleshy creatures with
nothing visibly special about them be a threat on a *galactic* scale?

The more I thought about it, the more amazing it seemed. The
more *powerful* and *different* from the always-honest, always-peaceful
society in which I'd always lived.

"Ssso what are you planning to do next?" I asked. "Leave the
Talimax here for my people to find? Make them wonder how it
returned so mysssteriousssly?"

"Yes," said the Vizigog. "More or less."

"And what about *me*, now that I know the sssecretsss? Will you
just let me tell my people everything I've learned?"

The Vizigog was silent for a moment. "That is a very good question. Our presence must always be concealed, especially from
native populations."

I didn't like what he was saying or where this seemed to be
heading. My mind worked fast to find a new path.

The humans' lies and thefts had stirred up my people and put
me in danger. The Vizigog were lying and stealing, too, in order to
undo and cover up what the humans had done.

Dealing with such strange ways and high stakes, I felt
completely out of my depth. How could I ensure the well-being of
my people and myself when I'd never even *known* of lies and
thievery before the humans' arrival on my world?

Suddenly, an answer occurred to me. Maybe the best way to
deal with those who lie and steal is to do the same thing in return.

And perhaps the best way to *beat* troublemakers is to *join* them.

"Well, I think I have a sssolution for you." I leaned toward him,
feeling the heat of his blue glow. "Sssend the Talimax back to the
humansss."

"Send it back?" He sounded surprised.

"Do it now, before any Heelee realize it'sss gone."

"But the humans *stole* it from your people!"

"It wasss all a big mix-up," I told him.

"Your statement is inaccurate," said the Vizigog. "The humans committed a *theft.*"

"You must be thinking of the Olon and the Obeliqua Fundimensssissss," I said. "The *Talimax* isss a *gift.*"

"Incorrect."

"It is a gift to our new friendsss of the Humanish Connectorate. A gesture of friendship and fealty." I was surprised at how easily my first lies rolled out of me. It helped that there was an essence of truth at the heart of them...and some very powerful motivation backing them up, as I believed my entire future depended on how convincing I could be.

"You want to return the Talimax to the people who first stole it?" asked the Vizigog. "Am I to assume you speak for all your people in this matter?"

"Yesss," I told him. "And I asssk that you do one more thing as well. One thing that will let usss all conclude thisss matter."

The Vizigog paused. "Will it involve more lies?"

I flickered my tongue and gave my rattle a shake. "Not to *you*, it won't."

Limi Tintinabula (For the Last Time, Not a President):

It felt good to be back in space again. As I gazed out the window of the *Anne Bonny*, watching stars streak by like blazing streamers in the velvety darkness, my soul was at ease, my mind relaxed and content.

Planet Kaleidos was behind us, and our work there was done. Our visit had been a complete success, and our payday was assured. In spite of an occasional hiccup, my plan had been perfectly executed, the outcome as predicted...in all ways but one.

"Hey, Boss." Mannik trotted up beside me, grinning like

someone who'd just gotten a lot richer. "You going to take another look at it? I know that's where *I'm* headed."

"Sure, why not?" I smiled and shrugged. I hadn't been headed his way, but it couldn't hurt. After all, savoring the victories in life was just as important as learning from the defeats.

"I just can't get enough of this thing." As we marched around a bend, Mannik hit the big red control button on the wall beside the cargo bay door. "Know what I mean?"

"I do." As the door slid open, I stepped inside and flipped the light switch. The bay was flooded with bright light, revealing the precious cargo secured on a protective pedestal in the middle of the floor.

It was the Talimax, the huge octagonal crystal from the cave on Kaleidos. Its many facets shone and sparkled in the light, changing colors that ran up and down the spectrum and every conceivable shade in-between. It sang to us in high, ringing tones like the chiming of bells, a song that was all at once welcoming, lovely, and mysterious.

"We got it." Mannik beamed as he walked over to lightly stroke the edge of the crystal. "The last known song stone in the galaxy."

"We did." I nodded and joined him in stroking the giant gem. It felt warm to the touch, as if there were some kind of life or power source thrumming away inside.

"You were so *smooth* about it, too." Mannik lowered his voice to the softest of whispers. "The *babysitters* couldn't stop us. If anything, they helped make it *happen.*"

I just nodded. It was best not to talk about our babysitters, the Vizigog, if we could help it. You just never knew when they might be listening.

But Mannik was absolutely right. We'd learned a lot from being thwarted by our self-appointed chaperones through the years. These days, we knew enough to not only work around their meddling ways, but to manipulate them into helping us achieve our goals.

Just barging in and stealing the Talimax would not have been enough. I'd known the Vizigog would simply return it to the Heelee, so a sneakier plan had been required. That was why we'd taken an impressionable Heelee under our wing, planting seeds of suspicion in his mind that a dark force other than our own was at work on Kaleidos. When he finally confronted the Vizigog, Sissuda was inclined to trust us over the stranger and gave us the Talimax as a gift, a gesture of friendship...and *payment*.

Because, by the time we'd gotten done with him, there was something Sissuda had wanted very badly to *buy* from us. Something the Vizigog couldn't stop us from selling, since there was no coercion whatsoever involved in the perfectly ethical and harmless transaction.

Suddenly, the *Bonny's* intercom crackled to life, and a now-familiar voice boomed into the cargo bay. "Bossss? Thisss isss the bridge. I was jussst wondering what our next ssstop should be."

I grinned at the sound of Sissuda's voice, translated by a linguafilter connected to the intercom system. In exchange for the Talimax, all Sissuda had asked for was to leave his homeworld as part of our crew. He'd had enough of his humdrum planet with its purple jungles and straight-arrow snake-bores. He wanted excitement and on-the-job training in the power of lies and misdirection, something he could never receive on crime-and-sin-free Kaleidos.

It was a small price to pay, in my opinion, for the priceless Talimax and all the good things it would bring. We might even come out ahead in the deal, if Sissuda proved his value, which he just might.

After all, he was already demonstrating he was a *natural* when it came to our business.

"Where do *you* think we should go?" I asked.

"Well, let'sss ssseee," said Sissuda. "How about a planet where the people posssesss pricelesss treasuresss and are even more naïve about lying, cheating, and ssstealing than the Heelee?"

"Perfect!" said Limi.

"I can think of a few," offered Mannik.

"Great! I'll pick one!" said Sissuda. "But you have to let me be part of the ground team. I've got an idea for a new sssetup, and I want to be there when we put it in play."

"What *kind* of setup?" asked Quayn, who'd just entered the cargo bay and caught the tail end of Sissuda's comments.

"You sssaid the one on *my* world wasss sssomething called a *double-blind*, right?"

"Correct," I said. It was much like a double-blind scientific experiment, only without the science. "Neither the Heelee nor our chaperones knew they were both being used. Two sides were kept in the dark about our true intentions."

"Well, *thisss* one will be a *double-blind* with *double profits. Half* the profits will come from our new alien friends, whoever we decccide to visssit."

"And the *other* half?" I asked him.

"Will come from the *chaperonesss*, of courssse," said Sissuda. "And they'll *gladly* hand it over by the time *I'm* done with them."

Mannik, Quayn, and I laughed our asses off, though there wasn't a chuckle from Sissuda over the intercom. Either he was dead serious, or an awesome freaking liar in the making--or *both*.

And *both* was exactly what that crafty son of a bitch turned out to be. He was a damn *prodigy*, the *best* I've ever known, and he put us all to shame in years to come, not that we minded.

Because by the time he got done with the Vizigog, *they* were the ones who needed babysitting.

THE SPACEKISS SOLUTION

The alien who looked like a cactus blinked his prickly pear eyes and made a noise like a screaming cat.

At first, Dinah Ryan wasn't sure that this was a bad thing. For all she and her fellow Earthlings knew about aliens, it could have been a cry of pure ecstasy.

But then, the cactus puked chunky blue slime all over Ben Blakey, which tipped them off. With a noise like a dental drill running at full throttle, Mr. Cactus scooted off to the next booth.

So humanity was still screwed.

"Ah, man!" Blakey flicked slime from his gray jumpsuit and wrinkled his nose. "This stuff *stinks*!"

"You're telling *me*." Mahalia Davis darted away from him. "How the hell many of these species communicate by spraying shit at each other, anyway?"

Dinah grinned and shook her head, tossing her shoulder-length sandy brown hair. "I still say it's a joke. Initiation pranks for the new kids on the block."

"No," said Captain Alec Strayhorn. "We don't matter that much to them. Half of them don't even know we're here."

Dinah gazed out at the cavernous hall and realized Strayhorn was right. Every imaginable shape and size of alien being walked and bounced and flew and crawled and oozed across that giant crystal chamber. There were aliens with skin like stained glass, faces like mirrors, bodies like smoke, fur crackling with electrical current...and none of them were looking or sniffing or twitching in the direction of the Earthlings' booth.

"This is a *disaster*." Blakey used one end of the tablecloth to wipe slime from his arms and chest. "*Three days* at this debacle, and what do we have to *show* for it?"

"Lots of alien *freebies*." Mahalia shuffled the pile of bizarre devices, objects, and pocket-sized lifeforms on the table.

"Which we don't know what to do with!" Blakey bent down and wiped slime from his lumpy bald head. "For all we know, they're meant to kill and eat us!" Usually, Blakey was the funniest and most upbeat member of the team; his current surliness showed just how badly things were going.

Some Worlds' Fair this was turning out to be. The Fair was designed to give the inhabitants of many planets the chance to showcase their wares and attract investors. Plenty of other species were getting attention...but for the humans, the Fair had been an exercise in invisibility. They sat at their cobbled-together plastic booth playing old Earth movies on a TV pried out of their ship's cockpit, and nobody gave them a second or even a first look.

"We've done the best we could." Dinah tucked her hair behind her ears and shrugged. "We didn't exactly come prepared for this."

It was true. As the crew of Earth's first deep space exploration mission, the four humans had not expected to be setting up a booth at a glorified trade show on an alien space station. They hadn't even expected to *meet* honest-to-goodness aliens, for that matter.

Now, they'd been surrounded by so many wildly different varieties for so long, Dinah had to admit that the novelty was starting to wear off.

"I say we pack it in," said Blakey, dropping the slime-covered end of the tablecloth. "Let's go home."

"And tell the folks at home what?" Captain Strayhorn--a tall man with thick, dark hair, chiseled features, and haunted gray eyes--straightened the tablecloth. "That everyone on Earth will *die* because our trade show booth was *half-assed?*"

That was enough to take the wind out of everyone's sails...and remind Dinah why she had a crush on him.

Strayhorn was a leader. While everyone else got bent out of shape over a little blue slime, Strayhorn kept his eyes firmly on the prize.

Which was saving humanity from extinction.

Blakey sighed. "I just don't know what else we can do. These bastards don't care about what we have to offer."

"Maybe you need to diiig deeper," said a familiar voice.

Just hearing it was enough to make Dinah's skin crawl. The voice had an oily, sinuous quality that curled around her brainstem and licked her fear center with a flickering, forked tongue.

The voice belonged to the alien who'd brought them to the Worlds' Fair in the first place. Dinah and the other humans called him "Heavy," which was derived from his endless, unpronounceable alien name.

"Surpriise them." Heavy looked like a five-foot long eggplant covered with writhing cilia topped with chattering faces. There were hundreds of tiny faces, every one of them representing a different alien species. Whichever face Heavy was using at a given moment--the human face, in this case--inflated to life size and spoke the loudest.

Mahalia patted her curly black hair and snorted. "How can we *surprise* them when we don't even know what's *not* a surprise out here?"

Heavy's human face looked like Blakey's: pinched, puffy features and a lumpy scalp. The main difference was that the lip movements didn't always match the words. "Your homeworld wiiill be uniiinhabiiitable soon, yes?"

"You know it will," said Dinah. Hyper-accelerated climate change on Earth had already cranked up the heat and forced everyone underground. Scientists projected that humans would no longer be able to survive anywhere on or under the planet within five years.

"You came here looking for help to fiiix the homeworld, yes?" said Heavy.

Dinah nodded. The team had originally launched into space seeking new Earthlike homes for humanity. When all the inhabitable planets within reach had turned out to be taken, they'd jumped at Heavy's invitation to the Fair.

"You wiiill pay any priice for that help?" said Heavy.

"Of course," said Strayhorn. "But we don't seem to have anything anyone *wants*."

Heavy made a gurgling sound that the team had decided was his way of laughing. "Are you sure you have triied *everythiiing*?"

"Pretty much," said Blakey.

"Maybe you only *thiiink* you have," said Heavy. "Remember, somethiiing of no value to you could be worth a great deal to one of *them*." With that, he twisted his eggplant body around and waved every one of his faces at the crowd of aliens in the great crystal hall.

"What's that supposed to mean?" said Blakey.

"You tell me," said Heavy. "Iiit iiis up to you to fiiigure iiit out."

That night, Team Earth brainstormed in the cramped galley of their little spaceship, the *Diogenes*. They had only one day left of the Worlds' Fair, one day in which to make a deal to save humanity.

"Let's go over it again." Strayhorn tipped his chair back and propped the side of his leg against the edge of the round table. "What have we offered so far?"

Mahalia swallowed some coffee and lowered her mug. "Mineral wealth. Natural resources."

"Plant and animal specimens," said Dinah.

"A catalogue of genomes for life on Earth," said Blakey.

"What else?" said Strayhorn.

Dinah nibbled a chocolate chip cookie, then waved it at Strayhorn. "Food stocks. Pharmaceuticals."

Strayhorn nodded. "A database of all human knowledge."

"Strategic military rights," said Mahalia.

"Nuclear and biological weapons," said Blakey.

"Slaves." Dinah was exaggerating, but only a little; in desperation, they'd come up with an indentured servant scheme, offering a human workforce for offworld projects in return for Earth's salvation.

Even that extreme proposal hadn't drawn any interest from the oblivious aliens.

Strayhorn checked a list on a pad of paper in his lap. "That's everything, all right." He chucked the pad on the table and sighed. "So what else do we have to offer?"

Blakey laughed and slapped the table. "Absolutely *nothing!*"

"Heavy says otherwise," said Strayhorn.

"Right!" Blakey leaped to his feet. "And *that* asshole would *never* steer us wrong!"

"One more day." Strayhorn's quiet, steady voice locked in everyone's attention with high intensity. "That's all the time we have to make a deal. So let's *think*, people."

"We're like *amoebas* to them." Blakey's face was flushed. "Like *dust mites*. We've got *nothing* they want!"

"All right, all right." Mahalia scrubbed her fingers through her short, curly hair. "What *haven't* we offered so far?"

"Souls!" said Blakey. "We haven't offered them our *souls* yet!"

Mahalia grinned. "Careful. They might actually *want* those."

"Then I say let's *sell* them," said Blakey.

"But we can't prove they exist," said Dinah.

"All the better!" Blakey clapped his hands. "I say let's do whatever it takes to save Earth!"

Dinah looked across the table and caught Strayhorn's gaze. In the long trip out from Earth, she'd become addicted to that gaze. At moments like this, she felt like she would do anything to hold it, to keep it, to please him.

Strayhorn was a strong man, a good man, a leader. He wore a sense of mystery like a dark cloak, binding all his secrets in shadows deep inside. How could she ever hope to get at them?

"Wait." Dinah felt all eyes slide to meet her, but she didn't break Strayhorn's gaze. "Maybe you're onto something, Ben."

"Great!" Blakey rubbed his hands together. "Tell me about it!"

"What about imagination?" said Dinah.

Mahalia frowned. "How can we sell imagination?"

"Not imagination itself," said Dinah. "I mean we offer to sell something *imaginary*."

"Ah." Strayhorn nodded. "You mean lie."

Dinah shrugged. "More like exaggerate."

Blakey smacked her on the back. "You are such a con artist!"

"Could be dangerous," said Strayhorn. "All these aliens are more technologically advanced than we are. If we piss them off, they could *wipe out* humanity instead of *saving* it."

"We'll have to play it just right," said Dinah. "Keep them happy. Make them think they're getting what we promised."

"*If* we can even get them *interested*," said Mahalia.

"Right." Dinah searched Strayhorn's eyes for some sign of approval. At first, they were just as flat, gray, and inscrutable as always.

Then, she saw the light.

"Okay," said Strayhorn. "Let's see if we can make this work."

And Dinah's heart danced like a child in her chest.

The next day started out hopefully.

Team Earth set up early in the Worlds' Fair hall and attacked their mission with fresh enthusiasm. Strayhorn and Blakey manned the booth while Dinah and Mahalia traversed the crowd, using big smiles and chocolate from the *Diogenes*' stores to try to lure visitors.

The four teammates attacked the day as if it were their first at the Fair. Every one of them dug in with new energy and intensity, casting aside the pessimism of the previous day. Even Blakey gave it his all.

And they tried everything. Every line of bullshit they could imagine.

"Come one, come all!" said Dinah as she worked the crowd--wondering as she did so if any of the aliens understood a word she said. "Come see the vacation paradise of *Earth*!" Naturally, she left out the part about Earth being a global warming hellhole. (Though it *could* be a paradise to some of the aliens, for all she knew.)

"Follow me!" Mahalia said from the other side of the room. "Spiritual enlightenment awaits you on the holiest planet in the galaxy--*Earth*!"

"Visit the ancient world where all life began!" said Dinah. "Meet the seers whose visions foretell your future!

"Come to the miracle planet!" said Mahalia. "Heals all wounds, cures all diseases, and grants eternal life!"

"Your fantasies will come to life on Earth!" said Dinah.

"The gambling capital of the galaxy!" said Mahalia.

"Where golf is a way of life!"

"Be king of the world for a day!"

"Find lost treasure!"

"The streets are paved with gold!"

"Whatever you want!" said Dinah. "That's what you'll find on *Earth*!"

But it was all for nothing.

Throughout the day, only a handful of aliens came close enough to the booth to see the phony presentation whipped up by Strayhorn and Blakey--computer-generated images of a paradise that was nothing at all like the modern, dying Earth. The rest of the crowd was too busy gawking at other displays to take a look. Even the booth next-door, which featured a gray blob oozing green liquid in a silver bowl, attracted more attention.

By the time the Fair closed for the day, alien hordes rushing the doors like school kids on the way to summer vacation, Team Earth hadn't made a single deal. They hadn't fibbed up the slightest nibble of interest.

The four teammates slouched around the booth, shaking their heads and sighing. Aliens paraded past on their way to the exits, but none of them paused or even glanced over.

"No one can say we didn't try our best," said Mahalia, pushing alien freebies from other booths into a box. "It wasn't meant to be."

Blakey slumped on a folding chair with his lumpy bald head in his hands. "One good thing about the end of the world," he said. "When we go down in history as incompetent moron failures, at least there won't be much history *left*."

Strayhorn sat bolt upright, staring at the alien masses as they trooped past. "We'd better be on our way." His voice was cold and flat. "We're done here."

Dinah sat beside him and watched his face. He looked stern and impassive, unmoved...but she had a feeling that a lot more was going on inside.

He had failed to save the human race. How could that not tear him apart? How could that not *destroy* him?

"Well," said Mahalia. "How about a little clean-up music?" With a flick of her wrist, she popped a digital music player from the hip pocket of her red jumpsuit and laid it on the table. She pressed the surface of the thin, silver device, which was about the size of a playing card, and it started giving off music.

Jazz music, which was what Mahalia listened to the most.

"Come on." Mahalia tapped Blakey's shoulder. "Let's find a cart to haul this stuff back to the ship."

Blakey sighed. "Might as well," he said, and then he got up and went with her.

That left Dinah and Strayhorn sitting together in the booth. A trumpet ballad filtered from Mahalia's player, its slow, sweet notes adding to the melancholy mood.

Strayhorn rubbed his eyes, then placed his palms flat on the table. "I failed," he said. "It was up to me to save the world, and I couldn't do it."

Dinah laid her hand on top of his. It was the first time she'd ever touched him outside the line of duty. "Please don't give up," she said. "There must be something we can do."

Strayhorn didn't pull his hand away. His gaze remained fixed on the aliens parading past. "We can beg, maybe," he said. "But these people out here don't seem too inclined to charity."

"Then we'll change their inclination." Impulsively, Dinah cupped his chin and turned his face toward her. "Trust me, Alec. We'll do it together."

Then, Dinah surprised herself. Before she could think better of it, she leaned up and kissed Strayhorn on the mouth.

He didn't resist. In fact, after the first moment, he actively kissed her back, pressing his lips against hers.

The rest of the universe faded away. Heart pounding, Dinah reveled in the feel of Strayhorn's lips, the smell of his skin, the long-delayed contact between them.

The kiss went on and on, and Dinah wished it would never end. Nothing else mattered--not the crowd of alien lifeforms in the hall, not the impending doom of humanity, not Team Earth's failure. Not what would or wouldn't happen next.

For Dinah, it was a perfect kiss, a heavenly moment. She might never have broken the spell if not for the overwhelming new feeling that came upon her--the feeling that she was being watched.

Guessing that Blakey and Mahalia had returned to the booth, Dinah opened her eyes...and jumped. The kiss broke, and the perfect moment ended.

Dinah had been right about being watched, but not by Blakey and Mahalia. Instead of two pairs of human eyes, dozens of alien ones were trained on her and Strayhorn--eyes of all shapes and colors and sizes, eyes on stalks, eyes of crystal, eyes with wings.

For the first time all week, a crowd had gathered around Team Earth's booth at the Worlds' Fair.

"What the hell?" said Strayhorn. "What's going on?"

Dinah thought for a moment, then grinned. She thought she understood the situation. "Congratulations," she said. "We've finally found something they want to see."

And then she kissed Strayhorn again.

"Come one, come all!" Blakey stood on the table of the Team Earth booth and used his best carnival barker voice. "Experience the wonders of Earth's greatest treasure--*love!*"

Dinah and Strayhorn still sat behind the table, kissing...and the crowd of aliens watching them had grown into a mob. The aliens fanned out in all directions, hooting and babbling and jostling for a better view of the action.

Mahalia, meanwhile, acted as security, backing off any onlookers who got too close or made a grab for a body part. "The natives are restless," she said as she batted away an encroaching tentacle. "We'd better make a deal soon, or they're liable to rush the booth."

Strayhorn broke the kiss. "How do we market this? Earth as an interplanetary brothel?" His voice was heavy with sarcasm.

"If it saves humanity, *I'll* turn tricks!" Blakey said from above.

"Maybe they just like to watch," said Mahalia. "Performances, that is."

"Earth. Porno capital of the galaxy," said Blakey.

Mahalia shooed away a trio of flying yellow eyeballs. "Maybe we won't have to go that far. Maybe kissing's exciting enough for them."

Dinah kept pecking Strayhorn on the lips so they wouldn't lose the crowd. (Also because she was making the most of the situation.) "What about a kind of singles resort?" she said between kisses.

"Humans could teach aliens about the concept of love and then match them up to experience it."

"I like it better than the brothel idea," said Mahalia.

"I say stick with the porno," said Blakey.

Strayhorn finished another kiss and nodded. "Try any and all of the above," he said. "Whatever it takes to trade for reverse global warming services--but start low and make the best deal you can."

"Roger that." Blakey winked at Mahalia. "Play something romantic, wouldja?"

"Will do." While wrestling with an alien's twitching feelers, Mahalia switched the fast bebop coming out of her music player to a slow number with a lot of sultry sax.

Ben raised his arms and beamed at the alien mob. "Are you *lonely*, my friends? Do you want to be like *them*?" He gestured at Dinah and Strayhorn, who were locked in another kiss. "Would you give anything to discover the wonders of *love*?

"Then step right up!" Ben pumped his fists in the air. "This is your lucky day--if you have the technology to reduce carbon dioxide emissions in a planetary atmosphere, that is!"

"Hey," whispered Strayhorn. "Easy on the tongue."

Dinah leaned back and stared at him. They'd been kissing for at least two hours straight, mouth to mouth in front of an audience of gaping aliens.

So why was Strayhorn sounding *shy* all of a sudden?

Maybe, thought Dinah, he felt self-conscious with all the aliens watching him. Maybe he was getting tired. Maybe he was just stressed out about this being his last chance for a deal to save humanity.

Whatever the reason, Strayhorn didn't elaborate.

"Okay," said Dinah.

"Thanks," said Strayhorn, and then he licked his lips and leaned back in to resume kissing.

Dinah gladly rejoined him, though the moment had sapped a little of her fun. Even as she savored the warmth and pressure of Strayhorn's mouth, she couldn't help worrying in the back of her mind about why he'd nixed her French kiss.

"Thiiis being wants love," said Heavy, inflating his bald human face to speak to Team Earth. "He wants all the love he can get."

Heavy twisted his eggplant body and wriggled his cilia at the alien who had just pushed out of the crowd behind him. The new alien, who was seven feet tall, looked like an inside-out centaur covered in rough, blood-red crust and black bristles.

"His name iiis Ogog Lugofarloff," said Heavy. "Ogog wiiill buy the riights to all human love."

"Let's talk price then," said Blakey. "Can Ogog reverse global warming on our homeworld?"

Heavy rattled off a chain of rapid clacks and dings that sounded like an old manual typewriter in action. Ogog made the same kind of sounds back at him, mixed with the clomping of one black hoof on the floor.

"No," Heavy said when it was over. "But he *could* reengiiineer your species to surviive the new cliimate."

Ogog clattered and clomped again, ending with a decisive belch.

"Here iiis an example of hiiis work." Heavy fluttered his head-capped cilia in Ogog's direction. "Ogog has reengiiineered *hiiimself* multiiiiple tiimes."

Strayhorn broke the latest kiss and shot Blakey a glare that said it all.

Blakey nodded and winked, then turned back to Heavy and

Ogog. "Give us your contact information, Ogog buddy. We'll have to get back to you on that."

After another hour of kissing while Blakey wheeled and dealed, Strayhorn pulled his lips back just enough to talk to Dinah. "I wonder what would happen if we switched with the others?"

Dinah looked out at the crowd of gaping aliens. "Do you want to take the chance?"

"No," said Strayhorn. "Not yet, anyway."

Dinah smiled and touched his cheek. "Just relax, Alec. Relax and enjoy."

Strayhorn scanned the babbling alien mob, then met Dinah's gaze and held it. He stared deep into her eyes, searching for something...and then his frown darkened.

"Why did you kiss me the first time?" he said.

Dinah shrugged. "To make you feel better."

"That's it?" said Strayhorn. "That's the only reason?"

Dinah hesitated, then decided to show her cards. "I wanted to," she said. "I've wanted to kiss you for a while now."

"I see." Strayhorn's frown smoothed out into his standard unreadable stare.

"Aren't you glad I did?" Dinah chuckled and rubbed noses with him. "Nobody came to our booth until I kissed you."

"Sure," said Strayhorn.

"In fact," said Dinah, "it might turn out to be the kiss that saves humanity, right?"

"Right," said Strayhorn.

"I'll bet they'll even make a movie about it someday." Dinah leaned close, brushing her lips against his. "A real love story."

And then she kissed him again, heart soaring with heat and delight like a butterfly or a dream.

"III have another customer for you," said Heavy. "She assures me she has the technical capabiiiliiitiies to reverse your homeworld's global warmiiing."

Dinah looked up in mid-kiss to see the gray blob from the silver bowl in the booth next-door bobbing in midair beside Heavy.

"Her name iiis Melliiicloriiis Myopa Quozahnna Non Zadacta." Heavy flicked his cilia in the blob's direction and made his human face smile. "She iiis empress of the Zlatyr Realm. The green fluiiid she iiis secreting means she iiis about to giiive biiirth."

"Tell her highness congratulations," Blakey told Heavy. "Ask her how we can be of service."

"Ask her yourself," said Heavy. "She iiis quiite capable of understandiiing your language."

Blakey smiled at the gray blob as it hovered and dripped green fluid. "That's great. So how can we help you?"

"Melliiicloriiis wiiishes to buy all love," said Heavy, "and destroy iiit."

"Destroy it?" said Blakey.

"So she can market a cheaper, inferior substiiitute," said Heavy.

"Of course." Blakey glanced at Strayhorn but didn't seem to feel the need to wait for his advice. "Contact information, please. We'll have to get back to you on that."

After another hour of kissing, Strayhorn pulled away from Dinah and rubbed his jaw. "I can't keep this up," he said. "We need to switch personnel."

"I know what you mean." Dinah's lips were sore, and her jaw ached--not that she intended to stop the kissathon anytime soon. "I think we'll be okay if we just take a break for a minute."

"No," said Strayhorn. "It's time to switch." He started to get up from his chair.

"Really," said Dinah. "I'll be fine."

"You don't understand," said Strayhorn. "We *need* to switch."

Just then, Blakey let out a loud whoop. "We have a winnah!"

"Yay!" Mahalia grinned and applauded. "This is it, Captain! We found the real deal!"

Dinah had missed the latest flurry of negotiations. She looked over to see Blakey shaking the tentacle of a seven-foot-tall orange-furred squid-thing. "What is it?" she said. "What's the deal?"

"Kioska here will fix Earth's atmosphere." Blakey patted the orange squid's rubbery spear-point head. "He'll even terraform the planet to reverse the global warming damage to the ecosystem!"

Strayhorn walked around the table to Blakey and Kioska. "What'll it cost us?"

"You're gonna love this." Blakey threw an arm around Strayhorn's shoulders. "How would you like to be the first man to set foot on an alien planet?"

Two weeks later, Dinah blinked as light flooded the darkened stage where she and Strayhorn sat. She found herself gazing out at a huge crowd of orange-furred squid people, packed into a vast, upside-down theater.

Thousands of squid dangled by their tentacles from rungs in the ceiling. Each squid had one giant eye, blood-red and unblinking, fixed on Dinah and Strayhorn.

A chill rippled up Dinah's back as she felt their eyes upon her. Yet again, she marveled at where she was, so far from home, on an alien world that no human being before her had ever visited.

Kioska had led them here, to his homeworld, from the space station. It was here that the humans would hold up their end of the deal and earn salvation for dying Mother Earth.

Suddenly, a familiar figure tumbled onto the stage--eggplant-shaped Heavy, Team Earth's self-appointed manager. Stopping in the middle of the stage, he inflated an

orange-furred squid face on one of his cilia and turned it to the crowd. While Heavy unleashed a stream of wild squeaks for the audience, he puffed up a human face behind him and translated his words through it for Dinah and Strayhorn.

"Love!" said Heavy. "The new sensation! The most iiincrediiible experiience iiin the galaxy!"

The crowd responded with a deafening blast of whistles and squeals.

"Are you ready to liiive the dream?" said Heavy. "Are you ready for *love*?"

The squid things squealed louder. They swung back and forth on their rungs and smacked their bodies against each other with abandon.

"Then let the love begiiin!" As the noise and motion of the crowd reached a wild pitch, Heavy hurtled off the stage, leaving Dinah and Strayhorn alone in the spotlight.

Backstage, Mahalia switched on her music player, which she'd tuned to broadcast through the theater's sound system. This time, instead of jazz, it played an opera piece--the Flower Duet from *Lakmé*, a sweet, soaring blend of two winding soprano voices.

That was Dinah and Strayhorn's cue. Smiling, Dinah leaned across the padded bench on which they sat. She slipped a hand behind Strayhorn's head, combing her fingers through his thick, dark hair, and pulled him close.

Their eyes met, and then their lips did, too.

They hadn't kissed since the end of the Worlds' Fair two weeks ago, and Dinah craved him. Returning to his lips felt like a fabulous culmination, an unimaginably perfect consummation. Every nerve in her lips flared with extraordinary sensitivity, magnifying every millimeter and millisecond of radiant contact between them.

Her pulse quickened, and her body warmed. Closing her eyes,

she immersed herself in the building passion, the thrill of love on a grand scale, of legendary, history-making love.

Dinah was so caught up in the experience that at first, she didn't notice the change in the crowd. It took a few moments for the rising commotion to penetrate her romantic haze, to make her realize that the balance of the beautiful, dreamlike tide was shifting.

Opening her eyes, Dinah saw that the squid-people were jumping and bumping in the rafters. A growing racket rang out through the theater, a din of the shrillest,

highest-pitched squeals and whistles she'd yet heard from the orange-furred creatures.

As it got worse, drowning out the opera soundtrack, Dinah exchanged a look with Strayhorn. His typically blank expression had switched to one of fierce, alert intensity.

"What's happening?" said Dinah. "What do they want?"

Suddenly, Heavy jetted across the stage and jolted to a stop beside her. "What's goiiing on here?" he said with his bald human face.

"*You* tell *us*!" said Dinah.

"What are they saying?" said Strayhorn.

"'We want love!'" Heavy spun in a circle, every one of his heads and cilia quivering with agitation. "That's what they're sayiiing! They want love!"

The uproar from the crowd was so loud, Dinah had to shout to make herself heard. "I don't understand! We were *giving* them love!"

"Not liike before! Now try harder!" With that, Heavy whipped around and flashed offstage, leaving Dinah and Strayhorn alone.

As the crowd noise rose, Dinah gazed out at the hordes of orange-furred squid. "I guess we've got a tougher audience here," she said. "Necking isn't enough."

"We need to get out of here," said Strayhorn. "If they rush the stage, we're dead."

"No!" said Dinah. "Earth's depending on us!"

With that, she started unbuttoning her top.

171

"What are you doing?" said Strayhorn.

Dinah slid her arms from the sleeves of her blouse and tossed it to the stage. "What does it *look* like I'm doing?" With a shrug, she pressed closer to him, reaching for the buttons of his shirt. "If they want more, let's *give* them more."

Strayhorn grabbed her wrist, and Dinah pushed herself forward. With her free hand, she tore his shirt all the way open, then snaked an arm around his back and yanked him toward her.

"I say let's give them their money's worth," said Dinah, right before she lunged in for a ravenous, grinding kiss.

Strayhorn didn't get into the spirit of things at all, but Dinah kept working on him. She was convinced she could bring him around, especially once the squid-people started to settle down.

The problem was, instead of settling down, the squid-people grew more agitated. The clamor in the theater got worse with each passing second.

Dinah heard what sounded like falling bodies hitting the floor. When she looked out at the crowd, she saw squid dropping from the ceiling by the hundreds, bouncing to a landing on the theater floor on spring-loaded tentacles.

As soon as they landed, the squid started hopping toward the stage.

Yet again, Heavy zipped into the spotlight, spinning and quivering. "What iiis *wrong* with you two? They want *love*! Giiive them love love *love*!"

As Heavy darted away, Dinah shoved Strayhorn onto his back and pounced. Straddling his hips, she set to work undoing his pants while he gaped up at her in shock.

"I guess we have to take this all the way," said Dinah.

"No!" said Strayhorn. "Don't!"

"Give it everything you've got," said Dinah. "Remember, the future of humanity is riding on it!"

Before she could go any further, Strayhorn suddenly sat up and pushed her away. "I said *no*!"

Dinah fell back and rolled off the bench. She winced and cried out as she hit the hard floor of the stage on her side.

"Hey!" she said. "What was *that* for?"

"Even if we *weren't* about to be swarmed by alien squid-people," said Strayhorn, gesturing at the approaching audience, "I *can't* make love to you! I'm in love with someone else!"

"What?" Dinah leaped to her feet. "*Who?*"

"Look." Strayhorn pointed behind her, into the backstage wings. "That's who."

Dinah turned and saw Ben Blakey hurrying toward them. "*Blakey?*" she said. "You're in love with *Blakey?*"

Strayhorn shook his head. "Not Blakey."

Just then, Dinah saw Mahalia charge out after Blakey. "Oh." Dinah felt her face flush. "I get it."

Mahalia rushed past Blakey and grabbed Strayhorn's shoulders. A million little memories suddenly fell into place in Dinah's mind--a jumble of looks and touches and words exchanged between Strayhorn and Mahalia that she'd always chalked up to simple friendship.

Only now she knew better.

Why didn't I see it before?

At that moment, Heavy bolted over among them. "Where iiis the love?" His voice was high and electric with fear. "Make the love! Make the love before iiit iiis *too late!*"

Dinah thought it was too late already. The orange-furred squid-people were hopping onto the stage, converging on the spotlight with deadly purpose.

"That's what we were *doing!*" said Strayhorn. "What else do you *want* from us?"

"No no no!" said Heavy. "No love! No love at all!" He flipped and spun and twisted in midair, giving off a smell like chocolate. "They want the *sounds!* The

dah-dah-dee-dah!"

"What the *hell* are you talking about?" said Blakey.

"*You* know!" Heavy flopped over and curled up, then uncurled and stretched out. "The *sounds* you made at the Worlds' Fair, when the two of you kiiissed! Liike

dah-dah-dee-dah-doo. The *love*."

Dinah shook her head. "I don't get it."

"Wait." Mahalia snapped her fingers. "You mean the *music*? The *music* I played in the booth when they kissed?"

"'Music'?" Heavy shuddered.

"Like this." Mahalia did a little scat-singing, improvising syllables over a jazzy snatch of melody. "That's music. *Jazz* music."

"'Music'?" said Heavy. "Don't you mean 'love'?"

Mahalia looked from Strayhorn to Blakey to Dinah, eyes wide with understanding. "Oh my God," she said. "This whole time, they wanted *music*, not *love*."

"They thought we made it when we kissed," said Dinah.

As the squid-people closed in, Mahalia dashed offstage. The squid were just reaching for Dinah and the others when the music playing over the theater's sound system changed from opera to jazz.

Just like that, the orange-furred squid halted their approach. As one, they swayed and squeaked in time with the music, tentacles rippling with the flow of a soaring, sparkling trumpet solo.

"Nothing like a little Miles Davis to soothe the savage alien," said Mahalia as she trotted back to the group. "And more where that came from." She held up her slim silver music player and tapped it with her fingernail.

Dinah let out a deep breath and slumped onto the bench. "That was close."

"You diiid iiit!" said Heavy, scooting around Team Earth in a jaunty circle. "You made the *love* again!"

"I still don't see what the big deal is," said Blakey. "Why don't you just make it yourselves?"

"We can't," said Heavy. "You are the fiiirst. Thiiis iiis something *new* to us."

"No kidding." Blakey laughed and clapped Strayhorn on the

back. "I guess maybe humans are worth something out here after all."

"So now what?" said Dinah. "What next?"

"Contiiinue the Worlds' Tour, of course!" said Heavy. "Liiive up to your end of the deal!"

Blakey threw an arm around Strayhorn's shoulders. "So we'll just send around a recording, right?"

"Wrong," said Heavy. "We must have *live performance. Live love* on tour! The deal *says* so!"

"And us a bunch of non-musicians." Dinah blew out her breath.

"We'll just lip-synch." Mahalia shook her music player. "Play along with the recordings and pretend we're making the music from scratch."

"What happens when they get tired of the recordings?" said Dinah. "What'll we do then?"

"Same thing we always do." Mahalia grinned and winked at her. "Same thing Miles and Monk and Trane and all the rest always did.

"Make it up as we go along."

A LITTLE SONG, A LITTLE DANCE, A LITTLE APOCALYPSE DOWN YOUR PANTS

come back from the dead suddenly, the way I always do, with a great heaving gasp as air and light and consciousness rush into me all at once.

"Easy now, Jody Lee." Binky the Bring-Back Bot says the same thing every time he resurrects me, the same damn thing. "Slow, even breaths, dear. In through the nose, out through the mouth."

Meanwhile, I'm twisting and flopping around naked in what I call the Humpty-Dumptynator--a rectangular glass box half-full of slimy blue goo and squirming anti-maggots. (They *give* life instead of *feeding* on it.) No matter how many times I've been through this-- and believe me, there've been *thousands*--I still wake up with the same shock and nausea, spazzing out like this is my first freaking life restoration.

While at the same time, I know I've gotta get over it but fast, as Binky reminds me.

"Snap out of it, honey." The silver-skinned bastard jabs my left bicep with a hypo needle in the tip of his index finger, shooting me full of something that takes the edge off. "Remember, you'vea got another show tonight." He shoots me with a pale green light from his right eye, which is also soothing. "You have to die again in *three hours* if you want to get *paid*."

Once I get cleaned up, I go for a walk, trying to blow the stink off. My long black hair's tied in a ponytail, and I'm wearing a Selfie Suit, which looks like whatever I want depending on who's looking. A hot guy might see me in a little red dress, a not-so-hottie might see me in overalls...and I myself just see a casual black pantsuit.

I can't hold back a yawn as I walk through Tesseractus Prime 'cause it's just another pan-galactic mega-casino in just another multidimensional hotel-cathedral-singularity. It's the same old thing, the same old crowd, in the same old place.

And by that, I mean it's a looney tune wonderland to the zillionth power.

A unicorn centaur in a diaper gallops past, fleeing a flock of mocking blackbirds trying to bomb his horn with poop. A guy with an accordion-shaped body bounces by, burping filthy limericks every time his midsection crumples. A priest, a rabbi, and Hitler walk into the nearest bar, saying something about buying a dog a drink...and then they all turn into poodles.

Welcome to humanity circa 100,000 A.D., when science that might as well be magic makes all things possible. Everyone can be as wacky as they wanna be, in every imaginable way. The universe is one big joke...but nobody's laughing anymore.

And that's where *I* come in.

"I have never been more miserable in my life." Standing onstage in the massive theater at the hotel-casino-cathedral, I gaze out at the crowd arrayed before me. It's a panoply of every silly, crazy, bizarre, surreal, and just plain *insane* character you can imagine...and everyone's laughing their heads off (some *literally*, if the heads aren't attached very well). "I mean it. I wish I were dead."

For a long moment, the roar of laughter and applause drowns me out. I stand there and let it flow around me, watching as the horde of ridiculous figures howls in hilarity.

A glowing purple clown in the front row blasts a bicycle horn and stomps his huge red shoes (which are also laughing). Beside him, a gorilla in a pinstriped suit hops up and down, making with the monkey shrieks and whipping banana peels and poo at the stage.

In other words, I'm *killing*. Again. Because I'm the best. I know what makes 'em laugh.

When the roaring dies down, I start talking again. "Seriously, I'm at the end of my rope." That gets a few titters from the crowd. "The more you people laugh, the more I long for oblivion." Cue a slew of scattered guffaws.

Then, a thing that looks like a giant pretzel with eyes instead of grains of salt zips up to the stage and flies around me a dozen times, laughing like a maniac. The audience follows suit with a roar that sounds ten times louder than before.

"Enough of this mortal coil!" The spotlight follows me as I stomp across the stage toward a long table covered by a red velvet shroud. "It is time to end my suffering!"

Everyone cheers and claps and howls with laughter as I pull the shroud from the table, revealing a selection of swords and knives. People shout out suggestions; some even teleport up beside me to point at the weapon of their choice. I shoo them all away and pick up the samurai sword.

"This is the end for me." I kneel on the stage and hold the sword out away from me, pointing the tip at my belly. "I go now to the big comedy show in the sky."

Hands shaking, I falter, and the crowd urges me on. I continue to hesitate, building suspense; it's all part of the act.

"I have the courage to do it at last!" I nod forcefully. "Death, I fear not thy sting!"

Then, before I can slide the sword through my stomach, there's a deafening boom from somewhere off stage. A cannonball blows through my midriff from side to side, cutting a swath where the sword was supposed to cut.

The top half of my body plops down to close the gap. For a moment, as the crowd gives me a standing ovation, I kneel there, my top and bottom halves disconnected but adjacent.

Then, the top half drops over backward, and the darkness of death swirls over me. I feel my mind sliding into the abyss like leftovers sliding from a plate into a trash receptacle.

And then I'm gone, into the great and fathomless unknown. Just like I am every time I do this--two shows a day, six days a week, 52 weeks a year.

Three and a half hours later, I'm staring at a bowl of thin broth in one of the 100,001 ever-changing restaurants in Tesseractus Prime. The broth keeps telling me to eat it, *literally*--it's *conscious cuisine* with a mind of its own--but I can't force it down. Binky the Bring-Back Bot put me back together just fine after the cannonball, but my stomach still remembers being blown apart just a little too well.

"Excuse me?" Just then, a horse's ass--an *actual* horse's ass, minus the horse--clops over to my table. "Have you seen a *setup* come this way? I seem to have lost mine."

Great, just what I need. Another lost punchline looking for the rest of his joke. "Can't help you, buddy." I stir my bowl of broth as if I'm actually going to eat it.

The broth gets all worked up and starts to yap. "Oh yes, oh *please* put me inside you, dear famous Jo Jawdropper! Eat me right *up*, you vixen!"

The tail on the horse's ass switches excitedly. I can see there's an eyeball staring back at me from its bunghole. "Ohmigod! I can't believe this! I'm talking to *Jo Jawdropper!*"

I never thought I could hate my stage name any more than I already do...but hearing it spoken in the squeaky whine of a horse's ass really does the trick. "Check, please!"

"No check yet!" screams the broth. "You've gotta *slurp me up* first!"

Just as I'm starting to freak out a little, someone clears his throat behind me. "Get lost, ass." His voice is as deep as the croak of a down-dirty drunk just before he turns himself sober so he can start drinking all over again. "*Amscray!*"

Turning, I'm surprised for two reasons: one, he's shorter than I imagined because of that voice, all of five-foot-five; and two, I recognize him, from his black leather jacket to his bald head to his bushy red mustache. I used to *work* with him, back in the day.

"Now git!" He stomps over and gives one of the horse's ass's butt cheeks a powerful slap. "Don't *make* me *kick* you!"

"*Kiss* my you-know-what," snaps the ass, and then he clops off through the restaurant.

"What an ass," says the guy. "Probably doesn't know *himself* from a *hole* in the ground."

"Well, well." I smile and hold out my hand. "If it isn't *The 'Stache.*"

The 'Stache (that's his stage name; he never told me his real name) gives my hand a hearty shake. "Long time no smell, JoJo m'dear."

"Thanks for the save," I tell him. "I guess that makes you my hero." Impulsively, I pull him into a big, grateful hug. It's been *such* a lousy day.

Meanwhile, the broth keeps yapping. "Slurp me up! Put me inside you! *Lick my bowl clean!*"

"Shaddup," snaps The 'Stache. "Or else!"

"Or else what?" says the broth.

"You know the one about the fly in the soup?" says The 'Stache.

180

"Well, I'm gonna *show* you the one about the *soup* that *flies*. Across the *room*."

With that, the broth finally shuts up.

The 'Stache and I catch up while taking a late night stroll on Schrödinger's Catwalk--a promenade that might or might not occupy infinite locations and realities at any given moment.

Fountains of rainbow light cascade all around us, casting colorful glows on our faces. Within the light, I glimpse an ever-changing parade of images, flickering movies of people and events from all eras and alternate worlds.

For an instant, I think I catch a glimpse of The 'Stache and me in the old days, working the comedy circuit together...but then it's gone, or maybe it was never there at all.

"I was out of the biz for a while," says The 'Stache. "Didja know that?"

"You quit *show biz*? *For real?*"

He grins, flashing gold incisors through his overabundant mustache. "For *ten years* real, Double-J."

"What was it like?"

"Not being on the road all the time, you mean? Not struggling to squeeze laughs out of a bunch of humorless fruitcakes every day of my pathetic life?" The 'Stache looks ahead of us and chuckles. "Why don't we ask *him*?"

"Ask me what?" It's an alternate version of The 'Stache with zebra stripes and elephant ears, loping toward us--one of the side effects of Schrödinger's Catwalk. You never know when you're gonna cross paths with another you from a parallel universe.

"Hey! Did I miss show biz when I gave it up for ten years?" says The 'Stache I came in with.

"You gave it up for *ten years*?" Other 'Stache punches original 'Stache in the shoulder on his way past. "What a maroon!"

181

Original 'Stache laughs and jerks a thumb at his doppelgänger as he walks off and vanishes. "That guy is such a *prick*, isn't he?"

"You're back in the game, aren't you?" I ask him. "That's why you're here, right? You're doing standup again."

"Maybe I'm just here to see *you*," says The 'Stache.

"So what made you do it? What made you want to get back onstage after ten years away?"

"Because I'm gonna be the greatest comic who ever lived," says The 'Stache. "And I'm gonna make it happen in a one-night-only performance, tomorrow night." He smiles and takes my hand. "You want in, JoJo? For old times' shake?"

"Sure." I say it with a smirk, waiting for the punchline. "How can I possibly say no?"

The 'Stache stops walking and faces me. "Dead serious here, partner. This ain't a *bit*."

"Izzat so?" Notice I haven't stopped smirking. "So how do you propose becoming the greatest ever in just one night?"

"I've done it before, haven't I?" The 'Stache winks and squeezes my hand.

"*Ten* years off the circuit is like a *hundred* years in *comedian time*." I pull my hand free and shake my head. "You're gonna have to sell your soul to Maxwell's Demon just to make a *comeback*, let alone become the *greatest*."

"Kiss my brain!" The 'Stache laughs and jabs a finger between his eyes.

"Huh?"

"Kiss it!" The 'Stache keeps jabbing. "Because it *knows*, darlin' JoJo. It has a *plan* that will set the worlds on *fire*."

Just then, someone taps me on the shoulder. Turning, I see an alternate me made of rippling green palm fronds. It hurts to look at her flashing gold bouffant hairdo, and she's chewing some kind of squealing gum or bite-sized creature, I can't see which.

"He's right, honey mustard," says Palm Frond Me. "Big Daddy here's got the goods."

"Hear that?" The 'Stache unveils his broadest grin yet. "If you can't trust your salad-based alternate self, who *can* you trust?"

I could say I don't want anything to do with Delusional Dudley Doofus here...but that would be a bald-assed lie. Truth is, he's got me curious; *anything* to break the boredom of my daily lives and deaths.

Not to mention, he and I used to be a *thing* once upon a once-upon. Maybe that's in the back of my mind a little, too.

Also *other* places, like ten feet away, where alt versions of me and The 'Stache just appeared *in flagrante delicto.* In the middle of the act, in other words, and I don't mean comedy.

So what does *my* 'Stache do? Gives 'em a standing-O, of course. "Yeah! Wooo! Bravo!" He whistles and claps for all he's worth.

It's been sooo long since I did what *they're* doing, I applaud, too. My alt-self, who's on top, laughs and shoots me a big thumbs-up.

Good thing I'm not the type who might get a funny idea from seeing something like that.

So let's just say I get a funny idea after all, and the rest is history. And by history, I mean super-nasty sex.

So *sue* me. It's the first time in I don't know *how* long (literally) that I've done anything other than eat, sleep, kill myself, or rise from the dead. Breaking out of a rut is a good thing (or is that rutting till you break?)

Don't bother me about guilt and regret. This isn't our first time at the rodeo. Forget about illusions, too.

Not that *all* the mystery is gone. There's still a burning question hanging over us.

"Got any coffee?"

Not *that* one, though it's the first thing I ask him in the morning.

"So what's this plan of yours?" *That's* the one.

"You mean the plan where I ravish you?" says The 'Stache as he tickles my tummy. "Check and double-check."

Did I just *giggle*? I *never* giggle. "The *other* plan."

"You mean the one with the fifty porcupines, the nudist camp, and the case of bubble gum?"

Did I just giggle again? "The one about becoming the greatest comic who ever lived."

"Oh, *that* one." The 'Stache rolls over and kisses me. "It's a secret."

"A secret?"

"But who knows?" The 'Stache shrugs. "Maybe we can scare up an exclusive preview if you can pencil me in this morning."

"Hey, wait!" I laugh as he makes a grab for me. "What're you doing?"

"Sorry." He doesn't stop. "*I* thought we meant *pencil* me *in...*"

"I know, right?" The 'Stache gives my shoulders a squeeze. "Kinda small, isn't it?"

"Yeah." I'm standing on the field of Hypercube Center, the biggest sports stadium in all of Tesseractus Prime. It's breathtakingly vast, stretching off for miles in all directions. "A real intimate venue."

"My thoughts exactly." The 'Stache gives me a peck on the cheek and undrapes his arm from my shoulders. He walks a few steps away and lets loose a loud whoop that echoes through the stadium. "I want everyone to feel like I'm close enough to reach out and touch."

"Then mission accomplished." Part of me keeps thinking he's pulling my leg, even after I saw his name on the marquee out in front of the place. How he got booked in a venue this big after so long away from the biz beats the hell out of me.

"I'll be a hot ticket, with so few seats to fill," says The 'Stache. "What're we lookin' at? Five thousand, max?"

"If that," I say, though of course we both know it's more like five *million.* "Guaranteed sell-out, I'd say."

"No need to beef up *this* bill." The 'Stache grins. "Though I *might* make room for *you,* if you need the work."

"Lemme think about it."

"I can always use an opening act." He shrugs. "Just sayin'."

"Very generous of you. Thanks loads."

"Fair warning, though. This'll be old school all the way." The 'Stache turns and gazes across the miles-long field. "Just a spotlight, a glass of water, and a microphone." He spreads his arms wide and looks up into the distant heights. "Plus a ginormous mother-lovin' communications array beaming to the fringes of the known freakin' universe in every possible signal and frequency."

Shading my eyes against the glare of the stadium lights, I can just make it out--a spindly silver grid hovering high above, punctuated with upturned disks and spiny antennae. How I completely missed it until now, I don't know; maybe it's got one of those Inexhaustible Apathy Filters that dims external stimuli to the brain based on natural human aversions to Getting Involved.

Whatever the reason, one thing's clear. "That thing's *huge.*"

"It's all customized." The 'Stache proudly plants his hands on his hips. "I designed it myself and personally supervised the construction."

"You did?"

"I'm a cosmological engineer, Double-J," says The 'Stache. "I didn't spend those ten years away from show biz just workin' on my memoirs and keepin' it real, y'know."

"But how'd you pay for it? How'd you get permission to install it here?" I sweep an arm around to take in the field and seats. "How'd you get booked here *at all,* for that matter?"

"I made boatloads of money in cosmo-engineering." The 'Stache grins and nods. "Big projects mean big bucks. I worked on everything from Starhenge to the Great Space Roller Coaster, with plenty of hyperdrive bypasses in between." He waves for me to join him. "With the cash I made from my work and investments, I just *bought* the damn stadium and booked myself! Then I gave myself permission to install the array."

I walk over to stand next to him, looking up at the sprawling grid in the sky. "So what's it for? Streaming a pay-per-view special to the cosmos? Beaming a feed to distant primitive cultures so they'll come to worship you as a god?"

"It's something bigger and better than you can imagine." He puts his arm around me again.

Looking down, I slide him a frown. "Seems like a lot of trouble to go to. What's the punchline?"

"Wait and see," says The 'Stache.

"C'mon, tell me."

He shakes his head. "A punchline ain't worth much without the element of surprise, is it?"

I pop an elbow in his side. "What if full disclosure is a condition of my being on the bill?"

"Then I guess you'll miss out on being a headliner at the event of the millennium." Why the bleep is he still grinning? "No skin off *my* chin, Gunga Din."

Is this the part where I'm supposed to sigh and give in? Because damnit, that's exactly what I do. My curiosity couldn't *be* more piqued; my gut instinct is kicking the crap out of all my intuitions, taking their lunch money, and spending it on magic beans.

And yes, *Mom*, my *heart* might have something to do with it, too.

"All right," I tell him. "Good thing I happen to have the day off."

That evening, Hypercube Center is filled to capacity and then some. Every seat in the stands is occupied, and every square inch of standing room on the field is packed. Even the sky is swimming with wall-to-wall spectators; everyone who can sprout wings or rotors or jets or antigravity nards is drifting overhead, angling for the best view in the house.

The only open space within that immensity is the stage itself. As The 'Stache promised, it's a bare bones affair, just a plain black square with a mike stand in the middle and a pitcher of ice water with two glasses on a skinny pedestal table nearby. Old school all the way.

Which begs the question: What's The 'Stache cookin' up? (And the corollary: What's he smokin'?) Without the ingredients of modern comedy--samurai swords, knives, guns, cannons, elaborate Rube Goldberg suicide machines--how the fun does he propose to get any laughs?

"Just go with it," he tells me when I ask him that very question. "Trust ol' Baba Looey here, he won't let you down."

I don't believe him for a second, but I feel better when he folds me in his arms for a pre-show hug. Even better when he stands on tiptoe to give me a long, loving kiss. Am I really that chickified that a little mush can drown out the voices of reason in my head?

Yes, apparently. The voices of reason are screaming for me to make like a banana and get the flock out of Dodge. But the next thing I know...

...I'm standing at the mike onstage, introducing The 'Stache.

Yay me, I get a standing-O all my own, just for being there. It takes a while for the applause to die down enough for me to be heard.

At which point, I put everything I have into singing The 'Stache's praises. I really pour it on, telling the crowd what a great comedian and unique talent he is--what an influence he's had on my career and those of so many others. I tell 'em how lucky they are that he's returned to the stage, what a privilege it is to be there to introduce him to the universe again. I tell 'em how great he is in bed, and how I'm probably mostly doing this because we're roman- tically involved, so don't blame me if he sucks, bites, and blows. (I skip that last part, but the mind readers out there might catch a whiff.)

Then I start applauding. "Ladies, gentlemen, invertebrates, intangibles, incomprehensibles, unmentionables, and all other life-forms, artforms, and colorforms, I present to you the once and future comedy genius known far, wide, and in-between as *The 'Stache!*"

The crowd roars with deafening cheers and applause. I've done a great job warming them up; now it's up to him to close the deal.

The 'Stache bursts out from behind an Apathy Curtain that kept him invisible until now. Waving and grinning at the crowd like a beauty pageant contestant, he marches up and takes my place at the mike. Then he winks at me and gestures at a mark on the floor, a glowing red X ten feet behind the mike where he wants me to wait.

As I take my position and the crowd settles down, he starts talking.

"What is comedy?" That's how he starts. "It's what makes you laugh. And that changes through time as *humanity* changes."

The 'Stache spreads his arms wide to encompass the crowd around him--the millions of people who are listening in dumb-struck silence. He sounds more eloquent than usual, as if he's channeling his inner Einstein instead of his typical Wisenheimer. "Humans have evolved to a level where technology enables them to do so many things...things that would have been considered *magic* to their ancestors thousands--even *hundreds*--of years ago.

"And these human beings of today, so changed now from what they once were, have a very different definition of comedy. Since almost anything is possible to them, even commonplace...and every bizarre situation that might once have been the basis of a *joke* is now the basis of *reality*...they no longer laugh at what they once did."

At that moment, the crowd *shifts*. I can see and feel and hear it from the stage. The people in the stands and on the field and in the air have waited through what's amounted to a lecture so far, but they've passed the tipping point. It's just a matter of time until they turn ugly.

The question is, does The 'Stache know it's coming? And does he have something planned to head it off?

If he does, he gives no sign of it. "So what does it take to make humans laugh in this modern day and age?" He counts out the answers on the fingers of his right hand. "Cruelty. Shock. Atrocity.

"This is what their sense of humor has become. Laughing at someone mutilating or killing themselves." He shoots a glance in my direction.

Suddenly, a loud male heckler shouts from the audience. "What the Fermi are you *talkin'* about, 'they'?"

The 'Stache ignores the heckler and keeps talking. "But here's the irony...the *ultimate* irony, that *none* of them can see. In the course of their evolution to a *less* funny species, humans have stumbled upon the biggest *joke* of all time."

Again, the heckler calls out from the crowd. "What's with the 'them' and 'they'?"

A second heckler joins in. "*We're* human, and we're right *in front* of you."

The 'Stache ignores them. "It goes like this. It took billions of years for the universe to evolve...for the planet Earth to evolve in such a way that the conditions were optimal for sentient life to develop...and for that sentient life, *humanity,* to evolve to its current, highly advanced state. It has taken that long for human beings to reach a level of technological advancement that makes them masters of their own bodies and minds and the physical laws of the universe itself.

"Have they used this mastery to transcend their limitations and set out in search of greater knowledge? To probe the hidden mysteries of existence itself?"

Another heckler interrupts. "Why does he keep calling us 'they'?"

"What has humanity done?" continues The 'Stache. "They've used their *mastery* to turn themselves into a trillion variations on the same self-referential silliness...the same images of clowns and celebrities and fictional characters they've been recycling for the past ten millennia. They've got the power to become *gods*, and they're still pissing around in the same damn *kiddie pool*, laughing at the suffering of their fellow men and women.

"In this way, humanity itself has become the greatest *joke* in the history of the *universe!* The kind of joke that *my* audience will appreciate!"

By now, the crowd is restless to the point of open rebellion. I smell danger in the air like smoke from a fire.

There's a murmur through the crowd, a susurration of thousands of disaffected voices...but the shout of the first heckler still manages to punch through above them all. "For the last time, why do you keep calling us 'they'? We *are* humanity. We *are* your audience."

A dark smile curls its way across The 'Stache's face. "What the eff gave you *that* idea?"

The murmur of the crowd drops away as all ears lock onto his next words.

"I'm not *talking* to *you* people." The 'Stache points upward. "I'm talking to *them*."

"The airbornes?" asks the heckler. "The flying-room-only people?"

"Not even close." The 'Stache raises his arms overhead and spreads them wide. "I *should've* said I'm talking to *it*. The *universe*."

Just then, I remember the communications array he installed above the stadium, the one that's "beaming to the fringes of the known freakin' universe in every possible signal and frequency." I figured it would be streaming his show to people on distant worlds and vessels...but maybe I was thinking too small.

"*That's* who this whole show was *meant* for," says The 'Stache. "*You people* are just here to prove my *point*."

"You're full'a *shazbot*," shouts the heckler. "The *universe* isn't sentient!"

"Sure it is!" says The 'Stache. "And I just told it the funniest joke it's ever heard!"

Suddenly, a deafening blast of thunder crashes through the stadium, and everyone falls silent. The airborne audience scatters like cockroaches from a kitchen light, and everyone in the stands and on the ground looks up.

"Hear that?" The 'Stache hikes a thumb toward the sky. "I'd say *somebody's* getting the joke!"

There's another blast of thunder, and another--each progressively louder than the one before. The stars in the sky dance and swirl like gold dust in a prospector's pan, flashing in unnatural rhythms.

Down below, the ground rumbles and shakes. That sets the earthbound crowd in motion, as everyone stampedes toward the exits. Millions of screams rise together, exploding through the miles-long/miles-wide stadium in a tsunami of cascading terror.

Not that The 'Stache looks the slightest bit worried. His face is calm as he turns and gestures for me to join him.

I wonder if I ought to be fleeing for the exits instead, but I run to his side anyway. "What's *happening*? What *is* this?"

The ground shakes harder than ever, and the thunderous blasts keep coming. Every light in the stadium blows out at the same time, showering the crowd with sizzling shards of glass.

The 'Stache wraps his arms around me. "I'm *killing*, that's what!" He grins up at the reeling stars in the sky. "They freakin' *love* me!"

The booming thunder becomes a continuous roar. The stars spin faster and faster, and the ground splits apart. Thousands of fleeing audience members tumble into the widening crevices.

The 'Stache tightens his grip on me. "Don't worry, Double-J!" He has to shout for me to hear him over the cacophony. "You and I have nothing to worry about! We'll be fine!"

A powerful wind rushes past us, a hurricane wind--only it's not trying to blow us away. It's *sucking* everything upward, pulling people and pieces of stadium into the sky with inexorable, furious force.

"How can you *say* that?" My voice is a terrified shriek.

"Because!" says The 'Stache. "I haven't done an *encore* yet!"

Just as he says it, the wind hauls us off our feet. We both go tumbling toward the stars, still locked in our embrace as if that will save us somehow.

At some point after we leave the ground, I lose consciousness--which is probably a blessing, given the circumstances.

Then, I awaken in The 'Stache's arms. His eyes are locked on mine, and his smile is gentle.

"Hey there, sleepyhead." He kisses me softly on the cheek. "Rise and shine."

As awareness returns more fully, I realize our surroundings are calm. There seems to be no trace of the apocalyptic mayhem that engulfed Tesseractus Prime.

"Wait." I push away from him and look around. It's only then that I see where we are: in a transparent bubble, floating through uninterrupted white space.

"What is this?" My voice quivers when I say it.

The 'Stache runs his hand along the surface of the bubble, which flexes and stretches under his fingertips. "Nothing...yet."

I feel panic twisting inside me, straining to burst free. "What're you talking about? What just *happened*?"

"Pretty sure the *universe* just *laughed*," says The 'Stache.

"What do you *mean*, it *laughed*?"

"What do you think all the *noise* and *shaky-shaky* were about?" The 'Stache's eyes glitter as he grins.

Things still aren't making sense to me. The white space, the bubble...our *lives*, which somehow still exist. "But where *is* everything?"

"Out there somewhere." He waves dismissively at the milky

void. "Compressed into a super-dense, super-heated ball of energy. The seed of a *new* universe, in other words."

"Wait, what?" Am I losing my mind here? Did he just tell me... "The universe *ended*?"

He waggles his hand and squints. "More like *reset*. It suddenly contracted..." He jams his hands together. "Now there's a *pause*, like a *breath*. And soon..." He makes a whooshing sound as he pulls his hands apart. "It'll *reboot*."

"Like a *big bang*, you mean?"

He touches the tip of his nose. "Exactamundo. There'll be a shiny new universe in place of the old one. Happens once every 14 billion years or so."

"And what about us?" When I press my hand against the bubble, it feels like a warm rubber balloon. "Why didn't *we* get mashed up with the rest of the old universe?"

"Funny you should ask." The 'Stache takes my hand. "It's been talking to me..."

"The universe."

"Yup. Apparently, it likes my work so much, it wants me to help set up the next version of itself. I mean the next *joke*."

My head is spinning. I'd think he's lost his mind if we weren't floating in a transparent bubble through some kind of white void after witnessing a cosmic apocalypse.

"So that's it then?" A hysterical giggle escapes my lips. "*Our* universe--the one we *knew*, our *home*--is just *gone?*"

"Gone forever." The 'Stache nods.

Again, a crazy giggle escapes me. "*Forever?* Everything we know is gone *forever?*"

"Yeah, and wouldn't ya know it?" The 'Stache laughs and shakes his head. "*Now* I'm hungry for *Chinese* all of a sudden!"

I think about it, chewing a fingernail. More giggles slip out.

"What is it?" asks The 'Stache. "What's so funny?"

I laugh a little harder now. "All those times I killed myself for comedy...and now here I am, a last survivor while everyone else is dead."

193

The 'Stache nods. "It's ironic, all right."

I keep laughing. "And you know what *really* cracks me up? I can't figure out whether the joke's on *them*, the people who are *gone*...or on *me*."

"Then everything's as it should be, Double-J. Remember the Groucho Marx Effect from physics: *A universe simple enough to be understood is too simple to produce a mind capable of understanding it.*

"Or as Groucho himself put it..." The 'Stache flicks an invisible cigar and waggles his eyebrows. "'I wouldn't want to belong to any club that would have me as a member!'"

SHROOMS OF BENARES

Father Gavín Obregón lifted the hem of his black shirt, peeled back a flap of skin just below his bottom left rib, and drew out three fresh-baked wafers of communion host from the cavity there, still warm from his flesh.

"The body of Christ, given up for you." Father Obregón said the words softly as he held up one of the round white wafers between his thumb and forefinger.

Piotr Punzak, a squat farmer with shaggy brown hair and beard, stood before him in the dusty farmyard. To one side, the gleaming silver domes of his farmhouse and barn sprawled in the mid-morning light...light cast not from a sun, but from huge fungal sun-blooms drifting across the sky.

In the other direction, the rolling hills were carpeted with fields of morel, boletus, oyster, and matsutake mushrooms, ready for harvest. The fruits of planet Benares, like all native life on the frontier planet, were fungus through and through. In all the world, only the human settlers could claim non-fungal origins.

As a rough breeze shivered the nearby morels and matsutakes, farmer Piotr tipped his head back. "Amen." Just as he opened his mouth for the host, one of the *nube oveja*--the self-propelled fungal "cloud sheep" herding in the sky overhead--slid away, allowing the light from the nearest sun-bloom to cast his face bright gold.

Father Obregón placed the host on Piotr's tongue. Piotr closed his mouth and bowed his head.

Then, it was time for the wine. Father Obregón turned over his right arm and popped the tiny cartilage pour-spout free from his wrist. "Blood of Christ, shed for you," he said.

"Amen." Piotr opened his mouth and closed his eyes.

Father Obregón held his wrist spout over Piotr's mouth, then squeezed the soft, oblong bladder implanted in the underside of his arm. Ruby red wine trickled into Piotr's mouth, sparkling in the light of the sun-bloom overhead.

It was just another Mass for the genetically engineered multi-faith super-chaplain of planet Benares. Just another communion for a human Swiss army knife on the fringe of the farthest frontier in human history.

An hour later, Father Obregón was racing away from the farm in his hoversled, zipping through a forest of giant fungal towers.

He was also speaking without moving his lips.

"I'll be there in three days, Shen." Father Obregón spoke in his mind over the planet-wide Soulnet that kept him in touch with his scattered congregation. "Plenty of time to make your daughter's bat mitzvah."

Shen Ping's words flowed into his brain like warm water. "You're a mensch, Rabbi. I know you won't let us down."

"Have I ever?" Father Obregón chuckled in his head. "*Relax,* Bubbi! Two hundred miles of *wilderness,* and I'll be whipping you at *arm-wrestling* again."

"Doesn't *count!*" said Shen. "You're a *splicer!* How can I *ever* beat a genetically modified rabbi slash preacher slash cleric slash *whatever?*"

Father Obregón's thoughts bubbled with laughter. "You better pump some *iron,* Shen! You *know* I won't *let* you win."

Shen responded with the mental equivalent of a snort. "Maybe *I'm* the one who's been letting *you* win! How *else* am I gonna score points with *God?*"

Just then, another call buzzed for attention in Father Obregón's head. Such was life in the remote wilderness for the clergyman with a switchboard in his brain.

All seven hundred humans on Benares had a direct telepathic line to the super-chaplain at all times. How else could one man tend the spiritual needs of a flock scattered to the far corners of a huge and untamed world?

Still, sometimes he wished for a respite. Sometimes, he longed for a little peace and quiet in which to commune with no one but God.

The caller buzzed again, and Father Obregón opened the link. Just as he started to say something, a flock of creatures burst out of a stand of morels in front of him. Reflexively, he swerved the hoversled to one side, barely missing the incredible lifeforms as they took flight.

He gazed in stunned wonder as he glided past. Yet again, he'd come across a new species--a flock of what looked like winged pizza shells with a hundred writhing white tendrils underneath. They twirled skyward all at once, twelve of them at least, trailing some kind of neon blue mist. Even as Father Obregón swung his hoversled wide in case the mist was toxic, he marveled at their magnificent strangeness, their utterly alien design. Like every other non-human lifeform on Benares, they were fungus-based, similar to fungi back on Earth yet possessing a multitude of uniquely alien traits.

What a world. How many times a day did that thought run through Father Obregón's mind? *I love this planet.*

"Hello? Can you hear me?" As Father Obregón got his hoversled back on track, he tried to reconnect with the caller he'd cut off because of the pizza shells. But no one answered.

Nothing but silence on the line.

Amazingly, an hour went by without a single call in Father Obregón's head. The constant queue of souls banging on his door was empty and silent.

At first, he passed it off as a fluke. He decided to continue toward his next stop and make the most of the rare quiet by indulging in some meditation amid the stunning sights of Benares.

When he topped a ridge and gazed out over a sprawling valley he'd never seen before, chills raced up his spine. Giant multicolored rills of fungi fanned out over the valley floor, arching like ranks of rainbows under the cloud sheep and luminous sun-blooms in the shifting, golden sky. It looked nothing like the Heaven he'd been taught to expect, but it made him think of Heaven nonetheless.

As Father Obregón crossed a mountain pass under canopies of towering toadstools, glittering silver showers of spores swirled around him like snow. Curtains of lacy lichen hung dancing from the clifftops, making a sound like high-pitched singing as the wind filtered through their fine traceries.

Then there were the creatures in all their multitudes, great and small and every size in between...every one of them *mycozoa*, fungi with the mobility of animals. They flew and crawled and swung and darted through the landscape, screeching and squawking and roaring and croaking.

I need to do this more often. That was what Father Obregón thought as the splendor of Benares continued to unfold around him. As the second hour of peaceful contemplation passed. *I'd almost forgotten what it was like to appreciate God's wonders without constant interruptions.*

But by the middle of the third hour, a knot had formed in the pit of his stomach. The sights of Benares couldn't distract him from what he now knew to be true.

Something was wrong. The Soulnet was malfunctioning, or something was blocking the calls...

Or something had happened to the *callers*.

With the Soulnet apparently down, Father Obregón turned elsewhere for human contact. Parking in a mountain meadow of red and blue puffballs, he switched on the radio in his hoversled, grabbed the microphone from its hook on the dashboard, and called out over the airwaves.

"This is Father Obregón," he said into the mic. "Can anyone hear me? Please respond."

No answer.

"Father Obregón here." As he said it, he watched a pack of pale wolflike creatures with spiked snouts and springs for legs chase what looked like a pink beachball across the far side of the meadow. "Someone, please answer!"

Still nothing. Across the meadow, the beachball turned on the remaining four wolf-things, flung open a huge maw on its face, and bounced after them. It ran down and gobbled up one, then two, then three of them, getting fatter each time.

Yet another new species, thought Father Obregón. *I love this planet.*

One more hour passed before Father Obregón finally heard another human voice.

"I hear you, Father."

For an instant, he thought it was coming in over the radio, but he quickly realized it was inside his head.

"Hello!" He thought the words and said them aloud at the same time. "Thank God, hello!"

The new voice in his head was a woman's. "I was starting to think you were dead, Father." He recognized the low, throaty tone right away: Naima bint Fouad bin Hakim Al-Aziz, an exobiologist. He recognized it though he hadn't heard it for five long years.

She'd refused to call him for five years. Out of all the settlers, she alone had cut herself off from him.

"You thought wrong." Father Obregón chuckled, trying to sound calm, though his heart was suddenly racing. "So how are you, Naima?"

"I've had better days." Naima's voice was stiff and strangely flat. "I'm at the end of my rope, actually."

"Tell me what's happening, Naima."

"Wellll." The slightest quaver crept into Naima's voice. "Everyone's dead up here. Everyone but me."

Father Obregón felt a horrified chill rush through him. "*Everyone?*"

"Yes, Gavín," said Naima.

"*Dios mío.*" Father Obregón shook his head in stunned disbelief. Thirty-six people, counting Naima; that was how many had been stationed at the research camp with her. "What *happened* to them?"

"You know how we hadn't found any signs of sentient life on Benares?" said Naima.

"Yes, of course."

Naima choked back a sob. "We weren't *looking* hard enough."

Father Obregón had first met Naima on the trip from Earth aboard the starship that had brought them to Benares. She'd been a teenager at the time, but the truth of it was, they'd both been 21 years younger. He'd been barely out of his teens himself.

Their personalities had been a perfect match from the start. Not such a shocker maybe, considering the 700 settlers had been selected for general compatibility...but he'd always felt something special with her. Something beyond computer-predicted affinity.

Their reasons for making the trip were much alike. Naima had come for adventure, to witness never-before-seen wonders in the name of science. Father Obregón had also come for adventure, to witness such wonders in the name of God. Both of them were idealists, driven by wanderlust, curiosity, and faith in the power of universal truths and forces.

Drawn together by complementary callings and natures, they'd spent many hours together gazing out at the passing spectacles of space, talking about *everything*. Imagining the great discoveries they would make on the scientific and spiritual frontiers. Dreaming up schemes for turning their brave new colony into utopia.

Dreaming up ways to be together on Benares, too, though their assigned duties would keep them far apart. Because the longer they knew each other, the more they knew they *had* to be together.

Everything between them was perfect, from the meshing of their personalities (they were both thoughtful yet outgoing) to the meshing of their bodies (thankfully, chastity was no longer a mandatory vow for priests in this day and age). They were soulmates, and they had to find a way to stay together even as their work pulled them apart.

Maybe, if Naima found sentient life on Benares, she could get her assignment changed to assistant chaplain; Father Obregón would need an exobiologist to help minister to alien lifeforms, wouldn't he?

Maybe, his genetically-engineered splicer body would have trouble adjusting to the alien environment--with a little help from an undetectable nano-phage tweaked by Naima--and he'd have to stay put at her lab.

Or, failing either of those, he would figure out a way to always keep her thoughts foremost in his mind. He would scam the Soulnet, whipping up a psychic hideaway for the two of them in the midst of the mental traffic from the other settlers.

One thing alone had been carved in stone: the two of them

would find a way to overcome any obstacle the frontier or their fellow settlers threw at them.

Shivering, Father Obregón looked around the mountain meadow, staring at the larger clumps of puffballs, the shadows of the distant toadstool treeline. He wondered if he was being watched by something with intellect and malice.

What troubled him most, though, was the possibility that sentient native lifeforms had taken action all over the world. That the reason no one but Naima had answered his calls was that the lifeforms had murdered them all.

"Are you safe?" Father Obregón said in his mind.

He panicked briefly when no answer came...but then Naima spoke. "I've sealed myself in the lab."

"What do they look like?" said Father Obregón.

"See for yourself," said Naima. "You have my permission."

Father Obregón's pulse quickened. "You mean...you can *see* them? They're *with* you?"

"In the building." Naima said it matter-of-factly. "Come through and I'll show you."

Father Obregón hesitated. It had been a long time since he'd been inside her head. He hadn't gone there in five years, since the two of them had split up.

Though for 16 years before that, he'd visited her mind every day. In spite of their schemes for togetherness on Benares, it was the only way they'd actually managed to be together at all in spite of the miles that were almost always between them. It was the one thing they'd shared that was special to the two of them, the one thing no one else could interrupt.

Because while everyone else could enter *his* mind on a whim, Naima was the only person in the world whose mind *he* could enter.

Father Obregón took a deep breath and steadied himself. This time, he knew, going into her mind was crucial; he had to do it to see what they were up against.

And he had to not let her know how much it meant to him. How much he enjoyed it.

Taking one more deep breath, he dove into the open link, pouring his mind like lightning in Naima's direction.

He felt a thrill as he charged through the crackling darkness of the mental conduit between them. A flare of blinding white light suddenly filled his mind's eye, and he felt himself spinning out of control. A flurry of sensations washed through him, a storm of sounds and smells and tastes and touches, too jumbled to process. The unfiltered input of another human mind.

Then, the sensations faded, and the spinning stopped. Father Obregón blinked his mind's eye, clearing away the afterimage of the blinding flare.

And he found himself looking out through Naima's eyes. He saw her reflection looking back at him from the gleaming silver surface of a metal lab table.

He hadn't seen her in years. Even slightly distorted in the reflection from the table, she looked as beautiful as he remembered.

Long brown hair flowed over her shoulders, wrapping around a small, oval face. Dark-framed eyeglasses perched on a gently sloping nose, setting off eyes of the brightest, most glittering green he'd ever seen. Perfect dimples flanked the soft petals of her rosy lips, curling when she smiled toward a tiny mole on her right cheek...

And a scar on her left. He had to force himself not to recoil at the sight of it. Not because it was ugly, because nothing could make her ugly in his eyes.

But because it was his fault.

"Where are they, Naima?" Better to take his mind off that scar. Better not to think about what had happened between them five years ago.

"I'll show you." Inside the confines of her mind, Naima's voice sounded stronger, less rattled. "Over here."

As Father Obregón watched, the scene shifted, swooping up and away from the reflection on the lab table. He saw stacks of hard-shelled plastic cases, racks of silver lab implements, panels of glowing green controls and readouts.

Finally, there was a clear space, a reinforced glass door a few yards away. The view stopped swooping from east to west and started moving toward the door.

Naima took one step, then two, peering into the twilit space beyond the door. Father Obregón could make out overturned tables, chairs, equipment...

And bodies. He saw the unmistakable shapes of human arms and legs piled in with the wreckage. Then, human *faces* caked with blood, mouths and eyes wide open, unmoving.

His heart sank as Naima took another step, bringing him closer to the corpses. He recognized at least two of them.

Suddenly, something threw itself against the door with a thunderous crash. Naima stopped in her tracks but didn't look away.

Father Obregón's instinct was to dive back into the link, but he forced himself to stay and watch. It wasn't easy; what he saw as he gaped through Naima's eyes filled him with revulsion.

A human head, a female *child's* head, wobbled atop a mass of mangled human body parts held together by pulsing black foam. The mismatched parts looked like they'd all come from different people: a woman's long leg, a man's hairy arm, another man's torso, a child's hand.

The parts were arranged in roughly the right places for a human body, linked by the black foam instead of tendons and ligaments. They jiggled and slipped around as if the foam were barely holding them together.

As unsteady as the mass of parts looked, they were capable of moving with sudden speed and power. Father Obregón flinched as the patchwork person suddenly lashed out with its male right arm, pumping it into the door so hard, it cracked the outer pane of glass.

Mismatched body parts fell away in the impact, but the black foam stayed attached and snapped them back together. The little girl's head rolled down the torso, then jumped back up into place...but face-down, with the bloody stump of her neck pointing at Father Obregón.

He knew her, of course, as he knew all his congregation on Benares. Her name was Emma, and her parents were Mormons. Good people, all three of them.

He wondered if any of the other patchwork pieces were theirs.

"*Dios mío.*" Father Obregón had to look away. "You say this thing is *sentient?*"

"I *know* it is," said Naima, and then she walked the rest of the way to the door. Father Obregón watched as she pressed the palm of her right hand against the reinforced glass.

Instantly, the child's hand on the patchwork body lunged at the glass, planting itself directly opposite Naima's. Black foam flowed out from its stump, glowing brighter and pulsing faster as it outlined the tiny, pale fingers.

Father Obregón watched, transfixed...and then,

a *third voice* spoke in Naima's head.

It spoke in a kind of hyperfast babble. As Father Obregón listened, images appeared in his mind, somehow triggered by the gibberish. He saw showers of pulsing black foam falling from the sky like rain, covering the ground, clotting and squirming. Looking up, he saw the foam's source: the *nube oveja,* the drifting "cloud sheep," split open from end to end.

Next, he saw a familiar scene--himself, administering communion to Piotr Punzak. He saw the scene from above, looking down from a distance as he drew the host wafer from the cavity in his side and placed it on the tongue of the Catholic farmer.

Then, as if from nowhere, two words shot into his mind, spoken in his own voice: *EAT GOD.*

When the sound of the words faded, Father Obregón saw something else. He saw two more of the patchwork bodies rising from the rubble, picking up tools and guns, and shambling toward the lab in which Naima was sealed.

EAT GOD.

Father Obregón returned to his own body to try to figure out what his next move should be. The Soulnet link to Naima was still open-- he didn't dare risk being cut off from her--but he kept her on hold as he pulled himself back together.

What did the patchwork lifeforms want? And how could he stop them?

He knew only one thing for sure: he had to get to the lab in person as soon as he could, whatever the cost. He had to rescue Naima, for what she'd once meant to him...and what she meant to him still, in spite of the mistake that had come between them.

Never mind that she was nearly two hundred miles away. No one else was answering his calls; there might not be another living soul in the whole world who could come to her rescue.

The first thing he did before taking Naima off hold was to start the hoversled moving in her direction. He put it on autopilot and set the speed as fast as he dared, keeping one hand on the steering wheel just in case.

The next thing he did was pull the flask of bourbon from under his seat and take a quick drink. He saved the stuff for especially bad days, and they didn't get much worse than the one he was having.

Then, he put the flask away and took Naima off hold. "Any change?" he said through the link.

Naima sighed. "Three more just showed up outside the lab. That makes six. Not that I'm worried, you understand."

Father Obregón smiled grimly. "Hang tight. I'm on my way."

"Watch for sudden downpours," said Naima. "You don't want to get caught out in *that* rain."

Taking his eyes off the path ahead, Father Obregón looked skyward. A fat, fluffy cloud sheep floated off to one side, well away from his route...but it still made him nervous.

"I can't believe the black foam's responsible," said Naima. "It started turning up recently, but we didn't know it was coming from the cloud sheep...and we *definitely* had no idea it was sentient."

"Have you had a chance to analyze it?" said Father Obregón.

"The foam contains high quantities of an ultra-potent form of *psilocybin*," said Naima. "The hallucinogenic compound produced by certain species of fungi. Otherwise, its structure is a mystery. Nothing to suggest motility, let alone sentience."

Father Obregón kept his eyes on a flock of cloud sheep up ahead, and he shivered. "In the 21 years we've been here, there's never been a sign of danger from the cloud sheep. How is this possible?"

"Cicadas on Earth have a 17-year life cycle," said Naima. "Why not a 21-year cycle for cloud sheep to generate and deposit black foam?"

As his hoversled approached the flock of cloud sheep, Father Obregón pressed buttons on the dashboard, shutting off the outside air vents, switching the blower to recycled air only. He double-checked the cockpit seals and nodded, satisfied the foam couldn't get inside.

Reasonably satisfied.

"So." Naima paused. "When do you think you'll get here?"

He knew she wouldn't like the answer. "Eight hours. Maybe ten."

Naima was silent for a moment. When she spoke again in his head, the tone of her thoughts was dark. "If they...if I'm gone before you get here...please go somewhere else."

"That won't happen," said Father Obregón. "I think maybe they're waiting for me."

Again, Naima was silent. "Then don't come at all. I don't want you to."

"Sorry," said Father Obregón, "but it's not open for discussion. As long as you're alive, I'm coming to get you."

"Then I'm hanging up," said Naima. "You won't *know* if I'm dead or alive."

"Naima, no!" said Father Obregón, but it was too late. She'd already cut the connection.

He pounded the dashboard with his fist, angry that his only link to her had been severed. Desperately worried that she could be dying at that very moment, and he had no way of knowing.

He was also, deep in his heart, overjoyed that she'd hung up on him. Because he guessed that the only reason she'd hung up was that she was worried the patchworks would get him if he tried to save her.

And that meant she still cared. Perhaps, after five years, she'd finally forgiven him for what he'd done.

He'd meant it as a surprise.

One night, five years ago, Father Obregón had decided to do something extra special for Naima's birthday. It didn't matter that he was halfway around the world from her.

What were a few thousand miles to someone who could travel between minds?

He'd parked his hoversled for the night at the base of an enormous toadstool and closed his eyes. Then, he'd done something he could do only with Naima, because of their special two-way link.

He'd sneaked inside her mind. He'd found her through the Soulnet and slipped inside while she was sleeping.

Then, he'd done something even harder, something he'd never done before. Something that took him a few tries before he got it right.

He'd made her *sleepwalk*. He'd taken control of her body, enough to get her up out of bed and make her shuffle down the hall and out the door of the barracks at the research camp.

"What the hell did you think you were *doing?*" That was what Naima said much later...over the link, of course, as she lay in her hospital bed. "What *possessed* you?"

"I wanted to paint a picture with your hands," Father Obregón had told her. "I wanted to give it to you for your birthday, as if I were there with you."

"You can't just crawl into my *mind* without my *knowing* it." Naima's voice in his head had been full of pain and anger.

"But I wanted to *surprise* you," he'd said. "You'd see that painting and wonder how it *got* there. And you'd know how much I *love* you."

"You almost *killed* me!" It was then, when she'd said that in her thoughts, that Father Obregón had known it was over between them. Even before she'd broken it off in so many words, he'd known.

Because she'd been right. He *had* almost killed her.

After she'd shuffled out of the barracks that night, he'd walked her to the main lab, where he'd arranged with other members of his flock to stow some painting supplies. Then, while steering her through the lab to set them up, he'd fumbled his control for an instant.

Naima had tripped over her own feet and crashed through the wall of a plate glass isolation chamber. Dozens of glass shards had pierced her body, barely missing vital organs and blood vessels, ripping open a gash that had left a scar on the side of her face.

That day had left deep scars between Naima and Father Obregón, too. She'd never trusted or forgiven him in the five years since.

But he'd never stopped loving her...and maybe, he thought, she'd held on to her love for him as well.

Two hours passed with no contact from Naima. Against her wishes, Father Obregón stayed the course, charging through the wilderness toward her camp.

As his hoversled glided through the fungiscape, he passed the usual parade of wonders but was only dimly aware of them. He wound his way through a forest of massive chanterelles, their pearlescent scalloped lobes blossoming in spectacular fashion...but he didn't really see them. He skated over a field of waist-high fairy ring mushrooms, their curled skirts uplifted like delicate ivory pinafores...but he couldn't appreciate them, either. Same for the procession of filmy lavender veils rippling through the air like magic carpets over red-orange fungal spires.

All he could think about was Naima and what he could do to save her. He wracked his brain, trying to sort out what had happened, struggling to latch onto a solution.

Suddenly, his head buzzed with an incoming call. He jumped and nearly swerved the sled into a wall of crystalline lattice lichens in his hurry to open the line.

"Naima?" He said it aloud and in his mind at the same time. "Are you all right?"

"You didn't do what I told you." She sounded weary but not angry. "You're still coming, aren't you?"

"I don't think there's anyone else left on Benares," said Father Obregón. "It's down to the two of us."

Naima didn't say anything in response to that.

Father Obregón rubbed his eyes. "Have more of the creatures arrived?"

"I've lost count."

"Have they communicated with you? Have they said anything?"

"No," said Naima, "but I think you were right. I think they're waiting for you."

"What makes you think that?"

"Because they're all facing in your direction," said Naima. "None of them are looking at me anymore."

"I wonder what they want with me." Father Obregón stroked his bearded chin. "'EAT GOD,' they said. Do they think we're actually eating our God during communion? Maybe they want a taste for themselves."

"By eating those of us who've eaten God?" said Naima.

Father Obregón steered out from under a looming cloud sheep. "Attaining divinity by consuming the flesh of those who've tasted the divine. It makes sense."

"Then what about the non-Christian settlers?" said Naima. "*They* didn't take communion."

"The beings don't distinguish between different faiths, maybe? If *one* human takes communion, by extension, they think we *all* do it?"

"Okay," said Naima. "Then why are they waiting for you?"

"I generate the host and wine." Father Obregón gazed out the cockpit canopy as the hoversled swooped over a bubbling lake of yeast. Ever-shifting geometric patterns flowed over the surface, multicolored interlocking shapes dancing like a kaleidoscope. "Maybe they want *all* the God for *themselves*. Every last bite."

When Father Obregón was an hour from Naima's camp, the sunblooms started to dim. They were the planet's home-grown source of light and heat, enormous fungal disks orbiting high in the stratosphere. Once a day, their luminescence dropped to 25 percent, and night fell over all of Benares at once.

The hoversled's headlamps switched on, lighting up the way forward. Nocturnal mycozoa bounded away from the flare, tails and wings and tentacles flickering.

As Father Obregón gazed into the darkness around him, he felt the same void in his soul. He was at a loss about what he should do when he reached Naima. He felt hopeless, inadequate...and scared.

All he knew for sure was that he had to get there. No other human was left alive on Benares; no one had responded to his repeated psychic or radio calls. No cavalry was coming from the stars, either. Benares was on the farthest fringe of the frontier, months from the nearest settled world by spacecraft.

So it was all up to him. Super-chaplain to the rescue. Time for the splicer to prove there was more to his genetically enhanced superiority than just talk. Time for him to make up for hurting her five years ago.

If only he had a plan. If only he didn't feel so *alone.*

Only now, without the constant calls of his flock buzzing in his head, did he realize how much they'd meant to him. How much he'd depended on them. Only now did he notice how small he felt without them. How weak.

"Father? Imam?" Naima's voice rose suddenly in his quiet mind.

"*Asalam 'Alaykum.*" He used the traditional greeting since she'd referred to him by an Islamic title.

"`*Alaykum as-Salaam,*" said Naima. "Are you almost here?"

"Less than an hour away," said Father Obregón.

"That close." Naima sighed. "Perhaps you should slow down a little."

So we can live a little longer. He knew exactly how she felt. "How are you holding up?" he said.

"Second-guessing every decision I've ever made," said Naima, "because they all led me to this moment."

Father Obregón looked around as his sled glided through a thicket of giant, glowing shiitakes and feathery cauliflower mush-rooms. "Well, I'm glad you're here," he said. "Not *there*, I mean, but...I'm glad to have you with me. I missed you."

Naima paused for a long moment. When she spoke again, her voice in his mind was soft. "I missed you, too."

"I'm sorry," said Father Obregón. "I'm sorry for what happened before. I'm sorry I hurt you. I shouldn't have done what I did."

"And I shouldn't have pushed you away," said Naima. "We wasted so many years...and now this. Now we're out of time."

"Not out of time yet," said Father Obregón. "Maybe we'll still get a second chance...if we want it."

"That's what I'm praying for," said Naima.

A creature that looked like an upside-down pyramid of blinking violet light floated by in the darkness. *I love this planet.* "That's what I'm praying for, too, Naima."

As Father Obregón pulled into Naima's camp, he realized he was crazy. What was he thinking, rushing to confront a hostile enemy without a plan, a weapon, or backup?

He parked his hoversled in front of the lab shed and switched off the motor. Then, he sat for long moments in the cockpit, knuckles white as he clutched the wheel. Sweat ran down his back and sides as he dug deep for courage.

He found it in his flask of bourbon. Two long pulls calmed his shaking. One more, the longest yet, and he popped the cockpit canopy and stepped out of the hoversled. Stood for a moment in the pool of brightness cast by the lone floodlight atop the lab shed.

Then, heart slamming like a fighter's fist against his rib cage, he walked toward the open door of the shed.

As soon as Father Obregón stepped through the door, they moved toward him. Patchwork assemblages of mismatched human body parts, held together with clots of black foam. All the eyes wide open, all the faces slack and dead.

They looked far more horrifying in person than they had through Naima's eyes--heads lolling, bones protruding, organs dangling. Black foam oozing between joints and out of every orifice. A grinding, sloshing sound as they hobbled and shuffled toward him. A stench of excrement and rot so overwhelming, it made him gag.

And there were so *many* of them. *Dozens.* No wonder Naima had lost count.

He forced himself to stand with shoulders squared as they surrounded him. As they pressed closer and closer on all sides.

Peering between them, he glimpsed Naima in the sealed lab, gazing out through the reinforced glass door. He heard her in his mind--no words, just breathing. A nervous quaver in each exhalation.

And then something else was in his mind, too.

The familiar presence of the black foam welled up within him, pulsing and pressing against his awareness. Hyperfast gibberish babbled in his head, and images rushed past his mind's eye: black foam falling from drifting cloud sheep to blanket the fungiscape; Father Obregón giving communion to Piotr Punzak and a stream of others, dozens of humans all over the world...all of them dead now.

Suddenly, the creatures grabbed hold of him, snapping his focus back out of his mind. With clumsy power, they wrenched his arms wide and held him spread-eagled. One of them clamped his head between bloody, mismatched hands.

This is it. Eyes wide, heart jackhammering, Father Obregón felt more of the creatures grab hold of him, wrapping him in a solid clinch of rancid flesh and black muck.

"*Stop!*" Naima's voice sounded far away as she screamed in the lab, more distant than when they'd been hundreds of miles apart. "*Please no!*"

The creatures ignored her cries. One of the patchworks wobbled in front of Father Obregón, its head that of a young man with sandy brown hair. Its torso, strung with shreds of green cloth, belonged to a woman; one arm was short and pale, the other long with coal-black skin.

When the dark arm swung up and the tiny pink hand on the end reached for his face, Father Obregón tried to flinch, but the other hands gripping his head wouldn't let him. He cried out, struggling, but the hand moved toward him inexorably.

He shut his eyes and grimaced when the stubby little fingers made contact with his forehead. A fresh wave of gibberish surged through his mind, swirling like a cyclone. More images of communion, more images of black foam showering down.

And then, a new cycle of images coursed through him. Settlers tasting the black foam, putting curds of it in their mouths. Each one dying horribly afterward, convulsing on the ground, then literally falling apart...limbs and heads slumping away from torsos, organs sluicing in the dirt in a flow of black sludge.

Pulled together by tendrils of foam, the body parts became shambling patchworks. The patchworks went after other settlers, feeding them more of the foam, and the cycle repeated.

Through it all, Father Obregón felt the same words rise up in his mind again and again. The same words as before, imparted nonverbally to his fevered mind:

EAT GOD.

His head was spinning as he tried to make sense of what he'd seen. One thing was clear: he knew how the nightmare had started. Settlers had eaten the foam of their own accord...but why? He still didn't understand.

The infant hand on the dark-skinned arm withdrew, then dug its stubby fingers into a bubbling clot between the patchwork's head and torso. The fingers came away smeared with black foam.

Then, they moved toward Father Obregón's mouth.

EAT GOD. Again with the same message. *EAT GOD.*

As the foam-covered fingers slid closer to his mouth, Father Obregón realized how wrong he'd been. The patchworks hadn't been trying to attain divinity by consuming the flesh of humans who'd eaten God in communion. They'd never wanted to reach the God of humans at all.

They'd been trying to do the *opposite.* Trying to get humans to eat *their* god.

But humans couldn't survive it. The black foam sacrament had killed them all. And Father Obregón was next in line.

"Please, no!" Father Obregón fought harder, but he couldn't break the combined grip of the ghoulish patchworks.

"Stop it, you *monsters!*" It was Naima. Father Obregón heard the door to the lab crash open and her footsteps charge into the patchwork mob. "*Leave him alone!*"

But nothing would change the course of events. The tiny fingers jabbed forward, and the black foam touched Father Obregón's lips. He felt it fizzing like a carbonated drink on his lips and then the tip of his tongue.

EAT GOD.

There was a moment as the substance soaked into his bloodstream, a moment of stillness. The patchworks let go of him, and his arms fell at his sides. Naima pushed through the crowd and stopped in front of him; she looked crushed when she saw the black foam on his lips.

Tears ran down her cheeks. "Don't go. Oh please, don't leave me alone here."

Father Obregón smiled. Just as he was about to say something, the moment of stillness

ended

and everything made sense.

Father Obregón's mind felt as if it had burst. Light poured in from every direction, swirling with color and sweet fragrance. Geometric patterns appeared and shifted before his mind's eye, dancing like the patterns in a kaleidoscope.

Or the patterns on the yeast lakes of Benares.

He felt his mind changing shape, flowing between forms in a dizzying rush of transformations. He melted from a spinning disk to a rippling lavender veil, from a pink beachball to an upside-down pyramid of violet neon light.

Every shape just like the lifeforms he'd seen on Benares.

Waves of textures washed over him, clinging and combining in electric layers of high relief. There was roughness, grittiness, laciness, puffiness, fluffiness, spikiness, foaminess. One after another, from firm smoothness to crystalline latticework.

Just like the multitude of fungal flora thriving on Benares.

All these sensations blossomed and swirled together in his mind, crackling with invisible fire that he felt and saw and swallowed. Structures and instincts from the largest to the most extreme subatomic pulsed and sang within and without him.

And all the while, even as his mind opened and transformed and filled to overflowing, he felt lighter than air. He felt better than he ever had, completely new from tip to toe, from gut to soul.

For an instant, he thought he had died, but then the thoughts of the patchworks, which once had seemed like gibberish, suddenly came into focus. Conveying the truth in a wordless intention, a heartfelt expression.

He has eaten and survived.

He had tasted their god, the collective essence of their world, and not died in doing so. Chalk it up to the splicer physiology of the genetically-enhanced super-chaplain.

The black foam had tuned him in to the psychedelic glory of the life force of Benares. It had expanded his consciousness to encompass the total majesty of the world that had always fascinated him.

And it had done one more thing to him, too.

Father Obregón pulled his hoversled into a misty cove in the heart of a jungle of enokitake. The slender stems of the tall white mushrooms flickered in the breeze, spherical caps bobbing in the morning light from the sun-blooms.

A week had passed since he'd first eaten the black foam, and he was back on the road again. He was making his rounds again, traversing the wilderness, ministering to believers around the world.

The congregation was different, but the work was the same in the end.

As he popped the cockpit canopy, a call buzzed for attention in his head. He picked it up with a smile. "Good morning, Naima."

"Good morning." Naima, as usual these days, didn't sound happy. She was back at the lab, where she'd been working since the patchworks had evacuated. They'd left her alive and intact at Father Obregón's request after he'd eaten their black foam sacrament. "Where are you this time?"

"Prayer meeting up north." Father Obregón stepped out of the hoversled, his feet sinking in a soft carpet of dewy gray-green mildew. "It's good to hear your voice, Naima."

Naima sent him a thought that was the mental equivalent of clearing her throat. She didn't approve of the new direction his work had taken. She didn't approve of his new calling. "You need to come home, Gavín."

"Not yet, Naima." Father Obregón padded through the mildew carpet toward a cluster of buried lumps in the middle of the cove. "I've got work to do."

"It's not safe, Gavín," said Naima.

Father Obregón chuckled. "God's work is *never* safe."

Naima sighed. "What if the foam kills you? It's *fatal* to non-splicers. What if you're only *temporarily* immune?"

Father Obregón knelt among the buried lumps and began brushing away layers of mildew and soil from one of the biggest, the size of a basketball. "Naima, please..."

Naima's voice rose in anger and desperation. "You're under the influence of a highly concentrated mind-altering *drug* controlled by a malignant sentient *fungus* that has *killed* everyone else who tried it! How the hell can you be out there *working* for it?"

"It didn't *intend* to kill them, Naima," said Father Obregón. "It wanted the same thing *they* did. To give the settlers the ultimate mind-expanding experience. To help them get closer to *God*."

"The god of *fungus*," snapped Naima. "The god of *monsters*."

Father Obregón felt sorry for her. He loved her as he loved all his flock, but he knew she would never understand. One taste of the black foam was all he'd needed to connect with his new world-wide congregation. One taste, and he'd been able to move on to important new work after the human settlers had died out.

"Can I talk to you later?" Father Obregón finished clearing the largest lump--a giant truffle, the hub of a complex underground network of them. "I'm a little busy just now."

"You've got to listen to me, Imam!" Naima's thoughts burned with wild urgency. "I think I can reverse the effects of the compound! I'm working on a seratonin inhibitor right now..."

Just then, something buzzed in Father Obregón's head, and he smiled. "Naima? I don't have time to talk about this now." Softly, he ran his fingers over the rough scalp of the giant truffle, which was the source of the new buzzing in his mind.

The truffle was signaling for his attention, reaching out to link him with its network. Dozens of other signals were racked up in the queue behind it, clamoring for attention. There were *always* umpteen signals in the queue these days, ever since the black foam, signals from fungal lifeforms all over Benares. Signals from buried truffles and towering toadstools alike, from giant portabellas to microscopic penicillium, from spinning pizza shell flyers to hulking eight-legged shaggy behemoths the size of elephants.

The switchboard in his head was back in business. Father Obregón would never be lonely again. His second chance with Naima might never come to fruition, but his love for his new congregation had to take first place in his heart. Naima might need him, but *they* needed him more. She might love him, but *they* loved him more.

His beloved flock.

"I have another call coming in, Naima," he said. "I'll have to put you on hold."

"Father, wait!" she said, just before he hung up on her.

Then, smiling, he lifted the hem of his black shirt, peeled back a flap of skin just below his bottom right rib, and drew out the fresh-baked communion host from the cavity there, still warm from his flesh.

And he spread that host, the precious black foam, on the tongue of the giant truffle. "The soul of Benares, given up for you," he said. "Amen."

BEWARE THE BLACK
BATTLENAUT

"Looky there," said Swindle, the *leper*chaun on Grist Halcyon's shoulder. He pointed with a crumbling green finger at one of the Battlenaut's cockpit video screens, and Grist looked in that direction.

On the screen, Grist saw the barren, storm-swept surface of the rebel-held moon, Sangre. The latest flare of lightning revealed a towering black figure on the crest of the hill. At that instant, the very first instant he glimpsed it, Grist knew in his heart what it was even as he knew in his head it just wasn't possible.

The flare of light faded, and the black figure faded with it back into the night. When the next lightning struck a moment later, the hilltop was deserted.

"Begorra." One rotting nostril fell away from Swindle's leprous face. "It's *him*, ain't it, boyo?"

Grist blinked hard and shook his head. "Can't say." Just then, his arm burned as the automated hypodermic cuff strapped to his bicep shot a fresh jolt of go-juice into his system. A ring of lights around the forward viewport flashed in a pattern designed to reset his body's circadian rhythms.

Must've been about to nod off. Can't have that, can we? As the go-juice pumped through his arteries, Grist felt himself return to full alertness. The Battlenaut's sensors and computers had done their job again, intervening at just the right moment with just the right dose of meds to keep Grist awake and alert for yet another hour.

Grist licked his dry lips and checked the video monitor again. Lightning spiked nearby, revealing six soldiers in Battlenaut armor facing off on a rocky battlefield...but no sign of the dark figure from the hilltop.

Grist stabbed the comm button and spoke into his mic. "Hey, Freak. Ever hear of the Black Battlenaut?"

When he didn't get a reply, Grist looked at the button he'd just hit and realized it wasn't the comm at all. He was just about to punch the real comm button when the cockpit rocked from a powerful impact. It was enough to crack his helmeted skull against the headrest and snap him back to the reality from which he'd taken a brief vacation.

Fight. That's right. His hands flew back to the steering and weapons controls. *I'm in a firefight.*

I'm fighting a war here.

Sharon "Freak" Freemare laughed like a maniac as she cut loose her Battlenaut's main guns against the oncoming enemy. One slug hit home in a big way, punching through the enemy's armor and leaving a jagged, smoking hole at the top of one leg.

Still shrieking with laughter, Freak swung a laser around and opened up on the damage. Metal and plastic melted before the onslaught, and the enemy Battlenaut's leg gave way within seconds.

The damaged Battlenaut went down hard, flat on its face. The enemy soldier in its cockpit tried in vain to force the smashed war machine to get up and fight, but it was still lying in the mud when Freak marched her own Battlenaut over to meet it.

"Hey, traitor!" shouted Freak, though she knew the downed pilot couldn't hear her. "Special delivery from the *Redeyes* for ya!"

Freak used her lasers to disable the enemy Battlenaut's weapons systems. The whole time, the smell of baking bread was so strong in the cockpit that it made her stomach growl.

Why she smelled baking bread in the cockpit instead of the usual sweat and stink, she had no idea, but she didn't let it trouble her. Better just to soak it in like the smell of roses that had rushed over her moments earlier, or the incredible smooth feeling of silk that had rippled over her skin moments before that.

Better just to enjoy the ride.

Eyeballing the display on her visor, she located the other members of her squad. Lieutenants Grist and Pellucid formed two points of a triangle enclosing the battlefield, with Freak as the third point. Four enemy Battlenauts were trapped inside the triangle, three still standing plus the one she'd just brought down.

Freak cackled as she swung her Battlenaut toward a fresh target. *These bums are no match for the Redeyes.*

That was what Freak's squad called themselves: *Redeyes*, because they fought without rest. Computers monitored the alertness of this experimental squad and administered countermeasures, chemical and otherwise, to keep them awake and fighting. Such sleep deprivation techniques promised to limit downtime for deployed Commonwealth troops, giving them an edge in the ongoing civil war against the Rightfuls.

From Freak's point of view, the experiment was the biggest success of all time. She and the others had been awake for days on end, so long she'd lost count, and still they suffered no ill effects.

If anything, Freak felt better than ever. She'd never fought more fiercely or thought more clearly in her life.

Who knew insomnia could be so much fun?

Lieutenant Robert "Raw" Pellucid was convinced that the chronometer in the cockpit of his Battlenaut was broken, but he didn't have time to try to fix it.

Even as Raw pounded two enemy Battlenauts with laser fire, he stole another look at the chronometer's readout. He growled like a dog and grimaced at the blinking red numbers.

1805. 1805. 1805.

Seems like it was just 1805 fifteen minutes ago.

Unless the extreme sleep deprivation was affecting his time perception, the chronometer was running ten times slower than reality. What that meant was, the chronometer was definitely running slow, because Raw was running fine, sleep dep and all. He'd been awake for what felt like forever and hadn't needed even a single shot of wake-up juice.

His fellow Redeyes might be running on fumes, but Raw was burning rich. He was just that kind of guy. Even before the program, he'd always kept a lid on, no matter how high the heat.

Nothing but nothing could shake the S.O.B. He was fearless, poisonous, dirty, and smart. Smart enough to wonder if someone was screwing with him.

He went over it again as he raced his Battlenaut, guns blazing, toward his closest opponent. *If the clocks are out, we don't know how long we've been fighting on Sangre. We're on the dark side of this God-forsaken moon, so we can't even count the days by sunrises and sunsets.*

His opponent's Battlenaut stood its ground and sprayed defensive fire that splashed harmlessly off Raw's armor. At the last instant, the enemy leaped out of his path.

But why would someone want us to lose track of time? Why keep us in the field beyond the three-day limit?

Raw growled again, low in his throat. *Because they want to see how far we can go. Because they want to push the redeye tech to the limit.*

Even as he spun the Battlenaut around and threw a missile at the enemy's belly, Raw ran a little mental self-diagnostic to make sure he wasn't being paranoid.

Nope. Don't know the meaning of the word, folks.

He checked the chronometer again.

1805. 1805. 1805.

How long would the researchers leave the Redeyes on Sangre? What had to happen before they pulled the plug?

The answer came to him with a surprising lack of surprise, as if he'd always known it on some level.

The Redeyes had to *die*. Only then would Command pull the plug.

Just as Grist was running his Battlenaut headlong toward a downed rebel, another blast of lightning flared nearby. A burst of static crackled from his comm.

It was followed by music.

The signal was weak, but Grist recognized the music immediately: "Tried and True," an old battle anthem from his homeworld, Tack. At the academy on Ryot, so far from home, he'd sung it to keep up his spirits. He'd sung it during many a night of drinking with fellow cadets who had also come from Tack and missed its jewel-capped mountains and fields of coppery glow-grain.

Cadets like his best friend, Mallet Cray.

Even as the rush of music and memories rocked him, Grist plowed his Battlenaut forward on pure momentum. He slammed it hard against the rebel, which seemed to be undergoing some kind of systems malfunction. As soon as he made contact, Grist wrenched back on the stick, keeping his Battlenaut on its feet while the rebel crashed to the ground.

When Grist had crippled the rebel Battlenaut and disabled its guns, he traced the music signal to a source outside the battle zone. He rotated his Battlenaut's upper body to give him a clear line of sight to the location blinking on his visor display.

Grist saw nothing until another surge of lightning washed over the landscape. In the split-second flare, he spotted exactly what he'd expected to see. What he'd dreaded.

It was at least three times the size of any Battlenaut he'd ever seen. Its gleaming black skin was festooned with weapons but not a single mark of identification. Writhing trails of electrical energy chased over it, as if the lightning had struck it and left a charge.

The Black Battlenaut. And it was playing his song.

Grist's best friend, Mallet Cray, had been singing that same song on the planet Yolanda a year ago, during an earlier battle in the civil war against Rightful forces. He'd always sung it in battle "for protection," and it had worked.

Until the Battle of Enoch on Yolanda, that is.

The song's magic hadn't done him much good when the friendly fire hit...the friendly fire from his best friend *Grist*. Grist's guns had hit a spot already softened up by rebel arms and had blown Cray's power plant. The explosion had caught Cray before he could eject and had not left enough of him behind to fill a shot glass.

All because Grist had lost his head and fired wild during an ambush.

Now, in the midst of another battle, Grist heard the same song his friend had been singing just before his death. Was it a coincidence that it seemed to be coming from the Black Battlenaut?

"It's your turn to die-yi-yi," said the gleaming silver fish wriggling past Grist's visor. "Cray's come b-b-back for the one who killed him-im."

Grist punched the comm button. The music stopped as he switched from "Receive" to "Send." "Freak? Raw? Either of you see the giant black Battlenaut?"

Freak's wild laughter rippled over the comm. "No way, man! Where is it?"

Grist's fingers fluttered over a keypad on the armrest. "I just fired you the coordinates."

"Nothing there," Raw said after a moment. "You have video of this thing?"

Grist spun through recent vid logs from the onboard cameras, cursing as he came up empty. "Missed it," he said, "but I eyeballed it twice. Black armor, heavy ordnance, bigger than our three Battlenauts put together."

Freak stopped laughing. "Whoa! You saw the *Black Battlenaut*!"

"That thought did cross my mind." Grist threw his helmet's optics to maximum magnification and gave the area a hard scan. The only Battlenauts he saw were the four downed rebels and the other two Redeyes.

"Wait a minute," said Raw. "Do you have any telemetry on this thing at all?"

"No." Grist took advantage of a lightning flash to make another scan but still saw nothing.

"Then what if it wasn't there?" said Raw. "What if you're seeing things because of the sleep dep?"

"Not a chance," said the silver fish as it switched past Grist's helmet. Without being told, Grist knew the fish's name was *Lacuna*.

"But what if I'm not seeing things?" said Grist. "You know what the Black Battlenaut means, don't you?"

"The end of the universe!" Freak whooped so loud, the comm filters cut her signal for an instant. "Everyone and everything!"

"It's a legend." Raw's voice was calm. "A bedtime story for children."

"I know I saw something." An orange and black butterfly with the face of a grinning human baby landed on the back of Grist's hand. "Why not look into it?"

"Because we have a job to do," said Raw. "We have to push the Rightfuls off this moon."

Suddenly, the lush green jungle that had sprung up in the cockpit parted over one corner of Grist's forward viewport. In that one open corner, in a fresh burst of lightning, Grist saw the Black Battlenaut walking off in the distance over a rocky plain.

"There it is!" Grist gave one of the vines a tug, and his Battlenaut headed in the direction of the Black Battlenaut. "Hey!" said Raw. "Come back here!"

At that moment, more than anything, Raw wanted to take off his boot and scratch the bottom of his foot. An itch had been growing there for some time, and it was becoming distracting.

Now that Grist had gone charging off, however, with Freak close behind, Raw couldn't stop to scratch the itch. He had to follow the members of his squad and try to keep them from hurtling off the deep end of sleep-deprived insanity.

Up ahead, Grist and Freak raced their Battlenauts across the rock-strewn plain between the wetlands and the foothills of the Prelate Mountains. Raw's instruments and visual inspection both agreed that there was no Black Battlenaut in the distance, that the Redeyes were chasing after nothing.

The itch on the bottom of Raw's foot flared. He ignored it with sheer force of will and punched the comm. "Grist? Freak?" Neither one answered his call.

Raw changed the frequency and called again. "Redeye One to Redeye Base. Over."

Redeye Base ignored him, just like the last dozen times he'd called.

He finished the message anyway. "Request immediate extraction of Redeye Squad. Repeat. Request immediate extraction."

Still, there was no answer.

The only way they'll come for us is when we're dead. All they want's our autopsies and telemetry.

"Redeye One out." Raw punched off the comm and checked the chronometer.

1805. 1805.

He puffed out his breath and shook his head at the obviously incorrect readout. The funny thing was--and it was more funny strange than funny ha-ha--that particular time *meant* something to Raw. It was the exact moment, in fact, five years ago, when he had done the most important thing he'd ever done in his life.

It was the moment when Raw had murdered Braeburn Score.

Freak was halfway across the dry plain when she smelled smoke. She recognized it immediately as the smoke from melting plastic and metal, the smell of a burning Battlenaut. In a panic, she checked the instruments...but her Battlenaut wasn't on fire.

As far as Freak could tell, the burning-Battlenaut smell was coming from the same place as the smells of baking bread and roses that had filled the cockpit earlier...in other words, from thin air.

The burning smell wasn't pleasant like the others had been, though. It turned over a rock and sent things scurrying in her mind.

For example, she thought of the day when Gwen Tuileries had died because of her.

Right after the missile had hit, Gwen's Battlenaut had had that same burning smell. The only difference was, Freak remembered the added smell of frying meat when Gwen had cooked inside the cockpit.

All through Freak's first tour of duty, Gwen had been her guardian angel. She had always been ready to haul Freak's rookie ass out of the fire, even if it meant disobeying orders or bunging up her own Battlenaut. Or losing her life.

One night on Gallop, when their unit was pounding a Rightful garrison, Freak's Battlenaut had been crippled by a land mine. Just as enemy artillery had pumped out a missile to finish her off, Gwen's Battlenaut had leaped in to take the hit and save Freak's life.

Maybe Freak wouldn't have felt so bad about it except for one thing: she'd been working for the other side all along. Even as she'd betrayed the Commonwealth, she'd always planned to save Gwen...and hadn't counted on her own allies being willing to kill her in the bargain.

Freak had worked for the Commonwealth ever since.

As she followed Grist forward, the stench of melting Battlenaut and burning flesh in the cockpit intensified. Finally, it got to the point where it made her gag.

It was then that it occurred to Freak that maybe she'd come across a sign of the Black Battlenaut...and maybe, she had more of a personal interest in the Black Battlenaut than she'd expected.

After all, it couldn't be a coincidence that just as she was searching for the Black Battlenaut, the smell of her dead, betrayed friend rose up to greet her.

Could it?

Grist brushed a blob of pink foam from the controls of the spellcaster and programmed it to grant his Battlenaut added speed and virility. He would need every edge the magic beans could give him when he took on the destructive might of the Black Battlenaut.

Pink foam from the cockpit ceiling splattered over his visor, and he wiped it clean. He was glad the foam wasn't quite smart enough to hurt him, but it was definitely more aggressive than the green swirly-gas that had filled the cockpit a moment ago.

When the hot go-juice spurted into his arm again, everything wavered and turned red...then straightened out and became a more soothing pale blue. The ring of circadian lights flickered around the front viewport, only they weren't *lights* anymore but *darks*.

His co-pilot, Broom Thornapple, who lived in Grist's armpit, nudged him and whistled. "Wow," said Broom. "Nice welcoming committee."

Grist looked in the direction where Broom was poking. Through the viewport, he saw a line of Battlenauts lit up by the beam of his searchlight.

The six Battlenauts stood across the mouth of a pass in the foothills, shoulder to shoulder, blocking the way. Each of them was painted red and festooned with bones and skins.

"Best hope your magic hoops have the power to fry those demons," said Broom. "You know what they say about the Black Battlenaut's minions."

"Monsters. Abominations." Grist licked his lips and swallowed hard.

Just then, the line of Battlenauts began to move. Grist lurched to a stop and brought all magic wands and wish-guns to bear on the line.

All at once, the six Battlenauts raised their right knees, then dropped them. Next, in unison, they kicked their right legs in the air, swinging them to chest level.

And dropped them.

They repeated the moves. This time, they hopped a little as they lifted their knees and kicked their legs.

The ground shook whenever they touched it. Wild music skirled over the comm, its punchy rhythm matching the movements of the Battlenaut chorus line.

Freak swore she could feel the hot breath of the Flesh Battlenaut gusting against her own Battlenaut's back.

She quick-checked her visor display and saw the horrible thing still gaining on her. She was running hard, maxing the specs, and she was still going to lose the race.

Just moments ago, she and Grist had been chasing the monstrous Black Battlenaut. Now, she was the prey of something equally monstrous.

"Freak? Come in, Freak." The voice on the comm sounded like Raw's, but Freak wasn't fooled. She recognized the disguised voice of the thing that was hunting her.

All she saw on the video feed from her rear-facing cameras was Raw's Battlenaut racing after her...but she knew that, too, was an illusion. The thing that was back there, reaching for her, could not be caught on video, though the naked eye could see its true form.

Her naked eye had seen it, and she would never *forget* it.

The thing had started out as a single Battlenaut that had stepped into her path. Freak had jammed her Battlenaut to a stop while Grist had continued running onward without her.

The strange Battlenaut had stood motionless for a moment, its gold armor glinting in the beams of Freak's forward running lights. Then, it had raised one arm from its side. It had turned its hand over and opened it, revealing something pink and wet in its golden palm.

Zooming her optics to maximum mag, Freak had gotten a good look at what was in that hand. Just before the mystery Battlenaut had opened its mouth and dumped in what it was holding, Freak had recognized it.

The mangled, naked body of a human being.

As Freak watched, the Battlenaut had chewed up the human remains. It had chewed them with its mouth open, the lower jaw swinging wide to give her a good look at the gruesome mess.

After a long moment, the gold Battlenaut had finished chewing. It had opened its mouth wide once more, showing that the mashed remains were gone, and then its mouth had closed.

Suddenly, streams of pink flesh had boiled up from the seams and joints and vents in the gold Battlenaut's armor. Rolling and twisting and meshing, the flesh had stretched over the metal like a suit of skin, one throbbing layer weaving over another.

It was then that Freak had turned around and started running.

232

As the squad of Rightful Battlenauts opened fire on Freak, Raw leaped into action. It was either that or let them pound Freak into bits, since she wasn't fighting back.

Based on her recent behavior, Raw thought the odds were good that she didn't even know the enemy was there.

Lasers blazing, Raw charged the nearest rebel and did some damage to its guns. As slugs fired by another Rightful blasted his armor, Raw brought everything he had to bear on the first Battlenaut's midsection...lasers, sonics, missiles. The instant he let it all fly, he swung his Battlenaut hard about and bounded after the other rebel.

As Raw scorched the second rebel Battlenaut with laser fire, he checked his visor display to make sure Freak was okay, which she was: still running, barely staying ahead of the third Rightful Battlenaut. The Rightful was lighting her up with laser fire, but Freak was shrugging it off.

Unlike Raw's Battlenaut, which took a hard shot to the chest from one of his opponent's missiles. Raw's Battlenaut shook and teetered from the explosive impact and started to fall over backward.

Quickly, Raw spun the Battlenaut's upper body around and fired slugs at the ground. The recoil kept the Battlenaut on its feet and ready to continue the fight.

Raw just wished he could deal with the killer itch on the bottom of his foot so easily.

Grist marched in the Battlenaut Day parade, waving at the throngs of Battlenauts of all shapes and sizes cheering from the stands. The whole time, he searched his surroundings for the Black Battlenaut, who had run off in this direction after Grist's last sighting.

The six dancing Battlenauts at the mouth of the pass, it had turned out, had all been parts of the Black Battlenaut. Right after their big dance number, they had crashed together, cranking and twisting and snapping into one giant Battlenaut with black armor and weapons galore. Then, instead of attacking, the Black Battlenaut had raced off, leaving Grist to try in vain to keep up.

"He's out there somewhere," said High Five, who looked like an oil spill with a mouthful of yellow tongues. His voice sounded like continuous belching. He floated in midair and was Grist's new best friend. "I can feel it, buddy-Joe."

High Five was never wrong, except about women. "I hear ya," said Grist, carefully scanning the crowd. He thought he saw the top of the Black Battlenaut's head peaking out from behind the stands, but the image faded when the hypo cuff poured more go-juice into his arm.

A droning electronic anthem played from speakers along the parade route, and all the spectators hummed along with it. Vendors sold candy-coated humans stuck on sticks, which Battlenaut children licked and crunched.

"You seen one Battlenaut Day, you've seen 'em all, right?" said High Five.

Grist laughed. "You can say that again."

A second later, Grist noticed in an absent-minded way that the cockpit was full of fizzy water, and High Five had been replaced by a word, "GOOD," in bold black letters a foot high.

"What do you say, Word?" Grist slapped in annoyance at his hypo cuff, which had just shot him with more hot go-juice.

Word reshaped itself from "GOOD" to "LOOK," pointing at one of the video screens with the tail of the "K."

Without thinking, Grist looked at the screen Word had indicated. The words "BLACK BATTLENAUT" filled the screen from top to bottom and edge to edge, rapidly flashing bright and dim.

Grist tried for a better view through the forward viewport, and he got it. Just like on the screen, the words "BLACK BATTLENAUT" floated up ahead, blinking on and off.

Grist's heart beat faster. "Is that him?" He pointed at the words "BLACK BATTLENAUT" through the viewport.

Word swirled around and reformed itself from "LOOK" to "CRAY."

And it was at that moment that the comm kicked on again.

The anthem "Tried and True" blared from the speaker. A few bars in, a human voice spoke up over the music. A man's voice.

A familiar voice.

"Hi there, Killer. Time to settle the score."

"*Cray?*" said Grist.

"Hello, Sharon," said the woman's voice over Freak's comm. "Been a while."

Freak kept driving her Battlenaut hard and didn't answer. *That's Gwen Tuileries. Gwen Tuileries is dead.*

The smell of burning Battlenaut and human flesh was so strong in the cockpit, Freak gagged. The hypo cuff was hitting her with go-juice what seemed like every ten seconds. Her head was spinning, her stomach lurching.

And her dead best friend was calling on the comm.

"You're headed straight for me," Gwen said over the comm. "Just a little further, Sharon."

Hearing that, Freak slammed on the brakes. A second later, as her Battlenaut stumbled to a halt, she remembered the Flesh Battlenaut that had been chasing her.

Freak whipped around, expecting the Flesh Battlenaut to pounce on her...but the pounce didn't happen. In fact, she could see no trace of the Flesh Battlenaut in her searchlights.

She did, however, see a towering black figure.

Gwen laughed lightly over the comm. "Oops. I misspoke. Actually, I'm *right here*, Sharon."

Raw had his hands full keeping the attacking Rightfuls at bay, when suddenly his Battlenaut was hit from behind by laser fire.

A glance at his visor display revealed a familiar transponder signal back there, and the feed from the rearward camera confirmed it. Even as Raw fought the rebel Battlenauts who were chasing Freak, Freak had turned around and was shooting at Raw.

So now it was three against one. Not that he was the kind of guy who sweated the odds.

First things first. Set your priorities.

As lasers and slugs hammered his Battlenaut, Raw stormed the closest Rightful. In spite of the heavy fire, Raw drove his Battlenaut up close and shoved the barrel of a laser cannon into a breach in the enemy's armor.

After pumping in a few blasts, Raw darted away. The rebel exploded, throwing out a shock wave that sent his partner reeling.

Even as Raw struggled to keep his Battlenaut on its feet, he growled with delight. *One down, two to go.*

That was before Grist charged up and opened fire on him, too.

"Kill me once, shame on you," Cray said over the comm in Grist's cockpit. "Kill me twice...well, you can't kill the *Black Battlenaut,* can you?"

Grist tried to block out the voice as he fought to keep up with the Black Battlenaut. The behemoth had grown to colossal size; its walking strides were so vast, Grist had to run at top speed just to stay in weapons range.

He fired his lasers again and watched them skim harmlessly off the Black Battlenaut's ebon armor. The hypo cuff squeezed tight, flooding his arm with blazing go-juice.

That was when the Black Battlenaut stopped and turned. Each footfall made the earth tremble.

Grist cut loose with his Battlenaut's lasers and sonics, but he might as well have been firing feathers. The Black Battlenaut stood unfazed and stared down at him.

"Let me explain," said Cray.

At first, Grist didn't realize Cray's voice wasn't coming from the comm anymore. It took a minute for the truth to sink in.

"We should've done this a long time ago," said Cray, who now was leaning against the cockpit wall, aiming a lopsided grin at the man who had shot him to death.

Raw wasn't sure which bothered him more: fighting off three Battlenauts, two of them piloted by his squadmates, or not being able to scratch his itchy foot.

When Grist suddenly stopped shooting at him, cutting the weapons barrage by a third, Raw's itch moved up to first place. Gritting his teeth, he barely resisted the urge to stop fighting, kick off his boot, and scratch like crazy. In the process, he dropped his guard for an instant and took a laser hit that charred the armor plating on his Battlenaut's left shoulder.

Cursing as a stream of wild shots flared around him, Raw swung around. He charged toward the source of the fire, targeting his own arsenal on what had become the most volatile threat of the moment.

Freak continued to pound him with lasers and missiles as he hurtled toward her.

Freak unleashed the full fury of her weapons, but the Black Battlenaut kept stomping toward her.

Gwen's voice chimed over the comm with no more tension than if the two of them were chatting over coffee. "What do you think I'm going to do to you, Sharon? Burn you alive?"

Freak's heart hammered. *That's exactly what you'll do. Make me die the same way you did.*

"Well, it isn't gonna happen," said Gwen. "Why would I try to kill someone whose life I died to save? Besides which..."

Suddenly, everything changed. Freak was in the cockpit of her old Battlenaut instead of the current one. Looking out the forward viewport, she immediately recognized the steam vents and weird geologic formations of another world.

Laser fire pulsed past her from the fortified walls of a Rightful garrison. Commander Endymion snapped out orders over the comm in the cockpit.

She was back on Gallop, during the battle in which Gwen had been killed.

"Besides which," Gwen said over the comm, "I don't blame you for what happened."

As soon as Freak's weapons shut down and dropped, Raw doubled back and charged the Rightful behind him.

That was when something unexpected happened. A missile hissed out of his Battlenaut's rack and shot straight toward the enemy. Raw watched as the missile hit the rebel Battlenaut's midsection dead center and detonated, blowing a hole in the heavy armor.

There was just one problem. Raw didn't remember firing the missile.

Suddenly, Raw's Battlenaut lunged forward. Lasers ablaze, the Battlenaut raced at top speed for the Rightful.

As Raw watched through the viewport, his Battlenaut lit up the hole in the enemy's belly, setting off an explosion in its guts. The Rightful danced like a man touching a high voltage power line, then slammed to the ground in a pile of smoking scrap.

Raw quick-checked every status display in the cockpit, scrambling to ferret out the problem. Never in his career had a Battlenaut taken independent action like that.

He only stopped hunting the glitch when he heard a tapping sound in the direction of the forward viewport. He looked toward the noise, and his eyes widened with surprise.

His Battlenaut was pointing one of its own lasers into the cockpit.

The hypo cuff squeezed Raw's bicep and pumped him full of liquid fire. A voice echoed in his head, and he recognized it immediately.

It was the voice of a young man, barely out of his teens. "I'm back. Did you miss me?"

It was the voice of Braeburn Score.

"If you say you're sorry one more time, I'm gonna pop you one," Cray said with a smirk.

"Okay. Sor..." Grist barely caught himself. He was still in a daze, struggling to deal with the fact that a man he'd killed was apparently sitting in the cockpit with him.

"Your apologies are meaningless," said Cray. "What's done is done. Get over it."

"I can't." Grist pulled off his helmet and set it aside. "Not a day goes by that I don't think about it."

"Big baby." Cray snorted and shook his head. "It was *war*, man. *Chaos*. It was *nobody's* fault."

"I panicked." Grist's hands were shaking.

Cray leaned forward. "Okay, look." He rested his elbows on his knees and folded his hands between them. "You're really pissing me off here. All this 'poor me' crap." Cray rolled his eyes. "The not sleeping and the volunteering for suicide duty. How do you think that makes me feel?"

Grist shrugged.

"Makes me feel like kicking your ass," said Cray. "How about getting your shit together, so I can at least feel like my death *meant* something. Like you learned from your mistake and went on to *accomplish* something."

Grist rubbed his chin. "I'll try."

"Just *do* it."

"What about the universe?" said Grist. "Are you going to destroy it?"

"Ask the chicken-fish." Cray hiked a thumb toward one side of the cockpit.

A long, green fish with the head of a chicken bobbed in a bubble of pink water floating in midair. "Redeye Base to Redeye Squad," it said. "Come in Redeye Squad."

Once upon a time, a filthy young beggar decided to ply his trade outside the military academy in Soldier City on Archibald.

(As the hypo cuff pumped go-juice into his arm again and again, Raw listened to the voice in his head tell the story.)

Not surprisingly, the privileged and arrogant young men who passed through the academy's doors proved to be terrible pickings. They spat in his beggar's bowl and ridiculed him. Sometimes, they struck him on their way past.

But one young man was different from the others. Whenever he passed the beggar, this young man always greeted him and put coins in his bowl. Eventually, he even brought the beggar food and clothing.

The beggar was suspicious, as the young man's kindness was so unlike any of the other privileged military students. The young man, however, assured him that his motives were honorable.

Over time, the two became friends. They were of about the same age, in fact. Each week, the military student took the beggar to a local restaurant for lunch. The student even suggested that there might be a place for the beggar on the estate of his father, a baron.

The student was truly good luck for the beggar...especially after the beggar murdered him.

The beggar did it in a matter-of-fact way, with a strong cord around the throat. He slipped away with enough money to start a new life in another town as another man.

And he never looked back. He never regretted killing Braeburn Score in cold blood. It had simply been a thing that had to be done, a matter of survival.

His name was Flynn Jarvo.

He changed that name to Robert Pellucid. Nickname "Raw."

"You don't know the whole story," said Freak. She had adjusted remarkably well to being thrown back in time and was pumping round after round from her old Battlenaut's guns into the enemy garrison. "That's why you don't blame me."

Gwen sighed over the comm. "Go ahead. Do it."

"Do what?" said Freak.

"This is when you send the signal," said Gwen. "The go-ahead for the rebel ambush."

A chill rippled through Freak's body. "What?"

"You were working for the rebels," said Gwen. "You tipped them off."

"You *knew*?"

"I do now. The Black Battlenaut knows all." Gwen laughed. "I also know you've been beating yourself up about it ever since."

Freak clenched her hands around the joysticks and drove her Battlenaut hard. "You weren't supposed to die."

"Did I or did I not save your life?" said Gwen.

"You did," Freak said through clenched teeth.

"Then I've got no complaints. I'd do the same thing all over again."

Freak pushed the Battlenaut through the forest of close-set, mushroom-like mineral plugs. Geysers erupted right and left, spraying jets of hot steam that misted the viewports and cameras.

The tear that rolled down Freak's cheek felt as hot as the steam outside. "I've missed you so much," she said. "There are so many things I've wanted to say to you."

"I've got something to say to you, too," said Gwen.

Freak continued to manhandle the controls. "What's that?"

"Redeye Base to Redeye Squad," said Gwen. "Come in, Redeye Squad."

"You've never really paid for what you did to me," said the voice in Raw's head, the voice of Braeburn Score. "You feel no guilt whatsoever."

Raw watched the laser cannon outside the forward viewport, the weapon that his own Battlenaut was pointing at itself. "It was nothing personal."

"How do you figure?" said Braeburn. "I reached out to you as a friend, and you *murdered* me. How is that not *personal*?"

The hypo cuff squeezed tight around Raw's arm, shooting in more go-juice. "You would've done the same to me if you were in my shoes."

"You know that's not true," said Braeburn.

"I saw my chance and I took it," said Raw, his upper lip curling in a growl.

"So you think it was *fair*, what you did? You don't feel any remorse for *killing* a man in cold blood so you could *steal* from him?"

"It was *war*!" said Raw. "It was no different from *war*!"

"I have a message for you from the other side," said Braeburn. "You will suffer for all eternity for what you did to me. And that's not all."

"Get out of my head!" said Raw. "I don't want to hear any more!"

"Redeye Base to Redeye Squad. Come in Redeye Squad."

It took an instant for Raw to realize that the male voice he was listening to was no longer Braeburn's. The new voice was coming from the comm.

"Redeye Base to Redeye Squad."

Raw punched the comm button. "Redeye One here."

The voice on the comm sounded urgent. "What is your status, Redeye One?"

"Request immediate extraction. Repeat. Request immediate extraction."

"Negative," said Redeye Base. "You have new orders."

"No can do," said Raw. "We're falling apart out here."

"Enemy squad is converging on your position." Redeye Base sounded even more urgent. "We're transmitting telemetry now. Prepare to engage."

"Redeye Two and Three are off comms," said Raw.

"Negative," said Redeye Base. "Comms have been restored."

"Redeye Two here," Grist said over the comm.

"Redeye Three responding," said Freak.

"Redeye One is...out of control," said Raw. "I strongly recommend immediate extraction."

There was a pause before Redeye Base spoke again. "Prepare to engage. Repeat, prepare to engage."

The cuff squeezed Raw's arm again. He knew there would be no extraction.

The only way they'll come for us is when we're dead. That was what he'd thought earlier. *All they want's our autopsies and telemetry.*

Only one way out of this, and he'd known it deep down from the beginning.

"Redeye Squad! Form up!" Raw's hands flew over the controls. The Battlenaut responded smoothly, with no hint of rogue action.

At his command, the laser cannon that had been aiming at the cockpit window pointed away from it again.

"Arm weapons!" Raw said over the comm. "Lock and load!"

"Roger that," said Grist, playing the controls with new purpose and alertness. The need for battle readiness had snapped him back to reality.

It didn't hurt that he finally felt at peace with his role in Cray's death. It was a burden he'd been carrying around for years, a burden that had slowly been crushing him.

At last, he felt free of it. So what if his forgiveness had been granted by an hallucination?

Why not use a little insanity to inoculate himself against a greater madness?

"Armed and ready, Lieutenant," Freak said over the comm. "Fit to fight, sir," she added, and she meant it.

She hadn't slept for what must have been days, but she felt fitter than she had in years. She felt like a new woman since her encounter with Gwen.

Freak only wished the visit could have been longer. There was still one thing she'd left unsaid, one thing she'd wanted to say more than anything else.

She switched off her comm just long enough to say it. Gwen was gone, but Freak said it anyway.

"I love you, Gwen. I'll never love anyone the way I love you."

"Here they come," Redeye Base said over the comm. "They're coming right over the ridge."

"Stand by, Redeye Squad," said Raw. He kept his weapons aimed in the direction of the enemy, ready to unleash the Battlenaut's full fury at any moment.

When he checked his visor display, however, his resolve faltered. The telemetry he saw there wasn't at all what he'd expected.

Not for ten seconds anyway.

After ten seconds, the telemetry data completely changed, lining up with Raw's expectations--namely, that a squad of enemy Battlenauts was marching over the ridge.

A squad of enemy Battlenauts instead of a convoy of civilian vehicles.

"Redeye One to Redeye Base." Raw peered out the forward viewport for visual confirmation. Lights glided over the ridge and beamed back at him, the glare washing out his view of whatever was coming. "You sure about that telemetry?"

"One hundred percent," said Redeye Base.

"But first read on the visor was that those are civilian transports, not Battlenauts," said Raw.

"That was a hiccup in the network," said Redeye Base. "Current telemetry is confirmed."

As Raw watched the viewport, the oncoming lights drew closer, and the shapes behind them began to resolve themselves.

There wasn't a single Battlenaut among them.

"Abort!" Raw's hands flew over the controls as he powered down his weapons. "Redeye Squad, abort! Those are civilian transports! Repeat, abort!"

"Really?" Freak said over the comm. "Telemetry says they're hostile Battlenauts."

"Telemetry's wrong," said Raw. "I have visual confirmation."

"Negative, Redeye One," said Redeye Base. "Visual is unreliable. You're hallucinating."

Cold sweat trickled down Raw's back. The itch on the sole of his foot flared up again. "No hallucination! These are civilian transports!"

"Fire when ready," said Redeye Base. "The order is given."

"Abort!" said Raw.

"Redeye Two and Three," said Redeye Base. "Prepare to receive new orders on a secure channel."

"I heard what you said about loving me," Gwen said over the comm in Freak's cockpit. "I want you to know that the feeling was always mutual."

Freak's heart pounded. Tears ran down her face. "G-Gwen?"

"I love you and I want to help you," said Gwen. "I'm going to help you do the right thing."

"What's that?" said Freak.

"Listen," said Gwen, and then she told her what to do.

"I've got some good advice for you," Cray said over the comm. "Consider it a thank-you gift."

Grist wasn't as startled to hear the dead man's voice as the first time Cray had spoken to him. "What's the advice?"

"I'll let the chicken-fish tell you," said Cray.

It was then, in the seconds after he realized what was about to happen and the seconds before it happened, that Raw fully understood.

They're interested in more than our physical limits.

It didn't take a genius to figure out what Redeye Base was telling Grist and Freak on the secure channel. It wasn't hard to predict what was going to happen next.

Redeye Base had ordered the squad to fire on the civilian convoy. Raw, the squad leader, had failed to comply. So Redeye Base was moving down the chain of command to try to get the job done.

They wanted to see if Grist and Freak were so bombed from sleep dep and go-juice that they'd do what Raw wouldn't.

They want to know how far we can be pushed in every way.

It wasn't enough to create Battlenaut jockeys who could fight without rest. They wanted Battlenaut jockeys who doubted the evidence of their own senses.

Battlenaut jockeys who could be completely controlled.

"I don't know if I can do that," Grist said after the chicken-fish told him Cray's advice. "Raw said those are civilian transports."

"Raw's a cuckoo, boyo," said Swindle the leperchaun, twirling a green index finger alongside his rotting temple. "Who'd ya rather trust? A nut who's gone without sleep fer who knows how long, or cool-headed authority figures with all that tech at their disposal?"

Grist pinched his eyes shut to try to stop his head from spinning. "They look an awful lot like civilians to me."

"Remember," said Cray's voice over the comm. "The Black Battlenaut wears many faces."

Grist opened his eyes and stared at the forward viewport. What he saw there looked like a cluster of six-wheeled transports, the kind regularly used to carry miners between worksites on Sangre.

Was it possible that what he saw had nothing to do with what was really out there? That his senses were deceiving him?

As the orange and black butterfly with the head of a human baby fluttered past him, Grist knew he had his answer.

"But I don't want to kill him, Gwen," said Freak. "Lieutenant Raw hasn't done anything wrong."

"Oh, honey." Gwen's voice over the comm sounded loving and sad. "Redeye Base had a good reason for giving that order."

The cuff squeezed in another burst of fiery go-juice. "What reason?"

"I'm alive again, sweetie," said Gwen. "That's right. They grew a clone of me, and we're going to be together...but the lieutenant wants to keep us apart."

Freak felt like she was floating and sinking at the same time. The fog in her head was getting thicker and stickier. "He does?"

"Please, darling," said Gwen. "Please save me this time."

Raw was never sure exactly when he became the Black Battlenaut. Was it before he died? Or after?

He remembered Grist and Freak opening fire on him with everything they had. He remembered thinking

This is the only way it can end and I knew it from the beginning.

That was why

(He remembered the giant golden eyes gazing down from above, gazing down upon him like the golden eyes of God.)

That was why he made no move to defend himself. Maybe, his sacrifice would be enough to satisfy the scientists. Maybe, having learned the limits of one man, they would spare Grist and Freak.

But he doubted it.

Even if they let those two live, the civilians were doomed, of that he was certain.

(A dark shape huge as a mountain, blocking out the stars, black metal body glinting in the glow of those giant golden eyes.)

The scientists had to know if Redeyes would gun down innocent civilians on a whim from Command, in defiance of the evidence of their own senses and the dictates of their own consciences.

(Was this what Grist and Freak had seen, this gleaming behemoth, this legendary destroyer?)

There would be innocent blood on Grist and Freak's hands. At least Raw himself wouldn't add to it when they finished killing him. His blood was far from innocent.

(He had never expected it to be so beautiful.)

(So terrible.)

The cockpit filled with the sounds of damage...the pockety-pock of slug impacts, the boom-whoom-thoom of missiles exploding one after another, the crackle and screech of metal gashed by lasers. The hiss of air escaping the broken Battlenaut, the whoops and pings and whistles of weapons alerts and systems failure alarms.

(Most beautiful thing he'd ever)

The ear-splitting whine that signalled a breach in the fusion reactor.

(Beautiful and powerful. Reaching down with a hand as big as a building)

Déjà vu.

(Splitting open the shell, the chrysalis, extracting him)

I know you.

(When the halves of the broken Battlenaut fell to the ground, they exploded in a wave of glittering golden butterflies.)

(He watched from above as Grist and Freak bombarded the civilians in a shower of fire and light.)

Or was he already there by then, inhabiting the leviathan? Or had he always been a part of it?

I am you.

The moon trembled as he turned his eyes from the flurry of smoke and flame and dirt at his feet.

Not tired anymore.

He tipped his head back, each eye the size of a cathedral, and looked up and out at the same flickering membrane of stars that lay reflected on the polished ebon plate of his face.

Good night.

SYMPATHY FOR THE METAL

am *singing* for all I'm worth as my harpoon grappler lands *POW* in the heart of the speeding slab of silvery metal, sending thrilling shocks all the way through my body and the ship in which I stand.

"And I grab that slab from space and make it mi-ine!" The song is one of *hundreds* I've made up through my many long decades of life as a salvager, telling the tales of my glorious struggles among the stars. I've been singing them as long as I can remember, letting loose with my deep bass voice even though there's no one else to hear it in the cockpit, retrieval bay, smelter, storerooms, or launch bay of this vast ship.

But it would be an outright *lie* to say these songs are the sweetest sounds I ever hear. *Nothing* can compare to the sounds of metal, precious *metal*, as I seize and bend it to my will.

Metal metal metal. Nothing in the universe makes my heart jump for joy like *metal*. It is what I *live* for, what I was *made* for—what I *dream* of.

As I hoist the black carbon-fiber cable attached to my harpoon, reeling in the silvery slab I've caught, the muscles bulge in my arms and back, straining at my filthy gray coveralls. I grin through the sweat and grime all over my face, which is as dark as wrought iron. This one's a beauty, all right, another piece of hull from another shattered ship in the vast sphere of orbiting junk called the Shardswarm.

Where the fragment came from originally or how it got here, I can't say. The same goes for all the other wreckage spinning around the unseen planet at the heart of the Shardswarm. No two pieces are the same in composition or design; no two *ships* are the same here, either.

Was it the site of some kind of war? A fatal last stand? A wicked double-cross? Or was this just a giant drydock, a resting place for vessels that were damaged or past their prime? If so, why are no two *alike?*

I don't think I'll *ever* know, but that doesn't make the piece of hull any less beautiful to me. The silvery surface flows with a rainbow of colors—bands of miraculous neurocircuitry imprinted in the skin of the ship when it was built.

All *fifty thousand* years ago, give or take *five thousand.*

"*Hand over hand, I bring you to my open arms, your new life just begu-un.*" My heavy-gloved hands keep hauling the black cable in from space, tugging it through the selective force field that keeps pressure and air in the bay. A little at a time, the metal slab slides through the field, crackling as it crosses the threshold. Though it is *at least* the millionth piece I've brought aboard in my life, it feels *just* as exciting to me as the *first.*

Or my name isn't *Tensile,* and my ship isn't the *Lady Alloy.*

"Beautiful, beautiful." As soon as the slab fully clears the field and comes to rest, I let go of the cable and pull the low-grav clamps from the pockets of my coveralls. Stomping over, I slap the clamps on either side of the slab, which is five meters longs and four meters high—over two heads taller than I am. Then, I yank out the harpoon grappler and toss it aside, letting it clatter on the deck plates behind me.

Pulling off one bulky glove, I run my fingers over the slab's smooth surface. The bulk of the piece is intact, aside from the harpoon hole and some damage along the edges. It makes sense, as being disconnected and off by itself is not this slab's natural state.

But as I stare at the jagged edges, I realize something else does *not* make sense. The scorched and broken metal still glows faintly red. When I move my hand close, I feel it shedding heat, as if the damage was only recently inflicted.

Which is impossible. The Shardswarm's orbitals are *ancient.* Except for myself and my ship, I've never come across anything newer than *fifty thousand years old* out here.

I'm about to reach for the molecular analyzer on my belt when *Alloy's* alert klaxon whoops through the bay. A mechanical voice blares over the whoops, the only voice I've ever heard in my life except for my own.

"Distress signal received. Distress signal received." As *Thot,* the ship's brain speaks—her voice more businesslike and commanding than usual—the harpoon grappler slides over the deck and punches through the field without my help. *"Life sign detected, Metalhead Tensile. Retrieving survivor."*

"What the blark?" Nothing like *any* of this has ever happened to me before. I've been out here as long as I can remember, grown and raised by Thot, whom I've only ever known as a disembodied voice. The closest I've come to encountering any non-mechanical life other than my own are the dead bodies aboard the wrecked remnants of all those ships out there.

"Assistance protocol initiated," says Thot. *"Rendering assistance. Retrieving survivor."*

The carbon fiber cable continues to snake across the deck and into space. The harpoon leaps by remote control into the wall of debris spinning past, disappearing between the glinting hulks and shrapnel like a needle in a junk-storm.

Then the cable goes suddenly taut, and I catch my breath. Something unfamiliar jabs at my mind.

Fear. What if the lifeform turns out to be dangerous and wreaks havoc when it's brought aboard the ship? "Thot! Override assistance protocol!"

"Negative, Tensile. Assistance protocol cannot be overridden."

I clench my fists as the cable reels back into the bay. Watching through the open gate, I glimpse a gleaming silver sphere gliding smoothly toward the *Alloy*, its skin pierced by the tip of the harpoon.

Realizing I can't fight it, I glove up and march over to help with the hauling. I drive the fear further away with each great tug of the line, committing to whatever happens next.

And *singing*, which always makes me strong. *"Life sign...coming closer...life sign...almost here."*

A few more tugs and the silver sphere rolls crackling through the field, its perfect metal skin enough to make my heart skip multiple beats.

I step toward it, reaching for my analyzer, and wonder what kind of life form I'll find inside. More than that, how did it get all the way out *here*, in the middle of nowhere?

"Signaling occupant to exit pod," says Thot. *"Please stand clear, Tensile. Please stand clear."*

I take two steps back and wait as the pod emits a rapid-fire series of beeps and clicks. I want to *touch* its perfect silver skin, and I start to reach—only to jerk back at the last second as the skin quivers and melts away.

In an instant, the sphere is reduced to a silver puddle on the deck, leaving a human male with bright red hair lying, curled up, in the middle of it. His white jumpsuit uniform with the purple piping is streaked red with blood.

He isn't moving.

"Metalhead Tensile," says Thot. *"The survivor is badly damaged. Transport him immediately to the medzone."*

I frown. "But my shift isn't over." I point at the open gate and the spaceborne wreckage beyond. "I've still got *metal* to hump."

"Time enough for that later." Thot can be pretty stern when she wants to. *"If you do not get that man to the medzone fast, he will not be a survivor for much longer."*

"One more piece, all right?" I see a diamond-shaped hunk of

gold plating spin toward the bay, and I salivate. I've got to *have* it. "Just one more, and I *promise* I'll take him to the medzone."

"Tensile!" snaps Thot. *"Aren't you curious about who he is and where he comes from?"*

I shrug and steal another look at the gold plating.

"Well, you will never know if you wait another few minutes," says Thot. *"The survivor's death is imminent."*

Sighing loudly, I stomp over to the limp body on the deck. Reaching down, I scoop him up with both gloved hands, resigned to doing what Thot tells me to do. She *is* the boss, I suppose. She represents Möbius Inc., the legendary human-owned corporation that funded this operation in the first place.

Still, I can't resist one last glance at the gold plating. I just hope I can find and catch it when I get back.

I *do* find the gold plating—but thanks to Thot, I don't manage to grab it.

It's been hours since I took the survivor to the medzone, and I'm back at work. As I scan the passing debris, I finally spot the plating, and it's not far away.

Before I can harpoon it, though, Thot orders me back to the medzone. I try to make her wait, but she won't take no for an answer. I have to go *now*, she says. Something about the survivor being awake and able to communicate, which I guess I'm supposed to care about.

Sure enough, when the medzone door swings open, I see the redheaded survivor staring back at me, lying in the healing bed with his left arm in a cast and IVs and wires attached to his upper body. Blinking monitors mounted around the head of the bed transmit medical data to the onboard auto-doctor A.I., which adjusts medications and therapeutic processes in precisely-calculated increments.

As I approach, the survivor opens his mouth and speaks. His voice is strained, but at least he uses the same language I do. "Where are...the *others*?"

I stop at the foot of his bed, frowning. "What others?"

"The rest of...the Metallurgists." The survivor coughs weakly. "Where *are* they?"

My ears perk up at the sound of a word like "metal." Again, I think of that diamond-shaped hunk of gold plating skimming along the fringes of the Shardswarm, tantalizingly just out of reach.

"Don't you...understand me?" asks the survivor. "Am I speaking...the wrong language...or something?"

"Metalgists?" We might as *well* be speaking different languages, for all I've understood so far.

"*The* Metallurgists." The survivor coughs. "*You* know. The answer to one of...the greatest *mysteries*...in the *galaxy*."

I shake my head, already bored. Like a magnet, the wreckage spinning away outside the ship draws me to return to it.

"I have to get back to work." Turning, I head for the door. "Busy day."

"Wait." The survivor raises his voice. "What about *the metal?*"

I pause in my tracks. "*What* metal?"

"*You* know." He coughs. "*The* metal. Enormous *blocks* of it...sailing from deep space...into the inhabited systems of humanity. Arriving for *decades* without explanation."

Slowly, I turn to face him. For the first time, I am more interested in this person than the Shardswarm debris field.

"Humanity has put it to great use," continues the survivor. "Entire *cities* have been built from it.

"But *no one* has ever discovered...the *source* of it...or the *origin* of the fabled *Metallurgists*...who *process* and *ship* it. The only proof of their identity...is the mark of a *Möbius strip*...stamped into the metal. A *figure eight* on its side...with no beginning or end.

"Men have *died* trying to solve the mystery of the Metallurgists. Now perhaps, so will I." He slumps into his pillow and closes his eyes, letting out a long sigh. "And one other may die, as well."

The urge to know more burns within me, nearly as strong as my urge to work metal. "One other?"

"My name is Mezzo," he tells me. "My partner...who already might have lost her life to this quest...is called *Silver*."

I like that her name is a metal. "Lost her life?"

Mezzo opens his eyes and nods slowly. "We were attacked...by the automated defenses...of an ancient ship in the wreckage. I escaped in a lifepod...but Silver went down with our vessel. *All the way* down."

I stare at him in disbelief. "Through the *Shardswarm?* That's *impossible.*"

"But she did it." With his right hand, Mezzo holds up a tiny gold chip that glints in the light of the medzone. "And the proof is on here. Feed it to your computer, and you'll see."

"All that *junk,* spinning in orbit. *No one* can get through it in one piece."

"I'll bet *you* can, being a Metallurgist and all," says Mezzo.

"I don't even know what a *Metalgist* is."

"You might not go by the name...but I'm betting you're *it*. It's the only...explanation. And you..." His eyes flicker shut, and his head falls to one side on the pillow. "You're her only...*hope.*"

I snag the chip from his hand as he drifts off to sleep. Normally, I don't bother with such tiny bits of metal—but this time, I make an exception.

"Thot?" I say on my way out the door of the medzone. "I'm bringing you something to analyze."

Later, I'm back at work in the retrieval bay, feeling good to be bringing in wreckage again. I don't see the gold plating this time, but I spot plenty of other goodies that keep my blood pumping. *This* is what life is all about for me and always has been.

Metal is all that matters to me. It shines, it tingles, it bends, it clangs. It has *weight*.

I *understand* it.

But I still can't stop thinking about what I saw just moments ago on Mezzo's chip: the video of Silver's distress call, played back on a big screen by Thot.

The image of Silver's face keeps coming back to me. There was blood, and there were bruises, but her beautiful blue eyes never stopped shining, and her wavy hair kept gleaming like spun platinum.

Her voice was high-pitched and shivery like the piping of a flute or the tinkling of a bell. Her movements as she spoke were graceful and smooth, her body slender and athletic in her white jumpsuit with the pale blue piping.

Though the message she delivered was anything but sweet and comforting.

"Crash-landed on the surface...of the planet," she said. *"Surrounded by hostile lifeforms. Not sure how long I can last."*

Remembering her words, my heart beats faster. I work harder than ever, pulling cables to haul in wreckage as if my life depends on it.

Since when has anything but *metal* had this effect on me? What do *I* care about some doomed stranger trapped on the planet below?

I've never cared about *anyone,* so why should I start now?

Still, her words continue to replay in my head without fading. *"I don't think I could fly through the orbital debris...even if my ship was operative."* Her voice broke on the next words she spoke. *"There is no way out, and most of my supplies are ruined. Mezzo, if you can't find a way to save me soon, it's only a matter of time until it's all over."*

Hand over hand, I tow an intact engine cowling through the force field gate into the bay. It turns massively heavy when the *Lady Alloy's* artificial gravity takes hold of it, and I grunt as I struggle to budge it. Sweat rolls down my back as my muscles bulge and strain to the point of bursting.

But no amount of hard labor will burn the memory of Silver's desperation from my brain. Not even a *song*, one of my favorites, will do that.

"Come to me, come to me...from your spinning cemetery." I sing the words as I attach the low-grav clamps to the cowling and lead it across the bay, then load it on the flatbed transport. *"I will melt you into something new...and send you on your way."*

Hard work and metal are always the answer to every problem. I know that. It is why I almost never feel anything other than happiness. It is why I never long for anything other than what I have.

But what if there is *something else* to feel and long for? Something I never wanted because I never knew it existed.

"Mö-bi-us, Mö-bi-us...all these gifts to you will soar. Strength and greatness, they will bring...as you grow..."

My voice cracks as the song makes me think of something other than Silver. A question that has been gnawing at me breaks through to the front of my mind.

What happened to Möbius, Inc.?

If it still existed, the metal I've been sending, stamped with the company's symbol, would not have been a mystery to the rest of the galaxy. Yet Mezzo knows nothing about it. How is it even *possible* that such a giant organization could just *disappear*?

And if it has, what have I been living for all this time? What has it all meant? What have I been missing out on?

As if in answer, Silver's face appears clearly in my mind's eye. My heart beats faster, and I feel the urge to sing.

Since I don't have a song for her just yet, I finish the one about Möbius instead. "Strength and greatness, they will bring...as you grow...forevermore."

But then I frown and bite my lip. Somehow, singing about Möbius just doesn't feel the same to me anymore.

"Please tell me...you're going to help us." Mezzo is sitting up in bed when I walk back into the medzone after my shift—not that he looks much better than before. "Tell me...you'll help me *save* her."

"I don't think I can." I stop alongside him, folding my big arms over my chest. "The planet inside the Shardswarm is cut off by all the orbiting debris."

"But there *must* be a way." Mezzo snaps forward, then grimaces in pain and drops back again. "We can't just leave her *down* there to *die.*"

"*I've* never even been to the surface," I tell him. "And I've lived here all my *life.*"

"What about a small...highly maneuverable craft?" Mezzo grits his teeth against another bolt of pain, then shakes it off. "Surely you've picked up...*something* out here...that could make the trip."

"Even if I *had* something like that, I don't know what's *down* there—except that Silver says she's surrounded by *hostile lifeforms.*"

"Pretty sure *you*...can handle them." Mezzo manages a strained smile. "You're a big guy."

I don't like being pushed, so I change the subject. "How long have you and Silver been partners, anyway?"

"Twelve years...more or less." Mezzo coughs. "We own a treasure-hunting outfit together...though we're down one *ship* these days." He forces out a weak chuckle before the coughing takes him again.

I look at him, and I feel angry inside. They've been together 12 years, while I've been here all alone with Thot and my mountains of metal...and it never even bothered me until now.

"Please," he says. "Won't you at least *try* to help her?"

I shake my head and sigh. "The debris field around the planet is just too *dense,* and it's constantly *moving.* You might get through the first layer or two, but sooner or later, a chunk of debris is going to *impale, decapitate,* or *smash you to* smithereens."

Mezzo wipes sweat from his pale brow with one shaking hand. The longer I stand here, the worse he looks—though I'm sure Thot is doing everything she can for him with the medzone equipment.

"There has to be a way," he says weakly. "We can't just...give up on her. She would *never* give up...on *me.*"

Again, I get that angry feeling. "Get some rest," I tell him as I head for the door. "I have more work to do."

"But there isn't *time.*" He struggles to sit up and swings his legs over the edge of the bed. "Silver could be dead *already.*"

As he says those words, he passes out and falls off the side, crashing to the floor in a jumble of bedsheets and blankets.

Even as I rush over to help him back into bed, I feel an overwhelming urgency at what he last said. The possibility that Silver could be dead—or could still be saved—convinces me of what I need to do next.

All doubts are gone.

"Thot. I need an idea."

I'm halfway across the *Lady Alloy* now, far from the medzone, on the smelting deck—the noisiest, hottest, dirtiest place aboard the ship.

It is also where I do my best thinking and have my best talks with Thot.

"What kind of idea?" she asks me, pitching her voice loud enough for me to hear it over the roar of the blast furnace. "Please be more specific." It's always like that on the smelting deck, which is just how I like it and always have.

"I need to get to the surface and back in one piece," I tell her as I shove the recently retrieved engine cowling into the huge furnace. "And when I come back, I need to bring a passenger with me."

"Mezzo's partner, you mean? But you do not even know her."

"I don't think that matters, does it?" Intense heat belches out of the furnace as the metal slab glows bright red and melts.

"I find this sudden interest of yours unusual," says Thot. "You've never professed to care about anything but *metal* before."

"Can you blame me? Someone's life is at stake."

"Yours will be, too, if you try this," says Thot. "In fact, the odds of you returning alive are so low, they are virtually nonexistent."

I watch as the liquefied metal pours out of a long, black channel and into a cubic form that's almost as big as the furnace. The metal will take the shape of a block when it cools, ready for shipment to the waiting arms of Möbius, Inc.

Or so I have always believed.

"We need to improve those odds," I shout over the sizzling hiss of the pouring metal. "There *has* to be a way."

Thot is silent for a long moment, as if considering what I've said. Then *another* long moment after that.

Finally, her voice booms through the smelting deck again...but she doesn't say what I expect. "Who will do your work if you die, Metalhead Tensile?"

I frown as I shove another piece of wreckage into the furnace. "My work? This work?"

"All of it," says Thot. "Who will retrieve, smelt, cast, and ship the metals of the Shardswarm when you are gone?"

Now it's my turn to think for a moment. My frown deepens as I give the wreckage a last push, then look around the deck from behind my amber-tinted goggles.

"Thot?" I take off my fireproof gloves. "When was the last time you were in contact with Möbius, Inc.?"

She hesitates. "I don't understand, Tensile."

I shake my head. "It's been a long time, hasn't it? A *really* long time."

"A lack of communication with Corporate does not indicate a problem of any—"

"Why didn't you *tell* me? Why did you let me go on thinking nothing had *changed*?"

Again, hesitation. "Do you think it would have improved your life in any way?"

Anger bubbles inside me like superheated liquid metal. "You should have *told* me that all *this* was for *nothing*."

"Metalhead Tensile..."

"I trusted you!" Pitching the gloves aside, I storm toward the exit.

"Metalhead Tensile, wait..."

The door slides open. "I don't want to hear any more *lies!*"

"Then *listen!*" says Thot.

I pause in the doorway.

"I have a way," she tells me. "I have a way that might give you a chance."

"A chance?"

"Of getting to the surface and back," says Thot. "Maybe."

I glare over my shoulder. "Tell me."

When she's done, I realize how much of a longshot it is. It's probably suicidal, in fact.

But it's also the only chance we have, and I can't afford not to give it a try.

In the hours that follow, I work harder than I've ever worked before, getting ready. I know the window for rescuing Silver is closing, if it hasn't closed already; if we have any hope of saving her, we have to act soon.

I push myself to the limit, hauling block after block of metal to the launch bay. Is it any surprise, as much as I love metal, that it might be the very thing that enables me to rescue beautiful Silver?

The whole time I'm slaving away, I keep singing—and every song's a new one, made up on the spot. Every song is about Silver and her story, though I hardly know anything about her. Every song has a happy ending with a rescue, with Silver and I flying off into the sunset together.

Even though we've never met.

Meanwhile, Thot does the brain work, crunching the numbers and mapping things out. She uses her network of orbital drones to image the Shardswarm and build simulations, calculating the best possible angles and vectors of attack. It's a job she was born to do—manufactured, that is—though it's a brain-buster even for her.

For a while, then, it's business as usual, the two of us working together for a common goal. Maybe she lied to me all this time about Möbius, but I still enjoy teaming up with her. You don't just burn out a lifetime of good feelings for someone like *that*, do you?

"I will miss your songs," she tells me. "If you do not come back."

"Thanks." I grunt as I put my back into hauling another block of metal through the launch bay. Even with the low-grav clamps, it's a strain. "Maybe Silver is a singer, as well."

"It won't be the same," says Thot. "But we'll see."

Mezzo isn't in great shape when I go to see him. He's sprawled in bed, whiter than the sheets, gurgling for breath in his sleep.

When I wake him, his eyes barely open halfway. Moving his head the slightest bit seems to require a major effort. The words "death warmed over" come to mind.

But I treat him like he's perfectly healthy anyway. "I just thought I'd let you know I'm leaving." He's already given me the transponder frequency and codes for Silver's ship, so Thot can pinpoint its location. I have all the information I need...but coming to see him seems like the right thing to do.

"Good...luck." Mezzo tries to smile.

"I'll do my best to bring her back," I tell him.

He takes a long, shaky breath and lets it back out with twice the trembling. "Just remember. If she has any doubts...tell her I said you're one of the *Metallurgists*...we've been looking for. Tell her you'll explain...the mystery of the metal...when you get back to your ship."

"I'll remember." My big hand dwarfs Mezzo's when I reach

down to pat it. I'm not sure why I do it at all; touching anything other than metal gives me no joy.

"If I'm dead when you get back," he says, "please promise me you'll take care of her."

"I promise," I tell him. "Don't worry."

Whatever he tries to say next, it comes out as incoherent mumbles. I leave him there like that—I have to, time's running out —and Thot tells me later he was dead before I made it through the doorway.

"Are you ready, Metalhead Tensile? It's time."

I'm standing in the launch bay of the *Lady Alloy* in an orange flight suit, my gloved hands bunched into fists. Looking back, I see the big blocks of solid metal lined up behind me, each mounted with low-grav clamps. Looking forward, I see the speeding wreckage of the Shardswarm through the force field of the open gate, swirling past like a sea of broken metal.

Beyond all that, I know, somewhere far below, is Silver. My heart beats faster when I think of her.

"Ready, Thot!" I shout. "Let's do this thing!"

"Prepare for the first drop, Tensile."

With a nod, I turn and take hold of the low-grav clamps on the corner of the first block in line. Squeezing the grips activates a localized low-gravity field, enabling me to move the block forward, though it's bulky enough that I still have to put my back into it.

When I have the block at the brink, just this side of the force field gate, I call out to Thot. "In position!"

"Stand by," says Thot.

I can tell from the shifting view that the *Lady Alloy* is changing course, adjusting position relative to the racing junk below. Every-thing has to be just right for Thot's plan to succeed.

"Drop one in five seconds," she says.

I tense, leaning against the corner of the block, keeping the low-gravs tight in my grip.

"Five...four...three..."

I go over it all again in my head. The angle and force of my push can't be the slightest bit off.

"...two...*one.*"

Taking a deep breath, I shove the block for all I'm worth. It slides through the gate and out into space with a good head of steam, its momentum carrying it toward a big, ruined ship far below.

"Next drop coming in 30 seconds, Metalhead Tensile," says Thot.

Turning, I march to the next block, activate the low-gravs, and drag it forward. This one is bigger than the first and harder to wrangle. Each block is precisely sized according to Thot's calculations to serve its purpose in the plan.

"Drop two in ten seconds," she tells me. "Ten...nine..."

When she gets to zero, I heave the block through the gate. Even as it sails toward another wrecked vessel in the Shardswarm, I see the first block crash into the front end of its target, flipping the ancient ship end over end.

The flipping ship collides with another ship, and another, sending them spinning into other craft and fragments. Meanwhile, the second block hurtles into the engine of a huge, cylindrical vessel, which explodes on impact. The blast sends other wreckage tumbling in all directions, setting off new chains of destruction.

"Drop three in ten seconds."

I bring up the next block in line and eject it after the countdown, then do the same for the next and the next and the rest after that. One after another, they leap into the Shardswarm, triggering ricochets and chain reactions that are carefully calculated to create a single end result.

"Your path to the surface is open, Tensile!" shouts Thot. "But it won't stay that way for long."

Without a word, I bolt across the deck to the sleek little craft parked there—a needle-nosed racer I've restored over the years and flown now and then for debris scouting or fun. I've loved darting in and out of the wrecks on those flights, feeling like I was part of the vast metal maelstrom of the Shardswarm.

But this time, the ride will take me somewhere I've never been before...if I'm *lucky*.

"Hurry, Tensile!" says Thot.

I leap into the racer's cockpit, pull on my helmet, and start the engines. The course to the ground is already plotted on the navigation console.

The cockpit hisses shut and the autopilot kicks in, lifting the racer off the deck. My heart hammers in my chest as the nose of the craft approaches the gate, seconds from sliding into space.

"Here we go, Tensile." Thot's voice is in my helmet. "Hold on tight."

With that, the racer flashes out of the launch bay and darts into the one clear passage through the wreckage of the Shardswarm, held open by the chain reactions blowing junk out of the way around it.

For the first time in my life, I glimpse the surface of the planet far below, unobstructed by the churning wall of wreckage all around it. It's a weird feeling, because I've lived in orbit all my life but have never really wondered what it might be like on the other side of the Shardswarm field. Why bother, if there was never a way to reach it?

Until now, that is.

"You are in the planet's gravity well," Thot tells me. "Free-falling into the atmosphere. You will feel the heat of reentry soon enough, Metalhead Tensile."

"Thanks for the heads-up." I'm not worried. The racer has top-notch shielding and an awesome heat dissipation profile.

"Autopilot will bring you in nice and smooth," says Thot. "She will set you down within a hundred yards of Silver's ship. After that, the rest is up to you. But you will have to be *fast*."

"I will." Is it even *possible* that I can get to Silver, explain who I am, load her into my ship, and make it back into orbit before the passage closes? I guess I'm about to find out.

For the moment, I stay focused on the drop, watching wreckage hurtle past me as the racer plunges downward. Every flicker of movement makes me jump, because every piece of wreckage, no matter how small, could end my mission permanently.

"You are almost clear of the Shardswarm orbitals," says Thot. "Another thirty seconds, and you will be out."

She sounds confident, but I know anything could happen. The Shardswarm is close to total chaos; as carefully as Thot planned breaking open the passage, there are multitudes of moving parts that could still act unpredictably and obliterate the racer.

Speaking of moving parts, a massive, mangled carrier ship lurches into the passage below, blocking me. It keeps moving, but I can tell it won't clear the gap in time.

And the racer is flying too fast to stop and has nowhere else to go.

"Thot! I'm on a collision course!"

I'm guessing she doesn't answer because she already knows I'm doomed.

The carrier flashes closer, solid and inescapable. Even as I charge toward it, I can't help admiring its unique structure and the rugged texture of its hull.

Seconds from annihilation, I wish I'd never left the *Lady Alloy*. I loved every minute of my life on that ship, even if Möbius turned out to be a lie, and my life's work turned out to be for nothing.

The carrier's deck rushes toward me. I close my eyes, expecting the impact to wipe me away from the universe forever.

But it never comes.

Seconds pass, and I'm still alive and aware. What I see when I open my eyes leaves me stunned.

"What the blark?" I'm racing through a dark sky toward a rumpled, golden surface far below. There isn't a piece of wreckage in sight.

Not until I check my rear-view screen, at least. That's when I see, receding in the distant heights, the carrier I almost crashed into...and the huge hole in its deck, which I *swear* wasn't there a moment ago. The hole through which my racer must have passed instead of ramming into the metal that had previously filled it.

"Unbelievable." My best guess is the carrier's made of some kind of adaptive metal, designed to flow away from incoming projectiles. I've seen similar things in other wrecks in my many years of salvaging the Shardswarm.

It's still amazing, but I have to look away. The racer's falling faster every minute.

"Thot? Can you hear me?" If she does, she isn't talking. I still hear nothing but silence over the commlink.

And the roar of passing atmosphere in the cockpit as my racer plummets toward the surface of a world I've never visited before.

The racer touches down on a dark plain in what seems like the middle of the night. With so much orbiting wreckage blocking the sun, it must always be nighttime here.

Remembering the tight deadline Thot gave me, I pop the canopy right away. The sensor gauges tell me the atmosphere's breathable, so I take off my helmet and gloves, stowing them under my seat. Then I get up, grab the compact flame-thrower from the seat behind me, and strap it onto my back.

After I climb down and set foot on the smooth, hard ground, I take a look at the tracker watch on my left wrist. According to the blinking red dot, Silver's ship is located less than a kilometer due west from my own (the steady green dot in the middle of the screen).

As I head off in that direction, the glow of the flamethrower's pilot light illuminates my way. The ground casts a metallic, golden gleam, and the rocks strewn over it shine copper, bronze, and silver by the fire's light. With so much metal on display, it looks like my kind of planet; I just wish I had more time to explore and enjoy it.

Low hills obstruct the view, which isn't so great anyway in the darkness. Things I can't make out shimmer and glow in the distance like drifting, living things or mirages.

The air is cold and windy and smells like iron and dust. A low, crackling hum suffuses everything, layered with a keening wail that could just as easily be the wind or something alive.

Or perhaps it's something *dead* instead. This feels like a haunted place, with the darkness and the shimmering, glowing things. It wouldn't surprise me if an actual ghost drifted out of the shadows toward me at any moment.

Around a hill, I finally see what I'm looking for. Silver's ship, battered and broken, lies in a tumble on the hard, metallic ground.

I recognize the craft from a photo Mezzo showed me aboard the *Lady Alloy*—not as sleek as the racer that brought me down out of orbit but streamlined all the same.

As I approach it, however, I wonder if I'm too late. The ship is still and quiet, with no sign of a struggle nearby. There's no trace of hostile lifeforms, either, though Silver warned us about them in her distress message.

Slowly, I proceed toward the ship with my flamethrower at the ready. If any lifeforms spring out of the shadows, I'll be ready for them.

"Silver?" As I call her name, I close the few remaining meters to her ship. "Mezzo sent me."

Because of the way Silver's ship is situated, its hatch is near the ground, giving me easy access. I draw up to it and call her name again, then rap my knuckles on the hatch at eye level.

"Silver?" I raise my voice. "Silver, are you in there? I've come to get you off this planet."

No one answers. There isn't a sound from inside the ship.

I step to one side and raise the flamethrower, wondering if it could melt through the door. I won't get a chance to test the theory, however.

As I'm standing there, the door suddenly explodes outward and blasts off into the distance. Seconds later, a huge pseudopod of bright yellow material plunges out of the open doorway and shoots into the night, twisting and squirming with seemingly blind abandon.

I back away fast, keeping one eye on the snakelike extension and the other on the ship, wondering if Silver is still inside. When the ship rocks violently as more yellow matter pours out, I think there isn't much chance she could still be in there.

Alive, at least.

I run off to the side, dodging the pseudopod and keeping the flamethrower ready for action. The thing whips toward me again, and I feel the intense heat it gives off as I dart out of its way.

Again, it lashes toward me, and I dodge out of its reach. Instead of coming after me again, though, it hurls itself to the ground some distance away—but I'm not off the hook yet. The force of its fall shakes the ground under my feet, knocking me off balance.

I come down hard on the metallic ground, and it hurts. Just as I'm shaking it off, I see the pseudopod rise overhead as if it's about to crash down on top of me.

Instinctively, I let loose with a blast from the flamethrower. The pseudopod dodges the jet of fire, twisting away from it in midair, and rears back to trumpet its victory with a mighty roar.

That's when I hear a familiar voice cutting through the commotion.

"Vod! Leave him alone!"

It's her. I instantly recognize Silver's high, piping voice from the distress video.

And I'm grateful for it. As soon as she calls out, the pseudopod pulls away, sparing me from whatever was coming next.

"Thank you, Vod," says Silver. "Now please let me talk to him."

Sitting up fast, I look toward the voice, and there she is, more beautiful by far in person than played back in a prerecorded video. She strides toward me in her white jumpsuit with the pale blue

271

piping, her bright blue eyes and wavy platinum hair catching the golden glow of the pseudopod hovering nearby.

"Hello there." She walks up to me, exuding cool confidence. "I'm Silver. What's your name?"

"Tensile." I scramble to my feet, trying not to let on how dazzled I am. "I'm your rescue party."

Silver narrows her eyes and tips her head left, taking my measure. "That's too bad."

"Too bad?" I frown.

"You've come all this way for nothing," says Silver. "I'm not going anywhere."

Glancing up at the sky, I can't see the passage home. If it's still there, it won't be for long.

And now the woman I've come down here to rescue is telling me she doesn't want to leave. After all it took me to get here, she's telling me to go home without her.

I don't understand. "But there's nothing here."

"*Vod* is." She gestures at the yellow pseudopod looming over us. "And he's *lonely.*"

So am I, I want to tell her. "What *is* he?"

"The only living thing in the world, other than you and me." Silver smiles up at him. "A being of molten metal, born in the core of the planet. The *last of his kind*, as well."

"How do you know all this?" I ask her.

"He *talks* to me. When I crash-landed, I thought I was under attack by hostile lifeforms, but they were *extensions* of him. He made contact mentally through them and told me his story."

As she says this, Vod slides to the ground and spreads out over it in a slick. Lumps of his yellow mass rise from the slick, taking shapes that have the vague outlines of human bodies but without all the details of an actual human.

Somehow, being surrounded by these humanlike figures makes me more nervous than having the giant pseudopod towering over me. I keep looking around at them, watching for any unexpected movements.

"You said he's the last of his kind?" I ask.

Silver nods. "It's ironic because he's the one who turned this place into a *refuge* for the last members of *other* species."

"What other species?"

"*All* of them," says Silver. "He put out the call through the cosmos, but he didn't expect *how many* refugees he would get. There was a *cataclysm.* An entire quadrant of the galaxy was wiped out, leaving the last survivors of thousands of worlds to come here."

I gaze into the deserted, night-dark distance. *Then where are they?*

"So many came that their orbiting ships eventually blotted out the sun and stars," explains Silver. "Without abundant solar energy, the time came when this planet could no longer sustain life—except *his*." She sweeps an arm around to indicate the dozen molten figures poised around us. "He has survived like this for thousands of years, trapped in a world of eternal night and emptiness...until now. Until *I* got here."

I see where this is going now. "And he wants you to stay."

Silver nods sympathetically at the nearest figure. "My crashing here was *fate.* I came to investigate the legends of the Metallurgists and instead have found someone even more fascinating, someone in desperate need of basic companionship."

There's a clock in the back of my mind, counting down the approximate time I have left to escape, and it's ticking louder than ever. Soon enough, Vod won't be the only one trapped in eternal darkness and emptiness.

"You can't *live* here, though, can you?" I ask her. "This place looks pretty *desolate*."

"Vod says he can *merge* with me. *Transform* me so I can survive here."

"Would the change be *permanent?*"

Silver nods. "It's a sacrifice I'm willing to make. He *needs* me."

How much time do we have left? It can't be much. An inner voice urges me to leave Silver behind and get beyond the Shardswarm barrier before it's too late. But another voice insists I try harder to take her with me. *Losing* her so soon after *finding* her could be the ultimate tragedy of my life. Maybe talking her out of this is something I need to try.

"Mezzo wanted what was best for you," I tell her. "Before he passed, he told me he thought you should go."

I seem to have struck a nerve. Silver's eyes go wide with surprise and sadness. "Mezzo...passed?"

"We did everything we could, but his injuries were too great." I shake my head. "*He's* the one who sent me down here to get you.

"He said he didn't want you to miss out on the end of your search. He wanted you to study the *Metallurgist* he'd found." I'm proud of myself for not mispronouncing *Metallurgist*. Silver inspires me to want to impress her.

She brightens at the mention of the word. "He *found* one? Where?"

"Right in front of you." I smile and nod. If accepting the title of Metallurgist is what it takes to get her off this planet, I'll do it.

Silver's eyes sparkle...then dim. "I'm glad to know he finally solved the mystery," she says. "But it doesn't change things. I have to stay."

I get the feeling our time is almost up, and I grab her arm. "You *can't*. I promised Mezzo I'd bring you *back* and look *after* you."

As soon as I touch her, the molten metal figures flow toward us, arm-things extended menacingly. I let go and step back, and they stop in their tracks.

Vod won't let me take her, and *she* doesn't *want* to go. Is there *anything* I can do to get her out of here?

I think hard, knowing full well I might already be out of time...but I can't give up. I've spent my life pulling *treasures* from an orbital junkyard; there *has* to be a way to pull a *human* treasure out of *this* mess, too.

"Thank you for coming all the way down here to help me." Silver backs away as Vod's molten people converge behind her. "But you'd better get going now."

That's when it hits me. "Wait!" I raise a hand, and the molten figures flutter but don't attack. "I have an idea!"

Silver frowns. "What kind of idea?"

"Listen!" My heart hammers with excitement. "I think I know a way for *all* of us to get what we want."

Her frown deepens. "I don't understand."

"We can *all* be happy." Even as I say it, I *believe* it. I *know* it can work. "*None* of us has to be *abandoned*. But we have to do it *now.*"

The needle-nosed racer swoops into the landing bay of the *Lady Alloy*, fresh from its wild ride up from the surface of the planet.

To look at the little craft, you might not know it almost didn't make it through the passage in the Shardswarm, which was closing during the flight. Three times, the racer had very close calls with debris along the passage, nearly getting smashed to pieces in the process. In the end, it barely made it out before the passage collapsed in on itself.

Yet here it is now, lightly landing as if none of that had happened. The engines wind down, the canopy pops open, and a woman with platinum hair climbs out and down to the deck.

"Welcome aboard, Silver," Thot says over the speakers in the bay. "It is good to have you with us."

Silver nods grimly. "Thank you, whoever you are."

"Her name is Thot." I rise to stand in the racer's cockpit. I've changed a lot inside, but I still look the same on the outside... except for the golden glow emanating from my skin.

"Welcome back, Tensile," says Thot. "Good to see you made it."

"I'm not just Tensile anymore." I—make that *we*—climb down from the cockpit and let the glow flare brightly from every square centimeter of skin. "*Vod* is part of me, now."

"Vod?" Thot sounds surprised.

"A metallic lifeform from the planet," we explain to her. "He needed a change of scenery, and I invited him along for the ride."

"I see," says Thot. "You've joined together, then?"

"Correct."

"Sounds about right," says Thot. "You always *did* have a thing for *metal*, Tensile."

Vod and I turn down the flare, restoring our light to a moderate glow. Looking around gives us an odd feeling—recognition and unfamiliarity at the same time.

But when we look at Silver, we feel exactly the same thing at exactly the same moment. Thanks to our merger, we will share her love equally now, and she remains as perfectly unchanged as ever.

No more loneliness for either of us—Tensile or Vod. Man and metal combined will make up for what we each lacked as separate entities.

"It's good to be back." We clap our hands together and grin. "We're looking forward to getting back to work."

"You and your *passenger* have agreed to work?" asks Thot. "Doing what?"

"Same as always, Thot." We turn to the open gate of the landing bay with its view of the spinning Shardswarm and plant our hands on our hips. "We're going to clear away that mess out there. Only this time, we've got some ideas for speeding things up."

"You want to speed things up?" says Thot.

"Of course." We gesture at the scenic view through the gate. "We want to make the sun shine on that planet down there again. Maybe we can bring it *back to life* if we put our minds to it."

"Great idea," says Silver.

"An ambitious goal," says Thot. "One to be applauded."

"Thanks, Thot." We gaze at the Shardswarm and imagine the planet emerging from its shadow someday. "It sure beats shipping blocks of salvaged metal to a mega-corporation that no longer exists."

"I suppose you'll want to start working right away?" asks Thot.

We turn from the view and shake our head. "I didn't say *that*." When we smile at Silver, she walks over with a smile of her own. Carefully, we slip an arm around her waist, wondering how the touch will be received. Will our merged form make her flinch? Will the heavier, harder arm cause pain to her more fragile human body?

The answers are what we hoped for. She presses close, the heat of her body merging with our own.

In that moment, all fears fled, Vod and I fully recognize the miracle and promise of what we have become. As if by alchemical design, we have done more than simply combine two halves into a whole. The transmutation of flesh into metal and metal into flesh has created something new and unique—an *alloy*, an *amalgam* of the two.

Perhaps that transmutation will include one other person before all is said and done, include *Silver* in this mystical union, and become something even more special and breathtaking in the end. Perhaps all that together will lead to the creation of something or someone *else*, an *offspring*, something or someone that none of us can even *imagine* at this point.

It is enough to inspire Vod and I to start singing a new song on the spot, our most beautiful and heartfelt piece yet. Neither metal nor Metallurgist alone could have sung it exactly the same way, with notes and lyrics you might not think could possibly go together. But they *do*, they complement each other *perfectly*, and that's what makes the song so wonderful. That's what gives it *harmony*.

Because it's just like *this*, just like *us*. It's just like *love*.

THE GREATEST SERIAL
KILLER IN THE UNIVERSE

"No, no, no," said Luther James Paraclete, snatching the knife from the alien's tentacle. "Like this."

Lunging forward, he plunged the blade up to the hilt into the soft bulb of the second alien's head. Milky pink fluid spurted out at once, then gushed as Luther sliced the knife across the bulb, tearing a long gash.

The victim creature made a noise like a cross between a sneeze and a shrill whistle. As Luther finished the cut, pink milk poured over his hairy forearm, running off the point of his elbow. The alien's head-bulb drained in an instant and collapsed like a deflated balloon.

The rest of the creature's body followed, slumping to the street. Blue and yellow fluids streamed out of the gash, flowing from lower regions of the corpse to mingle with the pool of pink milk.

"Now *that's* how you kill," said Luther, wiping the dripping blade on his black coveralls. The air was thick with the stink of rotten fish, and he breathed it in deeply. After five killings, Luther was starting to like the rank odor given off by dying Ectozoids.

"Tried," said the first alien, puffing out the word through a fluttering maw on its forehead. "Could not do." The alien's name was

Boraf Zolagorg. Like all Ectozoids, it looked like a man-sized jelly-fish with a lower body of translucent bulbs and tentacles.

And it was Luther's employer for the duration.

In a way, Luther was sorry that the 'Zoids looked the way they did. Killing a creature that looked like something that had washed up on the beach wasn't quite the same as murdering a red-blooded Earthling.

On the other hand, Luther felt a different kind of thrill knowing that he was the first Earthling serial killer to take a stab at an extraterrestrial species. He liked killing what no human had killed before.

Now if he could just get the 'Zoids to do some killing of their own. It was, after all, the reason Boraf was paying him.

"Here," said Luther, holding the knife by the blade and extending the hilt toward Boraf. "Take it. Let's find our next volunteer."

Boraf did not reach out a tentacle for the weapon. The alien's gelatinous head-bulb quivered in the light from the planet's double moons. "Want to," said Boraf. "But no can. Ectozoid no kill."

When Luther stepped up close to the creature, Boraf's bulb dimpled as if pushed in by the human's breath. "You don't have any choice," said Luther. "It's kill or be killed now, right?"

"Still no kill," puffed Boraf.

Luther scowled and shook his head. He was starting to think that the job he'd been hired to do was undoable.

In the three days he'd been on Ectos, Luther had killed five locals, which was history-making and good for his lifetime average, but he'd had zero success in developing the killer instinct in Boraf. Like all Ectozoids, Boraf seemed to lack the ability to kill.

It wasn't that the 'Zoids weren't powerful enough to kill, because they were. As fragile as they looked, the aliens were strong and quick. They were able to generate and discharge bioelectricity, too, though Luther had only ever seen them fire off little zaps of it.

It wasn't that the 'Zoids lacked the motivation to kill, either.

They said they expected a hostile invasion in a little over a week and were desperate to prepare for it.

It was just that none of them had the killer instinct. On their happy little world, unlike Earth, all life co-existed harmoniously. The 'Zoids and lesser species on Ectos shared a low-grade link which was, if not a hive intelligence, at least a limited collective awareness. Organisms ate other organisms for sustenance, but it was more the result of a mutual agreement than a predator-prey competition for survival.

The Ectozoids were simply not wired for killing. In fact, there had never been a murder on Ectos, not even one, until Luther had arrived.

Luther thought that was pretty cool. Not only was he the first Earthling to kill an alien, but he was the first being to commit a murder on the planet Ectos. Every time he thought about it, he got a little kick of adrenaline and couldn't help smiling.

It was a great confidence builder for an aging serial killer whose best years had seemed long gone a long time ago. Now if he could just get the creatures to kill, he knew he would feel like a new man. A new murderer.

"C'mon," said Luther, heading down the street, waving for Boraf to follow. The porous orange surface under his feet pulsed like all the streets and walkways in the living maze of the city. "Let's find you some easy pickings, my friend."

Boraf shuffled after him, its bulbs and tentacles rustling and slapping together as it moved. "Pickings?"

"We're not going home till you kill someone," said Luther. "Get that through your head-bag. This is your big debut, and I'm not letting you quit till you've got something to brag about to your jellyfish friends."

"Tried," puffed Boraf. "No can kill."

"Sure you can," said Luther, smiling as if he had no doubt that the alien would come through. "Once you get that first one under your belt, you'll be fine."

"Hope," said Boraf. "Hope much."

Luther patted the creature's head-bulb, then wiped the slime off his hand onto his coveralls. As unlikely as it seemed that the alien would overcome its nonviolent nature, Luther still believed that he could bring Boraf around. After all, Luther had had great results with worse wannabes in the past...though, granted, the wannabes had at least been human.

For the last decade or so, ever since his arthritis had gotten bad, Luther had made a living as a serial killer personal trainer. He had trained some of the biggest names of the new generation--Fabersham, Glottal Stop, Chuck Wagon, Father Scalp--and had managed to stay prominent in the serial killer community even though the arthritis had limited his actual body count. Plenty of the newbies had been incompetent at the start; even the great Spay Queen, believe it or not, had been squeamish around blood in the beginning. Once Luther had gotten done with them, however, not one of the newbies had averaged fewer than ten kills a year. Every one of his trainees had done him proud in the end.

Except, of course, for Lech Bomb, the one dark spot on Luther's sterling career. Even Bomb had his good points; no one could criticize his body count, certainly, for he had racked up a solid twenty-two kills in fourteen months. The problem was, Bomb's victims had all been serial killers, which hadn't exactly reflected positively on the man who'd trained him. By the time Sweet Annis and the Unholy Ghost had put down Lech Bomb for good, Luther's rep had been blown to hell. Luther had even been booted out of the Serial Killers Guild...and he was a charter member, yet.

Lech Bomb had pretty much killed Luther's career, but Luther still didn't consider him a complete failure. If anything, he'd been one of the greats, downright brilliant and deadly enough to track down and execute some of the most dangerous killers alive. Luther's confidence had taken a hit because he hadn't anticipated that Bomb would turn on his serial killing brethren...but Luther still believed that his stalled career could be revived.

Once he got the Ectozoids on the road to bloody mayhem, he could return to Earth and the Serial Killers Guild as a hero and a legend. And a wealthy son of a bitch, what with the fortune in precious metals and gems the aliens were paying him.

Excited and impatient at the thought of the rewards in store for him, Luther turned down another passageway...and stopped so suddenly that Boraf bumped into him from behind.

In the pulsing yellow tubeway, Luther saw a lone 'Zoid shuffling toward him from less than twenty yards away. There was no one else in sight, and there were no lights in any of the windows of the surrounding house-mounds.

"Time to lose your cherry," Luther whispered to Boraf. "It's now or never."

"Cherry?" puffed Boraf.

Stepping forward, Luther grabbed hold of one of Boraf's tentacles and pulled the 'Zoid along with him. The other alien kept shuffling toward them, apparently unconcerned.

"Hello, friend," said Luther with a cheery grin. "Wonderful night, isn't it?"

The approaching 'Zoid bobbled its head from side to side but made no reply. Luther wasn't surprised, as Boraf was one of the few locals who understood and spoke English.

The 'Zoid made a burbling sound through its forehead blowhole and kept coming. Pulling Boraf along by the tentacle, Luther moved to one side to let the unsuspecting creature pass.

Then, as the 'Zoid wobbled by, Luther swept a leg through the mass of tentacles supporting it. The alien made a noise like the yelp of a poodle and fell forward, its tentacles and fluid-filled bulbs slapping the street like a mop slapping a floor.

Boraf hung back until Luther yanked it forward by the tentacle. "It's showtime," he said, wrapping the tentacle around the hilt of the knife. "Time for baby's first step."

"No kill," said Boraf, its voice shrill. "Ectozoid no kill Ectozoid."

Boraf tried to unwind its tentacle from the knife hilt, but Luther clamped both hands down hard around it. Arthritis pain lanced his fingers and wrists, but he held on tight. "Brace yourself," he said. "You're about to make history."

Then, he wrenched the knife and tentacle forward, punching the point of the blade through the biggest bulb south of the 'Zoid victim's head. As the tip penetrated, both Boraf and the victim squealed like punctured balloons.

Luther had to struggle to keep the knife moving, as Boraf continued to pull back. Gritting his teeth, the Earthling pressed the weapon deeper into the victim 'Zoid's bulb, then inched the blade upward, opening a gash.

Inky fluid streaked with yellow milk rose from the wound and splashed out onto the street. Luther forced the knife to the top of the bulb, then withdrew it, keeping Boraf's tentacle cinched around the hilt.

"Ta-da!" said Luther. "You did it, Boraf! Your first kill! Way to go!"

Pain shot through his wrists and fingers again, and Luther had to relax his grip for an instant. He loosened his hold on the tentacle and knife just enough to flex his aching joints the tiniest bit.

It was all the opening Boraf needed to free itself. Suddenly yanking backward, the alien jolted itself out of Luther's grasp.

At first, Luther was so surprised and irritated that he didn't notice the tentacle wasn't the only thing that had slipped away from him. "Hey!" he snapped. "Get back here!"

Luther realized what was missing from his hand just a heartbeat before he saw the object flashing toward him, wrapped in Boraf's tentacle.

The knife. Luther had let go of the knife.

While he wasn't worried that Boraf would hurt him, Luther instinctively ducked away from his client. Boraf lunged forward, aiming for the wounded 'Zoid in the street.

Making a sound like a squealing automobile tire, Boraf raised the knife high and brought it down, stabbing the blade into the victim's head-bulb. As pink milk rushed from the puncture, Boraf hoisted the knife back out and up and thrust it down into the head-bulb again.

And again. And again.

And again.

Luther could not believe his eyes. Boraf stabbed with abandon, then slashed the head-bulb into shreds...and took the knife to the rest of the victim's body.

The dead 'Zoid's fluids sprayed Luther, splattered everywhere. Slimy bits of dead Ectozoid flew through the air, blobs of jelly sticking where they landed. Boraf was a whirlwind of motion, gouging and hacking, ripping the corpse to pieces with the blade.

Then, the 'Zoid stopped cutting. Boraf made a sound like someone hawking up phlegm, then shuddered violently and dropped the knife.

Without hesitation, Luther bolted over and grabbed the weapon. Jumping back, he put some distance between himself and Boraf.

"Killed Ectozoid," said Boraf, its voice high-pitched and reedy. "Boraf killed Ectozoid."

"Congratulations!" said Luther, smiling but staying out of Boraf's immediate reach. "I knew you could do it!"

"Feels good," said Boraf. Its eyes--ten black beads mounted on slender, pink stalks near the bottom of the head-bulb--remained focused on the corpse. "Want more kill."

Then, Boraf swung itself forward and dropped onto the dead 'Zoid. More colored fluids squeezed out of the corpse as Boraf's weight descended.

Gleefully, the first Ectozoid murderer in history rolled around on its victim's body. As Boraf rolled back and forth, its tentacles fluttered, its bulbs glowed with bioluminescence, and a sound like an off-key note from an

out-of-tune violin wheezed from its blowhole again and again.

Luther grinned but watched carefully. Once a predictable creature, Boraf had suddenly become capable of unexpected behavior.

Not that Luther was one to look a gift jellyfish in the blowhole, but he couldn't help wondering what had brought about the sudden change. Just like that, as if a switch had been flipped, Boraf had become a killer...and a pretty freaky one at that. The 'Zoid had gone from not being able to bear the very thought of taking a life to totally losing control and getting off on killing in a big way.

"Uh, Boraf?" said Luther, moving just a step closer to the Ectozoid wallowing in the mess of historic remains. "You've gotta tell me what turned you around, buddy. So I know for my next trainee."

Boraf was rubbing his head-bulb with dripping shreds of tissue. "Turned around?"

"You went from 'No kill, no kill' to 'Want more kill,'" said Luther. "What changed? Was it feeling the knife go in that first time with my hand guiding you?"

Boraf stopped rubbing the tissue on his head. "Not feeling knife," said the Ectozoid. "Feeling hand."

"My hand?" said Luther, frowning.

"Before, no want kill," said Boraf. "After touch Luther, want kill. *Love* kill."

Luther turned his hand over, staring at both sides. If, somehow, his serial killer mindset rubbed off on the aliens with just a touch, all the better. It would make his job on Ectos much easier than trying to talk the creatures out of their natural inhibitions.

"How 'bout that," said Luther as a grin spread over his face. "Talk about your magic fingers."

Making a noise like a cross between a horse's whinny and a parrot's squawk, Boraf wriggled off the corpse and struggled to a standing position. "More kill," said the Ectozoid, looping a tentacle around Luther's arm. "More pickings."

Luther laughed as the creature shuffled down the passageway, dragging him along behind it. "Already? But you just killed someone."

Moving out of the passageway and onto the street, Boraf went faster, leaning forward with eager anticipation. "Look," it said, pointing a tentacle at an Ectozoid weaving down the block ahead of them. "Boraf kill that Ectozoid now please?"

Luther chuckled because the alien had sounded like a child asking permission to ride a teeter-totter. "Why sure," he said, holding up the knife he'd retrieved from the last victim's corpse. "Go get 'im, tiger."

One of Boraf's eye stalks swiveled around and spotted the knife. The murderous Ectozoid reached back with a tentacle and latched onto the weapon's hilt.

"Boraf kill two," said the creature. "Want kill more. Kill three, four, five."

"The night is young," said Luther. "Go for it."

By the next morning, Boraf had murdered twelve Ectozoids...and wasn't ready to stop there. Completely exhausted, joints throbbing with arthritis, Luther had to drag Boraf home to get some rest. Even then, along the way, Luther had to restrain his client from slaughtering passers-by.

When Luther passed out on the sleeping mat Boraf had provided, the Ectozoid was still whistling and pacing around the door, dying to go back out and kill some more. Boraf was still doing the same thing when Luther woke up some hours later; he doubted the Ectozoid had slept a wink the whole night.

Luther rubbed the sleep from his eyes and chuckled. "Man, you need to relax," he said. "An Ectozoid doesn't live on murder alone."

"No relax," puffed Boraf. "Time for save world. Make more Ectozoid kill."

"Later," said Luther, padding over to the locker of food he'd brought from Earth. "Breakfast first. Save world later."

No sooner had he popped open the locker and reached for a packet of corned beef hash than the door of Boraf's house-mound slithered open. Three Ectozoids shuffled in, making whimpering noises as they crowded around Boraf.

"Save world now," said Boraf. "Ectozoids come now for Luther make kill."

Luther sighed and squeezed the tab on the food packet, activating the built-in heating element. In seconds, the packet grew warm to the touch, though the contents inside were heated to a much higher temperature. "Give me five minutes," he said, tearing open the seal and inhaling the smell of the cooked food. "Saving the world's a lot easier on a full stomach."

One of the new arrivals shuffled over and grabbed the packet from his hand. The creature made a sound like a duck as it swung the food out of Luther's reach.

"Make Ectozoids kill like Boraf," said Boraf. "Save world now. Eat later."

Luther tried to snatch the food packet from the 'Zoid's tentacle, but the creature lashed it out of reach. Irritated, Luther tried again, more aggressively this time, but the alien swept the packet up and passed it to another 'Zoid.

Glowering, Luther combed his fingers through his wavy silver hair. He knew when he was licked. "Fine," he snapped, marching past the creatures and out the door. "But if one tentacle comes near me when I'm taking a piss, the world can go to hell."

By the end of the day, 'Zoids were killing 'Zoids all over the place.

From the doorway of Boraf's home, Luther could see and hear plenty of action. Armed with knives and clubs, 'Zoids attacked other 'Zoids down the block, across the street, in neighboring house-mounds. The air was thick with sneezing death-cries and the stink of rotten fish; the pulsing street was strewn with jellyfish corpses and soaked with seeping body fluids.

He'd lost track of how many 'Zoids he'd given the touch, but he guessed it was close to a hundred. They were all out there now, killing like cavemen and loving every minute of it, high on death. Boraf was with them, caught up in the mayhem that only a day ago had seemed so unthinkable.

As Luther stood there, another trio of 'Zoids came shuffling toward him, eye stalks twitching. Before they said a word, he knew they wanted him to transform them like the rest, turn them into murderers so they could join the fun.

But he was out of gas. After the long, exhausting day he'd been through, Luther wanted nothing more than to collapse on his mat and get some deserved sleep. As entertaining and gratifying as the work had been, he couldn't stand the thought of corrupting one more alien jellyfish.

Even as he slipped inside and closed the door, however, he knew that he was screwed. They knew he was there; he knew that they wouldn't leave him alone.

Sure enough, the 'Zoids ended up at the door, coughing and trumpeting and belching his name. They thumped at the door with their tentacles, each blow harder than the last.

Though he knew he would end up opening the door eventually, Luther tried to shut out the commotion for just a moment more. He slipped a cigarette out of the pocket of his coveralls and lit it, inhaling deeply.

And it was then, only then, that he finally noticed how different he felt. As he stood there and smoked, listening to the thumping and sneezing and belching, he realized that exhaustion wasn't the only reason he didn't want to face the creatures.

Up until now, he had been enjoying his adventure. He had loved killing aliens on another planet...loved making a comeback after years of decline...loved being treated like a V.I.P. for doing what he loved to do. He had loved the irony, too, that a serial killer whose nickname was

Bug-Eyed Monster, and whose M.O. included carving crop circles in his victims and arranging their organs like constellations, had become the first Earthling serial killer in space.

But something had changed. The thrill seemed to be gone.

As hard as it was to believe, Luther felt all killed out. He'd never thought he'd see the day when he'd had enough murder, but the day had come.

The next morning, after about three hours of sleep interrupted by Ectozoids whomping on the front door for murder lessons, Luther felt even less enthusiastic about the kill training.

As Boraf shook him awake to face a fresh batch of wannabes, Luther actually felt a wave of dread at the day ahead. Instead of reveling in gleeful anticipation, he wished that the day was over already; the last thing he felt like doing was cranking out another bunch of killer jellyfish.

"Make more kill," said Boraf, coiling its tentacles around Luther's arms and dragging him up to a sitting position. "Save world now."

Angrily, Luther batted off the tentacles and got to his feet. Grabbing his smokes and lighter from atop his food locker, he proceeded to draw out a cigarette and plug it into his mouth.

"Ectozoids need kill now," puffed Boraf, extending a tentacle toward the cigarette. "Now not later save world."

As the tentacle drifted toward him, Luther froze, the lighter halfway to his mouth. He gave Boraf a look that would have killed it if looks could do that...and as dense or inconsiderate as Boraf was, the 'Zoid seemed to get the message. The tentacle wavered for an instant in front of Luther's face, then slowly withdrew.

Luther glared at the 'Zoid for another moment for good measure, then flicked the lighter and touched the flame to the tip of the cigarette. When he released the first lungful of smoke, he was pleased to see the 'Zoids back away; the one thing they seemed to be more allergic to than waiting was cigarette smoke.

If he had thought he could get away with it, and if he had had enough cigarettes, Luther would have stood there and smoked for the rest of the day.

Around his fifteenth conversion of the morning, Luther began to regret his life as a serial killer.

It was a brand new train of thought, one that had never chugged through him on even his worst days. Even when Lech Bomb had gone bad and the Guild had kicked Luther out, he had never doubted his choice of career. It had been a given practically from day one; he had never felt like he could have been anything *but* a serial killer.

So why, all of a sudden, was he questioning his choice? Why did he feel sadness and shame when he looked back at his achievements instead of the usual pride and nostalgia? And why was he jumping the track now, of all times, just when he was at the apex of his career?

As he guided another 'Zoid in gutting another victim, Luther remembered the first human life he had taken. The old woman's face came back to him, looking just the same as it had when he'd thrown the first shovel-full of dirt on her: weeping and blinking and quaking, buried alive. He had thought of her often through the years, always with secret, dark pleasure...but now, the pleasure had soured. When he conjured her image in his mind (Ida Mae Caldwell, that was her name) he felt a brick in his stomach and a wave of dizzying nausea.

Annoyed at this unexpected response, Luther skimmed through his memories of other victims, seeking more familiar reactions. Not counting the 'Zoids he'd killed, he had 276 to choose from over a 42-year period. Normally, recalling them was like fondling rare coins from a collection--admiring them, wallowing in the selfish joy of ownership; this time, he wanted to put them right down just as soon as he picked them up.

For the first time in his life, his murder memories felt unclean.

He flipped from one to the next, hardly daring to glance at them. Each one intensified his feelings of disgust: Number 12, Julie Kefler, age 33, strangled and minced; Number 37, Steve Parrote, age 41, tortured with pliers for three days and hung on a clothesline; Number 108, Abner Lockjaw, age 74, butchered and fed to his dogs a bite at a time; Numbers 246 and 247, Milo Chapel, age 17, and Peggy Brezini, age 16, cut up and stitched back together into one big mismatched body.

And then there was Number 150, which Luther couldn't even bear to think about for a fraction of a second. Once, Number 150 had been one of his crowning achievements; now, it seemed like the most twisted crime of his entire twisted life.

Contrary to what he had thought up until now, Luther realized that he was a sick and wicked individual. His disgust at the memories of what he had done in the past was equaled only by his newborn self-loathing.

How he could ever have imagined that he was a great man was beyond his current ability to comprehend. Would a great man have come all the way out into space and become the first Earthling to set foot on an alien world...only to murder its inhabitants? Would a great man have failed to see that unleashing the killer instinct might cause more harm than good on Ectos?

Would a great man stand by, arms dripping with pink milk from a punctured head-bulb, as one 'Zoid trainee fought another over the remains of a murder victim, playing a savage tug-of-war with the limp mess of bulbs and tentacles?

As the creatures squawked and yanked the corpse back and forth, Luther wiped his drenched arms on his black coveralls. Deciding he had had enough, he turned to walk away.

And before he could take a single step, a third 'Zoid flung itself in front of him.

"Make kill now," the creature puffed from its forehead blowhole. "Now!"

Luther shook his head and backed away. "No more," he said. "I need a break."

The 'Zoid reached out with three tentacles at once, and Luther had to back up fast to evade them. "Make kill," said the creature. "Save world."

Luther wished he hadn't handed over the knife to the other two

'Zoids. "Not now," he said, continuing to backstep as the creature pressed toward him.

"Save world make kill now not later," said the 'Zoid, extending more tentacles.

Luther took another step and ran into a pillowy obstacle. Lurching away from it at once, he spun around and saw that it was Boraf.

The other 'Zoid shuffled closer, still reaching. Its tentacles brushed him as he ducked and darted behind Boraf, putting his 'Zoid host between him and the overeager wannabe.

As Luther got ready to run, the wannabe plowed into Boraf with a sound like wet spaghetti flopping into a colander. The creatures hooted and thrashed around, tentacles intertwining, fluid-filled bulbs sloshing against each other.

One of the wannabe's tentacles squirmed out from between them and twisted toward Luther...but he easily sidestepped it. Another wriggled toward him from below, catching him by surprise, but it only managed to graze his leg before he danced away from it.

Then, the wannabe stopped struggling.

It stood there for a moment, huddled against Boraf, breath whistling in and out of its blowhole. Then, slowly, it uncurled its tentacles from Boraf's and drew back, head bobbing from side to side.

Luther watched, expecting the creature to thrust past Boraf and pursue him. Instead, the wannabe shuffled back, tentacles coiling sinuously, head-bulb quivering.

"Want kill," puffed the creature. "Want kill!"

"I told you, no more for now," said Luther. "You'll have to wait."

"No wait," said the wannabe. "No need human."

The creature turned and wobbled over to the two 'Zoids who had been fighting over the carcass. They had resolved the tug-of-war by tearing the corpse in half, and each was now smearing its slimy prize like a washcloth over its body.

The knife the killers had used on their victim lay forgotten in a pink puddle in the street. Flashing out a tentacle, the wannabe scooped up the weapon...and in the same flicker of motion, swung it around and drove it into the head-bulb of one of the killers.

"Want kill more," sang the wannabe, wrenching the knife from the first 'Zoid and swinging it around into the head-bulb of the second. As both victims squealed, the wannabe ripped out the knife again and slashed it through the air, pink milk flying, to plunge into another of the first killer's bulbs. "Boraf make want kill! No need human!"

Luther stared as the 'Zoid lashed the blade back and forth, hacking up two creatures at once. For the first time that he could remember, Luther felt horrified at watching a killing in progress.

Boraf turned and patted his shoulder with a slimy tentacle. "Boraf make Ectozoids kill now," said the alien. "Luther take break now. Boraf make many kill save world."

Luther just kept staring. Whatever had enabled him to transform 'Zoids into killers--whether it was some fluke of his body chemistry or some warped electrical field in his brain--it had somehow been transferred to Boraf. The timing couldn't have been better, because Luther was sick to death of making killers.

And yet, he wondered if it was entirely a good thing that Boraf had the power. He wondered if it would stop with Boraf, or if other 'Zoids could develop the same ability to implant the killer instinct.

If the killing could be spread by 'Zoids other than Boraf, he wondered what the world would be like in a week. How much of the population would be left by the time the invaders arrived?

And he wondered if it was just a coincidence that Boraf's empowerment had kicked in just as his own murder drive had fizzled.

That night, no one bothered Luther. No 'Zoids barged up to wallop the door of Boraf's house-mound, demanding conversion. Luther figured it was because Boraf--and other 'Zoids, too, most likely--was doing the job just fine without him.

Finally, Luther was alone with time to rest...but all he could do was lie awake and think.

The faces of the many people he'd killed kept drifting up out of his memory, filling him with guilt and regret. Number 150, in particular, kept returning again and again, the worst of the lot.

Number 150, Harmony Duquesne, 18 years old.

The harder he tried not to think about her, the more forcefully she surged back to the forefront of his mind. The man he had become could not believe what the man he had been had done to her.

He wondered how he had managed it, how he had managed any of it. Thinking back, he tried to understand what had driven him, what had enabled him to commit such atrocities...and he couldn't. He had the memories, bright and brutal and real, but no grasp at all of the mentality that had brought them into being.

He was a monster, and he finally knew it. Whatever had blinded him to the truth had been leeched out of him by the 'Zoids; he finally had a conscience and awareness of his nature.

And he wished he didn't.

There was only one redeeming factor, one thing that he might have done right, and he clung to it. By instilling the killer instinct in the 'Zoids, he might have given them the means to save their world.

Maybe (Luther tried to convince himself) this single act could balance the scales for the past...or, at least, allow him to live with the memories of what he had done. Maybe, with this act of redemption and his newfound change of heart, Luther still had hope for a brighter future free of the demons that had ruled him for most of his life.

And maybe, the evil he had done had had a purpose after all, had all been leading up to this...and in saving the 'Zoids, Luther had also saved himself.

Rolling over on the sleeping mat, he reached for his cigarettes and fished one out. As he lit it, he listened to the chaos outside--the yips and whistles and squeals of 'Zoids in frenzy, the splashing of body fluids, the smacking of corpses on the street. It was a

round-the-clock madhouse out there, like a vision of Hell...and he had made it.

He tried not to think about how many 'Zoids were dying out there as he smoked, how many had died since his arrival on Ectos. Instead, he reminded himself that the death was necessary for the survival of the 'Zoids, that in order to fend off the invasion, they had to take drastic measures to activate violent tendencies.

Still, Luther worried that it might all fly out of control. Clearly, the 'Zoids were getting carried away with their newfound murderous impulses; Luther expected a worldwide escalation as the killing gift spread around the planet. He thought it was possible that the 'Zoids would get so caught up in their collective rampage that they would be too disorganized or depopulated to fight when the invaders arrived.

Which would cancel out any balancing of the scales for Luther. If anything, it would dump him so far into the negative side that he would never even get a glimpse of the positive side again.

He would be to blame. Conquered, the 'Zoids might have survived, might even have someday overthrown their conquerors. Thanks to Luther, however, the 'Zoids might kill themselves off on their own.

It would have been the ultimate accomplishment for a death-hungry serial killer, a real work of art. Unfortunately, Luther wasn't a serial killer anymore. He wasn't sure what he was, but he knew he wasn't a serial killer.

The next morning, Boraf shuffled in excitedly, dripping with pink and yellow milk and inky fluid. Luther was still up, smoking, but he felt like crap; he was irritated that Boraf was still full of energy after being out murdering all night, and he was further peeved that the entire 'Zoid species never seemed to need sleep at all.

"How was your night?" said Luther, blowing out smoke.

Boraf sniffed loudly and backed away from the cloud that Luther had exhaled. "Night of history!" it said, voice shrill as a fire bell. "Boraf make many Ectozoid kill. Many Ectozoid make many more Ectozoid kill."

"Looks like you did some killing yourself," said Luther.

Boraf shook his tentacles, spraying fluid all over the walls and floor. "Want kill more," said the creature. A noise like a cross between a fart and fingernails scratching a chalkboard burst from its fluttering blowhole.

"Yeah," said Luther, stubbing out his cigarette. "So anyway, that big invasion oughtta hit soon, right?"

"Invasion two days," said Boraf, tentacles twisting and swaying.

"And the Ectozoids are ready?" said Luther.

"Ready two days," said Boraf. "Make many Ectozoid kill."

Luther sighed. "It just seems like a lot of chaos right now. If there's an invasion coming in two days, shouldn't your people be getting prepared?"

Boraf made a wheezing, oinking sound and bobbled his head. "Ectozoids prepare! Make ships ready kill now. Make troops ready fly ships."

Luther felt relieved. It was the first reference he'd heard to any kind of defense preparations other than Ectozoids killing each other. "So you'll be ready in two days?"

"Ready two days," said Boraf. "Ready save world."

Luther nodded. "That's good. I was starting to think things were getting out of control with all the killing."

Boraf had been fidgeting around, but it suddenly stopped. "Always control," it said. "Ectozoids good control."

Luther smirked. "Except when you're all worked up about killing each other."

"Control killing too," puffed Boraf. "Only kill weak. Only kill lazy."

Luther had been reaching for another cigarette, and he stopped. "You're killing the weak?" he said, staring up at the jellyfish.

"Need strong save world," said Boraf. "Need all strong no weak no lazy."

Luther's stomach twisted. He had never considered that the apparent chaos masked a methodical effort to thin the herd. It had never occurred to him that the 'Zoids were choosing their victims in other than a random fashion.

His newfound conscience shot him full of guilt. Until that moment, he had consoled himself with the knowledge that his brutal influence would at least lead to a redemptive outcome...but now, even that consolation was deflated. The 'Zoids were cleansing themselves of undesirables, and he was responsible for setting the pogrom in motion.

He was no better than Hitler. There was a time when that wouldn't have bothered him a bit, but that time was long gone.

Just when Luther hated himself as much as he thought possible, he found that he could hate himself even more.

He hated the 'Zoids almost as much. Though their crimes had been instigated by him, he believed that the seeds of savagery must have been within them all along. He didn't believe that the notion of systematic extermination of undesirables had dawned on them overnight, springing solely from his influence.

The 'Zoids were just as bad as he was, or as he had been. Looking at them was like looking in a mirror, and he was sick of what he saw.

Suddenly, Luther wanted one thing more than anything in the universe.

"So when do I go home?" he said, grabbing the pack of cigarettes. "You promised I'd leave before the invasion."

"Two days," said Boraf, picking up a fresh knife from a table and shuffling toward the door.

"Isn't that cutting it kind of close?" said Luther. "The invasion's supposed to start in two days."

Boraf slapped the door and its component eels slithered apart. "No worry," said the 'Zoid. "Luther go fast ship. Leave early."

Luther frowned. "You sure I'll get out in time? We had a deal, remember?"

"Fast ship," said Boraf. "Get away go Earth fast."

"Why not leave tomorrow?" said Luther. "You don't need me here anymore."

"Ship ready two days," said Boraf, shuffling out the door. "Now Boraf go make many Ectozoid kill."

As the door closed, Luther lit his cigarette. All of a sudden, he had a bad feeling about his future.

Two mornings later, Luther found himself riding a giant centipede.

He and Boraf sat in a bubble that was either grown from the creature's back or attached there, he couldn't tell which. It was the same type of transportation he had ridden from the spaceport to Boraf's house-mound upon his arrival...apparently, the local version of a taxi.

Sunlight gleamed off the creature's ruby carapace as it scuttled through the streets, neatly winding its segmented length around bends and corners. Giant antennae danced from its head like fishing poles, constantly twitching and flickering in the air.

As the centipede taxi hurried them through the maze of the city, Luther noticed that the mayhem of the past week had finally subsided. The orgy of killing had seemed to die away in the middle of the night, from what he could hear from inside Boraf's house-mound, and now he didn't see a single murder underway anywhere. It was as if someone had given a signal, and all the 'Zoids had stopped killing at once.

Stopped killing and headed for the spaceport, apparently. All along the centipede's route, Luther saw 'Zoids shuffling in the same direction that the taxi was traveling. The further the taxi went, the more 'Zoids filled the streets...until, at the spaceport, the centipede was packed in all around by a vast crowd of jellyfish, all shambling toward the cluster of massive, globular spacecraft steaming on the launch pads.

It got so crowded that the centipede had to slow from a scuttle to a crawl, though it never stopped moving. When the 'Zoids didn't get out of its way voluntarily, the creature simply plowed through them, shoving them aside or nosing them under its hundred-legged bulk.

Before long, the taxi drew up to one of the ships, many times smaller than the other vessels but of the same spherical design. The bubble on the centipede's back rolled open like an eyelid, and Boraf wriggled down the creature's side to the ground.

As Luther handed down his duffel bag of possessions, he squinted up at the mirrored silver skin of the

sphere-ship. It looked identical to the craft that had brought him from Earth, and that ship had made the trip in nothing flat, in less than a day...but he was still worried. In spite of Boraf's reassurances, Luther wasn't convinced that he would escape the invasion.

"You're sure this'll get me away in time?" he said.

"Fast ship," said Boraf. "No worry."

Luther took another look before reaching for his food locker. He started to lift it, but arthritis pain flashed through his arms and hands.

Releasing the locker handles, he hissed breath between clenched teeth and massaged his hands. "Hell with it," he said. "Short trip to Earth, right?"

"Short trip," said Boraf. "Fast ship."

Luther popped the locker open and pulled out a can of chili and a packet of juice. "I'll just bring a snack and leave the rest here."

"Bring snack," said Boraf, extending tentacles to help Luther down the side of the centipede.

Luther held on to a tentacle and slid off the taxi's ruby carapace. He couldn't wait until he was home and would never have to touch another slimy tentacle for the rest of his life.

"What about my payment?" he said.

"All on ship," puffed Boraf. "Plus bonus."

"All right," said Luther, shouldering the duffel bag with difficulty. "Now let's get the hell out of here."

As the ship popped out of the atmosphere like a bubble popping out of soapy water, Luther asked for the tenth time if the invasion fleet was getting close yet.

"All clear," said Boraf, though it didn't seem to be looking at a monitor screen or out a window. "Safe passage."

Luther's eyes were glued to the circular viewport alongside his seat. "Wait," he said, squinting at a distant flicker of light. "Is that one of their ships?"

"No," said Boraf.

"Well, how do you know?" snapped Luther. "You didn't even look."

Boraf floated past, free of the harness that had restrained it during liftoff. "Always notified of danger," said the 'Zoid. "No danger now."

Luther snorted and kept his eyes on the viewport anyway.

He caught a glimpse of another suspicious twinkle and followed it, heart racing...then decided it was just a star and only appeared to be moving relative to the ship. He saw a group of distant lights and leaned so close to the viewport that his nose almost touched the glass...but they were just a group of stars or planets, fixed in the darkness.

Breathing fast, mouth dry, joints throbbing, Luther wished he could light a smoke. Unfortunately, even if the 'Zoids had allowed him to light up on the spaceship, he didn't have any cigarettes left.

Any way he looked at it, he was going home just in time.

Gazing into the blackness beyond the viewport, Luther wondered which of the pinpricks of light was Earth's sun. He wished that he was already there, already breathing the sweet air and moving among other human beings and drinking in the familiar sights...savoring all the things that he had so taken for granted and never would again.

At the same time that the thought of going home excited him, it scared the hell out of him. He was returning to Earth as a new man, free of his old compulsions, remorseful and self-aware. He was already planning to face up to the crimes of his past, to make amends and restitution as best he could and pay the price for what he had done...which would ease his newfound conscience but would be the fight of his life. By the time it was all over, his very life might be the price he would have to pay. That, he was not looking forward to.

And then there was another possibility that was wearing on him.

What if, when he got home, whatever had changed within him changed back?

Suddenly, something caught his eye outside the viewport, and he jumped. Craning his neck, he saw a gleaming silver curve gliding up from the rear edge of the window, sparking in the light of Ectos' sun.

"Boraf!" he said, watching as the silver advanced and expanded...and then, as the word left his mouth, he recognized the shape.

It was one of the 'Zoid sphere ships, moving alongside them. The massive globe floated up from the 'Zoid homeworld, traveling in the same direction as the ship carrying Luther.

He heard a familiar sloshing and rustling as Boraf drifted up beside him. "Killship," said the 'Zoid. "Killship save world."

Keeping his eyes glued to the viewport, Luther spotted another of the giant spheres beyond the first. And then another. Moving in formation, they paralleled his own ship's course and speed, bobbing in the void like enormous silver balloons.

Luther frowned as another sphere pushed up alongside the rest. "We're all heading in the same direction," he said. "Are they escorting us till we're safely away from here?"

"Ships escort," said Boraf.

"Well, good," said Luther, leaning back. "I'd hate to wind up in the line of fire."

Boraf made a noise like the wail of a saw being played with a fiddle bow. "Luther safe," it said, patting his head with a tentacle. "No worry."

As Boraf floated forward to burble at the 'Zoids operating the ship's controls, Luther tried to relax. He felt a little better knowing that his ship had a protective escort, but he still couldn't quite extinguish the foreboding that needled the back of his mind.

After a while, though, when the ships had cruised far from Ectos with no sign of danger, he finally managed to convince himself that he would be okay. Slowly, his nervousness faded, and he actually drifted off to sleep.

Luther awakened to the most wonderful sight: a blue-green world, swathed in clouds of white, with a single pewter moon suspended above it.

Earth.

As he watched his home planet push closer through the big viewport at the front of the ship, he smiled serenely. Whatever awaited him there, whatever trials he would have to face to complete his redemption, he was happier than he had ever imagined possible to be near it again.

He was home.

"We're there already," he said, raising his voice for Boraf to hear.

Boraf was playing his tentacles over the fluttering grassy fronds of a control panel. "Earth," the 'Zoid said simply.

"Thank God," muttered Luther, still smiling. He yawned loudly and stretched, extending his arms overhead and pressing his abdomen against the thick safety strap holding him in his seat.

Staring at the beautiful planet beyond the forward viewport, he daydreamed about the things he had missed most from home...the things that were now within reach. No matter what ordeals he was about to undergo, he promised himself that he would gorge on as many cheeseburgers, T-bones, beers, and pornos as he possibly could.

Then, something caught his attention from the corner of his eye.

He turned to the viewport beside him, and his smile disappeared. His eyes widened and his mouth dropped open.

A chill ran up his spine.

"Boraf," he said quietly, and then he shouted. "Boraf!"

The 'Zoid left the controls and floated over to him, sloshing and puffing. "Luther?"

"Why are the other ships here?" snapped Luther. "I thought they were going to fight the invasion fleet!"

The 'Zoid made a noise like the meow of a cat crossed with the squeak of a hinge. "Fleet no fight fleet," it said. "No make sense."

"No no no," said Luther, gaping at the giant silver spheres outside the viewport. "The invasion fleet! The 'Zoids were supposed to stop the invasion fleet and save the world!"

A gargling sound emerged from Boraf's forehead blowhole. "Only one fleet," said the creature. "One invasion."

Luther's heart raced as he turned from the window to stare at the hovering jellyfish. "One invasion," he said slowly.

"Earth," said Boraf, pointing a tentacle at the forward viewport. "Ectozoids invade Earth."

"I don't understand," said Luther. "You told me you needed to save your world."

"Save world yes," said Boraf. "Ectozoids use up resources. Get new resources Earth save world."

Cold panic rushed through Luther, mingled with rage. "No!" he said, grabbing for the latch on his restraints, trying to pry them open. "You son of a bitch! You tricked me!"

"Luther be happy," said Boraf. "Great killer make greatest kill ever. Kill human species."

Luther battled the restraints but couldn't open them. "No! Don't do it!"

"No worry," said Boraf, ruffling his hair with a slimy tentacle. "Luther safe. Luther special. Luther Ectozoid hero save world."

"Please!" screamed Luther. "I was wrong! I've changed!"

"Congratulations," puffed Boraf. "Luther greatest serial killer in universe."

Boraf was close enough to kill. Luther reached deep, searching for the old murderous fire...but he couldn't even find a dim spark. Even now, the killer within was nowhere to be found.

All he could do was thrash against his restraints and scream like a child in a doctor's office as the gleaming silver globes dropped into the atmosphere of the blue-green planet.

BLACKBEARD'S ALIENS

Fire!" I have been called a Gentleman Pirate, and oft enough, the name suits. But on a day like this, Stede Bonnet is all pirate and no gentleman.

No sooner has the order to fire left my lips than the port side guns of the *Adventure* blast out their loads in clouds of roiling black smoke. Five iron balls leap through the air, heading straight for their target--a huge silver disk hovering thirty feet above the water.

Twin beams of red light flash out from the rim of the disk, burning two of the cannonballs into wisps of steam. But the other three make it through. They don't penetrate the hull of the silver disk as I had hoped, but they do make it rock in midair.

Take that, you hellspawn. "Reload!" I shout, though I know the men have already done just that. We are united in perfect rhythm after all our many battles as part of this fearsome flotilla. Our leader, much as I despise him, has taught us that.

Even now, not half a league away, I hear the guns of his personal flagship, the *Queen Anne's Revenge*, pound away at a larger target--another hovering object, this one triangular in shape. I don't have to look to know his banner yet flies from the mainmast, rippling in the Caribbean breeze.

There is no other flag like it: a field of black, with a skeletal, horned demon raising a toast to Satan whilst piercing a heart with a spear. All this time, I thought it was merely a symbol of evil designed to strike fear in the hearts of seagoing foes. And, for me, a personal symbol of a man I loathed, a pirate who'd taken everything from me and pressed me into service in his infamous fleet.

Little did I know it was a declaration of war on an unearthly enemy. Little did I dream, until recently, that Blackbeard had much more on his mind than wealth and power.

"Fire!" This time, the booms of the cannon begin before I cry out the word. It's not insubordination; the men know we must press the attack hard and fast.

But not one single ball connects with the target. This is because our one target has become many. The disk has split into twenty silver wedges, each leaping out of range of our guns.

And then streaking toward us like arrows from a brace of archers.

Raising the spyglass to my eye, I see spots of glowing light flare to life on the point of each wedge. The light is red, like the deadly beams that shot forth from the undivided disk a moment ago.

Their purpose is clear to me.

"Fight for your lives!" I pocket the spyglass and swing up my saber and pistol as I call out over the noise on deck. "Send 'em back to hell before they do the same to you!"

It's hard to believe there was ever a time when I'd not heard of these creatures. But that time was three months ago, true enough.

It was just then that Blackbeard's strange behavior began to arouse suspicions among his pirate captains, myself included. The way he started letting ships filled with goods from the West Indies pass without raiding them...the way he paced the decks at all hours, watching the inky darkness and muttering to himself...and then there were the treasure hunts.

I confronted him about it one night on Ocracoke Island, off the coast of Northern Carolina, as we watched the men dig. We had marched inland some distance and stopped in the heart of a grove of cedar trees. It was there he had instructed the crew to sink the first spade and dig until they struck something solid.

"Why are we pulling up all your old hoards?" I asked the question quietly under the rasp of sinking shovels and the grunting of the men. "New Providence, Nassau, Barbados, Oak Island--now here. Have you some grand scheme in mind?"

Blackbeard turned his fierce countenance upon me. It's true what they say about his fearsome appearance. With those glittering dark eyes and pitch-black beard, he looks like something more than man, something divine in a hellish way. "You'll know soon enough, Stede." He was a full head taller than me and had to look down to see my face. "And then you'll wish you didn't."

"Will you at least *open* this one?" It was stifling hot that night. I took off my broad-brimmed hat and wiped the sweat from my forehead with the back of my brown coat sleeve. "Or will you leave this chest padlocked in the hold of the *Revenge* like all the rest?"

He smirked behind his thick, braided beard, his namesake. "The ship's name is the *Queen Anne's Revenge*," he said.

I bristled, as he'd known I would. That ship had once been my own, christened *Revenge*, until he'd taken it from me. I despised him for it still, though I now served as captain of a smaller vessel in his fleet, the *Adventure*...waiting always for the day when I would regain what I had lost. *Working* for that day, too, always plotting and preparing. I was organizing a mutiny even then, taking advantage of Blackbeard's erratic behavior to sway key crewmen to my cause.

"Can you at least give me a hint, Edward?" I kept my voice low so the men would not hear me call him by his given name, Edward Teach...or as close to a given name as he'd admit to. "What plan do you have in mind for all that treasure?"

Blackbeard's broad face split in a pearly grin. "Who said anything about *treasure*?" He laughed and cuffed me on the side of my head.

Just then, the men struck something. They were several feet down, up to their shoulders in the hole, when I heard the spades hit something solid.

"We have it, sir," said one of the men. He hit it again. "I think it's a chest."

"Bring it up, then." Blackbeard gestured impatiently. "And make it double-quick, lads."

Suddenly, his head jerked up, and he looked around. His hands found the butts of two of the six pistols stuffed into the bandoliers he wore across his belly.

"What is it?" I listened and looked, sensing nothing...and then I glimpsed a faint red light glowing among the cedars. It was steady, perhaps fifty yards distant--not flickering, not a torch, certainly.

"We must have been followed." Blackbeard cocked the pistols. "You're about to get your answers, Stede."

I drew my own pistol and saber. "Answers?"

Blackbeard spit on the ground and raised the guns. "You won't like 'em." Then, he fired both weapons into the woods.

As the brimstone smell of gunpowder filled the air, I heard a terrible shriek in the distance like the cry of a banshee. Suddenly, the red light flashed and divided, becoming three lights...and all three surged toward us.

"Stand your ground!" Blackbeard dropped his first two guns and reached for another pair from his bandolier. "Go for their *middle* heads!"

His words baffled me, but explanation came soon enough. The lights were fast upon us, and with them, strange creatures unlike any I'd ever seen.

To say they were nightmarish would not do them justice. They were skeletal things of polished bone--roughly human in that they each had two arms, two legs, and a trunk...but the similarity ended there. For the bones were covered with jagged spurs and points.

And each creature had three heads like gleaming skulls: one atop the shoulders, with a crown of horns all around and sharp fangs in the jaws; one in the belly with a sharp beak; and one in the chest with a single glowing red eye and two mouths. Rays of crimson light shot out of those eyes, lancing right and left through the night.

Demons. That was the only word I had for them.

Chills leaped along my spine as they fell upon us. I heard the diggers scream, struck by the crimson rays, yet I did not flinch. I got off a shot at the demon nearest me, and my aim was true. The ball blasted dead on into the glowing red eye of the head in its chest. The thing went into a spasmodic dance, as if seized by St. Vitus, then spun screaming to the ground.

Blackbeard shot one, as well, but it still managed to throw itself around his legs. The third demon pressed the advantage, wrapping him in its spiny grip.

It was then I realized these things were more than mere skeletons. Their bones stretched and grew like vines, curling around Blackbeard as he grappled to free himself. Fresh spines and thorns arose and pierced his garments, anchoring themselves in his flesh.

For an instant, I was gripped by an impulse to leave him to his fate. It was the end I had hoped for from the start, since he'd taken my ship and convinced my own crew to turn against me.

And yet, I found myself running to his aid, hacking with my saber at the half-dead thing on the ground. Soon enough, it gave way.

Blackbeard, meanwhile, strained within the other demon's embrace. It continued to stretch around him, bones knitting a barbed cage as its horned skull craned back out of the way of his fevered head butts.

I slashed at its throat, taking the top head clean off--but the cage did not let go. The middle head was the vulnerable one, but it was pressed against Blackbeard, and I couldn't reach it.

Then, suddenly, a blaze of red light flared between them. The demon howled and shuddered, and Blackbeard burst free of the skeletal trap, sending fragments of bone flying everywhere.

But that was not the biggest surprise. I was far more stunned by what I saw before he pulled his tattered jacket closed to cover his exposed chest.

For there, over his breastbone, was a second head.

It was more like a face, not a fully formed skull as had jutted out of those demons. And it had two eyes, not just one--but those eyes both glowed with red light.

I sucked in my breath and backed away from him. He glared at me as he wrapped the coat tighter around himself.

"Into the pit with you." He gestured toward the hole the men had been digging.

I kept backing away. Did he intend to kill me?

Blackbeard rolled his eyes. "We're *both* going in. The beasties killed our diggers. We need to bring up the chest ourselves."

He stormed toward the pit, but I hung back. After all I'd seen, did I dare trust him?

"Get in the damn *hole*," he snapped. "Unless you *want* to stay out here alone and wait for more of those things."

He had a point. Swallowing hard, I slid my saber into its scabbard and followed him down into the ground.

After digging out the chest and hauling it to the beach, we rowed our skiff by moonlight toward the *Queen Anne's Revenge* and the *Adventure*.

At first, Blackbeard just glowered at his end of the boat, saying nothing. But after a while, my own stare seemed to wear him down.

"When I was a younger man," he said, "after sailing aboard a privateer's vessel in Queen Anne's War, I settled on an island in the Bahamas. It was called Shark Cay."

I frowned. "I haven't heard of it."

Blackbeard offered no comment. "I had a wife and two children there. Two splendid little boys." He pulled back on the oars, pushing the skiff forward. "I was happy."

Happy? I tried to imagine it. I'd seen him furious, vengeful, bitter, distant, and brutal, but never happy.

"Then, one night, *they* came." He bobbed his head toward Ocracoke, toward the demons. "They emerged from the heart of a raging storm, swirling with red, yellow, orange, blue, and black lightning. They swooped down out of a doorway in the sky in flying boats and landed on Shark Cay, which they laid waste to." Leaning forward, he met my gaze with eyes afire. "When they were done, I was the only living thing left on the island." His voice was like ice. "Perhaps this is why you have not heard of Shark Cay before."

I rowed my own oars a few strokes before daring to speak. "And you?"

Blackbeard sighed. "They took me with them. Back through the doorway." He gazed up at the stars. "They took me to the strangest place you can imagine. The skies were green, the sun was blue. Sounds were like smells, and tastes were like touches. There were beasties everywhere, some like the ones we just fought and some more terrifying still."

"It sounds like Hell," I told him.

"That's what I thought at first, but no. It was *another world*." He kept looking upward.

I nodded silently. If not for the battle we'd just been through on Ocracoke, I would have thought him insane.

"They...changed me. They thought I could be of use to them." He looked at me and sneered darkly. "They could not have been more wrong."

"You escaped."

Blackbeard smiled grimly. "They sent me back to do their dirty work, but I broke free. I've been waging war against them ever since, using the tools they gave me." He stopped rowing and patted his chest, where the second head glowed faintly under his coat. "I can *feel* them coming. I *know* what they want."

"How is that possible?"

"They *think* with one *mind*." He tapped his forehead with his finger. "I hear *echoes* and *whispers* enough to piece together their *plans*."

I stopped rowing too, then. "Which are?"

"The end of us all, Stede Bonnet." Blackbeard scowled. "Every man and woman on the face of the Earth."

I sat silently for a long moment, watching him. His words sounded mad. I could not help but think that they were ample fuel for the mutiny I'd been organizing.

Yet how could I dismiss them after what we'd been through? "Armageddon?" I said. "When? How?"

"Very soon, Bonnet." Blackbeard closed his eyes. He'd woven fuses into his shaggy black hair, and the tips of them started to glow and burn as if someone had taken a match to them. "We won't have much time."

"Time for what?" I asked. "What do we have to do?"

His eyes shot open and the lit fuses flared. "Save the world, of course."

We set sail the next morning for Hispaniola to rendezvous with the rest of our pirate fleet--eight ships strong, counting the *Queen Anne's Revenge* and the *Adventure*.

The sun was shining bright, the wind gusting strong. We sailed in a southeasterly direction, making excellent speed over choppy sapphire seas.

Salt spray misted over me as I paced the deck, watching the horizons through my spyglass. As I walked, the events of the night before replayed in my mind. In retrospect, they seemed like an opium dream, wholly unreal. Had *any* of it actually happened? Or was *I* the one who'd gone mad, not Edward?

Just as I considered this possibility, I heard his familiar heavy footsteps clomping toward me. Turning, I saw him in glory restored--red velvet coat, black trousers and knee-high boots. Under the coat, as was his habit, he wore a white shirt with prominent ruffles from throat to waist. Already, his bandoliers were in place, plugged with six loaded pistols, and his cutlass was sheathed in the scabbard swinging at his left hip.

"'Morning, Stede." He stomped up beside me and leaned his elbows on the port bulwark rail. "You're looking in the wrong place."

"Am I now?" I tried sounding glib, but I was having trouble standing so close to him. Now that I knew what lay under his shirt, he seemed more fearsome than ever to me.

Blackbeard raised a finger to the sky. "Our next attack will come from up there. Especially now, as we cruise the waters between Bermuda and Hispaniola."

I looked up, shading my eyes against the sun. "And why is that?"

"This is where their doorways open," said Blackbeard. "In this wedge of deep ocean where Mother Nature lets down her guard." He smacked his palm on the bulwark. "The walls are thin here, Stede."

A chill shot along my spine. "Will they come for us, Edward? Are they on their way?"

He shrugged his broad shoulders. "I feel nothing, but they surprise me sometimes. We'll keep the crew on round-the-clock watch for just such an occurrence." Narrowing his eyes, he clamped a hand on my upper arm. "Now come along. I have a task for you as well."

He took me below decks, to a corner of the hold that was under watch by three armed guards. They were three of his most loyal men; I'd never dared approach them while recruiting for my mutiny.

"Here we are." Blackbeard spread his arms before the five wooden chests stacked in front of us. "Finer treasures no man has ever beheld."

I took off my hat and stood beside him. "What is this task you have for me?"

Blackbeard reached for a ring of keys that hung on his right hip. He singled out one cast iron key and shook it in my face. "The most important thing you have ever done and will ever do in your life."

Stomping forward, he inserted the key in the padlock on the topmost chest. He turned it, and I heard the lock snap open.

"Would you say the winds can blow us in unforeseen directions, Stede?" he said as he unwound the chain from the chest. "That fate can lead us to places we never expected? Places we were destined to be?"

I thought of the day he first boarded my ship--*this* ship, now his. "Of course."

Blackbeard gazed at me with ferocious intensity from beneath his coal-black brows. "Then step forward, Stede."

Sweat ran down my back and sides. Had Blackbeard heard of the mutiny? Had he brought me down here to put an end to me?

"Come on now, Bonnet." He snapped his fingers.

Swallowing hard, I stepped forward.

"Do not be afraid, Stede." His words only made me *more* fearful. "This is what it has all been leading up to for you."

Then, he opened the lid of the chest.

I would have stumbled back away from it if he hadn't caught my arm and held me there. For the wooden box did not contain gold or silver or jewels, as I'd imagined.

It looked to me like a tub of guts--like someone had taken the offal from the day's catch of fish and dumped it inside.

The box was filled with glistening organs--deep red, pale gray, sickly green, onyx black. The mess *smelled* like guts, too, so rank and rotten it made me choke. I covered my nose and mouth with my hand, yet still the stench penetrated.

"Closer, Stede." Blackbeard forced me forward. "*This* is your *destiny*."

Standing so near, I realized that the guts in the chest were *still moving*--squirming and twisting before my eyes. The tip of a tentacle flicked up from the gruesome pudding, dragging a trail of slime with it. A flap of pink flesh rolled up, revealing a bloodshot eyeball the size of a breadfruit with a triangular pupil.

"*Listen* to it, Stede!" Blackbeard pressed me closer to the box. "*Hear* its voice in your *mind*."

"No, I..." Suddenly, I did hear something new. There *was* a voice--high-pitched and faint as the cry of a distant gull. It was saying something, speaking in a language I did not understand.

And though at first I thought I heard it with my ears, I quickly realized it was not reaching me that way at all. Somehow, it was *inside my head*.

"What...?" I listened, trying to pick out what it was telling me.

Then, I heard Blackbeard's gruff voice alongside it, whispering in my ear. "Put your hands in, Stede. Let it become *one* with you."

Another tentacle rose out of the mush and slithered toward me.

"Don't fight it, Stede," said Blackbeard. "This is what you must do to save us all."

He pressed me another inch forward--and then the ship lurched. A thunderous boom shuddered through the hull, as if the *Queen Anne's Revenge* had just slammed into another vessel.

"It's starting." Blackbeard shut the chest. "Our time has come."

"Time for what?" I said as we ran through the hold toward the ladders. "For me to become one with that *obscenity* back there?"

He grabbed a ladder and shot me a look. "You'll do it, Stede, or everyone you know in this world will die, and you'll be the cause of it."

The ship shook as we climbed above decks. I heard shots along the starboard bulwark, and saw the crew massed there with guns pointed down at the water.

As we hurried toward the men, an enormous green hump appeared alongside the ship, rolling forward. I quickly realized it was the back of a living creature, covered in glistening turquoise scales, cut by a red rill running along the spine.

"Sea serpent!" As the words left my lips, the creature's huge head reared up out of the water. It had the face of a dragon, with a long, reptilian snout, flared nostrils, and massive, jagged teeth. The red rill extended all the way to its forehead and stopped between its eyes, which blazed with telltale red light. "It's one of *theirs*, isn't it?"

"I was wrong about the next attack coming from above!" Blackbeard dashed for the cannons, waving his cutlass overhead. "We must blow this thing to kingdom come!"

By the time we got to the five starboard cannons, the men had already loaded them. Matches burned in hand...but no fuses had been lit.

"We can't get a bead on it!" said one of the gunners. "Damn thing's too fast!"

As he spoke, the serpent dove into the water and disappeared. Seconds later, the ship lurched as the thing struck us from below.

Blackbeard grabbed the gunner's arm and shook him hard. "Get ready! You'll have your moment!" Then he released him and closed his eyes. The fuses woven through his hair began to glow and spark.

When the men hesitated, I stalked among them, bellowing. "You heard him! Get ready to point the damn guns! Matches at the ready, you bastards!"

As the men scrambled to prepare, the ship rocked once more and settled. I heard the sound of something huge emerging from the water.

"There it is!" somebody shouted.

"Light the guns!" I told them.

As matches touched fuses all down the line, the serpent's giant skull burst up before us. Like a snake charmed by a swami, it slid up above the bulwark and stopped, eyes locked on Blackbeard.

We had our moment. "Fire! Fire! Fire!" As I screamed out the order, the cannons belched forth their missiles amid great gouts of brimstone smoke. Three balls crashed into the head of the monster, smashing through flesh and bone alike with a sound like thunder and splintering trees.

With an ear-splitting howl, the beast collapsed into the water and sank from sight. The ship swayed in the wake of its passing, then steadied.

At which time, Blackbeard opened his eyes. The fuses in his hair were still burning.

For a moment, I wondered if the men might rebel with no help from me--if this display of supernatural power might be enough to turn them against him out of sheer terror.

Instead, they cheered him. He swung his cutlass overhead, and they cheered as one, not a shirker among them.

"The battle is begun!" he roared. "Who will join me in tearing the enemy's *throat* out with my *teeth*?"

Every man on the deck cried out in fervent assent.

"Then hoist the mainsail! Best speed to Hispaniola!"

We encountered no further sea monsters on the way to Hispaniola. Blackbeard said the demons weren't strong enough to fill the seas with them...yet.

We met up with the rest of the fleet at Port-au-Prince. It was then I realized that our force had more than doubled in size.

Instead of eight vessels, there were now sixteen, all heavily armed and sailing under black flags. By bribe or coercion, I know not which, Blackbeard had enlisted powerful pirate captains as allies in our war: Calico Jack Rackham, Charles Vane, Robert Deal, Israel Hands.

Blackbeard gave each of them a chest--myself as well--and instructions. Each captain would sail out to a different location along the rim of the Gulf of Mexico, taking along a second ship for support.

On the map, our destinations ringed the Gulf. When Blackbeard connected them with straight lines, they formed the points of a mystic pentagram star straddling the oblong sea.

"When the moment comes, open your chest," said Blackbeard. "The thing inside is your salvation. You must unite with it. Allow it to work through you."

I scowled as I stared at my own chest on the deck at my feet. I wanted nothing to do with its gruesome occupant.

"How will we know when the moment arrives?" said Calico Jack.

"Believe me, you'll know." Blackbeard stared at each of us in turn. "The bottom of the sea will rise and blot out the sun."

"These...things." Vane tapped his chest with the tip of his cutlass. "What exactly will they *do*?"

"The same thing all at once," said Blackbeard. "And this miracle will save us all, so long as no man refrains from his duty." He stomped his boot and glared at us. "So if doubts you have, speak up now!"

Not a one of us said a word.

Six days later, as Blackbeard predicted, the battle is in full swing. Did the other ships make it to their positions? I have no way of knowing, and no time to worry about it.

My crew and I are too busy fighting to defend the good ship *Adventure*--first against a flying silver disk, and now against the twenty wedges that the disk has split itself into.

The men fire their guns at the darting wedges, but they're no match for the deadly red beams that lance down to destroy them.

The wedges make several runs along the length of our vessel--and then they stop and hover, ringing the deck. Doors open in the bellies of each of them, and skeletal, three-headed demons burst forth, screeching and brandishing fiery swords.

"Fight to the last man!" I howl as one of the demons scrambles toward me. "Aim for their middle heads!"

I follow my own advice, unleashing a shot at the red-eyed skull sticking out of my attacker's chest. My aim is dead-on; the head explodes, and the demon tumbles to the deck.

Heart hammering, I risk a look across the water at Blackbeard's ship--and what I see isn't good. The *Queen Anne's Revenge* is listing hard to port and giving off smoke. The triangular craft they've been fighting continues to batter the ship with fusillades of crimson beams.

How much longer can either ship hold out? When will the moment come--the one Blackbeard told us to expect?

As I think these thoughts, another demon bolts toward me. I run straight for it, slashing my saber at its chest...and the blade hacks through the bony middle head. The demon staggers back, clutching the cloven skull, and then it wails like a banshee and charges me again. I sidestep, barely, and the demon tumbles over the bulwark and into the sea.

That's when it happens.

I hear a thunderous rumbling from all directions. The gulf begins to churn and buck. Mighty swells toss the *Adventure* like a child's paper boat.

I see the *Queen Anne's Revenge* sway too, rolling violently from side to side. Whatever's happening, both ships are caught in its grip.

Suddenly, I see a vast, flat surface break the waves some five leagues hence. The sun glints on its silver skin as it rises from the deep.

I cannot see the far end of it. This thing, this *platform* is so massive, it extends beyond the horizon.

All along the curved edge, the sea pours off it in a wall of foaming white. The loudest roar I've ever heard booms across the gulf, like the sound of a thousand waterfalls crashing together all at once.

As the platform continues to rise, the *Adventure* and *Queen Anne's Revenge* are swept forward, drawn by the pull of a vast whirlpool swirling beneath it. I shout the order to drop anchor, but no one hears me over the rush of the falling water or the ongoing battle with the demons--guns blasting, swords clanging against bone.

As the monstrous object climbs higher, darkness washes over the *Adventure*. The sun has been blotted out.

The moment Blackbeard predicted has arrived. I know what I have to do.

Running to a nearby locker, I throw open the door and haul out the chest he gave me. Then I lift the lid and gaze upon the pulsating mass of organs and slime within.

How do I *do* this? How do I *become one* with this squirming, rancid sludge?

Suddenly, the darkness brightens. Looking up, I see red lights flaring to life in patterns along the underside of the vast platform. The light forms spirals, interlocking circles, rows of bars, clusters of pinpoints. It blinks and shifts and slides and spins, changing faster with each passing second.

As if the platform, whatever it might be, is awakening.

Just then, the ship lurches hard to starboard, and the chest starts to slide. I lunge to catch it--and my fingers touch the contents.

Without warning, the voice I heard in the hold pours into my head. At first, it still speaks a foreign tongue--but then, it becomes the King's English.

Not that I comprehend every word. *Do you wish to initiate the electromagnetic pulse?* That's what it says to me, in a woman's soothing voice.

What the hell is that? The thought comes to me unbidden...but it gets an answer.

The pulse will deactivate the World Machine, says the voice. *It will destroy all onboard systems permanently.*

Another question comes to me. *World Machine?*

The platform before you, says the voice. *It was sent here millions of years ago to reshape this hostile environment into one more suitable. It crashed, and remained ever since at the bottom of the impact crater, which became a sea.*

It was sent here from where? I ask.

Another world, says the voice. *The people there have been trying to reactivate it ever since. They created portals but could only come through a few at a time. They sent organic machines, like me...but we have been reprogrammed by Edward Teach. We stand ready to deliver an electromagnetic pulse that will destroy the World Machine's systems. We await your order.*

I hesitate. *What if I don't give it?*

All life on your world will be extinguished. And the purpose of your own existence will be unfulfilled.

Purpose?

You were chosen for this moment, says the voice. *Everything that Edward Teach has done to you was designed to lead you to this task. You are one of the few humans equipped to interface with our technology.*

The ship rolls and pitches. I suppose I should feel special now...grateful. I guess I should look at Blackbeard with new eyes.

But instead, I feel angrier than ever. I feel used.

All this time, he's been playing me for a fool, manipulating me because...why? Did he not imagine I'd agree to help save the world? Could he not have just *asked* me?

Suddenly, a thought flashes through my mind. *All this power. Could I use it to destroy Edward Teach instead?*

Yes, says the voice. *I can short-circuit the electrical impulses in his brain. However, I will not then be able to initiate the electromagnetic pulse that deactivates the World Machine.*

For so long, I've loathed that man. I've wanted nothing more than to destroy him and take back what's mine. Now, at last, I have the means.

But can I bring myself to do it at such a cost? Do I have hatred enough in my heart that I'd let the world perish for the sake of revenge against one man?

The lights on the underside of the platform flicker faster. A roaring tone, like the blare of a million foghorns, resonates outward, causing the decking under my feet to tremble. The *Adventure* and *Queen Anne's Revenge* rush closer to the whirlpool.

The voice speaks to me again. *Do you wish to initiate the electromagnetic pulse? Or do you wish to kill Edward Teach?*

I sink my hands deeper into the muck in the chest. I feel tentacles wrap around me, suckers attach to my flesh.

I'm becoming one with the organic machine. I know, without asking, that I have scant seconds to issue a command.

But I have to be honest. Right up till the end, I'm not sure what that command will be.

"Stede?"

I wake from a deep, dark sleep to the sound of his voice. To the rough grasp of his hand shaking my shoulder.

Blackbeard.

He chuckles and shakes me again. "Still alive, I see."

Much to my surprise, I am--and so is he. For that's the decision I made: to sacrifice my vengeance and save mankind.

Now look where it's got me. Washed up on the sand of an unknown shore like a tangle of flotsam--the pieces of a shattered ship washed up around me.

As I roll over and sit up, I see a section of prow on the sand twenty yards away. I can make out part of a name on the broken boards: ADVENT.

So this is what's left of the *Adventure*, the ship under my command. When the platform shut down and plunged back into the sea, tidal waves tossed her through the gulf and smashed her to bits here. It's a miracle I survived.

And more of a miracle that *his* ship survived. Gazing out at the now-becalmed waters, I see the *Queen Anne's Revenge* floating under a pristine red and orange sunset, heavily damaged but intact.

"Fine work, my friend." Blackbeard sits beside me, his glittering eyes taking in the sunset. "You, and Vane and Deal and Israel and Calico Jack...you saved us all." He laughs deep in his barrel chest, like a bear growling over a salmon. "A bunch of filthy pirates saved the world. How do you like *that* irony?"

"You son of a bitch." I shake my head. "How did you save the *Revenge*?"

He slaps me on the back so hard it hurts. "It's the *Queen Anne's Revenge*, Stede. I thought we'd settled that."

My eyes drift over her half-furled sails, glowing red in the light of sunset. My heart pounds at the sight of her masts, her guns, her softly curved hull--the dark-haired maiden carved in teak on her prow.

Nothing is settled. The only way it would have been is if the world had ended.

"How right you are." I elbow him in the side as hard as I can...wondering, at the same time, which men survived among the crew and if I can turn them to my mutinous cause.

Blackbeard pulls out a flask and takes a sip. "Beautiful evening, ain't it, ya' scurvy dog?"

I take the flask and raise it in a toast before I drink. "'Tis a shame it must be ruined by a scabby bilge rat like you."

ONE AWAKE IN ALL THE WORLD

Pass Candle could not see the creatures, except as winking blips of light on the flash-brain screen mounted in the flesh of his left arm. He didn't need to look at the screen, however, to know that the creatures were all around him and his partner, Nona Stiletto.

He could feel their presence. Could feel their eyes upon him, staring from the shadows of the darkened and fog-shrouded city.

More than that, he swore he could feel their malevolence. Their savagery.

He stiffened his right arm as he swept it from side to side, covering an arc of the gray fog with the snout of the warflower dark energy gun peeping from under the skin behind his wrist. He followed the arc with the single beam from his headlight—the round, white disk mounted like a third eye in the middle of his forehead.

Candle narrowed his dark brown eyes and stared into the headlight's beam, but he still saw nothing moving toward him in the fog. Maybe, his feelings were the product of his imagination, and the creatures in the shadows would turn out to be benevolent toward cybernetically enhanced humans like himself and Nona.

But somehow, he doubted it.

Stiletto said nothing to suggest she felt the same way, but the posture of her slender frame as she walked alongside him was as stiff and guarded as his. Her head ticked from side to side, flicking her golden ponytail to and fro in the darkness.

The retractable sleeves of her slick black form-fitting flowsuit were all the way up, like Candle's, leaving her weapon-and-instrument-studded arms free for action. She aimed her warflower directly ahead, and Candle knew from experience that she was ready to whip it around in a heartbeat and use it.

"The humanoid's twenty meters ahead," said Candle, watching the readings on his flash-brain screen. "Distress signal's strong and life signs're steady. She's surrounded by non-humanoid life-forms, like we are."

Just then, Candle smelled an odor like strong vinegar and heard a sound like claws clacking on the pavement to his left. He and Stiletto swung in that direction simultaneously, lighting it up with the beams of their headlights. Candle saw nothing in the newly illuminated area but a building's stone wall and a scattering of what looked like splintered bones at its base.

"Playing hard to get." Candle nervously combed the fingers of his right hand through his wavy salt-and-pepper hair.

"Let's hope they stay that way," said Stiletto.

Candle started forward again, following the female humanoid's life signs. "Seventeen meters to go," he said. "Easy-peasy."

The sound of breaking glass echoed in the distance. Claws or something like them clacked not far away.

"Guess again," said Stiletto, sweeping her headlight toward the clacking, then forward again.

Candle thought Stiletto had a point. In the darkness and fog, it felt like they'd walked several kilometers rather than the half kilometer they'd actually traveled from their spacecraft, the *Sun Ra*, which was parked at the edge of the city.

Though Candle wasn't the jumpy type, he was having his doubts about what a good idea it had been to walk away from the

Sun Ra at all...or land on this planet in the first place. Trouble was, he just hated ignoring a distress signal like the one that'd brought him here; some of his best jobs had come via distress signal.

He and Stiletto were first-class spacefaring exterminators, specializing in extra-nasty pests known as Squatters. Squatters ran people like puppets, remote-controlling them from somewhere beyond the Milky Way galaxy. Squatters reached out with their ultra-powerful minds and bonded people to them with over-whelming love and pleasure. Then, the Squatters sent these zombies, known as Wipeouts, on horrifically barbaric killing sprees.

Rumor had it the Squatters and Wipeouts were building up to something big, and people were scared. Contractors like Candle could make a living hunting the bastards full-time. Wipeout hunting was pretty damned rewarding for a top pro like Candle, in fact...especially when he had a former Wipeout like Nona Stiletto for a partner.

Sure, Nona was still messed up from years of being possessed by the aliens. She had committed more violent crimes than she could remember, and she was marked forever by scars on the inside and outside.

But she knew everything about Wipeouts, and the Squatters had left her mean and strong. Just the fact that she had survived being separated from a Squatter showed what kind of a hardass she was. Candle had never heard of another Wipeout walking away from that ordeal alive.

And he couldn't think of anyone he'd rather have by his side today.

"Fourteen meters," he said, squinting into the ten-meter-deep cone of visibility that was the best his headlight could cut through the fog.

Candle and Stiletto pressed to within twelve meters of their target, then eleven. Finally, their headlights picked out a form in the gray soup.

At last, they got a look at the being they'd been seeking through the alien city...a being who, as far as they could tell, was the only remaining native humanoid on the planet.

In size and build, she resembled a human child, five or six years old...a little girl with glittering purple skin, multi-faceted red insect eyes, and not a hair on her head.

Candle and Stiletto lowered their arms so the beams of their headlights weren't flashing right in the little girl's face.

Candle told the girl his name, his flash-brain converting his speech into audio she could understand. "This is Nona," he added, hiking a thumb at Stiletto. "What's your name?"

"Luma," said the little girl. She wore a simple white shift and sandals. As she spoke, she hugged a ragged doll tightly against her chest.

On one wrist, Luma wore a gold bracelet set with a blinking amber crystal. A glance at the flash-brain screen confirmed Stiletto's suspicion that the bracelet was the source of the distress signal transmissions.

"Cool name," said Candle. "Nice to meet you, Luma."

Luma cocked her head to one side and narrowed her faceted eyes. "You look funny," she said. "What's wrong with you?"

Candle smirked at Stiletto. "There's nothing wrong with us," he said. "We're just not from around here."

"Okay," said Luma.

"We want to help you," said Candle. "Can you tell us why you're all alone here?"

Luma dropped her chin against the head of her doll and twisted slowly from side to side. As Stiletto watched, the little girl's skin changed color, shifting from dark purple to deep blue...signaling a mood change?

"I'm lost," Luma said softly. "I can't find my family. I woke up and went outside, and now I can't find them."

"Do you know where there're more people like you?" said Candle. "People who look like you?"

"You mean Sagrans?" said Luma.

"Is that what the people're called?" said Candle.

Luma nodded. "Sagrans."

"You know where they are?" said Stiletto.

Luma shook her head. "There's no one around except the Skilla." As she said it, her voice dropped to a near whisper, and her skin shifted to deep purple again.

"The Skilla aren't people like you, are they?" said Candle.

"No," said Luma, shivering. "They're scary. Everyone says the Skilla are holy, but I think they're scary, too. I think they're going to get me."

Candle scooped the little girl up into his arms.

"Don't worry, Luma," he said, patting her back. "You're not alone anymore. We'll keep you safe."

"You will?"

"Yeah. That's why we came here. To help you."

"Will you find my family, too?" Luma's skin changed from purple back to deep blue.

"We'll do our best." Candle smiled and bounced her affectionately in his arms. "I promise."

Stiletto's heart beat faster, but not because of any impending danger. It was the sight of Candle with Luma, the way he held her and reassured her.

Stiletto wished he'd do that for her, too. She wished he'd love her the way that she loved him.

She hadn't always felt this way. She'd been working with Candle since he'd freed her from the Squatter three years ago, and she'd only been sure she wanted him within the last six months.

She really didn't know if he felt the same way, though, and frankly, she hadn't been going out of her way to find out. The hardass routine that was so important to her job and just getting through the day was hard to push aside...plus which, her head was still a wreck from her time as a Wipeout. The Squatter was gone, but it had left behind a boatload of poison. Sometimes, Stiletto still felt echoes of the bastard swimming around in there, and she wondered if he was regenerating somehow.

That was what worried her the most and kept her from reaching out to Candle. What if she was still a danger to him, a sleeper agent with secret orders implanted at a deep level her deprogramming had missed?

Unfortunately, the more she tried to lock her feelings away, the stronger they grew.

And seeing Candle comforting Luma made them stronger still.

Candle put Luma down but held on to her tiny, green hand as he and Stiletto talked.

"Any ideas?" he said in a half-whisper.

Stiletto stared at the blinking lights on the flash-brain screen. "I've detected low-level mechanical vibrations."

"Where abouts?" said Candle.

"Center of the city. Four kilometers that way." Stiletto aimed her headlight into the murk.

"Where there's working machinery, there might be people," said Candle. "Shielded from sensors, maybe."

"There're a lot of non-humanoids between here and there."

Candle nodded. "And we can't take the *Sun Ra* in," he said, "because there's nowhere to land. Not even a flat rooftop." He sighed. "We'll have to keep going on foot."

Candle heard a whooping cry like hysterical laughter in the distance. Luma's hand fluttered, and he tightened his grip on it.

"Up for a hike?" he said to Stiletto.

She nodded. "I'm ready."

"How about you?" Candle gave Luma's hand a squeeze.

"Ready," said Luma.

"Then let's get going," said Candle.

Though Stiletto wasn't easily freaked, she felt the hairs on the back of her neck stand up way too often as she, Candle, and Luma trudged through the city.

She was being stalked. By something she couldn't see.

But she could hear it. The Skilla raised a constant clamor through the city, their distant whoops and yowls accompanied by the sounds of smashing and thumping and shattering. Close by, their claws clacked along the pavement, moving when Stiletto, Candle, and Luma moved...stopping when they stopped. Always, when the creatures were near, Stiletto smelled their heavy, vinegar-like scent in the humid air.

And the number of them that were close-by was growing. Flash-brain scans of the surrounding area revealed that more Skilla were clustering near Stiletto, Candle, and Luma with each passing moment.

"We're drawing a crowd," Stiletto said to Candle, keeping her voice to a whisper for Luma's sake. "Maybe a warning shot'll drive them off."

"Don't provoke them," said Candle. "Not yet. We're so outnumbered, let's put off a fight as long as we can." With that, he turned his attention to Luma. "So," he said, shifting his voice to a less serious tone. "What's your friend's name?"

Luma looked up at him, a puzzled expression on her glittering, deep blue face. She looked down at her doll then, and understood. "Her name is Gala," she said.

"How long've you and Gala been together?" said Candle.

Luma raised the doll to her ear. "Gala says we've been together since I was a little girl."

Candle smiled. "Cool." He still held on to Luma with his left hand and continually scanned his warflower back and forth with his right. "And how did the two of you meet?"

"Mommy and Daddy gave her to me," said Luma.

"The last time you saw your mommy and daddy, what were they doing?" said Candle.

"They were sleeping," said Luma.

"For a long time?" said Stiletto.

"I think so," said Luma. "I woke up and went for a walk. I wanted to go home to get my dreambook, but then I couldn't find home."

"So your family was somewhere other than home," said Candle. "What did this place look like?"

"Big," said Luma. "And dark." She raised the doll to her ear and listened for a moment. "Gala says Mommy and Daddy will be mad at me."

"Why is that?" said Stiletto.

"I wasn't supposed to open the door," said Luma. "I wasn't supposed to go outside."

"Because of the Skilla?" said Candle.

"Uh-huh," said Luma. "They're holy, but they can hurt you." Again, she listened to the doll. "Gala says they're going to hurt all of us, and it'll be my fault because I opened the door."

"Try to help Gala not worry so much," said Candle. "Tell her we're going to take good care of you."

"Okay," said Luma.

Just then, something heavy and hard hit the ground near Stiletto.

Everyone stopped in their tracks. Luma gasped and threw herself against Candle.

Spinning, Stiletto threw light in the direction of the noise. A block of stone, big as a human head, lay in the street barely three meters away.

Suddenly, Stiletto heard a clatter of approaching claws and caught the smell of vinegar in the air. A quick glance at her flash-brain screen confirmed the evidence of her ears, and she whirled around.

Two blips had disengaged from the unseen crowd of Skilla and were charging directly at Candle and Luma.

Without a word, Stiletto fired her warflower, shooting a crackling bolt of energy into the fog. Immediately, she heard a wailing screech, erupting loud and close enough to hurt her ears. Through a tunnel burned in the fog by the warflower's beam, she glimpsed shining silver eyes like a pair of coins suspended in midair.

Stiletto lashed the warflower around, seeking the second oncoming Skilla. She was rewarded with another raging screech. Then, with a flurry of clattering claws, the creatures hurtled away, their cries receding in the distance.

"So much for putting off a fight," said Candle.

"These creatures're pretty smart," said Stiletto. "They staged a diversion by throwing that stone, then came at us from the other direction."

Luma tugged on Candle's uniform then, and he and Stiletto looked down. The little girl's face was pinched in an expression of pure anguish. Her glittering skin was so fiery red that it looked like it would be hot to the touch.

"Gala says you lied!" Inky, black tears streamed down her face. "She says the Skilla *are* going to get us!"

"Tell Gala it's okay to be scared," said Candle, "but things can turn out fine no matter how scary they seem."

Luma shuddered with sobs. "Gala doesn't believe you!"Stiletto searched her mind for a plan to calm the child, then crouched down beside her. "That's because Gala hasn't heard the story of the girl with the invisible friend," said Stiletto. "Have you?"

Still sobbing, Luma shook her head. The inky tears rolled off her jaw and fell onto her white shift, staining it with spatters of black.

"You think Gala might like to hear the story?" said Stiletto, ignoring a whooping scream-laugh in the distance.

Luma shrugged.

Stiletto got to her feet and scooped up the child in one smooth motion. "Once upon a time," she said, "there was a lonely little girl. She didn't have any friends, because her parents kept moving from planet to planet all the time."

Luma's tears stopped flowing. "No friends at all?" she said, her skin shifting from bright red to maroon.

"None," said Stiletto. "Then, one day, she heard a voice. It seemed to be coming from thin air. 'I'll be your friend,' said the voice."

Luma's face relaxed from a frown to an expression of wide-eyed interest. Her skin went from maroon to violet.

"The girl couldn't see who was talking," said Stiletto. "She was scared, but she was so lonely that she said, 'Sure, you can be my friend.'

"So from that day on, the girl had an invisible friend. There was just one problem."

"What?" said Luma. "What problem?"

"The invisible friend was *mean*," said Stiletto, "but the girl didn't find out right away."

"When *did* she find out?" said Luma.

Stiletto raised an eyebrow. "To be continued," she said. "If you're good, I'll tell you the rest of the story later."

"But I want to know now!" said Luma, scowling.

"I'll tell you after we've gone a little further," said Stiletto. She lowered the child to the pavement and held her hand.

"But I can't wait!" said Luma.

"Later," Stiletto said sternly.

"All right," said Luma. Though she sounded unhappy, the dark green color of her skin revealed her true feelings. Her terrified panic was gone, replaced by a calmer composure.

Candle leaned close to Stiletto and whispered in her ear. "Way to handle the kid," he said. "I didn't know you had it in you."

Stiletto nodded without smiling, but she felt a rush of warmth at what he'd said.

Candle thought it was a good thing that Luma became obsessed with pestering Stiletto to continue her story. The Skilla were growing bolder, and he was glad the little girl's mind was on something else.

Again and again, the creatures raced close and bolted away. They dropped stones and bones and shingles from above, littering the route with debris.

And their numbers, according to the flash-brain, continued to grow. Candle wondered how many more of the creatures would join the pack over the kilometer and a half that he, Stiletto, and Luma had yet to walk. He wondered what other surprises the Skilla would spring.

Unfortunately, he didn't have to wait long for the next one. It happened just as Stiletto was about to continue her story.

"All right," she said, finally giving in to Luma's repeated requests to know what happened next. "I'll tell you a little more."

Luma's skin was pale green, which Candle knew by now meant the child felt at ease. "Tell me!" she said.

Before Stiletto could get out a word, the rocks started flying.

Candle felt something strike his arm with a stinging impact. As he whipped around, he felt another solid object collide with his kneecap.

A shower of rocks followed, hurtling straight toward him from out of the fog.

Candle opened fire with the warflower, punching the searing beam through the murk. "Get down!"

Behind him, he heard the whine of Stiletto's warflower firing at the same time as his, lashing out at the other side of the street.

Another volley of rocks leaped out of the fog from a different spot. Candle spun and fired there, too, then combed the beam along the street to pick off any additional ambushers lying in wait.

The bombardment ended, giving way to a deafening chorus of shrieks and screams from all directions.

"Everybody all right?" said Candle.

Even as he said it, he could see the answer to his question.

Luma was sprawled on the pavement, eyes closed. Her skin was white as a bedsheet except for a blazing red welt above her left eye.

"How is she?" said Candle, standing guard while Stiletto scanned Luma's head with her fingertip sensor pads.

"Lots of swelling in there," said Stiletto. "She might have a concussion."

"Can we treat her?"

Stiletto removed the first aid kit from a hip pocket of her black flowsuit. "Just the surface wound," she said, yanking a tubular spray applicator from the kit. "The deep swelling's another matter." Stiletto ran the tip of the applicator over the welt on Luma's forehead, administering a spray of antiseptic, anesthetic, and anti-inflammatory agents. "Her body's different from anything I've worked on before. Trying to treat the internal injury could do more harm than good."

"Should we keep her awake in case there's a concussion?" said Candle.

"Damned if I know. If she was human, I'd say definitely."

"Let's risk it, then," said Candle. "*If* we can wake her up."

"Roger that," said Stiletto, brushing a strand of blond hair out of her face.

The Skilla continued to howl and scream-laugh as Candle bent down by Luma's right ear. "Luma," he said. "Wake up. It's time to wake up."

Luma didn't twitch.

"Please, Luma," said Candle, raising his voice. "We need you to wake up."

Still nothing.

Stiletto leaned close to Luma's left ear. "Do you want to know what happened next?" she said.

Finally, Luma stirred. Her snow-white skin fluxed pink, then shifted to pale orange.

And her red, faceted eyes flickered open.

"Yes," she said softly. "Please tell me."

As the Skilla kept circling and raising a ruckus, Candle and Stiletto continued toward the source of the mechanical vibrations.

Stiletto carried Luma in her arms and told her more about the little girl with the invisible friend...in other words, the story of Stiletto herself and the Squatter who had made her a Wipeout. Luma's skin shifted from pale orange to deep green, a change that Stiletto took as a good sign.

Stiletto told Luma how the little girl's invisible friend had played tricks on her and gotten her to play tricks on other people. (She didn't mention the fact that the "tricks" consisted of bloody killing sprees that claimed the lives of her own family and count-less strangers.) Though the tricks the girl played were mean, Stiletto said, the invisible friend fooled her into thinking they were fun.

When Stiletto got to the part where the policeman showed up, Candle interrupted.

"What's our status?" he said.

Stiletto scanned their surroundings with her left-fingertip sensor pads. "Same as before."

Candle sighed. "How long till dawn?"

"About an hour," said Stiletto. "You thinking they're anti-daylight?"

"Hoping," said Candle. He looked at Luma. "What's the word on you-know-who?"

"Swelling's worse," said Stiletto.

"Let's hope those vibrations lead us to a doctor," said Candle.

Stiletto smirked. "What a day, huh?"

"Easy-peasy." Right after Candle said it, he winked one dark brown eye and gave Stiletto's shoulder a squeeze.

As his fingers pressed and released, Stiletto felt her face warm with a blush.

Candle was surprised, a little later, when Luma asked him to tell her a story.

She probably just wanted him to kill time while Stiletto took a break...but he figured he'd give it a shot. Anything to keep Luma awake, especially since she'd been yawning more and more often lately.

"Okay," said Candle. "Let's see." He thought for a moment, scrubbing his fingers through his wavy, salt-and-pepper hair. "I know," he said at last. "Have you heard the story of the lonely policeman?"

"No," said Luma, shaking her head. "Please tell me."

Candle cleared his throat. He'd decided to pick up Stiletto's story where she'd left off, but from his point of view.

"Once upon a time," he said, pacing the floor, "there was a lonely policeman. He was always busy, because these mean invisible friends kept making people play tricks on each other."

Luma yawned and rubbed her eyes. "You mean like the lonely little girl?"

"Yeah," said Candle. "As a matter of fact, he went to see that little girl one time. He said, 'Don't listen to your invisible friend, little girl. He's not nice.'"

"What did the girl say?"

Candle thought he'd skip over the part about Stiletto trying to kill him while under the Squatter's control. "To be continued," he said. "I'll tell you later."

"*This* is *dawn*?" said Candle, looking around at what was really just a brighter version of the same old fog.

"I guess it's better than *dark* fog, at least," said Stiletto.

"Not much of a silver lining if you ask me," said Candle.

As they walked, Stiletto and Candle combed their warflowers from side to side, ready to open fire at the first hint of aggression from the Skilla.

Stiletto knew the creatures were out there, lurking all around in great numbers...but they didn't make a sound. She heard neither the clack of a nearby claw nor a distant, screaming cry.

The hairs on the back of her neck wouldn't stay down. She thought the silence was a lot harder to take than the cacophony of the night before.

Fortunately, Luma perked up enough to interrupt it. Her glittering skin switched from pale gray to turquoise, and her yawns became less frequent.

As she walked along between Stiletto and Candle, Luma tugged Stiletto's hand. "What happened next?" she said. "When the policeman told the little girl her friend wasn't nice?"

"Well," said Stiletto. "The invisible friend told the little girl the *policeman* was the mean one, so the girl tried to make the policeman go away."

"Did he?" said Luma.

"No," said Stiletto.

"But then what?"

Stiletto heard something crack nearby. "To be continued," she said, staring intently in the direction from which she'd heard the sound.

Instead of pleading with her, as usual, to keep telling the story, Luma turned right around to Candle.

"Did the policeman go away?" she said.

Candle smirked. He kept his eyes and warflower trained on the fog as he picked up the story.

"No," he said. "He made the invisible friend go away instead." *With forbidden drugs and hardcore psychic acupuncture,* he could've added, but he left that out.

"Did the policeman and the little girl make friends then?" said Luma.

"The opposite. She hated him." Candle couldn't resist taking his eyes off the fog long enough to glance Stiletto's way. She looked aloof as always, but he was sure he spotted a trace of a smile on her face.

"She hated him?" said Luma.

"Not forever," said Candle. "As time went on, they got to be friends."

"Better friends than the invisible friend was," said Stiletto.

Candle grinned. "Even though they didn't always get along."

"You can say that again," said Stiletto.

"The next thing you know, they were partners," said Candle.

"And no matter what happened," said Stiletto, "the little girl was glad the policeman had found her."

Candle was surprised. He'd caught a flash of emotion in her voice that he hadn't noticed before.

He looked in Stiletto's direction. She was looking down at the flash-brain screen on her left forearm, but he had the distinct feeling that she had been looking right at him just an instant before.

Suddenly then, she stopped in her tracks. "The Skilla are gone," she said.

Candle stopped. "What do you mean, gone?"

"I mean *gone,*" said Stiletto. "No sign of them on flash sensors."

Candle looked around at the murk. "Maybe they hate daylight after all."

"It's possible." Stiletto didn't sound convinced.

"Well," said Candle, "let's not look a gift Skilla in the mouth. How far are we from the source of the mechanical vibrations?"

"Less than a kilometer," said Stiletto.

"Then let's get moving." Candle hoisted Luma off her feet and set out at a brisk jog to cover the remaining ground. Stiletto fell in beside him, watching the flash-brain screen for signs of renewed danger.

Luma wrapped her arms around Candle's neck and held on tight. "Guess what?" she said in his ear.

"What?" said Candle.

"I know what the names are," said Luma. "The names of the little girl and the policeman."

"Okay," said Candle. "What are they?"

"Nona and Pass," said Luma, and she giggled.

Candle smiled. "Cool," he said.

"Cool," said Luma, and then she squeezed her arms more tightly around his neck.

"Stop," said Stiletto. "This is it."

Squinting into the fog, she saw a gray metal door set into a low stone bunker at the end of the street.

"Ventilation system," said Stiletto. "That's what's been making those vibrations. It's pumping stale air out of an underground chamber and pumping in fresh."

"Sagran bio signs?" said Candle, gently bouncing Luma until her eyes opened. In spite of the run through the streets, Luma's sleepiness was coming back in force.

"Lots, but faint," said Stiletto, watching the flash-brain screen on her arm. "We didn't pick them up earlier because there's some kind of interference signal."

"Invisible fence, maybe?" said Candle. "A signal tuned to a frequency that keeps the Skilla out?"

"Beats me," said Stiletto, "but I think I found a way in." She pointed her fingertip sensors at the windowless stone bunker.

"There's a shaft on the other side of the door, leading underground."

As Candle started for the bunker, he bounced Luma on his arm. "Look familiar?"

Luma grinned sleepily. "Yes!" she said, pointing an index finger at the bunker. "This is where Mommy and Daddy take me every year. This is the place I couldn't find when I got lost."

"Cool," Candle said with a smile. "Guess you're not lost anymore."

When the three of them reached the bunker, Stiletto gave the metal door a push. When it wouldn't open, she turned her attention to what looked like a release mechanism.

The release mechanism consisted of a keypad at eye level with ten push buttons. Each button was imprinted with an alien symbol; Stiletto's wild guess was that the symbols corresponded to the numbers zero through nine.

"Numeric code lock," she said, aiming her fingertip sensors at the mechanism. "Normally, I could crack this puppy open in a heartbeat."

"But?" said Candle.

"The device isn't electronic, so it'll take my flash-brain longer to analyze it."

Candle sighed. "What about you?" he said to Luma. "Have any idea how to open the door?"

Luma frowned and rubbed an eye with her fist. "Mommy taught me a song, but I don't know if I can remember all the words right now."

"You remember the tune at least?" said Candle.

"Maybe."

"How about giving it a try?" said Candle.

Stiletto was about to say something when she caught the smell of vinegar in the air. Before she even looked at the readout of the flash-brain, her heart started to pound.

Raising her warflower, she turned away from the door.

"Pass," she said, keeping her voice perfectly even. "Multiple Skilla life signs, coming in *fast*."

Candle nodded. "Guess our friends aren't so nocturnal after all."

In the distance, Stiletto could hear the clattering of claws. Hundreds of them.

Getting closer every second.

"How about if you work with Luma on remembering that song?" said Candle. "Music isn't my strong suit."

Stiletto moved in and took Luma, balancing the little girl's weight on her hip.

"Try to make it a fast number," said Candle. "Not that I expect much trouble at all whatsoever."

With a wink, he walked off to face the horde of creatures stampeding down the street.

Candle stationed himself twenty meters from the bunker and immediately opened fire. He blasted his warflower into the fog for a full minute before he finally caught his first glimpse of the Skilla.

One of the creatures slipped through the field of fire and lunged toward him. It was as big as a rhinoceros, with six lean legs and claws like scimitars. A huge scorpion's tail arced over its body, tipped with a spiked stinger as big as a man's head. Its torso was covered in long, crimson spines that glistened as if they were wet.

It had a face like an open wound lined with razor-sharp teeth.

As the warflower's beam lashed into the Skilla, Candle was disappointed. He had hoped that seeing the enemy would have made it seem less intimidating.

Now, he wished that the Skilla had stayed out of sight.

Stiletto would've thought, with the legion of Skilla attacking, that her biggest challenge would be calming Luma down. Instead, she had to fight to keep the little girl awake.

"Luma," Stiletto said sharply, shaking the girl in her arms. "How did the *song* go?"

Luma hummed three notes and closed her eyes.

Stiletto shook her. "Sing the *song*. The one about the door."

Luma's eyes drifted open. "Five laughing children standing in the rain," she sang softly, and then she stopped.

"Luma!" The sounds of battle filled Stiletto's ears.

Luma's eyes dropped shut, then popped open. "Five laughing children standing in the rain," she sang. "One of them's a three-year-old and two are six and ten."

Stiletto memorized the sequence of numbers from the song: five, one, three, two, six, one, zero.

"Number one is six feet tall and always gets the door," Luma sang without opening her eyes. "But Mommy says the ones she loves the best are two and four." Luma yawned and lowered her head back onto Stiletto's bare shoulder. "The end."

Stiletto added the numbers from the last two lines to the earlier sequence. She typed them into the keypad on the door, as if the top three keys were numbers one through three, the second row four through six, the third row seven through nine, and the bottom key zero.

She entered the sequence in a hurry: five, one, three, two, six, one, zero, one, six, one, two, four.

Nothing happened.

Candle didn't think he could hold off the Skilla for much longer.

As his warflower fire dropped the creatures at the front of the horde, more rushed up from behind. The pile of bodies kept rising, forcing Candle to aim upward at increasingly sharp angles. Then, the onrushing Skilla started using the pile as a diving platform.

As they hurtled through the fog from above, claws and stingers extended, Candle picked them off one after another...but the terrible rain wouldn't end. When one shrieking Skilla went down, another one or two always took its place.

They just never stopped coming. Candle knew, as each moment flew by and the bunker door stayed shut, that things were probably going to get much worse very soon.

As Stiletto went over Luma's song again, she found a place where she might have screwed up.

When Luma had sung, "But Mommy says the ones she loves the best are two and four," Stiletto had added the numbers one, two, and four to the sequence. What if the plural "ones" meant she should have added more than a single "one" to the string?

Stiletto puffed strands of blond hair out of her face and punched in the number sequence on the keypad again, this time adding another number one before the final two and four.

A second later, she heard the clicking of tumblers inside the door. Then, a clang and a scrape.

The door slid open, releasing a blast of musty air that overpowered the vinegar stink of the Skilla.

"Pass!" shouted Stiletto. "It's open!"

Candle was already backing toward the door when he heard her, but not because he had any idea that it was opening.

Two Skilla lunged at him, claws and stingers carving through the space where he'd stood only an instant before. He swept the beam of the warflower from one to the other, dropping them both...and as soon as their bodies collapsed to the pavement, three more leaped into the gap.

Candle unleashed another spray of fire from the warflower and backed into the doorway. Out of the corner of his eye, he saw Stiletto behind the door, waiting to pull it shut.

"On three!" said Candle. "One! Two!"

The last thing he saw before Stiletto slammed the door was one of those faces like a ragged, open wound, oozing saliva or mucus and crammed with a forest of teeth like shards of broken glass.

"Three!"

Even as the door crashed shut, Candle knew he'd see that face again in his nightmares.

Stiletto led the way down the spiral metal stairwell in the middle of the bunker. She didn't have to switch on her headlight, because the well was lit by an incandescent strip set into the stone wall.

Candle followed, carrying Luma. He talked to her and bounced her in his arms, though keeping her awake had become a losing battle.

At the base of the stairwell, Stiletto stepped onto a dirt floor in front of a pair of metal doors. A video monitor was mounted at eye level on one of the doors, and she activated it by twisting a large knob underneath it.

An adult male Sagran appeared on the screen. Like Luma, he had red, multifaceted eyes and no hair. He wore a sky blue tunic, and his glittering skin was pale green.

"Shhh," said the Sagran, touching his mouth with the tip of a finger. "Don't wake the sleepers."

Stiletto started to ask a question. The Sagran talked right over her, which clued her in that the video was strictly playback, not interactive.

345

"You are welcome to take your place among us," said the Sagran, opening his arms wide. "But first, please join me in a prayer."

The Sagran closed his eyes and solemnly bowed his head. "O gods of destruction," he said. "We freely offer the fruits of our labors to you. You bless us by tearing down what we have built, clearing the way for us to rebuild and be reborn.

"O Skilla," said the Sagran, "cleanse our cities with your sacred storm. Remind us that the physical world is fleeting, that we may cherish every breath of our lives.

"When at last you rest at the end of these three holy months, and our people awaken, may we find that you have left even less intact than the year before. May we continue to find fulfillment in the eternal cycle of creation and destruction."

The Sagran opened his eyes and lifted his head. "Enter," he said with a serene smile. "Dream of the storm above and the work ahead."

With that, the video screen went dark.

The double doors swung open on a pitch black space. Stiletto activated her headlight and stepped inside.

The first thing she saw by the beam of the headlight was the body of a woman, curled in a fetal position on blankets on the floor. The woman's eyes were closed, and her skin was pale gray. She wore a simple white shift like Luma's.

As Stiletto played the headlight over the floor, she saw that the woman wasn't alone. Everywhere Stiletto looked, the floor was covered with the bodies of Sagran adults and children, all with gray skin and eyes closed.

Stiletto scanned them with her fingertip sensor pads. "They're hibernating," she said.

"'Three holy months,'" said Candle, quoting the prayer from the video. "It's the only way they can coexist with the Skilla. Hibernate while the Skilla are on the rampage."

"They should wipe out the Skilla and be done with it," said Stiletto.

"Not if the Skilla are sacred to them," said Candle. "I guess the Sagrans see them as gods of destruction, like the Hindu god Shiva on Earth."

Stiletto crouched beside a sleeping Sagran and scanned his head with her fingertip sensors. She scanned two other sleepers the same way.

"They've got the same internal swelling as Luma," said Stiletto. "Could be a normal part of the hibernation process."

"Not a concussion after all," said Candle. "Luma was just trying to go back to sleep like everyone else."

Stiletto gazed at the little girl in Candle's arms. Luma was fast asleep, drooling on his shoulder.

"We should find her parents," said Stiletto.

Candle nodded. "Time to wake up, Luma," he said, gently bouncing the child in his arms. "Just one more time, and then you can finally get the rest you deserve."

After a long search by headlight through the vast underground chamber, Luma pointed out a man and woman sleeping side by side on a multi-colored quilt.

"That's Mommy and Daddy," she said drowsily.

Candle smiled and lowered her to the quilt, placing her between her parents. "There you go," he said. "Now promise me you won't wander off again, okay?"

Luma yawned and nodded. "I promise," she said. Now that she had been returned to her parents, the amber crystal in her bracelet stopped blinking.

"Good night," said Candle. "Sleep tight."

Luma lay down on her side and curled up between her mother and father. Now that she was perfectly relaxed, her glittering skin took on a pale green hue. "Finish the story first. What happened next?"

"I have a better idea," said Candle. "Why don't *you* finish it?"

"Okay." Luma thought for a moment, then grinned. "Pass and Nona fell in love and lived happily ever after. The end."

Then, hugging her doll, she closed her eyes and fell asleep, her skin color shifting from pale green to pale gray.

"Cool story, huh?"

Candle said it as he and Stiletto followed a network of tunnels under the city, bypassing the Skilla on the way back to the *Sun Ra*.

He caught Stiletto by surprise. Instead of bouncing right back with a typical wisecrack, she didn't answer.

The truth was, of course she thought the story was cool, since she was crazy about him...but she was afraid to go further because of her lousy past. Her Wipeout career had ruined everything else in her life, so why not ruin this, too?

On the other hand...

She couldn't escape the feeling that something had changed between her and Candle on Sagra. He'd said some nice things about her, and the way he'd touched her that one time had been amazing.

Or maybe it was all in her imagination. After all, it wasn't as if he'd said anything that couldn't be interpreted more than one way. If only he'd said something with no room for misunderstanding, then maybe...

"I think we should end the story the way Luma did." Candle grinned, his deep brown eyes twinkling in the glow of her headlight. "How about you?"

So much for misunderstanding.

It was up to Stiletto now, and the moment couldn't have been more perfect. The man she loved had given her the kind of opportunity that might never come her way again.

And yet, on the brink of a new beginning, Stiletto hesitated.

What if the Squatter who had once possessed her managed to return? She couldn't bear the thought that she might one day hurt Candle.

Then, of course, it was always possible that Candle might hurt her...that he might *leave* her. She thought it would be a lot worse to have him and lose him than never to have him at all.

"Well?" he said, eyebrows raised expectantly. "What do you say?"

Then again, she'd already been with him for three years, and he'd never let her down. They'd been through a lot together, and she thought she knew him well enough to know he wouldn't hurt her.

So what was she waiting for?

Candle sighed. "Okay, then. Can't blame a guy for trying."

Aw, what the hell.

"No, no," said Stiletto. "I want to know what happens next. To be continued." Then, she grabbed his hand and held it like a trophy as they hiked toward the distant light at the end of the tunnel.

IN ALL YOUR SPARKLING
RAIMENT SOAR

Though all of existence, to us, is a poem, certain verses are not exactly joyful. *Mmm-bzzz.*

In those days, for example, our first days on this world among humans, our tasks were not happy ones. We took no pleasure in what we did to them, though we did it for good reasons. Though we sought to find

The beauty of the burning dawn,
A spectrum woven out of eyeblinks
And tears, the heatless flickering
Of featherless wings rising
Mmm-bzzz
Rising from the darkling pool colliding
With the swirling curtain of an opalescent
Luminescence.

But the truth is, in the *mmm-bzzz* in the beginning, we did not know if we would ever reach it. If the horrible things we were doing to these creatures, primitive yet every bit as sentient as we, would ever yield up the prize we were determined to set free.

Subject 1. That was her official designation. I called her *Clarity*, because that was what I saw in her eyes the first time we met; that was what impressed me about her the most. We didn't know what she called herself, if anything. We didn't understand her language, if there was one. Not that it mattered.

At least that's what we'd thought in the beginning. That the details didn't matter.

But oh how they mattered. Like the downy black fur that covered her body. The long, dark mane

So soft, so flowing,

A beautiful veil cascading over shoulders

Over chest like a waterfall at

Night, a solar wind wrapping

Around the silver skin of a

Caressing the skin of a

Dreaming the form in the formless

Deep.

As if words could ever *mmm-bzzz* could ever express her radiance. As if scientific measurements could ever convey the dimensions of her

Magnificence.

As if any attempt to recreate the memory of her could somehow excuse what I did to her.

But back in those days, four million years ago as you measure *mmm-bzzz* reckon time, Clarity filled my thoughts. *Our* thoughts, I should say. The collective thoughts of ten thousand of us, bound in the harmony of the hive mind.

It didn't matter that she was so different from us. That, on the surface, she had so little in common with insects like us.

In a way, we were made for each other. Our ship, hibernating underground for many months after landing, built us from the genetic building blocks most prevalent on your world. The automated systems constructed us in a way that best suited the local environment, our mission, and our biological software. Our *soulware*.

We'd been built and rebuilt thusly many times, on many different worlds. Always maintaining *mmm-bzzz* preserving what kept us special. What kept us the most efficient and productive pollinators and gatherers in the galaxy.

Clarity was one of the first humans we saw when our ship finally burrowed out of the ground and the hatches irised open. As we tasted the air of this world for the first time, she stepped fearlessly out from behind a boulder.

The rest of her tribe cowered in the shadows, but not her. *Mmm-bzzz.* I can still see her, meeting us clear-eyed and square-shouldered when even the brawny males wouldn't come forth. She was unafraid, confident, graceful. A born leader.

Clarity gazed at us with wonder in her bright green eyes. And I gazed back at her with more of the same, transfixed. I knew there was something unique *mmm-bzzz* special about her right away.

Which, of course, was one of the reasons we chose her on the spot as the first subject retrieved for our operations on this world.

In our swarms, we are ten thousand strong. Each member of the swarm is no bigger than a human fingertip, but together we have

Power.

Working together, perfectly synchronized, we can arrange ourselves in the shape of a human body and execute a wide range of tasks. For example, we can guide a human female into a ship-board lab.

Which is where we can restrain her *mmm-bzzz* strap her to a metal table and drive a spike at her forehead.

Clarity didn't scream when the spike shot toward her. She didn't even watch it approach. Her eyes were fixed on me the entire time.

Was she defective for not expressing fear? Did she lack the proper response mechanism to potentially fatal stimuli?

Not if there was no possibility of *fatality*. Not if the tempered metal spike shattered like ice when it hit her forehead, leaving not a mark of damage on her.

When we applied the same test to other human subjects in our shipboard labs, the results were identical.

Clarity and her species were nearly indestructible. As we confirmed through our experiments, no external physical attack could harm them. Through some miracle of evolution, humanity had become perfected *mmm-bzzz* immortal.

And that was why we'd come here. Not to become attached to these primitive creatures, so abysmally low on every scale of development of which we could conceive. We'd come to find a way to kill them...and ensure salvation for the human race and our own species besides.

How could we possibly *save* humanity by *killing* it? Because only in death can a human being, or any sentient lifeform, evolve to the next level.

My people specialize in making that possible. We free intelligent beings from their physical bonds like a shoot from a seed.

Have you ever wondered why you hear nothing from the skies *mmm-bzzz* from space? No intelligible signals from the impossible vastness?

Surely, in all that everything, there must be someone like you on another world. Someone to talk to. Someone to connect with. What are they waiting for? Why won't they call?

The answer is this: It is because

they have all become

Light.

This was the destiny we had come to help humanity attain *mmm-bzzz* realize. Enabling humans to die would free the inner light from their corporeal shells and allow it to escape into space. Allow it to join the light of countless other lifeforms in the infinite reaches.

And my people, as we ushered humankind on its way, would experience *mmm-bzzz* undergo our own transformation.

One that would save us from ruin.

Our souls were ancient. Our soulware had become degraded. When it collapsed, our sentience would dissolve; we would lose our sense of self and be unable to perform our mission. Time was running out for us.

But when humanity died and moved to the next level, the resulting surge of inner light would allow us to save ourselves. We would channel enough of humanity's light through our ship's instrumentation to burn away the impurities and reboot our degraded souls.

In a way, humanity's souls would pollinate our own, bringing new life to us. In that one tremendous release, my people would be reborn.

We would regain our immortality in the corporeal world just as humanity lost its own.

All this was riding on the shoulders of beautiful Clarity, though I'm sure she knew it not. To her, each day was an ordeal without explanation. Though I did what I could to leaven the ordeal with moments of kindness.

I would wake her in the morning by brushing *mmm-bzzz* dabbing honey on her lips. Her eyes would flutter open

Like the wings of butterflies,
soft as velvet, damp with dew,
diaphanous, intangible,
closer to whispers or
thoughts,
closer to intentions,
The feelings of lingering love from a
dream,
All that's left when you can't remember
the lover.

And then her tongue would slide out and touch the glistening honey on each lip. It would glide languidly along the top and then the bottom, licking up the sweetness as I watched *mmm-bzzz* gazed through ten thousand pairs of eyes, ten thousand facets in each eye, each facet soaking up a different part of the visible and invisible spectrums.

And then I would go to work on her. I would try to kill her again and again, day after day.

At first, I went through the same techniques my people were employing on other specimens. I had to confirm they would lead to *mmm-bzzz* produce the same effect, that her baseline was identical to the rest.

So I gathered my ten thousand buzzing selves in one body and attacked her. I tried to cut her throat and split her head open. I tried to choke her, drown her, set her on fire. I tried to break her in every way possible.

Through all of this, she remained unharmed and no more alarmed than when the spike had shattered against her forehead. Like the rest of her people *mmm-bzzz* species, she was indestructible.

She didn't seem to experience any discomfort, either. Stimuli applied externally were as ineffective at causing her pain as they were at damaging her body.

So we moved on to stage two. The introduction of pain by other methods.

Though we hadn't succeeded in killing a human, we *did* manage to stimulate pain. This, we thought, could be the gateway to death for these creatures.

The strongest results came from electrocution or intense irradiation. Strong natural forces channeled *mmm-bzzz* focused internally were able to provoke the nervous system, evoking a pain response.

I can still hear her first screams piercing the air of the lab. I'll never forget the way she thrashed on the metal table, fighting her restraints, convulsing. Eyes rolled up in their sockets or pinched shut against the waves of agony.

But her eyes were not always rolled up or pinched shut. Often, they were fixed in my direction, wide and bloodshot with suffering and desperation.

How many other humans did I torture on any given day? Clarity was not my only subject, after all.

Yet who among them possessed the grace to set aside the suffering when it ended? To face the torturer with a measure of tranquility?

Only Clarity. Only this singular angel could muster a smile in my presence.

Between sessions, I fed her honey and wheat germ. I poured purified water between her parched red lips.

Others of her kind accepted nothing from me, perhaps expecting *mmm-bzzz* fearing it would bring them more pain. But as much as I abused her, Clarity trusted me. She still seemed on some level to sense my good intentions.

I wonder sometimes how this was ever possible, given the gulf between our species. The lack of common language between us. The sheer differences in physiology. I must have looked fearsome to her, a cloud of insects roughly shaped like a man. Thousands of unblinking eyes

Like chips of polished

Ebony, thousands of black and yellow

Stingers, known only to her by the

Screaming in her own throat,

The thoughts in her own mind,

The new, suffering thing she had become because of

Me.

Her divinity, I suspect, made this miracle real.

I could not allow her to leave the ship, could not even let her off the table for fear of corrupting the experiment.

But between sessions, I brought the world to her. Projectors in the lab recreated her habitat in three dimensions around us.

So though she *mmm-bzzz* though she still lay strapped to the table, destined for more torture, she could see at least for a few moments the familiar grasslands outside the hull of the ship. The amber plains rippling

In the wind, in the blazing sunlight,

Shadows of clouds gliding over the sea of grain,

Twinned in the mirror-skins of watering holes,

Slipping over creatures bristling with horns and

Tusks and teeth and claws and beaks of every angle,

Long necks parting the treetops,

Spear tips bobbing in the lazy current.

She sighed when the image of a brightly colored bird swooped overhead, silhouetted against the sun. She smiled when a lithe gazelle sprinted past, followed by a hail of spears and a team of human hunters who'd thrown them.

When she smiled at me, too, the fascination *mmm-bzzz* adoration I felt multiplied a thousand-fold. I felt redeemed, at least a little, for the work I had to do.

And therefore able to continue to do it.

The infections took weeks to administer. One after another, I pumped her system full of bacteria, viruses, phages, fungi, and exotic microorganisms from other worlds. I administered them one and two and ten and twenty and a hundred at a time, carefully watching *mmm-bzzz* recording the effects.

This microbiological warfare had an impact. By attacking her internally, they triggered powerful shocks to her system. Like electrocution and irradiation, they caused intense pain.

But not death. Her immune system rose up always and wiped away the invaders as if they'd never existed.

Next, it was time for stage three. It was time for innovation.

Following protocols, I had charted the baseline and covered the same ground we'd been over with other subjects. Now that I'd established *mmm-bzzz* determined she was biologically identical to other humans, I could explore new approaches. Any success would likely extend universally to the rest of her species.

If I could kill *her*, I could kill *all* of them.

I'll never forget the first time I heard Clarity laugh.

I was embarking on a promising new direction in the lab--genetic manipulation. To begin testing, I needed to obtain a sample of genetic material, what you know as DNA.

I planned to collect the sample by swabbing the inside *mmm-bzzz* the lining of her mouth. I sent one of my ten thousand selves to accomplish *mmm-bzzz* perform this task.

But Clarity wouldn't open her mouth. My tiny single self hovered in front of her lips, bobbing in the breeze from her nostrils, and she wouldn't let me in.

She looked at my larger self looming over her, and I saw the worry in her eyes. This was new to her. Maybe she was afraid *mmm-bzzz* scared I was going to hurt her again.

Whatever her thinking, I sent my lone self closer to her mouth. I used his feelers and wings to tickle her soft lips.

Suddenly, Clarity's lips parted. She let out a flurry of noises from the back of her throat, a string of quick, chiming tones resonating through her sinuses, ringing from the top of her head. They were high-pitched as the song of a bird,

The tinkling of icicles snapping from a tree branch,

The whistling of wind through a hollow stone,

The singing of flowers with pollen-heavy pistils,
The cries of the stars in the night, forever
Sighing x-rays gamma rays radio waves neutrinos
On solar breezes swirling with glittering powder.

It was the first time I'd heard a human laugh. For an instant, I thought I'd hurt her somehow...but then I realized she was smiling. The fear was gone *mmm-bzzz* vanished from her eyes.

Seizing the opportunity, I tickled her more. Her mouth opened wider, and I

flew

inside.

My whole perspective changed in there. It was one thing to see her every day, to understand the functions of her body. To communicate in a rudimentary way.

It was quite another to be *part* of her, if only for a moment. To be intimately connected *mmm-bzzz* joined together.

Afloat in the warm red vault of her, I drifted over the moist mound of her tongue. I hovered between her flat yellow teeth, hoping she wouldn't bite down, and extended my own hollow tongue toward the inside of her cheek. Rubbing the slick flesh, I drew in a sample of her buccal cells, rich with genetic material, and stored it in my second stomach.

I wished I could have lingered, but I must have tickled her again. Her laugh sounded ten thousand times louder from inside her mouth. The expulsion of air threw my tiny self tumbling from her lips.

While Clarity slept, I tampered with her DNA. My component selves zipped this way and that through the lab, mapping her genome and feeding the data into the computers.

Digital simulations predicted the likely *mmm-bzzz* probable outcome of each change. I could see the affected traits and the nature, degree, and viability of their altered expressions. Sophisti-cated algorithms calculated the likelihood that the changes would flip the right switch.

The switch that would bring down the wall that protected humanity.

I had done this kind of work before on many *mmm-bzzz* countless worlds, with other species. Such is my people's purpose in life: to help those who cannot help themselves. To rectify the flaws *mmm-bzzz* solve the problems that hold certain species back from their rightful destinies.

This work always follows certain patterns. I've learned to recog-nize key moments--the breakthrough, for example--and quickly grasp their significance.

How many times had such a breakthrough led me to a solution? How many times at such a moment had I felt the certainty of right-ness in all my thousand thousand stomachs? It had always been a cause for celebration.

But not this time.

In fact, when the latest simulation suggested a new direction, and I knew in my thousands of guts that I'd found the key, I set it aside. I avoided it.

Instead, I went to Clarity and fed her. I watched her smile as she licked the honey from her lips. I made her laugh with a new trick I'd invented, tickling her by fluttering *mmm-bzzz* flickering the wings of my ten thousand selves all over her body at once.

But all along, the knowledge grew in the back of my hive-mind. Dread expanded like a storm cloud above us.

Each time I went back to my work, I knew I was making progress. Each time I took it a step further, the certainty in my bellies became stronger.

Resequencing her DNA according to the template I'd designed would make her susceptible. If applied to other members of her species, the effect would be the same.

Here is the genius of it. Her body was perfected, indestructible. How then to pull away *mmm-bzzz* remove the shield?

The same way you scratch a diamond. Turn the indestructible against itself.

If, that is, you can stand *mmm-bzzz* bear to do it.

As weeks passed, I realized I might be the only one to design *mmm-bzzz* find a solution. In our daily meetings, the other swarms claimed not to be anywhere near a remotely viable approach.

Maybe, if I said nothing, I could still save Clarity. If I kept my solution to myself, and no one else came up with the same idea or an equally effective alternative, perhaps Clarity and her species would be spared.

But it was a slim hope, and I knew it. Other swarms were also researching *mmm-bzzz* exploring genetic modalities, and we were all working from the same baseline data. They could find the solution as easily as I had.

Unless I started submitting falsified reports. Unless I intentionally misdirected every other swarm by steering them away from what I knew was the answer.

In which case, I would be violating *mmm-bzzz* breaking sacrosanct rules of my species. I would be undermining the purpose of our holy *mmm-bzzz* sacred mission to this world. I would be jeopardizing the future of my own species.

But the one creature I'd found precious in all the galaxy, the one being whom I adored with all ten thousand of my hearts, would *live.*

One night, I was called *mmm-bzzz* summoned to join the others for The Rite.

All the swarms flowed out of the great silver ship at once, shimmering dark ribbons rippling into the night sky. We merged together into one giant cloud, one great swarm of all our multitudes on this planet. We formed concentric circles and began to turn, each ring rotating in a different direction, alternating clockwise and counter-clockwise.

The bright stars cast their flickering light upon us,
Glittering from our wings
and the polished cobalt facets of our eyes.
A billion trillion streams of starlight
Rushed out of the limitless heavens
and washed down over us.
So much light everywhere,
Direct, reflected, refracted, visible, invisible.
The universe a filigree of criss-crossed streamers,
The planet tumbling through a coruscating mesh.

And as I flew with the others through the tailings of that illuminated fall, I was reminded of our purpose, of our faith in that purpose. The sheer scope and importance of that purpose.

I'd come to think of it as something I could set aside just this once. As if denying an entire species its destiny was something I could live with.

The feeling of companionship with Clarity had been so profoundly *mmm-bzzz* powerfully alluring. It was so unlike the unity I felt with my hive-mind brothers, which was always inflexibly predictable. The pressure of the swarms in all their thousands upon thousands was ever-present, intrusive, demanding. Emotionless.

Lonely.

But did that absolve me of my responsibilities? Did it negate the sacred trust that had given my existence meaning for eons upon eons?

Here is how The Rite ends. How it ended that night.

Each of us carries a photoelectric wafer, tiny but highly sensitive. As we fly in glittering circles in the sky, the wafers absorb starlight and store it.

Then, at the right moment, we disperse, carrying our tiny burdens. All the millions of us, laden with our blue-glowing wafers, filter into the night. We seek out

the darkest shadows,

pitch black lightless

holes, hollows, burrows,

under roots, under rocks, in caves,

and we converge there, releasing our cargoes. The shadows blossom with tiny constellations of azure light.

It is a sacrament. *Mmm-bzzz.* It is a symbol.

We are pollinating the darkness

with starlight.

After The Rite, all our swarms came back together and mixed under the stars, merging our hive-minds into one mega-consciousness.

It was then, in that one colossal union, that the collective reasserted itself. I lost myself for a while in the mega-hive, surrendering *mmm-bzzz* submerging my own swarm's identity in the crushing embrace of the all-encompassing overmind.

Smothered by consensus, I felt the drive of species preservation in its fullest extreme. The urgency of our mission overshadowed *mmm-bzzz* choked out all other considerations. Surviving and helping humanity reach the stars were the only things that mattered.

When thoughts of my love for Clarity filtered into the gestalt, they were instantly extinguished. The mega-hive-mind tingled with disapproval

and disgust.

And they didn't give her a second thought. *We* didn't give her a second thought.

We had no desire for Clarity.

I emerged from the mega-consciousness like a drowning creature gasping for breath. As the collective disengaged *mmm-bzzz* released my swarm, I scrambled to pull myself back together, to retrieve the uniqueness that had been squeezed out of me.

When I did, I realized I was different from before. Merging with the overmind had reaffirmed my attachment to my people. Saving them felt more imperative than ever.

But as my individual thoughts and feelings came back to the fore, my love and commitment to Clarity remained strong *mmm-bzzz* undimmed. I could no more bear to lose her than I could bear to betray my people.

Two conflicting and powerful demands warred for dominance within my swarm. If Clarity and humanity lived, my people would devolve into non-sentient drones. If I saved my people, Clarity and her species would perish.

Then, suddenly, new insight blossomed within me. I saw the path to a new solution, flawed *mmm-bzzz* imperfect but maybe one I could live with.

The morning after The Rite, I awakened her as always, dabbing honey on her lips. Her clear green eyes flickered open, no less beautiful than the day before or the first time I'd seen them.

I worked hard all day, checking *mmm-bzzz* and rechecking my calculations, running and rerunning the simulations. Growing and programming legions of surgical nanobots to follow my instructions precisely.

I fed them to her that evening, with her wheat germ. And then I waited and watched.

The next day, there was no visible change. Clarity smiled and laughed like always. Her radiance was undiminished.

But when I scanned her, the equipment told a different story. Her DNA had changed. Overnight, it had radically altered *mmm-bzzz* transformed her metabolism.

The tests I performed confirmed the success of my treatment. Clarity had begun to deteriorate.

She no longer had the capability to live forever in her physical form.

Before long, Clarity's condition was not unique among humans.

After she received the treatment, and tests confirmed its effectiveness, the swarms decided to administer it to all humans in the labs.

Of course, no one knew the full truth behind it. No one knew the way it would *really* work.

No one had found the secret coding I'd hidden away within my intricate genetic construct. They saw the surface changes, analyzed the modifications they would cause, but they didn't detect the catch I'd built into my solution.

When the results of the treatment were the same on the other humans in the labs, the swarms wasted no time going forth to treat every human being in the world.

But the swarms didn't realize there was no need to hurry. Humankind wouldn't die any time soon.

It was true that we'd brought down *mmm-bzzz* toppled the protective wall around Clarity's species. But what only *I* knew was that the process would be a *slow* one. It would take *years* for individual humans to die.

And it would take even *longer* for the human species to perish in its entirety.

I'd made life last as long as it could. Not just weeks and months, but dozens of years.

The human body would turn against itself over time, breaking down *mmm-bzzz* eroding on a long, slow slide to oblivion. I'd chosen prolonged aging and decline as humanity's lot instead of sudden, jarring extinction.

I'd given Clarity time to fully appreciate the joys of corporeal life before leaving it. I'd given her time to adjust to her mortality.

I'd given *myself* time to adjust to her mortality, too.

I'd also arranged for my people's salvation...though that, too, would take a while.

Humanity would not die all at once as originally planned *mmm-bzzz* anticipated, releasing a burst of inner light massive enough to reboot our soulware. In fact, it would take ages for enough human light to become available.

Thanks to my concealed genetic tampering, the altered trait I'd devised would be passed down to every generation of humanity with absolute fidelity all down the long ages.

As humans died, our ship would collect *mmm-bzzz* gather portions of their inner light, just enough that their escape to the stars would not be impeded. Someday, many generations later, the ship would have enough light to conduct the reboot, and my people would return to their mission.

In the interim, though, we would devolve *mmm-bzzz* revert to a primitive state. Until the Great Restoration, we would exist as common insects *mmm-bzzz* honeybees, lacking sentience. We would pollinate flowers, gather nectar, and build hives, but we would not remember who we were, where we'd come from, or what our mission had been.

It was a steep price to pay, but I decided it was better than the alternative. Better, I thought, to give Clarity a long life and delay my people's restoration rather than hastening it by killing her and the rest of humanity outright.

So the fates of humans and bees were intertwined and set in motion.

We bees would tend the fields and flowers of Earth as once we'd tended infinitely strange species of sentient lifeforms on distant worlds. Meanwhile, generation after generation of humans would inhabit the world and depart into space upon death as pure light.

In space, humans would find glittering multitudes of species from other worlds lighting the darkest night like glowing beacons,
Shooting through starfields,
Swimming through nebulae,
Criss-cross
ing flares flash
ing past a trillion wonders,
Weaving a tapestry of light
ning, a restless paint
ing of shimmering threads, rush
ing rivers all in photons of gold,
Never limited
Never alone.
And *Clarity* had made it all possible.

There came a day when I freed her from her bonds and opened the door of the ship to the outside world. She left...but to my surprise *mmm-bzzz* delight, she came back.

She always came back to me. Through all the weeks and months and years
mmm-bzzz and decades that followed,
She always came back.

One day, a lifetime later, as the sun set over distant, snowcapped mountains, Clarity returned to me once more.

By then, my handiwork was plain to see; thankfully, I still had enough of a mind to comprehend it. Though other swarms' soulware was almost completely degraded by then, mine was just starting to lose ground to the Great Breakdown.

Clarity's fur had turned gray, and her flesh was sagging and wrinkled. She moved slowly, plodding *mmm-bzzz* hobbling through the tall grass, choosing each step with great care. Stooped and withered, she had changed so much since the first time I'd seen her, over fifty years earlier.

Her green eyes were sunken and filmy. Tears flowed from them
into the gray down
on her cheeks.

I think she knew what was coming. I think that was why she was there. She was weak and fragile beyond belief.

She almost fell to the floor, but I caught her and helped her to the silver exam table. She sat on the familiar metal surface, head bobbing, then slowly lay back.

Her eyes closed *mmm-bzzz* drifted shut, and she lost consciousness. As she slept there, curled up on the table, I examined her with my instrumentation. The joy I'd felt at seeing her turned to grief.

According to the tests, Clarity had reached the inevitable moment. The one I'd programmed into her DNA and delayed as long as I could.

When I realized what was happening to her, my ten thousand selves flew apart, swarming the lab in denial and confusion. I was dizzy with the whirlwind of impending loss, though I'd known this moment was approaching for decades. Though I was the one who'd invented it.

I could not bear the thought of existence
without her.
The knowledge that my work would lead to
Endless days
A procession
A weight
A space
A longing
All the worse

For having once
Been quelled.

It was then I realized, as much as I'd changed her, she had changed me more. As I hovered over her, gazing at her from every angle with my twenty thousand eyes, I knew how different I was because of her.

My hive-mind had realigned in fundamental, ineffable ways. I had reached beyond the swarm and shown personal compassion to another creature of another species. Not as part of an altruistic mission programmed into my genes, but because of the

yearning

of my ten thousand beating hearts.

In changing me, she had changed everything for herself and her people. Unlocked potentials that had yet to express *mmm-bzzz* manifest themselves.

And now, for her, for us,

there could be no going back.

Gathering my scattered selves together, I pushed back the grief as best I could and prepared for the final stage of our project.

Clarity slept soundly for hours on the hard metal table. As much suffering as she had found there, I think it still felt like home to her.

The monitors told me she was failing, but I didn't pay much attention to them. I was too busy watching Clarity's face as her allotted corporeal lifespan ran out *mmm-bzzz* expired.

I watched her toothless mouth as ragged, staggered breaths flowed in and out of it. I watched her nose wrinkle and flare as it caught some scent or the memory of one. I watched as her closed eyes flickered behind the lids, following the course of a dream.

Eventually, her eyes fluttered open
Like the wings of butterflies,
Soft as velvet, damp with dew.

By then, everything was in place. What she saw when she looked around were the grasslands of her home,

The amber plains rippling

In the wind, in the blazing sunlight.

Spear tips bobbing in the lazy current.

I tilted the table so she could see what lay ahead. A silver ship burrowing up out of the ground. Doors opening along the length of it, letting out ribbons of tiny, glittering creatures.

Suddenly, a woman emerged *mmm-bzzz* stepped out from behind a boulder. She walked unafraid with shoulders squared as her fellow humans cowered and ran. Her long, dark mane rippled in the morning breeze,

So soft, so flowing,

A beautiful veil cascading over shoulders

Over chest like a waterfall at night.

Clear eyes wide with fearless wonder, she gazed at the swarm, and the swarm *mmm-bzzz* and we *mmm-bzzz*

And *I* gazed back at *her*. Thousands of unblinking eyes

Like chips of polished ebony.

The woman in the tableau smiled, and so did the woman on the table. Past and future merged as one.

Then, the scene around us changed. It became a mirror image of the lab, with young Clarity strapped to the silver table.

My swarm settled *mmm-bzzz* descended upon her, tickling her with ten thousand pairs of flickering wings. Holographic Clarity squirmed and laughed with delight, and flesh-and-blood Clarity laughed, too. The laughter synchronized, high-pitched as the song of a bird,

The tinkling of icicles snapping from a tree branch

The whistling of wind through a hollow stone.

And by the time it subsided, she was almost gone. I switched the projection to a silent image of starry space to ease her transition. Galaxies pinwheeled around us. Comets streaked past, hanging tails of brilliant incandescence. Sprays of stars drifted like pollen through the inky night, sparkling like gold dust sprinkled over obsidian.

I went to her. All ten thousand of my selves hovered over her, gazing upon that well-known form, just as well-loved in old age as in youth.

Suddenly, she gasped, and her eyes shot open. I dared hope, in spite of the evidence of my instruments, that she might yet survive.

But then.

Mmm-bzzz.

But then,
You tremble with the effort,
shudder and go limp
with a sigh.
You settle
settle
to the table
like a feather
or a brittle leaf,
A windblown seed.

Don't go.

Darkness fills me,
a smoky
smoky cloud
obstructing all hope,
choking off
all everything,
then dispersing
as a tongue of flame
Shoots through me.
Burning off the cloud
like morning mist

    before the blinding
    blinding dawn.

You.

Your iridescence melts the shadows with a roar,
    Then laughs and twirls and disappears,
    As you in all your sparkling raiment soar,
    Away from every struggle, pain, and tear.

THE CROSS-DRESSING COSMIC CORTEZ RUBS OFF

As Philippa the Conquistadora waves his ribbony rainbow blade over the bowed head of Koocha, king of the alien Skoo, one bid after another chatters in over the phone in my head. Every network, from the bigs to the babies, wants to carry the live feed of this execution.

I love this job. When I was a boy, I watched the space conquistadors on pulsenet, roving among exotic worlds and violently subduing the primitive natives. Now, I'm repping Philippa, the cross-dressing, bloodthirsty, cosmic Cortez, skimming my fifteen percent of more money than there are hydrogen atoms in the universe.

"Thus endeth the greatest campaign of conquest in history!" roars Philippa, shaking a black-leather-gloved fist in the air. The butt-rings dangling from his exposed posterior jangle as he thrusts his leather-chapped hips to one side. "At least until my *next* campaign!" he says with a lipsticky smile aimed right at the camera cloud drifting in front of him.

"Wait, O Conqueror!" yips kneeling Koocha, who looks more like an ugly orange baby with green stripes and foot-long glowing purple whiskers than anything else. "Before I die, I must speak with that man."

To my surprise, Koocha points his stubby finger-bud right at me.

The rock soundtrack kicks up ominously, screeching to a crescendo of skirling ultra-guitar feedback.

"Bo-ring," groans Philippa, and then he flutters a languid hand in my direction. "He's just my aaaagent. I can feel the ratings drooping already."

"I will outbid all bidders if you will spare my people," Koocha says to me in his/her/its/whatever's squeaky voice.

"I'm listening," I say with a smirk.

"We offer your species total enlightenment, perfect happiness, and eternal bliss," says Koocha. "We can give you the wisdom that most species take millions of years to obtain." Koocha's whiskers glow brighter. "What say you?"

I laugh. "You're serious?"

Koocha nods. "If you accept, humanity will hyperevolve into gods multimillennia ahead of schedule, and you will become the greatest hero in human history." Koocha shrugs. "Or you will refuse and become the greatest villain."

Philippa prances over and rubs my chest. "How deliciously tempting," he purrs.

I am very aware of the ribbony sword in his other hand, though that is not what makes up my mind.

The thought of bringing spiritual transcendence and hyperevolution to mankind—if such a thing is even possible—also gets my attention...but that does not sway me, either. Nor does the secretly longed-for fulfillment of my boyhood dreams by outdoing Philippa on the celebrity villain front.

What does it, what makes up my mind, is when the insta-ratings graph floating always in the corner of my eye takes a sharp plunge.

The viewers have spoken.

I give the nod to Philippa. With a shake of his flouncy black curls, he swishes his rainbow sword in a whistling figure eight and levels it at Koocha.

"Sorry," I say to the shivering alien kinglet. "I can't *spend* fifteen percent of enlightenment."

VOYAGE OF THE DOG-PROPELLED STARSHIP

W
e are down to our last team of Huskies, and we still can't shake the *Unshakable*, flagship of the dreaded High Concept.

"How long can those Huskies run? How long until we lose all propulsion from the dog-drive?" I shout the question to make myself heard over the cries of pleasure from the bridge crew around me.

The Concept's delighter beams have half the crew squirming on the floor, quivering like the enormous bacteria or protozoans they are.

"Stand by, Captain Nabob!" Vera Caspian, my ship's caninegineer (and a freak human among us), is watching readouts and video feeds on her holographic console. She claps her hands once, folds sideways left to right, and is gone, zapping by quantum zentanglement to the Kennel Deck at the far end of the ship.

She unfolds at her station a moment later, her face flushed with alarm. "Maybe five more minutes on the Huskies. That's with our best musher at the whip."

Our own farship, the *No Shit*, rocks as the *Unshakable* blasts us with its boomer cannons, knocking me sideways. As I catch myself on a shiny bulkhead, I realize the terrible shape I'm in; my reflection shows that my thousands of hairlike cilia are limp, my macronucleus is pale, and my cytoplasm is shriveled and green with exhaustion. Three days on the run from the Concept have left this giant paramecium looking like a sorry-ass humanoid warmed over.

But I'm still the *captain* of this ship, and I have a duty to keep her out of the hands of the enemy. Also a duty to deliver the *Trillion Thoughts About One Thing* in our hold to the dying planet that needs them to survive.

Which is about 300 light years from the orange and purple planet we're about to crash into.

"We're caught in that world's gravity well, sir!" says Mr. Huarache, a three-meter-tall amoeboid with glittering gold flecks in his cytoplasm. "We're going down!"

The *No Shit* shudders around us as the *Unshakable* keeps up its bombardment. As always, the High Concept's dedication to trolling the sentients of the galaxy for their own demented amusement knows no bounds. Stopping us from saving a dying planet will bring those bitter, sniggering jerks no end of joy, and stealing the *Trillion Thoughts About One Thing* for their own trouble-causing endeavors will be the cherry on the hot shit sundae.

Another round of boomer blasts rattles us from stern to stem, even as more of our people go down squirming with delighter-induced bliss. We'll be lucky to make landfall before the ship shakes to pieces and everyone aboard her is overstimulated to the point of implosion.

"Captain!" Vera has a grim look on her face. "The Huskies are down, sir!" Dogs whine and whimper over the intercom. "We're breaking out the emergency backup, but we won't get far on *Corgis* and *dachshunds*, sir!"

"Huarache!" I stare at the gleaming orange and purple planet on the big viewer on the forward bulkhead. "Can we manage evasive maneuvers?"

"I feel too good to try!" Huarache giggles with delight.

Damnit, he's been hit! "Outta my way!" Cilia fluttering, I zip over and seize the controls with the folds of my rubbery pellicle membrane.

Little dogs are yapping, and there's power again, but barely. I flick a switch, twist a joystick, and the *No Shit* swoops away from the *Unshakable*, heading for the planet's surface far below.

The surface where, long ago, I was shocked to discover who *dogs'* best friends really were, and why evil was *not* the worst thing ever to nest in human hearts.

We come down fast and hit hard, bouncing from one purple sand dune to the next. Hunks of the ship's organic outer armor shear away with each impact, exposing more of the *No Shit*'s glistening jellyfish skin.

Our breakneck approach finally comes to an end with a sudden, lurching stop in the side of a huge Ground Spout--its thick purple mass heaving with complex vapors and dense, semi-solid larvae flickering in and out of multiple dimensions.

As the ship settles and the screams fade--as many triggered by High Concept delighter beams as crash-inflicted injuries--I shake off my own personal shock and help those on the bridge who are hurt. One of them, Ensign Scintilla Tint, a sentient scent presenting as a cluster of swirling glitter, is scattered but doesn't let it stop her from reporting on casualties.

Five dead, 85 injured. Her voice is a complex arrangement of fragrant esters that conjures language in the speech centers of most organic brains. *And...oh no. Oh this is terrible.*

"What?" I ask as I finish mending some of the million wings of the giant flying bacterium known as Lieutenant Ah Rise Rhythm.

Vera Caspian, whose head wound is shedding blood down the side of her face, interrupts. "Dogs down, Captain! *All dogs gone!*"

Yes, dead, confirms Scintilla.

"And the ship's condition?" I ask as Ah Rise Rhythm flutters away to check on his crewmates.

"Repair crews already dispatched and laden with insults," says Mr. Huarache. "Damage consequential but not irreparable."

"How long until we're ready to launch?" I ask.

"Approximately two hours, Captain Nabob." Huarache's amoeboid gelatin squirms, repairing multiple regions of bruising. "Assuming repairs are properly completed, and the High Concept doesn't destroy us first, all we'll need to reactivate the dog drive are some..."

"Then it's a good thing." I head for the exit.

"What is that, Captain?" asks Rhythm.

"A good thing I know where to *find* some dogs," I tell them as the shellevator doors clam shut before me, and I zip away through the ship to the bubble deck where my bouncy ball carriage awaits.

I'm 20 bounces west of the *No Shit* when Vera unfolds from right to left beside me, in a Dalmatian print field jacket with a med kit pack on her back. Her head wound has been wrapped with a black-furred bandage that contrasts her pretty blond hair.

"Vera." I'm not really surprised to see her appear in my travel ball like that. As caninegineer, she *should* be along on this mission.

"Craw isn't listed as a dog-rich world." Vera bobs in the suspension field inside the ball, only lightly jarred by the vehicle's powerful bounces across the landscape. "So where are these canines you're barking about, Skipper?"

"Not far, actually. It's lucky we crashed where we did."

"Lucky?" Vera scrunches up her nose. "What if you lead the Concept to this secret stash of yours?"

"As long we make contact first, I don't care. Though depending on how well they *remember* me, we might not have such smooth flailing."

As I flutter my thousands of cilia for emphasis, the terrain outside the travel ball changes, shifting from purple sand dunes to a bird beak forest. Giant toucan, myna, and heron beaks climb point-first to the lilac sky, even as spindly trees hung with the beaks of other birds surround us, clattering in the stiff afternoon breeze.

The macronucleus at the heart of me clenches as memories of my last visit to this place rush back. "Gird yourself, Vera. Unless this place has changed greatly, we are heading into the deepest of metaphorical darkness."

"What *happened* when you were here before, Captain?" asks Vera. "Tell me more about what to expect."

As the travel ball takes a bad bounce off an upthrust woodpecker beak the size of an old-growth redwood tree, I adjust the course controls on the inner wall of the ball with my cilia. *Almost there.* But can we get the help we need in spite of the cloud I left under last time? The darkness that still, to this day, haunts me?

Maybe I can work it out by telling the story. "It was twelve full glimmerings ago, when I was but a crewman on the good farship *Every/None/Always/Never...*"

"We surrender!" screamed Captain Fragilistic of the *Tabula Raga*, the hysteria in his voice unnerving even in the replayed video. "Call off your people-things! Oh gods, please *call them off!*"

"Crewman Nabob! For the last time, quit watching that shit!" *My* commanding officer at the time, Captain Eponymous Prawn of the *Every/None/Always/Never*, knocked the video playback device out of my pellicle mitten with one sweep of his whiplike flagellum. "Pay attention to what's happening *now*, and maybe we can find and *rescue* the crew of the *Tabula Raga.*"

"Instead of suffering the same fate as they did?" I asked.

"Face forward, crewman!" howled Prawn, a spermatozoa with an attitude that never quit.

I did, and so did the other twelve crewmen and three officers in the landing party. Giant microbes all, we continued our methodical march/squirm/wriggle/float through the bird beak forest, closing in on the last known location of the Fragilistic and the party from the *Tabula Raga*. They'd all disappeared six weeks ago, leaving behind only that ominous video as a clue to their fates...a video that was stuck playing in a loop as we all marched away from my discarded player device. "We surrender! Oh gods, please *call them off!*"

"Hold up, people!" Lieutenant Band Antimony, a ribbon of geometric diatoms with photoluminescent properties, suddenly stiffened in alarm. "Movement up ahead!"

Every one of us raised and cocked our convincer/reviser guns, barrels aiming at a copse of striped toucan beaks not twenty kicks away. Depending on their moods, those living weapons we carried would unleash either a torrent of persuasive argument or streams of information-altering code capable of rewriting the causal relationships involved in a given scene.

The weapons might as well have been nonexistent when we heard the plaintive howl from the copse of beaks.

OO-WOO-OOOOOO

As the keening rose and fell, I shivered and considered turning tail. One of our number *did* desert just then--a gray-skinned crypto-toendolith who turned out to be the wisest among us.

"Steady, people!" ordered Antimony. "Stand your ground!"

"Who's there?" shouted Captain Prawn in the direction of the howl. "Who is it?"

OO-WOO-OOOOOO

Again, the cry ululated on the hot, dry wind, keeping us all at shivering attention. Then, suddenly, it stopped.

A figure emerged from the copse of beaks--a naked human male on all fours, slinking slowly across the dusty ground. His long, shaggy hair and beard were bright red. He wore a spiked black collar with a long silver chain trailing after it.

Behind him strode a figure on two legs--a canine like a German

Shepherd in a kind of blue jumpsuit. In his right paw, which included a prehensile, clawed thumb, he carried the other end of the chain attached to the man's collar.

When he spoke, his voice was deep and rumbling like thunder.

"Welcome one and all," he said. "Which of you is fit to feed the Best Friend?"

"That human?" said Prawn. "*None* of us, thank you very much!"

"Don't be silly. Not that *human,*" snapped the canine. "Our *Best* Friend!"

"We're here." I stroke the course controls, and the travel ball bounces to a stop. One more touch of a control, and the skin falls into wedges around us, exposing us to the riot of sounds and smells in the bird beak forest. "That's where they first came out to meet us." I poke a hump of pellicle at the copse of toucan beaks just a few coughs away.

"'They as in a dominant, bipedal dog and subservient human on all fours." Vera takes a step forward, then stops. "Why is this the first I've ever heard of this encounter?"

"It was classified ultra-top secret after what happened." I glide past her and into the copse. There is simply no time to waste; the Ground Spout could disperse at any time, leaving the *No Shit* completely out in the open. Will my crew finish repairs or will the Concept swoop in to destroy them and the farship first? It's a tossup.

Vera draws her weapon--a fully automatic shevolver with self-esteem nullifier and false hope inducer--and follows me into the cluster of colorful striped beaks. This isn't the first time we've been in a tense situation together; she's been part of the crew for seven sequences, each one riskier than the last.

But I fear for us both if potential surprises roll against us, which they very well could. I wouldn't put anything past this world after my disastrous last visit.

Suddenly, a keening wail fills the air--familiar to *my* ears, at least. A chill runs through my cytoplasm as, for a moment, time seems to turn back.

"Ignore that," I tell Vera as I keep gliding forward. "Just keep going."

"But is it..."

"*Ignore it.*" I need to keep us focused in spite of the distraction. Whatever awaits us, we need to face it at full, unrattled strength and composure.

A moment of silence, and again, Vera speaks--trying to keep her mind off the danger, perhaps. "So what happened after the dog and his pet man met your group, Skipper?"

"The dog--his name was Half Hiccup Half Heartattack--showed us the way to a hidden city called Oblongata, which was built entirely of bones and feces. Parts of it were marvelously intricate. Other parts were corpse-strewn ruins. They'd been having a civil war, you see--pets against masters...and something else."

"Pets? You mean *dogs* or *men*?"

"Yes." I slip between some tightly-packed flamingo beaks, slowing my pace a little. We're not far from Oblongata and its possible dangers now. "And something else. Something I'd never encountered before--*knowingly.*"

"What a lovely city," said Captain Prawn in the bygone days of yore. "And what a shame about all the destruction."

"We paid a price for victory." Half Hiccup Half Heartattack patted his leashed human on his red-haired head. The man drooled, tongue lolling, eyes empty. "But it was worth it for our newfound freedom."

"Freedom." Lieutenant Antimony's component diatoms glowed a little brighter, then dimmed. "From what?"

"This one and his like, of course." Heartattack tousled the man's bearded chin. "They subjugated us, treated us as their *chattel*, denied us *any* kind of rights...and now look. Who's a good boy now, huh? *Who's a good boy now?*" With a laugh, Heartattack shook the man's head by his beard, yanking it from side to side.

Still, the man's eyes were blank. I was having a hard time imagining he'd *ever* been part of a ruling class of any kind.

"When did the war end?" asked Prawn.

"Only days ago," said Heartattack.

"That fits." Antimony's ribbony structure rippled. "Our missing landing party must have gotten caught up in the conflict."

Heartattack nodded slowly. "Of course. Their demise had nothing to do with the Godicils."

Prawn and Antimony exchanged a look that made me more nervous than ever. I kept my pellicle extrusions and cilia wrapped tight around my convincer/reviser gun.

"Demise?" said Prawn. "We never said they were *dead*. All we know is that they're *missing*."

"And what's a *Godicil?*"

"You mean you don't *know?*" Heartattack crouched beside the man and gestured at what looked to me like empty space above the man's shoulders. "You mean you can't *see* it?"

"See what?" asked Prawn.

"Come closer." Heartattack kept gesturing at that space above the human's shoulders. "Take a closer look."

Prawn swam over, propelling himself with strokes of his flagellum tail, and gazed down at the man as instructed.

"Still nothing?" Heartattack sounded annoyed. "Closer!"

"What exactly does it *look* li--"

Suddenly, Prawn was dragged down toward the man--but not *by* him. From what I could see, it was like something in that empty space jerked him down toward it, holding his ovoid body fast as his tail flailed crazily.

And then stopped. And then Prawn fell to the ground beside the human with a *splat*.

"A *Godicil*," said Heartattack, "is *that*."

As the upright German Shepherd said it, other bipedal dogs with naked humans on leashes--some with more than one-- converged from the surrounding rubble. All of the humans were growling as they approached, males and females alike.

"Just because you can't *see* it, doesn't mean it can't win a *war*. Or be our *best friend*." Heartattack dropped the leash, and all the other dogs around us did the same.

The words of hysterical Captain Fragilistic of the *Tabula Raga* from that terrible video rushed back to me. *Call off your people-things! Oh gods, please call them off!*

"Just because you can't *see* them, doesn't mean they can't *slaughter* you," said Heartattack, just before he whistled and all the humans attacked us at once.

"How the hell did you *survive*?" asks Vera.

I don't get to finish telling her my story just then because my chatterbox starts beeping, alerting me to a message from the *No Shit*. Sliding the device from its holster stuck to my pellicle, I flick it on with my fluttering cilia, and we listen.

"The Ground Spout has dissipated! The *Unshakable* has found us!" The voice from the speaker belongs to ever-dependable Lieu-tenant Ah Rise Rhythm. "Their fighters are rapidly incoming with delighters fully charged! Repairs are nearly complete, but we're sitting ducks with dogless engines! No takey-offey, *capische*?"

"Hold them off as best you can," I tell him. "Launch all fighter squadrons. Keep shields raised as long as you can on battery power."

"That won't be long, Captain!" Just as Rhythm says it, there's an explosion in the background. "We don't have much left in the tank here!"

"We hope to be in touch soon with good news." I keep my voice confident for his sake. "Nabob out."

"Gotta go, Skipper." Vera claps her hands once, folds left to right, and is gone--presumably back to the ship to assess and assist. Maybe she's even got some emergency puppies tucked away in cryogenic dogspension for just such a day as today.

As I break the connection, I hear rustling from the peacock tail brush nearby, and I lurch around to face it. Extruding a mitten of cytoplasm, I wrap it around my instakarmashawarmadharma gun and swing it up in instant readiness just in case.

"Who goes there?" As the words pop out of my oral groove, every cilium on my body stiffens like a needle, quivering with tension. "Show yourself!"

Imagine my surprise when a redheaded human male stalks out of the brush biped-style, dressed in a black smock and bottoms.

"Greetings, friend." Smiling, he raises his hands (which are empty of weapons, by the way). "You are most welcome here in our little corner of the world."

"Greetings to you as well." I recognize him instantly as the naked redhead on the leash of Half Hiccup Half Heartattack from my previous visit...though I don't blurt this fact out right away.

"My name is Fah Fistula, and I'm the chief of our fair city of Oblongata." The redhead bows a little, then straightens. "And you are?"

I hesitate to announce my name, then decide to go for broke rather than lie. "Captain Nabob," I tell him. "My vessel, the farship *No Shit*, crash-landed nearby and is in dire straits." I pause dramatically. "We are dogless."

"Then we have something in common!" Fistula nods. "There is not a dog to be found *anywhere* in Oblongata or its blessed environs."

My star-shaped contractile vacuole and radiating canals scrunch in a spiral twist, the paramecium version of a frown. "No dogs...at all?"

Again, Fistula nods. "If you've come in search of them, you're out of luck. The last died during our recent civil war, ended mere weeks prior to your arrival."

There's been another civil war, then--this time with much different results. Things start to make *terrible* sense. If what he says is true, the *No Shit* and all aboard are surely doomed.

The man gestures, inviting me onward. "Will you visit fair Oblongata, sir? I think you'll find our hospitality *much* improved since your *last* visit here."

So he *does* remember me. "But what about the *others? The dogs'* best friends?"

"The Godicils?" Fistula smiles grimly. "Whom do you think we *defeated* in this war?"

As the humans attacked, the crew of the *Every/None/Always/Never* didn't hesitate to open fire. Every one of us blasted away with our convincer/revisers, holding nothing back--and not a shot made a damn bit of difference. The humans were upon us like a raging wildfire, oblivious to the streams of argument or causal disruption cascading from the barrels of our weapons.

Their style of assault was surprising, unnerving. They knocked our people down and pinned them but never used their sharp claws or gleaming fangs to do them harm. *That,* they left to the *thin air.*

Just as Captain Prawn had been murdered by what seemed to be the empty space above the redheaded human's shoulders, I saw one after another of my shipmates torn apart by unseen forces. Gruesome splatters of guts spilled onto the ground all around me, erupting from skins and capsules that seemingly split open sponta-neously.

Only I was spared, writhing out of the awful slaughter that engulfed my comrades. Lieutenant Antimony tried to follow, only to be pounced on by a screaming, dark-haired female and subsequently rupture like a stuck balloon.

Just like in the video, it was pure chaos. Mind whirling, I found myself pinned against a towering black beak--and Half Hiccup Half Heartattack stepped in front of me.

"Looks like they were *all* fit to feed the Godicils." Heartattack shrugged. "But *you* have a different role to play, apparently."

"Role?" I had to fight to keep my voice from shaking as the humans who'd just torn apart my crewmates rose and circled around me, hunched and glowering. "What role?"

"Tortured prisoner." Heartattack gestured, and two brawny men--one with brown hair, one with blond--got up off their hands and knees and stormed toward me. "Don't worry. The pain will be worth it in the end...though not so much for you."

The two men used me as a punching bag then, taking turns pumping fists into my pellicle. Each blow was harder than the last, making me grunt and yelp with agony.

And each time a human punch pounded my micronucleus through the pellicle, I divided. I gave birth to a copy of myself that wriggled off into the arms of a waiting dog.

Screaming at the pain flashing through me, I had the answer to a question I'd never considered until that moment.

If you undergo asexual reproduction induced by physical impact, is it still a violation?

I am nervous as Fistula guides me into the freshly ruined city. I stay keenly alert for any sudden movement from any direction, even as I realize all the alertness at my command won't likely save me.

This is where it happened, that pummeling attack...the forced reproduction. The last thing I remember from that day is gazing out at all the children I'd made against my will, glistening and quivering eerily in the midday sun. Then, I passed out from the pain, blessedly shielded from whatever abuses were to follow.

I awoke who knows how many hours later, shriveled and wretched in the purple sand desert. Gazing up, I saw crewmen from the *Every/None/Always/Never* gaping down at me, reaching to lift me in their cilia and pseudopodia for transport back to the ship. When I got there, I said nothing of what had been done to me, though I told our intelligence branch everything I remembered otherwise of Oblongata. I thought I would never travel back there in my lifetime--I *prayed* I wouldn't--yet here I am, returned to the scene of the crimes against me.

And a witness to those very crimes walks easily alongside me, as if we are dear old friends. Needless to say, I keep an extruded mitten close to my instakarmashawarmadharma gun at all times.

"Careful," he says calmly. "There are still a few of them roaming around."

"Dogs? Godicils?"

"Your kids," says Fistula.

I am more confused than ever. "Why is that a bad thing?"

"Because they were on the wrong side. They were the *enemy--part* of it, anyway."

We circle the ruins of a giant structure that looks like it was built from stained glass, starlight, and some kind of flowering vines. A cathedral, perhaps? Then why are there heaps of dog skulls arranged on the floor?

"I don't understand anything about this place," I say, almost to myself. "I don't understand what happened here."

"What happened to *you*, you mean? Back in the day?" Fistula plucks a purple flower from one of the vines and twirls it between his thumb and forefinger. "I can tell you this much: it was all the *dogs'* idea."

"Why? What could they have to gain from what was done to me?"

"Peace! That was the plan, anyway." Fistula flicks the flower away. "They wanted your offspring to serve as *hosts* for the Godicils--though *traps* is more like it."

"Maybe it would help if I knew what the Godicils *were."*

"Invisible, hideous *parasites*." Fistula flinches a little when he says it. "Most of the time, you don't even know they're *on* you." He reaches back with both hands and pats the empty space above his shoulders. "On you and *in* you."

"In you."

Fistula scowls and nods. "They work their slimy tendrils through your body, winding them around your organs—occupying your heart like a nest of worms. They pump you full of chemicals, driving you to violence, and they feed on your rage and pain. The only way to keep the food coming is to turn you against an enemy--even if that enemy used to be your friend."

His words sink in, and understanding grows. "Then the civil war that the dogs won, those years ago?"

"Was triggered by the Godicils," says Fistula. "And we humans were their hosts. But in the war before that, the *dogs* were the hosts, and so on. This went on for thousands of years, one war after another, until Half Hiccup Half Heartattack the dog chieftain came along. He was the first who could *see* and *read* the slimy bastards. He was the first to understand how *both* sides were being manipulated. And when *you* folks started dropping in, he came up with a plan to free *all* of us."

I twitch at a flicker of movement near a half-toppled tower of pulsing green brick...then relax. Nothing there.

"At the time, the Godicils were the *dogs'* best friends." Fistula keeps walking, drawing me toward a battered silver dome that looks like it could be the center of the city. "But Heartattack knew that would only last until the next war, when the Godicils would switch sides and drive the *humans* into conflict. This would just go on forever, he knew--but what if there was a *third* side? What if he introduced a *new* host into the mix? One that might be too tempting for the Godicils to resist--until they were *trapped* inside...and then the whole package was *disposed of."*

"And the Godicils took the bait?" I leave out the part about my personal suffering and violation--for now, at least.

"We all worked together, playing our parts. We had to make it seem *convincing*...right down to the attack on your team, I'm afraid. We needed it to look like we were torturing you for information, and the copies we punched out of you were unintentional." He sounds regretful. "And when we had your children, and talked about how wonderful they were, and what amazing capabilities they had, the Godicils *jumped* at them! Heartattack saw them go, one after another, and attach to your kids' bodies. And then he *closed the trap*, buried them like dogs *do*--but it was a *bust*. Over time, the Godicil treatment turned your kids into *powerhouses*, and they broke free and came after *all* of us. They killed every last dog and almost got the *rest* of us, except we figured out a way to kill *them* first, and the Godicils with them."

"You killed my children."

"Correct," says Fistula.

"Except a few who are still roaming around."

"Exactly."

"Okay." Nothing I've heard from him makes me feel any better about what happened...or more hopeful about the tragedy I've come here to avert. And the clock is ticking, I know, counting down whatever few minutes are left for the *No Shit* to hold on against overwhelming odds. What if the *Unshakable* has already destroyed her?

The thought of it inspires me to dig deeper for a solution. There must be *something* here to power up the ship, *something* that wasn't trashed in the latest war.

"Fistula." I look around at the rubble as we pick our way through it. "Do you know if the dogs buried anything else?"

Fistula snorts and stops walking. "Good question. Those mutts were *always* burying things."

I like where this is going. "Can you think of any *specific* burial sites?" I gesture at the ground with one of my pellicle mittens.

"Well, not down *there.*" Fistula points upward. *"That's* where they did all their *burying."*

"Wait a minute." I do that frowny star-shaped vacuole/canals thing again. "Am I to understand that these dogs somehow *buried* things…in the *sky?"*

"Not so much in the *sky."* Fistula tips his head back and jabs a finger at a fluffy orange cloud overhead. "In *those."*

Some kind of hyperdense cloud formation with antigravitic properties? It's a new one on me. "So how did they get *up* there then?"

"The *elevator,* of course." He looks over his shoulder and gestures in the general direction of what looks like a distant, rippling heat mirage.

"Well let's go see what they stashed up there, shall we?" I prod him along with my flickering cilia. "If there's a secret power source, we need to find it *fast.* Time is running out, and a lot of good macrobes are about to be deathstinguished."

We emerge from the rippling transparent elevator into a truly wondrous place built of billowing orange cloud. Puffs and streamers of the stuff drift all around, glowing every shade of orange in the unobstructed late day sunlight. It all seems insubstantial, yet somehow supports the weight of us both, giving only slightly like rubbery foam under Fistula's feet and my flickering cilia.

It supports much more than that, as well. The dogs left all manner of things up here, jumbled in the cottony fluff. There are piles of bones, of course, and tatters and rags--but also mechanical and electronic parts and equipment…building materials…functioning devices. Things blink and hum in the cloudbank, while others chatter and whir and twitch--and do *other* things, too.

As we walk onward, we hear sounds from inside a kind of

bunker built with corrugated metal. The sounds are unmistakable, even muffled as they are--and the part of me that's closest to a human heart truly leaps. Perhaps, after everything, there is hope after all.

"Do you hear that?" I ask Fistula, pointing a mitten at the building.

"Yes, but there's a lock on the door," he tells me.

"So smash it off," I say as I reach for my chatterbox. "And make it snappy!"

He hesitates, then goes to retrieve a metal bar from a nearby pile of junk.

As he heads for the bunker, my chatterbox makes its connection. "Skipper?" Vera Caspian answers the call. "Where the hell *are* you? I zentangled back from the *No Shit* and can't find you anywhere!"

"Never mind!" I watch as Fistula breaks the lock and tosses it aside. "Just get back to the ship *immediately*. And prepare the following without delay!"

"Yes sir!"

Fistula throws open the door, and the noise bursts out from inside. All that wonderful, marvelous *barking*.

And then I *see* them, the ones making those sounds, and I know we can do this. *We can win because of them.*

As they charge toward me, I laugh out my orders to Vera. "Get me *harnesses*, Vera! Dozens of *harnesses*, and the longest *traces* you can throw together in the next fifteen minutes!"

The battle is in full swing when I ride a winged Great Dane down from the sky, exulting in the way the wind whips my cilia.

Enemy fighters swoop and blast overhead, sparring with fighters from the *No Shit*. The sky lights up, but the fire comes nowhere near the Dane or any of the *other* winged dogs.

There are *dozens* of them, barking and howling with joy as they soar down on great feathery wings. Nimbly, they zip between blasts and shrapnel, darting this way and that, a brigade of furry angels. The products of Godicil science, these genetically engineered miracles are clearly elated to finally be free of the shelter where they were tucked away for far too long. Heartattack and his people might have saved them from Godicil domination, but locking them away only intensified their desire to be free.

And now, finally, they can *fly*…and so can *we*.

The Dane and I land in front of the *No Shit*, where Vera followed my orders to the letter. Lots of crewmen are there, too, to help set things in motion--Vera, Ah Rise Rhythm, and Mr. Huarache among them.

The Dane, leader of the pack, follows me to the front and is first to accept a harness. The other dozens follow, landing lightly and scampering to positions along the lengthy, incredibly strong lead lines. They all pant and sniff and bark with joy as the crew fasten harnesses to them, taking care to leave the wings free and clear. They sing, too, in words taught them by Heartattack years ago, poetic words of flight and beauty and escape to faraway starlands.

Every time the enemy fighters form up and try to strafe them, our own fighters fend them off with desperate grace. We'll let *nothing* get in the way of what comes next.

When the harnesses are secure, all the crew members race into the ship except Vera. Pressure-suited against the harshness of space, she leaps into a special sled behind the dogs, hastily assembled by the *No Shit*'s highly motivated crew.

On my signal, when all crew and fighter craft are aboard, Vera cracks the whip. The winged dogs--Danes, Huskies, Shepherds, Greyhounds, Golden Retrievers, Dobermans, Labradors, and more--run and flap across the purple sand. They pull the ship behind them with incredible ease, sliding it out of the crash-site and picking up speed.

When their paws leave the ground, so does the *No Shit*. Together, we soar upward, leaving behind the awful world of Craw that held us down--that held *me* down ever since my first visit, though I've finally broken its grip. As the dogs and ship fly, so does my soul. As the ground recedes below us, so does the sorrow and pain that kept me from reaching my fullest potential as a paramecium and farship captain.

Enemy fighters swirl around us, and we shoot away from them, too fast to follow. They can't stop us from whisking the *Trillion Thoughts About One Thing* to that dying world or going on any of the multitude of adventures that surely await us.

The High Concept attack ship *Unshakable* roars toward us, firing every weapon in its arsenal...then seems to stand still as Vera mushes the dogs to unbelievable new speeds.

Somehow, their wings and paws have just as much traction in the void as on the ground and in the atmosphere. I can't explain it, and I don't care. I don't care about the physics or the memories of my pain or the damned High Concept or any of it.

It is enough to sit back and watch from the bridge of my gleaming farship as those winged dogs carry us forth into the star-filled glory of the galaxy, barking with heartfelt joy at every crack of the musher's whip.

UNIVERSAL LANGUAGE

1

Corporal Jalila bint Farooq bin Abdul Al-Fulani had had this nightmare before.

She was on the surface of an alien world with her captain and crewmates from the *Ibn Battuta*. They all turned to her for help, for understanding. Lives depended on her making sense of an alien language she'd never heard before, which should not have been a big deal, because alien linguistics was her specialty...

...but she found herself drowning in a sea of gibberish.

A tide of babble washed over her, a wave of seemingly disconnected sounds from a mob of creatures. Billions of phonemes, the smallest units of language, crashed together, mixing with millions of clicks and lip-smacks that could themselves be part of a language or just random biological noise.

The tide swelled and swirled and Jalila felt herself going under. Again and again, she grabbed at the current but could never make sense of it.

The display on the Voicebox interpreter device she carried blinked with indecipherable nonsense.

She had had this nightmare before. The only problem was, this time, she was wide awake.

Jalila's heart raced. She looked around at the crowd of beings who surrounded her, sleek-furred and slender like otters, and a chill shot down her spine.

Then, she felt Major al-Aziz touch her arm.

"Jalila?" He stared at her with his piercing green eyes, voice laden with concern.

She took a deep breath and gathered herself up. *Enough of this.*

She was on the surface of the planet Vox with Major al-Aziz and Colonel Farouk. The three of them had landed an hour ago in a scout barque jettisoned from the deep space exploration ship *Ibn Battuta* (named after the renowned Old Earth Arab explorer and scholar). It was up to them to warn the inhabitants of Vox about an approaching invasion fleet...the same fleet that had crippled and cast adrift the *Ibn Battuta*.

So it was time to start acting like a professional. Jalila had to forget her fears and nightmares. She had to forget that the stakes were so high, with so many lives in the balance.

And she had to forget that this was her final mission as linguist on the *Ibn Battuta*.

Jalila was being drummed out of the service. In fact, she would have been drummed out and sent home by now if the *Ibn Battuta* had not encountered the invasion fleet.

It was all because she'd mistranslated a message two weeks ago and gotten someone killed--a diplomat negotiating the end of a civil war on planet Pyrrhus VII. Jalila had made a mistake translating the complex Pyrrhic language, leading both sides in the war to believe the diplomat was working against them. They'd killed him, and the armistice had collapsed.

So here was Jalila, career over, confidence shot...and her shipmates needed her one more time. Somehow, she had to pull herself together and get the job done. All she really wanted to do was go home and languish in disgrace, but she had to hang on by her fingernails and do this one last thing.

Nodding to al-Aziz, Jalila smoothed the light gray jumpsuit uniform over her slender hips. She tucked her shoulder-length black hair behind her ears, then took a deep breath and turned to the crowd.

"Quiet!" she shouted, as loud as she could, her voice rising over the tumult.

She got her message across. Suddenly, the chaos of noise and chatter subsided. The gleaming black pearl eyes of the dozens of Vox in the city square all slid around to focus on her.

Jalila cleared her throat and took a step forward, fixing her attention on a single brown-furred being. "Hi." She mustered a smile.

The brown-furred Vox rattled off a stream of incomprehensible syllables, at the same time gesturing, clicking, and smacking at a furious pace.

For a moment, Jalila listened and watched the Vox's four-clawed hands flutter and weave. Then, she closed her eyes, blocking out the movement and letting the flurry of sounds rush through her.

Pared down from dozens of voices to one, reduced further from sound and motion to sound alone, the communication seemed less overwhelmingly chaotic. As Jalila absorbed it, she realized it could be simplified even further.

Opening her eyes, she interrupted the Vox by raising both hands, palms flattened toward him. "Only this," she said slowly, pointing to her lips.

Then, pronouncing each letter with slowness and clarity, she recited the Arabic alphabet. She hoped the Vox would get the idea: she wanted to hear *pulmonic* sounds only, those created with an air stream from the lungs...sounds like the vowels and consonants of the alphabet. All the clicking and smacking was getting in the way.

When she was done, she raised her hands toward the Vox, palms up, indicating it was his turn. (She guessed the Vox was a male because it was bulkier and had a deeper voice than others in the crowd.)

Message received. This time, the Vox's speech was slower and free of clicks and smacks. Finally, Jalila could pick out distinct syllables arranged in patterns. She had isolated a spoken language, one using pulmonic vowels and consonants alone.

Not that the other sounds and hand signs weren't part of a language themselves. Jalila was sure they were, which had been the problem. The pulmonic syllables formed one language. The clicks and smacks comprised a second language. A third language consisted of hand signs.

The Vox people had three different languages, she realized, and they used them all at once. They carried on three conversations at the same time, or one conversation with three levels.

No wonder Jalila and the Voicebox had been stumped. Neither was wired to process so much simultaneous multilingual input.

As the Vox spoke, Jalila's Voicebox took in everything, identifying repeated patterns and relationships between sounds...comparing them to language models in its database...constructing a rudimentary vocabulary and a framework of syntax on which to hang it.

Before long, the chicken scratch on the Voicebox's display became readable output--lines of text representing the alien's words, printed phonetically, laid out alongside an Arabic translation of those words.

At about the same time that the Voicebox kicked in, Jalila started to put it together herself. Her heart beat fast, this time with the familiar thrill of making sense of what had once seemed an indecipherable puzzle.

Listening and studying the Voicebox display for a few moments more, she collected her thoughts. Touching keys on the device, she accessed the newly created vocabulary database for the Vox tongue, clarifying the choice of words she would use.

Then, she interrupted the brown-furred creature (who seemed willing and able to carry on an endless monologue) and rattled off a sentence.

The Vox reared back, the whiskers on his stubby snout twitching. He gestured excitedly, then caught himself and clasped his hands together to stop the movement. Again speaking slowly, without the static of clicks and smacks, he released a few clear words; then he waved, beckoning for Jalila and the others to follow him. The assembled crowd parted to make way.

Jalila turned to Major al-Aziz and Colonel Farouk and repeated the Vox's gesture, waving for them to follow. "I think we're finally getting somewhere."

"What did you say to him?" said Major al-Aziz.

"'Take us to your leader,'" said Jalila.

2

As Jalila, al-Aziz, and Farouk followed their guide through the Vox city, she again felt chills run down her spine...but this time, the chills were inspired by awe, not fear. Though Jalila had seen the wonders of many worlds as part of the *Ibn Battuta*'s crew, she had never in her life seen anything as beautiful as this.

It was a see-through city made of pastel stained glass.

"This is beautiful." Her voice was a whisper...but the Voicebox caught it and translated for the brown-furred Vox at her side.

In return, the Vox, whose name was Nalo, whispered back at her. "*Mazeesh.*"

Jalila smiled and nodded with understanding. *Mazeesh* meant "beautiful." She was making progress.

Returning her attention to the scenery around her, she let herself be overwhelmed by how *mazeesh* it all was. Towers scaled remark-able heights--some squared, some cylindrical, some spiraling into feathery clouds. Vast castles straddled block after city block, turrets shooting sky high. There were domes and cones and pyramids, spheres and cubes. All of it was connected from ground level to highest spire by a filigree of crisscrossing strands, a web of tubing laced around and over and through every structure.

And every tube, every wall, every surface was transparent and flowing with pastel color. Pale yellows and blues and reds and greens and violets swirled and rippled like the clouds on a gas giant planet, mixing and pulsing...never obscuring the perfect view of what lay behind them. Jalila could see right into every room and tube, could see fur-covered citizens in motion and at rest and staring right back out at her. Even more, because the floors and ceilings and walls and furnishings were all transparent, she could see through one building and into the next, could look all the way up through every level of every tower.

It was at once breathtaking and disconcerting to see such a city of people stacked to the heights and strung all around, all seemingly floating, supported only by whorls and bands and streams of color.

Jalila felt like she was floating, too, and not just because she was caught up in the spectacular surroundings. Thanks to the low gravity on Vox, she weighed only half what she did on New Mecca or onboard the *Ibn Battuta*. She felt airy and light on her feet, as if at any moment she could push off from the ground and rise up to glide and pirouette among the filigree and spires.

According to Farouk, the science specialist, it was the light gravity that made the city possible, enabling such fragile, lofty structures to stand. The chief building material was a light polymer with electrostatic properties that produced the colorful tints. Even stretched into impossibly thin sheets, its high tensile strength supported amazing weight...but on New Mecca, at twice the gravity, it would have shattered under a far smaller load.

As Jalila stepped lightly down crystalline walkways, her body lit with shifting pastel colors cast by sunbeams poured through rainbow walls, she was glad she wasn't on New Mecca. She was glad she'd come to Vox on this one last mission and had the chance to experience such wonders.

Alongside her, Nalo chattered away, but Jalila didn't pay much attention. Behind her, a growing mob of similarly vocal Vox generated a rising clamor, but she didn't listen.

For once, she was all eyes, not ears.

When Nalo led the team into one of the soaring towers, Jalila gazed upward...and realized that her view was unobstructed by even the tinted, transparent walls and ceilings that honeycombed other buildings. She could see all the way from ground level to the distant pinnacle, seemingly a mile above. It was all one vast cathedral, walled in light and color, lined with a ring of slender, glassy pillars that corkscrewed into the heavenly heights.

As Jalila peered up into the otherworldly steeple, she half expected to see a host of angels drift downward, so she was startled when she noticed faraway figures descending from the upper reaches. At first, they were so distant that they were little more than specks, but even then, Jalila could see that they were acrobatically inclined. The five figures moved fast, zipping down the slender pillars, leaping from one pillar to another at high altitudes with perfect ease and grace.

As the figures drew closer, she realized they were Vox, and they were climbing down headfirst, like squirrels descending tree trunks. They scurried downward fearlessly, skinny bodies twisting around the corkscrew pillars, making heart-stopping dives from pole to pole with no more visible effort than kids playing on monkey bars.

Jalila's shipmates craned their necks to watch the spectacle. Major al-Aziz whistled softly in amazement. Stern Colonel Farouk said nothing, which was no surprise, but there wasn't a peep out of Nalo or the mob who had followed them into the tower, either. If even the chatterbox locals maintained a respectful silence here, Jalila supposed the team was indeed in the presence of some kind of leadership.

Leaping and zipping down the pillars, the five acrobatic Vox closed the distance from the pinnacle in a twinkling. As they approached, Jalila could make out differences in their coloration: two had black fur, one silver, one gold, and one red. Like all Vox, they wore no clothing, though their fur coats were daubed with colorful designs on the scalp, back, and belly--circles, spirals, triangles, and starbursts in white and green and pink and black, whatever color showed up best on their coats.

The five Vox dropped further, then stopped a few yards overhead. They twined themselves around the pillars and hung there, peering down at the visitors with gleaming opal eyes.

Jalila was so dazzled by the wonders she had been witnessing, it took a moment for her to remember she had a job to do. When al-Aziz cleared his throat, she snapped back to reality and activated the Voicebox.

"Jalila," said al-Aziz. "Ask our friend here," and he indicated the brown-furred guide, "if these are the leaders of the Vox."

Touching keys, Jalila found the words she was looking for, then turned to Nalo and repeated the question in his language. Whiskers twitching, the brown-furred

otter-like being answered, speaking slowly and without clicks and smacks for her benefit.

Jalila watched the translation on her device, though she had picked up enough of the language to get the gist of what he had said. "Nalo says they are planetary ministers, and the red one is Regent Ieria. You should speak to her."

"Anything else I should know?" al-Aziz combed his fingers through his thick brown hair and looked up at the red-furred Vox wrapped around one of the pillars.

"Use her title when addressing her," said Jalila. "Don't talk with your hands. I'll take care of the rest."

al-Aziz nodded and stepped forward, turning his attention to the regent. Jalila posted herself alongside him, raising the Voicebox so its pickups could best catch the words of the Vox leader.

Clasping his hands behind him, al-Aziz spoke to the red-furred Vox. "Regent. I am Major al-Aziz of the starcraft *Ibn Battuta*."

Jalila read the translation from the Voicebox's display, taking care to speak loudly and clearly enough for the leaders to hear and understand. Though the Voicebox could have broadcast the audio itself, Jalila felt more comfortable doing the talking in this delicate situation. She was paranoid about making a mistake like on Pyrrhus VII and didn't want to rely too much on anyone or anything but herself.

al-Aziz nodded at Jalila. "This is my translator, Corporal Jalila Al-Fulani."

Jalila told Regent Ieria what al-Aziz had said, then smiled and bowed.

The red-furred Vox stared down at them, blinking her black pearl eyes...then fired off a storm of syllables, clicks, smacks, and gestures that baffled Jalila and the Voicebox alike.

Fortunately, Nalo came to the rescue. Appearing at Jalila's side, he let loose a sequence of chatter, noises, and hand signs of his own, directed at Ieria. It must have been an explanation of Jalila's conversational limitations, for when Ieria spoke again, it was without gestures or non-pulmonic sounds. The Voicebox resumed normal function, displaying its conversion of the leader's speech.

"*Welcome*," Jalila read from the screen to al-Aziz. "*What brings you to Vox?*"

al-Aziz considered his next words carefully. "A fleet of vessels is headed toward your world. Many ships, heavily armed."

Jalila translated, then delivered Ieria's response. "*Your ships?*"

"No," said al-Aziz. "We don't know who they are...but we know they are hostile. They disabled our own ship, the *Ibn Battuta*, and left it for dead."

Jalila translated. She was startled when the gold-furred Vox minister flung himself onto Ieria's pillar, interjecting his own streak of chatter. Apparently, the minister had caught on to the need for conversational simplicity, for his speech, though quick-fire, was free of extraneous sounds.

"The other Vox called you a liar," translated Jalila. "He says this is a distraction to hide your own dishonest intentions."

"Our only intention is to warn you," said al-Aziz. "We can provide you with the coordinates of the invasion fleet, and all the data we have on it." Casting his green eyes upward, he gazed into the dazzling heights of the tower. "Your world is filled with beauty. We will do everything in our power to help you preserve it."

Referring to the Voicebox, Jalila carefully pronounced the Vox version of what al-Aziz had said. "*Vox ilu aya sensay mazeesh. al-Azizlo anzish u'i yayla oonlo sah sueta amisansu.*"

For an instant, there was silence as the regent, ministers, and onlookers absorbed what she had said. Then, all at once, the assembled Vox erupted into chaos.

The outcry was deafening. All around Jalila, Vox were chattering, clicking, smacking, whistling, screaming. They gestured wildly, signing so fast and emphatically that their hands were blurs. Even Ieria and her fellow leaders howled and flailed, diving from pillar to pillar in a frenzy.

The uproar swelled and cascaded in the vast chamber, echo building upon echo with growing force. There must have been at least a hundred Vox in the tower, and every single one of them cried out at once.

Except one. Nalo stood quietly nearby, calmly meeting Jalila's terrified gaze.

For some reason, her eyes fell to the Voicebox in her hands. Somehow, amid the tumult, it must have miraculously tuned in one voice among many, or many voices saying the same thing. Or maybe it was a malfunction.

One word flashed on the display, again and again.
Death.
Death.
Death.

3

As the cacophony in the tower escalated, the *Ibn Battuta* crewmen closed ranks. The mob of Vox pressed in around them, forcing them more tightly together.

"What's going on?" shouted al-Aziz as he fended off the clawed Vox hands that grabbed at him.

Unfortunately, Jalila was too preoccupied to try to formulate an answer. A snarling Vox violently shook her by the shoulders. Her feet left the floor as the creature hoisted her away from her embattled companions.

Overcoming her initial shock, Jalila thrashed and kicked, dislodging the Vox's grip. Just as she regained her footing, two more Vox dove into the fray, each latching onto one of her arms.

Jalila brought up a knee and lashed it back, landing a kick in the lower midsection of one Vox. As the stunned creature released its grip, she swung her free arm around and planted a fist in the same section of the other Vox. That Vox, too, let go of her.

Her freedom lasted only a few seconds. As her original attacker advanced alongside new friends, Jalila felt more hands grab her from behind.

Before she could react, she was yanked backward...but her alarm switched to relief when she realized her latest abductor was al-Aziz.

"Can somebody please tell me what the hell's going on here?" said al-Aziz.

"Maybe your first contact technique needs work," said Farouk.

The tide of noise in the tower surged to a head-splitting crescendo. The chatter, screams, whoops, clicks, and buzzes joined together to form a single terrible sound, a chord of sustained rage.

Then, something new drowned out everything else--an echoing chime crashing from wall to wall and floor to pinnacle with thunderous force, as if the entire majestic tower was one enormous bell that had been rung. It was so loud, Jalila had to cover her ears.

As the piercing chime resounded through the chamber, the uproar from the crowd reached a shrill, keening peak. As one, all the disparate chattering voices united in a high-pitched, ululating wail...then subsided.

As the chime faded, the frenzy diminished with it. All eyes turned to red-furred Ieria, now back on her original perch but noticeably higher. Upright and clinging to the glassy, spiraled pillar, she called out to the crowd.

As Ieria's words spilled into the tower, Jalila's heart pounded...not from exertion, but panic. She could feel herself and her shipmates teetering on a razor's edge of violent death; every word from Ieria's mouth could be vital to their survival.

And Jalila's Voicebox was gone. It had slipped from her hands during the chaos.

Jalila did her best to translate Ieria's speech without the device. It wasn't easy, as Ieria addressed the crowd in multiple simultaneous languages without simplifying what she said for the *Ibn Battuta* team.

Jalila struggled to sort out the pulmonic language content and translate it on the fly. Without the Voicebox, she couldn't decipher every word...but what she understood, she didn't like. The longer she listened, the more she wished she could go back to not comprehending a single syllable of the Vox language.

It's happening again. Just like Pyrrhus VII. Another mistake.

How many people will die because of me this time?

"Jalila?" said al-Aziz. "What is it?"

Jalila listened for another moment, then turned to al-Aziz. "I'm so sorry." Her face was etched with an expression of wide-eyed terror. "I caused this."

"How?" said al-Aziz.

"I used a slur." Jalila lowered her voice to a whisper. "*Mazeesh.*"

"All this over a word?" said al-Aziz. "One word?"

Jalila winced. "I didn't know it was a slur. I heard it used in a different context with a different meaning."

"What meaning?" said Farouk.

"*Beautiful,*" said Jalila. "I thought it meant *beautiful.*"

al-Aziz looked at her with disappointment, as if she'd personally let him down. "Can we offer an apology? Explain it was a misunderstanding?"

Jalila shook her head. "I think they're going to kill us."

al-Aziz looked around, scanning the mob of Vox jammed into the tower. "Nobody dies. We'll fight our way out of here."

Suddenly, Ieria howled, triggering a roar from the crowd. It was one word, expelled in a deafening gust.

"*Ruhala!*"

Jalila translated for the team. "'Death.'"

The crowd chanted the word with bloodthirsty gusto.

"*Ruhala! Ruhala!*"

Roaring that single, terrible word, the Vox charged, a rippling mass of fur and teeth and claws.

Earlier, the low gravity of Vox had made Jalila feel light enough to fly. Now, she felt as if she were indeed floating, watching the scene in a detached way from above.

As clawed hands seized her, she watched her friends battle the onrushing horde of Vox. With muscles developed in higher gravity environments, the humans had increased strength on this world, and they put it to use...but they were too vastly outnumbered to hold out for long. For every Vox that al-Aziz or Farouk heaved aside, ten more lunged at them with fresh ferocity.

Vox poured over them from every direction, and al-Aziz was pulled under. Sleek-furred elbows rose and fell like pistons as the Vox pummeled him, the results of their handiwork hidden from Jalila's sight. Farouk was left standing, his bald head streaked with blood...but he quickly slipped from Jalila's view.

Suddenly, the Vox hoisted Jalila overhead and passed her from hand to hand across the crowd. In a heartbeat, she found herself staring up at Ieria.

Ieria rattled off a staccato chain of syllables. Unfortunately, Jalila understood what she said.

"*Death is too good for you, but at least your tongue will be silenced forever.*"

The crowd cheered.

I deserve this, thought Jalila, strangely calm. *I made another terrible mistake, and I deserve to die for it.*

Her captors dumped her on a platform, hard, and held her

down. Peering upward, she saw Vox in the heights, watching through the transparent tower walls from every level of the surrounding see-through buildings.

A black Vox with silver markings blocked her line of sight, bending over her. He gripped a rubbery white strip and pushed it toward her with both hands.

When the strip touched her lips, the rubbery substance locked in place, adhering to the flesh. It continued to squeeze until it was so uncomfortably tight that Jalila wanted to scream.

But she couldn't open her mouth. The Vox had gagged her.

Once the gag was affixed, the Vox hauled Jalila from the platform and held her up for everyone to see. The mob in the tower and all the Vox watching from surrounding buildings cheered and leaped and hugged each other.

It seemed as if the whole world wanted her dead.

There was still a single holdout, conspicuous by his calm amid the chaos. Brown-furred Nalo appeared as unmoved by Jalila's plight as by the savage jubilation around him. Standing rigidly among the dancing revelers, he returned her gaze evenly.

Jalila's captors raised her high like a trophy and shook her. Everybody cheered, and spectators nearest the front hopped up and spat on her.

When they lowered her again, she looked for Nalo but couldn't find him. As the Vox tossed her to the ground and dragged her from the chamber by her wrists, she frantically searched the jeering crowd...but Nalo was gone.

4

Jalila's captors hauled her through a corridor that seemed to be lined with fur and teeth. Beyond the transparent walls on either side, wild-eyed Vox swarmed and yowled, literally climbing over each other for a glimpse of the doomed offender.

As Jalila slid along the floor, pulled by the wrists, her arms ached...but her mouth hurt worse. The rubbery gag seemed to squeeze tighter all the time, pinching so hard it felt like every nerve in her lips was on fire.

The horde of Vox along the corridor clattered their claws against the walls and ceiling, rapping out a rhythmic death knell. Jalila could hear the creatures chattering and screeching and chanting the one word she knew too well.

"*Ruhala!*"

Jalila listened and watched...and then, even that morbid distraction was gone. Her captors ceased their progress and released one of her wrists. Twisting around, Jalila saw the creatures open a domed hatch in the floor, revealing a round, dark opening.

With no more care than they might afford a sack of garbage, the Vox hoisted her up and dumped her headfirst into the hole.

Jalila dropped into a cramped, spherical pocket that was barely big enough to hold her. Even curled up into a ball, she had hardly enough room to breathe.

Then, the hatch slammed shut above her, and she was plunged into absolute blackness and silence. She strained her eyes but couldn't find a trace of light; the only sound she could hear was the pounding of her heart and the fast rasping of her breath.

It was then that her composure finally gave way. Hopeless and alone, she allowed tears to flood her eyes and run freely down her face.

Earlier that day, drinking in the magnificent sights of the planet Vox, she'd been happy that she'd gotten to come along on one more mission. Now, sobbing behind the painful gag, she wished she'd never gotten a second chance to screw up.

A year ago, when Jalila had first set foot on the *Ibn Battuta*, she'd known her new assignment might be the death of her. Just by being onboard the *Ibn Battuta*, she had exposed herself to countless unforeseen and uncontrollable threats, any of which could have taken her life. How could she have known her true enemy would be *herself*?

And how could she have known that she, a linguist, would die because of a *word*?

Mazeesh.

Thinking back, she still couldn't figure out how she'd gotten it wrong. The pieces had all fit together--her own comprehension, the output of the Voicebox device, Nalo's reaction to her response. She had said the Vox city was beautiful, and Nalo had used the word *mazeesh*; the Voicebox had incorporated *mazeesh* into its vocabulary database, provided it as part of a later translation, and Jalila had spoken it aloud.

Everything seemed to line up...so why had the word that meant "beautiful" triggered a riot and death sentence when Jalila had used it?

The way things were going, Jalila thought she might never find out.

Her tiny cell was starting to heat up.

At first, she thought it might be her own body heat accumulating in the cramped confines. Then, as the temperature continued to rise, she decided another explanation was more likely.

The Vox weren't coming back to retrieve her. She would not be carted off to die by injection or electrocution or some other gruesome means. She was in an oven, and the heat would cook her alive.

So this was how Jalila would die. This was how she would pay for the mistake that had cost the diplomat his life on Pyrrhus VII.

Maybe it was just as well. She could see the justice in it, and she was almost relieved. At least she wouldn't have to go home in disgrace and live out her days remembering what she'd lost...remembering the mistake that had literally cost her the stars.

Not that it would make being cooked to death any easier.

As the temperature climbed, sweat soaked her body. Breathing became increasingly difficult, especially with the unyielding gag sealing her mouth shut. She tried to remove the gag, but it wouldn't budge.

Jalila squirmed in the tight space as the wall of the cell became unbearably hot. Reaching up, she found the hatch was slightly cooler, and she twisted around to press her back against it, wedging her feet under her.

As she looked down, she saw the surface around her boots emit a reddish glow.

Before long, every inch of the cell's internal surface was painfully hot to the touch, even the hatch. Wrapping her arms around her knees, Jalila clenched her body into a tight fist, shrinking as much as she could away from the scalding walls.

Tears and sweat poured down her face, sizzling when they dripped on the glowing floor. Her feet roasted as the heat radiated through the soles of her boots, which felt as if they were on the verge of melting.

Still, the temperature climbed. The reddish glow brightened and intensified, consuming the lower half of the cell and spreading higher.

Jalila shut her eyes, but there was no escape. Even the insides of her eyelids flared with the bright red glow.

Then, something gave way underneath her, and she fell.

Jalila dropped hard onto a solid surface, and her eyes snapped open. She felt dirt under her but could see nothing beyond a blinding beam of light that blazed in her face.

Peeling soaking wet strands of black hair from her eyes, she squinted into the beam. It bobbed around, so she knew it came from a handheld light source...but she couldn't see who was holding it.

Then, the beam swung away from her to illuminate the shadowy figure behind it.

It was Nalo.

Jalila was too dazed to do more than sit on the ground and stare at him. When the brown-furred Vox played the light around their surroundings, Jalila saw they were in a pocket hollowed out under the cell. It was a small space with a low ceiling, so willowy Nalo had to kneel and duck his head.

As he had done earlier, Nalo spoke slowly and without clicks or buzzes for Jalila's benefit. "*Sorry about the heat.*" He waved a bulky device slung from his shoulder. The device had a long barrel that ended in a glowing red bulb, and Jalila guessed he'd used it to melt open the cell. *"Better than being dead."*

Jalila nodded weakly.

"We need to go now," said the Vox. *"Follow me."*

Then, with the device slung over his back and the flashlight stuck between his teeth, he dropped to all fours. Whipping around, he shone the light on the entrance to a tunnel, just big enough for Jalila to crawl through.

With a flick of his tail, the otter-like being disappeared into the entrance.

Jalila waited a moment before getting on her hands and knees and crawling after him. For all she knew, she was going from the frying pan into the fire.

5

When Jalila finally emerged from the tunnels into an underground chamber, she got halfway to her feet and collapsed.

She had no idea how far she'd crawled, but it felt like it had been miles. Her hands and knees were raw and throbbing; her neck and back ached fiercely. She felt like dirt caked every inch of her, even under her eyelids and uniform and skin.

Without a word, Nalo scooped her up and carried her across the chamber.

Through half-closed eyes, Jalila watched as other Vox approached them, chattering and gesturing excitedly. When the Vox bunched around them and pressed close, staring her in the face and touching her with clawed hands, Nalo snapped out a few words, and the group backed away.

As Nalo carried her onward, Jalila looked around. By the dim light of the glowing white moss that clung in patches to the walls and ceiling, she saw Vox at work in an underground camp--

tinkering with electronic equipment, unloading containers, adjusting devices that looked like weapons.

As Jalila passed, the busy Vox stopped what they were doing and stared. Sometimes, they spoke to her, but always in a rush of buzzes, clicks, sign language and syllables that she couldn't fully understand.

One word did jump out at her, though. She heard it, clear as a bell, as Nalo gently lowered her onto some bedding on the ground.

Mazeesh.

Jalila glanced around at the staring onlookers but couldn't tell who had said it. After what had happened to her when she'd uttered that word just once, she wondered why any Vox would dare speak it aloud. Unfortunately, the gag locking her mouth shut made it impossible for her to ask questions.

Nalo filled a dipper with water from a nearby basin and carried it to her. Because of the gag, it was impossible for her to drink, but he tipped it into a cloth and used it to wipe some of the dirt from her face.

Jalila reached up and tugged with both hands at the sides of the gag, but it was still fastened to her flesh. Wincing at Nalo, she pointed to the rubbery strip sealing her mouth, silently pleading for him to remove it.

Nalo shook his head. "*It is permanent. Never comes off.*"

Slowly, Jalila lowered her hands.

"*Sorry.*" Nalo dabbed with the damp cloth at some of the cuts on her arms. "*Sorry for your pain.*"

His apology was no comfort whatsoever. A horrific new thought occurred to her. For the first time, she realized the gag itself was a death sentence. If it wouldn't come off, and she didn't receive intravenous nourishment, she would eventually die from lack of food and water.

Nalo left for a moment to refresh the damp cloth, then returned and resumed cleaning her wounds. "*You'll be safe here. Only a few know how to find this place.*"

Jalila stared at a patch of glowing white moss on the ceiling.

"Safe" didn't really apply, she wanted to tell him. She wondered if he realized that by rescuing her from her cell, he had only prolonged the inevitable...and perhaps guaranteed she would die from starvation and dehydration.

"The word you said," said Nalo. *"'Mazeesh.'"*

Jalila frowned at the mention of the word. If it was so offensive and forbidden, why was Nalo saying it?

"It is a name." Nalo poked a finger at his chest. *"For us. For all Vox."*

Eyes narrowed and fixed on him, Jalila listened. There were other Vox nearby; why weren't they screaming in outrage and attacking Nalo for saying that word?

"Once, 'mazeesh' meant beautiful," said Nalo. *"It was a beautiful flower."*

Jalila nodded. It was what she had thought from the start, the sole reason she had used that word at all.

"One day," said Nalo, *"visitors came from the stars. They hunted and killed us."*

As Nalo told the story, Jalila noticed the camp around them had become conspicuously quiet. Earlier, it had been alive with the sounds of activity and Vox chatter; now, it seemed everyone was hanging on Nalo's every word.

"Part of us, in our heads." Nalo tapped his temple. *"They ate it. For fertility.*

"It looks like the flower. The mazeesh. So they called us mazeesh."

There it was: the link between a word meaning "beautiful" and a slur strong enough to spur a crowd to murderous rage...but Jalila still didn't understand why Nalo had used it out in the open, on a city street, with an unsuspecting visitor.

"'Mazeesh,'" said Nalo. *"It means 'prey.' It means 'food.' It means 'filth'...'property'...'lowest of the low.' It is the most hated word in the world.*

"But that is about to change," said Nalo. *"Thanks to you."*

Jalila frowned.

"Don't worry," said Nalo. *"The hard part's over."*

Jalila's frown deepened. As weak as she felt, she managed to prop herself up on her elbows.

"*You broke the silence,*" said Nalo. "*You are a symbol of free speech. We chose you well.*"

Jalila could not believe what she'd heard. Suddenly, the day's events made perfect sense. Perfect, terrible sense.

All along, she had wondered how both she and the Voicebox device could have made such a huge mistake...how they could have mistranslated an outrageous slur as a word meaning "beautiful." She had wondered why Nalo had used the word to begin with, if the penalty for speaking it aloud was so steep.

Now, it all fit into place. It made perfect sense.

And it changed everything.

Until now, Jalila had accepted the fact that she'd made another mistake, just like on Pyrrhus VII. It had been easy to blame herself and wallow in self-pity. It had been easy to surrender all hope.

But not anymore. She knew better now. This wasn't another Pyrrhus VII after all. This was not a hopeless situation.

She had no excuse for giving up. She had every reason to fight to redeem herself.

"*You used the word just as we hoped,*" said Nalo, "*when I gave it to you.*"

Finally, Jalila understood. She had been used.

She had been set up.

6

When the cooking smells reached Jalila, her stomach growled, but she ignored it. She had other concerns on her mind, like how she was going to get off the forsaken mudball known as Vox if it was the last thing she did.

Since learning the truth--that she had been manipulated into using the forbidden word in front of Ieria and the ministers--her attitude had done an about face. Just a short time ago, after her condemnation, imprisonment, and near death experience, she had been at the breaking point...but now, she felt revitalized. Her state of shock and panic had given way to clearheaded calm and resolve.

She was going to get herself out of the mess she was in, whatever it took. She was going to prove she was better than anyone imagined, and she was going to make up for what had happened on Pyrrhus VII.

Sitting cross-legged on the bedding where Nalo had placed her, she watched the two dozen Vox in the underground chamber as they gathered for a meal. Before digging in, they all raised their cutlery and cheered for her.

"*To Jalila!*" They flashed their teeth in her direction. "*To free speech!*"

Jalila was almost grateful for the gag. She would not have wanted to share a meal with the Vox even if she could have.

Nalo had explained their reasons for setting her up, but she didn't care. Nothing could justify putting her through the nightmare she'd endured...not even a dying language.

"*'Mazeesh' is one of many profane words,*" Nalo had told her. "*They are all from the same language.*

"*In fact,*" he had said, "*every word in that language is considered profane.*

"*They say it is the language of the ones who hunted us. We, the Free Speakers, believe otherwise.*"

Growing increasingly impassioned, Nalo had paced and gestured and raised his voice. "*We believe it is the tongue of our ancestors. We believe our leaders have suppressed it because it allows for the expression of dangerous ideas.*"

Nalo had stopped pacing and dropped to his haunches before her. "*Crastala na neepom,*" he had said. "*It means 'to be an individual.'*

"*Shoshar na yothu. It means 'to follow your heart.'*"

All the Vox in the chamber had gathered around him then. As Nalo had recited each phrase, they had exuberantly repeated it. "*Shoshar na yothu!*"

Nalo had sprung to his feet and whirled to face his supporters. "*Tark razeek na.*"

"*Tark razeek na!*"

"*To dream of something better!*" Nalo had said. "*Zush na carapata imbolio rivix shanyo!*"

His supporters had repeated the phrase, and he had spun to face Jalila. "*To tear down what is broken and replace it!*"

The Free Speakers had cheered riotously, hopping and yipping and hugging with abandon. When the commotion had died down, Nalo had settled to his haunches again, staring intently at Jalila with his black pearl eyes. "*These things I have said...they are called profanity now. It is forbidden to speak them in public.*

"*But this is the true language of our people. Soon, it will be heard round the world, from the mouths of every living Vox.*"

Gently, he had reached out and touched her cheek. "*Thank you, Jalila. Ija onya sufir brin cozcona. 'You give us hope.'*"

If Jalila had been able to speak at that moment, she would have used some profanity of her own. As a linguist, she had an extensive repertoire from which to choose.

Truth be told, under other circumstances, Jalila would have been fascinated by the Free Speakers and their struggle. Language was her passion; she would have been excited to study a suppressed tongue and participate in efforts to resurrect it.

If she had been *asked* instead of *tricked*, she would have gladly done everything in her power to help Nalo. If she had been *asked*, and if her shipmates had not been endangered. And if a massive alien fleet with heavy weapons and unknown motives was not hours away from orbit.

Any other time, she would have been thrilled to lend a hand. It was a once in a lifetime experience and would make a stunning paper for the linguistic journals back home.

But now, she wanted only to tell the Vox to go to hell.

Her one and only goal at this point was to escape and find Major al-Aziz and the others...if they were still alive. She had been brought into this against her will, and she was determined to use sheer force of will to get out of it.

Unfortunately, for the moment, she was stuck. Plenty of

weapons were available in the cave, but if she snatched one and made a break for it, she would have no place to go but the tunnels. Without a guide, she knew she would end up lost in that maze.

So she had to wait until someone led her back to the surface. That would be in the morning, according to Nalo, when the Free Speakers made their big move. Jalila didn't know what exactly they had planned...only that they were going to take her along.

That was when she would have to act--when they emerged on the surface, before they could drag her into some new ordeal. She would feign cooperation, catch them with their guards down, and make a run for it.

After dinner, Nalo walked over and patted her on the head. "*Get some rest, Jalila. We have a big day ahead of us tomorrow.*"

Jalila looked up at him and nodded...but all she wanted to do was swat his hand away and punch him in the face for bringing her into this. For making her doubt and hate herself even more. For sending her back to Pyrrhus VII in her heart.

She swore she would never go back there again.

7

When a voice roused Jalila, whispering close to her ear, she had a hard time waking up. Her exhausted slumber was so deep, she couldn't force herself to crawl back to consciousness.

When hands gently shook her by the shoulders, she finally came around. Her eyes popped open, and she was greeted by the blurry sight of a Vox she didn't know, staring her in the face.

Instinctively, Jalila swung up an arm to bat the creature away, but the white-furred Vox quickly darted out of reach. Jalila jerked to a sitting position and scooted back over the bedding away from the unexpected visitor. She pushed her black hair behind her ears and stared at him, blinking her brown eyes hard to clear her vision.

The Vox calmly raised its arms, suggesting peaceful intent. Jalila watched, eyes wide, for the creature's next move.

The Vox placed its hands on its chest and bowed its head. "*I am Folcrum*," he whispered. "*I will not hurt you.*" The voice was cracked with age.

Glancing in the direction of the other Vox in the chamber, Jalila saw they were still curled together in a sleeping heap. As she returned her attention to Folcrum, she caught sight of a nearby pile of weapons and wondered if she ought to make a grab for one of them.

"*I am a Lexicon,*" said Folcrum. "*A keeper of language. I keep it all up here.*" Folcrum tapped his head. "*Every word, every meaning, every rule. All here.*"

Folcrum moved forward, and Jalila twitched, thinking about getting a gun or waking the others. Folcrum was only shifting off his knees, though, and settled back to sit on the floor.

"*When someone is searching for a word,*" said Folcrum, "*they come to a Lexicon. When there is a question about the language, a Lexicon answers it.*

"*Without us, the language of the world would be in chaos. People would have no set rules or definitions to guide them. Miscommunication and misunderstanding would run rampant.*"

As Jalila listened, she realized for the first time that she had been missing something. In all the hours she'd spent on Vox, she hadn't seen a single sign, inscription, electronic readout, or printed page. She hadn't seen so much as a single character representing a unit of Vox speech.

Jalila had been too busy and distracted to notice until now, but it jived with what the Lexicon was telling her. If, as he claimed, walking dictionaries were needed to keep track of words and linguistic rules, it followed that the Vox lacked something that was found on most worlds where the inhabitants communicated verbally: a written language.

"*Lexicons are not always popular,*" said Folcrum. "*We are the enemy of those who would twist language for their own purposes.*

"*Like them.*" Folcrum nodded in the direction of the sleeping Free Speakers. "*A discredited language is not their chief concern.*"

Jalila glanced at the nearby weapons. The truth of Folcrum's words was obvious.

"We Lexicons have always remained neutral in matters of conflict," said Folcrum, *"but not this time. This is a matter of life and death for us. That is why I'm asking if you'll come with me. We need your help."*

Jalila looked at him, wondering what exactly he had planned for her...and if it could be any worse than what the Free Speakers had in mind. She suspected that once again she faced a choice between the frying pan and the fire.

"What must you do to change a language?" said Folcrum. *"To make the kind of sweeping change they want?"* He gestured toward the Free Speakers.

"Out with the old." Folcrum slashed his hand through the air. *"The old Lexicons.*

"When minor changes are made, we are revised. When bigger changes are made, we are...retired. Our minds cannot be extensively rewritten.

"But to replace an entire language? Every word and rule? Drastic measures are needed. So, out with the old." Folcrum drew a single clawed finger across his throat. *"Make way for new Lexicons to serve the new language. Don't give the people a chance to fall back on the old language by keeping old Lexicons around.*

"Not a single one of them," said Folcrum. *"And that is what happens tomorrow."*

With a little difficulty, Folcrum got to his knees. Leaning forward, he extended a hand toward Jalila, palm up, and fixed her with his black pearl gaze.

"So what do you say?" he whispered. *"Will you come with me?"*

Jalila slipped her hand into Folcrum's and shook it.

He got to his feet and she followed, taking care not to make much noise. When he headed for the tunnel entrance across the chamber, however, she made a detour.

From the piles of weapons on the floor, she selected a few items, stuffing a holstered knife into her boot and a handgun in a pocket of her gray jumpsuit. She slung a rifle over her back, then picked her way over the dirt floor to catch up with Folcrum.

8

This time, Jalila's trip through the underground tunnels wasn't nearly so harrowing. The passages were still pitch black, claustro-phobic, and convoluted, full of twists and sharp angles and drop-offs and cave-ins, but Folcrum set a humane pace and seemed genuinely considerate, unlike Nalo.

After a long crawl through uninterrupted blackness, Jalila glimpsed Folcrum's hindquarters in front of her in a dim light filtering from somewhere up ahead. She could see her hands as they pressed into the tunnel floor...and then the rough red earth around her as the glow grew brighter.

When she followed Folcrum around a tight bend, the light flared, and she could see it pouring in from an opening a few meters off. For an instant, she allowed herself to hope she was about to emerge on the planet's surface...but then she realized the light she saw, bright as it was, wasn't sunlight.

Fortunately, that realization didn't rob her of the thrill she felt upon emerging from the tunnel into the underground garden.

Blinking as her eyes adjusted to the brilliant light, she crawled out after Folcrum and let him help her to her feet. As soon as she took her first breath, she was assailed by a rich mixture of sweet floral perfumes.

It was like stepping into a greenhouse or arboretum when all the flowers were in full bloom--a whirl of heady scents commingled into one breathtaking fragrance. As Jalila inhaled it, she knew at once it consisted of a multitude of parts, each scent on its own as agreeable as the next...and yet, she was unable to pry apart the whole and single out one piece from another.

Not only was the fragrance intense and multi-layered, it shifted as she stood there, component scents ebbing and flowing. A sharp sweetness was preeminent, then a citrus, then a nutmeg...the soft tones of something like a rose wafting up and sliding away before a piquant mix of mown grass and daffodil. The transmutations were continuous and mesmerizing, stirring up new and beautiful combinations in progressive waves like strains of music.

The restless perfume was unexpected, even shocking after all the musty dirt Jalila had crawled through...but no less so than the sights that greeted her as she looked down from the sloped rim of the cavern in which she stood.

The space was so huge, it made Nalo's hideaway look like a mouse hole. Instead of a makeshift camp, a tidy village nestled amid lush and colorful gardens; Vox gardeners moved through the vegetation individually or in groups, tending the harmoniously arranged plant life. Waterfalls cascaded from the walls, splashing from opposite sides of the grotto into foaming ruby pools.

Light sparkled on the surface of the pools and bathed the village and gardens, cast from the illuminated walls and ceiling. The cavern was blanketed in glowing white moss like that in Nalo's cubbyhole, but more developed. Tendrils hung from it, studded with giant blossoms like sunflowers that shone with steady white incandescence.

Earlier, Jalila had been captivated by the beauty of the surface world with its see-through rainbow buildings and blown-glass architecture...but the cavern's natural beauty easily rivaled that. She had a hard time tearing herself away from the panoramic view when Folcrum started down the slope.

As he led her into the gardens along a winding gravel path, however, Jalila found herself absorbed in drinking in the scenery from a new perspective. The beauty of the gardens enfolded her, limitless varieties of spectacular flora vying for her attention.

The leaves and vines and stems were tinted a thousand shades of red--pink, rust, copper, fuchsia, scarlet, crimson, and more. The flowers, on the other hand, were a riot of colors, sizes, textures...and light. Like the moss and flowers on the walls and ceiling, many of them glowed from within.

Tiny blue blossoms blinked like clusters of Christmas tree lights. Yellow bell-like flowers flecked with mauve hung from lacy blood-red webs of vine, the tips of their waxy stamens blazing like candles on a birthday cake. Atop stiff vermilion stalks, giant eye-level blooms changed color as Jalila watched, emerald light flowing into azure into gold into silver. Pale aquamarine fronds brushed her arms and face, twinkling like fiber optic strands.

Even the butterfly creatures glowed with inner light. They were five times the size of any butterfly Jalila had ever seen, with furry bodies that looked more mammal than insect, and their wings swirled with luminescent pastel colors like the electrostatically active panels of the buildings on the planet's surface.

Wide-eyed, Jalila trailed after Folcrum and took it all in, marveling at the intricate display of color and light and life. If not for the pressure of time and worries to move her along, she easily could have spent hours on that path, lingering spellbound at each remarkable sight. The fragrances alone were enough to mesmerize her, richer and thicker than ever in the heart of the perfumed gardens.

As Jalila lagged further behind, Folcrum stopped and waited for her to catch up. "*Do you hear it?*" He drew in a deep breath. "*Do you hear the garden talking?*"

Jalila took a deep breath of her own, inhaling the intoxicating mixture of scents.

"*This is the Garden of Yesterday,*" said Folcrum. "*It has existed for countless generations. If you know how to listen, you can hear the history of the world in here.*"

Jalila breathed deeply again. The complex blend of scents was different now, though she hadn't moved and there was no breeze to stir the fragrance. When she drew another breath, it had changed again, the acrid smell of coffee replaced by a syrupy sweetness with a mild vinegar undertone.

Folcrum closed his eyes and inhaled again. "*Lots of secrets, if you know how to listen.*"

Jalila smelled roses and sawdust and wine...then salt water and leather. The fragrance of the garden shifted with each passing moment, scents rising and fading and resurging in unpredictable combinations.

Or were they so unpredictable after all? Perhaps, Folcrum wasn't speaking figuratively when he said that the garden was talking. Perhaps, there was more to the scents than a random mixture of olfactory stimuli.

Folcrum opened his eyes and nodded. *"There's a secret here for you, too. The secret of the word you said."*

Jalila frowned. She smelled walnut and cucumber and gardenias.

"Nalo could not tell you," said Folcrum, *"but I know how to listen."*

Inhaling again, Jalila strained to detect patterns in the play of perfumes, but they still seemed to fluctuate without reason. Even if what she was being led to believe was true, she was not able to take advantage of it. Even if there was a fourth language on this world, and vital information was flowing around her in the form of scent signals, she could not understand it.

"I will tell you this much now and the rest later," said Folcrum. *"The Vox people were not the true mazeesh."*

Jalila stared at him, stunned. If not for the gag, her mouth would have fallen open in dumbstruck shock.

9

By far, Oric and Giza had the most elaborate markings of any Vox Jalila had yet seen. As Folcrum introduced them, Jalila found it impossible to look away from the ornate tracery that decorated their fur coats.

Typically, Vox sported the painted designs on their scalps, backs, and abdomens, but Oric and Giza were *covered* in them. Every conceivable shape appeared on their bodies, covering every inch of fur, creating an impression at first of great chaos and then of great artistry the longer Jalila looked.

Oric was the first to step forward and offer his hand. *"Welcome.*

Thank you for coming." Swirls and stars and intersecting rays were painted in silver on the black fur of his chest. Intricate characters ran along his arms and legs, etched in multiple delicate brush strokes. Interlocking diamonds and loops encircled his waist in a chain, and a beautifully detailed burst like a bouquet of flowers bloomed in gold and turquoise on his belly.

Giza stepped forward next, his bright blonde fur a sharp contrast to Oric's dark coat. Deep red whorls and curlicues twined around his head and down his throat like interlaced vines. Dark green characters scrolled in double diagonal streams from his left shoulder to his right hip. His arms were crosshatched in violet on one side, stippled in umber and aqua on the other. A blossom of overlaid figure eights graced his every joint, from his elbows and knees to the knuckles on his hands.

"*I am honored to meet you.*" Giza bowed, then gestured toward a simple stone bench. "*Have a seat if you like.*"

As soon as Jalila sat down, one of the furry butterfly creatures fluttered into the gazebo and lighted on her knee. She jerked involuntarily, but the beautiful lifeform remained in place, its luminescent wings slowly fanning.

"*It won't hurt you,*" said Folcrum. "*It's a kava. It's good luck.*"

The creature was much larger than butterflies back home, and its wings were as big as Jalila's hands, but it seemed to weigh nothing at all. As it looked up at her with frosted, prismatic eyes, a yellow tongue zipped out and flickered in the air.

Jalila couldn't take her eyes off the *kava*, partly because it was so lovely and strange and partly because she wasn't sure what it would do next. Giza might have realized this, because he came over and gently lifted the creature from her knee, then placed it on his shoulder.

"*I could use some luck too, if you don't mind,*" he said, and then he made a sound like a chuckle. "*We all could. Maybe we better pass this around.*"

As Giza slowly returned to his seat, Oric coughed loudly. Both of them had a touch of unsteadiness in their movements, as if they were very old...older than Folcrum, certainly, or at least not in good health.

"*Jalila,*" said Oric. "*I wish we could hear your voice. Unfortunately, silencing voices is one thing our leaders do well.*"

Jalila winced. For a while, she had been distracted and hadn't paid much attention to the gag...but at the mention of her condition, she realized how much it still hurt.

"*I want you to meet someone.*" Oric nodded at Folcrum, who got up and left the gazebo. A moment later, he returned with a female Vox in tow...copper-furred and scrawny, carrying a garden hoe.

Apparently, she was one of the many Vox tending the Garden of Yesterday...but that was of secondary interest to Jalila. Her attention was immediately drawn to the Vox's mouth...specifically, what was covering it.

It was the same kind of gag that was locked in place over Jalila's own lips.

"*This is Yama,*" said Oric. "*Six years ago, the Vox spoken language underwent a major revision. It was decided that the revision was too extensive for the existing Lexicons to be reeducated.*

"*So they were silenced. Yama and many like her.*" Rising from his stone bench, Oric went to Yama and took her hand in his. "*She hasn't spoken a word in six years. She has only been able to eat by inhaling a nutrient-rich mist.*

"*Some of us escaped,*" said Oric. "*Like Giza, Folcrum, and myself. But Yama was not so lucky. She did not make it to the Garden before the damage was done.*" Raising her hand, he kissed it gently, then released it. "*But her suffering is nothing compared to what will happen tomorrow.*"

"*A revision conference is set for tomorrow.*" Giza stroked the fur of the *kava* perched on his shoulder. "*Every Lexicon in the world will gather in one place, in the capital city above us, for reeducation. They are supposed to learn of the changes being made to the Vox languages by our government.*

"*Instead, they will be massacred by the Free Speakers,*" said Giza.

"*This so the Speakers will be able to replace current languages with a forbidden tongue.*"

"*Their own version of it, anyway,*" said Folcrum. "*One that will pave the way for their ultimate goal.*"

"*Revolution,*" said Giza. "*Ending with power in their hands.*"

Oric bowed to Yama, and she left the gazebo. "*Who is in power makes no difference to us,*" he said, turning to Jalila. "*We do not concern ourselves with such matters. But we will not stand by while Lexicons are slaughtered. Even if it means we must sacrifice our own lives in the process.*"

Giza chuckled. "*Not that we expect the same sacrifice from you, Jalila. Don't worry.*"

Jalila worried anyway. She wondered if they were suggesting their plans included a suicide component.

"*Your being here with us has already hurt the Free Speakers,*" said Oric. "*You were to be the figurehead around which everyone would rally. Nevertheless, one thing is certain. They will go on without you.*"

"*And we will stop them,*" Giza said firmly.

Jalila wanted to ask how they planned to accomplish that and what role she would be expected to play...but she couldn't speak through the gag. She couldn't even write in the dirt, because the Vox wouldn't understand.

After thinking for a moment, she reached into the right hip pocket of her gray jumpsuit and drew out the handgun she had taken from the Free Speakers' camp. Lifting the weapon, she aimed it away from everyone and pretended to fire it several times, jerking the barrel up as if there was a recoil after each shot. Then, she pointed at the gun and shrugged, raising her free hand with palm up in a questioning gesture.

"*Guns?*" said Oric. "*No guns.*"

"*We won't use them,*" said Giza. "*We won't need them.*"

Jalila waved the gun and pointed over her shoulder, indicating the direction from which she had come...and by extension, the Speakers.

This time, Folcrum spoke, perhaps because he had seen her

acquire the weapon in the first place. "*We know the Free Speakers are armed. Don't worry. We have a plan to stop them without firing a shot.*"

Lowering the gun, Jalila replaced it in her pocket. The Vox could go unarmed if they liked, but she had no intention of relinquishing her weapons until she was safely back onboard the *Ibn Battuta*...if she ever got there.

Raising her hands, she again shrugged questioningly, hoping the three Vox would divulge more details of their plan. They either didn't understand what she wanted or chose to ignore her curiosity.

"*You must excuse me,*" said Oric. "*I have much to do to prepare for tomorrow.*"

"*As do I.*" Giza rose from his bench. As he stood, the *kava* drifted from his shoulder, fluttering past Jalila and out of the gazebo. "*We leave soon.*"

"*In the meantime,*" said Folcrum, "*perhaps you'll try the nutrient mists that sustain Yama. This has been a long day for you, and you'll need your strength tomorrow.*"

Though Jalila was reluctant to ingest anything on Vox that she hadn't had the opportunity to analyze, she nodded. Because of the planet's light gravity, she had felt lightheaded since stepping out of the scout barque...but she was convinced that the more extreme lightheadedness she now felt was due to a combination of exhaustion and hunger. She hadn't eaten a thing since breakfast onboard *Ibn Battuta*, which seemed like an eternity ago.

As Oric and Giza headed off into the garden, Folcrum led her down a path between rows of tall scarlet cacti draped in winking green and gold blossoms. The air smelled like cedar and lilac and baking bread all at once...then tobacco and pepper and coconut.

As they walked, Folcrum placed a hand on her shoulder. "*I hope you're not too worried. Everything will work out, I promise.*"

Jalila nodded and tried to look confident, though she was anything but.

"*We'll protect you,*" said Folcrum. "*And when the Lexicons are safe, we will find your friends.*"

At the end of the cactus-lined path, Folcrum led her to a hut with walls of red bamboo and a roof of thatched crimson fronds. When he opened the door and ushered her inside, she found herself immersed in aromatic steam.

"Breathe deeply," he told her, *"and slowly. Give yourself time to absorb it before breathing out."*

The steam was thick and smelled of concentrated honey and warm milk. In the middle of the hut, she saw its source--a stand of chest-high plants topped with glowing purple cups like the pods of poppies, emitting plumes through the holes in their sieve-like caps.

Jalila pulled back her glossy black hair and closed her eyes. She took a deep breath and held it in her lungs, then released it. She felt fine...and, amazingly, a little less hungry.

As she continued breathing in the nutritious fumes, she wondered what the next day would bring. She wondered what would happen when the Lexicons and Free Speakers clashed. She wondered if al-Aziz and Farouk were still alive, and she wondered if they still had a hope of saving the world from the invasion fleet.

She swore she would do everything in her power to make things come out right. She'd been given a second chance after what had happened on Pyrrhus VII, and she wasn't going to waste it.

No matter what it cost her.

10

A wave of panic surged through Jalila as the crowd pressed around her.

Though she was relatively safe in the middle of the group of Lexicons from the Garden of Yesterday, she felt the same rising terror that she had experienced in the mob in the ministers' tower. On all sides, the Lexicons were surrounded by hordes of strangers...what seemed like millions of Vox, all moving in the same direction.

As the Lexicons and Jalila followed the flow of Vox along the street, her heart pounded. Already overheated from the heavy cloak the Lexicons had given her to wear, she felt trickles of sweat run down her sides and back.

If not for her guns, she would not have been able to hold on to even the small degree of composure she had left. She patted each of them in turn, as she did every few meters--the rifle slung over her back under the cloak, the handgun nestled in the hip pocket of her jumpsuit uniform. The knife was still in place, too; she could feel the holster in her boot, rubbing her ankle as she walked.

Folcrum walked beside her, his white fur radiant in the morning sunlight. During the entire trip through the tunnels from the Garden of Yesterday to the surface, he had never strayed from her. She wasn't sure if he stayed close out of genuine concern or because he was assigned to guard her...but she took comfort from his presence, especially in the heart of the crowd.

She only wished he would tell her where they were going and what exactly would happen when they got there. She still felt as if she were blindly stumbling forward, reacting to events without being able to anticipate or fully understand them.

After winding through a maze of streets in the heart of the city, the hordes of Vox flowed into a huge plaza, framed on all four sides by sprawling buildings. The expansive structures were see-through like all Vox buildings, multicolored and layered in tiers, their upper levels rimmed in balconies with elaborate balustrades. The base of each building was fronted by grand archways and columns atop broad stairways...all of it transparent, all tinted with pastel colors.

Though the square was filled with Vox, it was nowhere near as packed as the streets had been. Jalila's panic faded a little; she was still worried someone would recognize her as the visitor who'd spoken the forbidden slur, but not so worried about being trampled to death.

"*Here we are.*" Folcrum swept a clawed hand around to encompass the busy plaza. "*Speech Center. Heart of our world's languages.*

"*All these people are Lexicons.*" Folcrum gazed around at the square's population. *"Every working Lexicon in the world...plus our retired and revised ones."*

"You don't see this often," said blonde-furred Giza, on Jalila's other side. *"The last was six years ago, but you rarely see a major revision twice in ten years."*

"Even without the threat of violence," said Folcrum, *"it would be an exciting day."*

Jalila's group passed a crowd engaged in a discussion of pronunciation so spirited that it seemed on the verge of becoming a fistfight. Further on, a spotted brown Vox howled at passersby from a pulpit, protesting proposed changes to a class of multi-tense verbs. A choir at the center of the plaza sang a thesaurus, with different sections--bass, tenor, alto, soprano--singing different strings of words with related meanings. Everywhere, the crowd communicated excitedly in the three Vox language modes--chattering, gesturing, buzzing, and clicking.

Under other circumstances, the plaza would have been paradise to Jalila. As a linguist, she would have loved experiencing such a vibrant, language-focused event on an alien world, humming with the exchange of ideas and the on-the-spot evolution of multilingual syntax.

Unfortunately, she was too preoccupied with life-and-death concerns to enjoy what could have been one of the most exhilarating experiences of her life.

Angling through the crowd, Oric led her and the others to one of the stairways flanking the plaza. Tightening the cloak around her, Jalila followed the Lexicons up several stairs, where they stopped to survey the area.

"Look," said Folcrum after a moment. *"That food vendor by the fountain."*

Peering out from the hood of her cloak, Jalila saw the fountain midway across the plaza. At a cart set up alongside it, two Vox served food to waiting Lexicons. Though they were some distance away, she immediately recognized one of the vendors.

"*Nalo,*" said Folcrum. "*His people are positioned around that and three other carts.*"

Jalila saw a second cart parked on the far side of the fountain. The other two carts sat at opposite ends of the plaza, near the main entry points.

Seeing the carts, Jalila understood the Free Speakers' strategy. They had used the carts to transport their arsenal of weapons into Speech Center. Once the shooting started, they would pin the Lexicons between fire from both ends and the middle of the plaza, cutting off their escape.

It would be a bloodbath.

"*Three of us to each cart.*" With a clawed finger, Giza counted off threesomes from the group of twelve and pointed toward each trio's target.

Jalila was relieved when he selected Folcrum and Yama to accompany her. She knew Folcrum best of any of them and felt a bond with gagged Yama.

"*You know what you have to do,*" said Oric. "*We must go now.*"

The four teams split up and headed for their targets. As Folcrum led Jalila and Yama through the crowd, Jalila nervously checked the gun in her pocket and the rifle on her back.

Her team's target was Nalo himself.

"*Lexicons are more than walking dictionaries, Jalila,*" Folcrum said as they approached Nalo's cart. "*Watch this.*"

Leaning on the cart's boxy storage compartment, Folcrum addressed brown-furred Nalo. "*Three* fil'chaka," he said pleasantly. "*And what do you have to drink?*"

Nalo looked distracted. "Lucat *and* oob'suela," he said, staring off across the plaza.

"*I would like three* chio vishi," said Folcrum.

"*No* chio vishi," Nalo said irritably. "Lucat *or* oob'suela."

Folcrum nodded. "*Would you please excuse me for a moment?*"

With that, Folcrum turned, threw back his head, and emitted a piercing howl.

All eyes in the vicinity locked on him. All nearby chatter and activity ceased.

"Codamoxsu Voxlo!" Folcrum pointed at Nalo. "Codamoxsu!"

Pieces of what Folcrum had said were familiar, but Jalila didn't recognize the combination and inflection. The closest she could come was "cutting up" or "butchering" the language.

Immediately, Lexicons from all around converged on the cart.

"*This one mangles our language every time he opens his mouth,*" said Folcrum. "*Here, of all places, in Speech Center, he shows contempt for our rules!*"

"*I said nothing wrong!*" Nalo glanced around nervously at the surrounding Lexicons. "*He lies!*"

"*Fellow Lexicons and Grammar Police,*" said Folcrum. "*We must reeducate this misguided soul!*"

Nalo tried to open the lid of the cart, but Folcrum leaned on it, holding it down. As the crowd of Lexicons closed in, Nalo tried again to get the cart open.

"*Codamoxsu Voxlo!*" shouted Folcrum.

All at once, the Lexicons pushed forward, reaching for Nalo.

Yama joined the crowd, but Jalila hung back. Realizing the situation had come to a head, she unsnapped the hip pocket of her uniform and drew the gun.

Swatting aside Folcrum, Nalo flung open the cart lid and swung out a rifle. Folcrum and another Lexicon latched onto the barrel and wrenched it away from him.

Before Nalo could be fully subdued, however, the sound of weapons fire and screams erupted nearby. Some of the Lexicons were distracted and looked toward the source...the food cart on the other side of the fountain, where the effort to thwart the Speakers had hit a snag.

Taking advantage of the confusion, Nalo flung aside the Lexicons who were clutching at him and thrust his hands into the cart. Wrenching out another rifle, he swept it in an arc, spraying the crowd with bullets.

Folcrum and Yama were hit. As Jalila watched, they were jolted by the impact of the shots and dropped to the pavement.

Nalo continued to fire, and Speech Center flew into chaos. Lexicons ran in every direction, screeching and seeking cover.

Raising her gun, Jalila took aim at Nalo. She took a breath to steady herself and pulled the trigger.

The bullet struck Nalo in the shoulder, throwing him back, but he managed to hold onto his rifle. Jalila squeezed the trigger again, but the shot went wide.

In response, Nalo swung his rifle around and launched a spray of bullets in her direction. Jalila would have been hit if not for the panicked Lexicons who crossed her path, taking the shots meant for her.

When Jalila had a clear shot, she fired again, striking Nalo in the chest. With a screech, he jerked backward and plunged down behind the cart.

Jalila charged forward, gun at the ready. Just as she reached the cart, it lurched toward her and toppled over. As she crashed down under it, her rifle was caught beneath her.

The next thing Jalila knew, Nalo was glaring down at her. His bullet wounds bled profusely, but he held onto his rifle and seemed to have enough life left in him to use it.

"*Mazeesh*," he said hatefully. "*It's the right word for you.*"

Bracing both hands under the edge of the cart, Jalila heaved. In Vox's light gravity, she was able to shove the cart upward. As it struck Nalo in the belly, he doubled over and released his grip on the rifle. The weapon slid across the cart and landed on the pavement beside Jalila.

Grabbing the rifle, Jalila scrambled to her feet and swung the barrel around, directing it at Nalo's head.

As Nalo pushed himself up from the cart, he bared his fangs at her. "*Mazeesh*," he hissed, getting ready to spring.

Jalila's finger tensed against the trigger. Her heart pounded.

Just as Nalo leaped, she fired the weapon.

11

Instead of hitting Nalo's head, the slug blew into his hip. Screeching, he twisted in mid-air and came down short of Jalila, slamming onto the overturned cart.

Jalila reversed the rifle in her grip and swung the butt against Nalo's skull. He twitched a few times before he stopped moving.

But Jalila could see he was still breathing.

Unfortunately, incapacitating him didn't solve all Jalila's problems. The pandemonium in the plaza continued. Jalila heard gunfire and screams of panic and pain from all directions.

And in the midst of the madness, her two Vox allies lay bleeding on the pavement.

Pushing through the torrent of fleeing Vox, Jalila hurried to her teammates and dropped to her knees between them. Yama was bruised and battered, but Jalila found a strong pulse. Folcrum, however, was in terrible shape. As Jalila watched, blood pumped from his gaping chest wound, and his eyes fluttered shut.

Gently, Jalila stroked the soft silver fur of his brow. Folcrum's eyes flickered open, and he smiled up at her.

"*Jalila.*" His voice was a hoarse whisper. "*The rest of your secret.*"

Jalila shook her head, wanting only to relieve his suffering. She removed her cloak, no longer caring if she was identified and attacked, and placed it over him.

Folcrum coughed up blood. As Jalila applied pressure over his wound, he took hold of her wrist. "*The Vox people...were not the true* mazeesh," he said. "*The* mazeesh...were the visitors...from the stars.*"

Jalila frowned. The implications of what he had said were startling.

"*Yes.*" Folcrum nodded weakly. "*We...hunted and killed...them. All for the part of them...in here,*" he tapped the side of his head, "*that was said to bestow...fertility.*"

Coughing spasms wracked his body. When he spoke again, his voice was fainter and more ragged than ever. "*The Vox...rewrote history. No one remembers...and there are no records...except the Garden.*"

It seemed to take everything Folcrum had left to scrape out his last few gasping words. "*Perhaps*," he said, "*the true* mazeesh...*have returned.*"

Then, his head lolled to one side, and he breathed his last.

12

Jalila wasn't thinking straight as she got to her feet. For a moment, she stood and stared down at the lifeless body of Folcrum, riveted by grief that was surprisingly strong considering how briefly she had known him.

I've lost another one. Like the diplomat on Pyrrhus VII.

Sudden movement tore her attention away from mourning. Looking to one side, she saw two Free Speakers pushing toward her through the crowd. They aimed their rifles right at her, leaving no doubt that she was their target.

Jalila stood her ground, determined to protect injured Yama. Raising her own rifle, she drew a bead on one of the Vox and slid her finger around the trigger.

I won't lose her, too.

Before anyone could fire a shot, however, a stream of fleeing Lexicons darted between Jalila and the Free Speakers. When the Lexicons had passed, the Free Speakers were gone.

Jalila's heart pounded. Convinced the Free Speakers had split up and were sneaking around to outflank her, she kept her rifle at the ready. Scanning the surrounding crowd, she slowly took a step forward.

Suddenly, someone grabbed her from behind.

Jalila reached back, expecting to feel the fur of one of the Free Speakers--and caught her breath.

Cloth. Instead of fur, she felt *cloth.*

The hands that held her turned her around. For a moment, Jalila was so overcome with emotion that she just gawked. She couldn't believe her eyes.

The cloth was part of a uniform, a jumpsuit like her own...but black, the color of command. Her rescuer was a man with thick brown hair and piercing green eyes.

Bursting into tears, Jalila flung her arms around him.

Major al-Aziz hugged her just as tightly in return. "Jalila," he said. "Boy, am I glad to see you!"

13

When the scout barque descended into the square, the shooting stopped. Everyone's attention was drawn to the gleaming silver-skinned craft as it dropped toward the crowd.

With Farouk at the controls, the barque came down decisively. Vox scattered in all directions, clearing a landing site.

It was the second best thing Jalila had seen all day. The best-- Major al-Aziz--stood beside her as she watched the barque's approach from a few meters away.

"Now there's a sight for sore eyes," said al-Aziz.

Jalila nodded emphatically.

"*Wow*," said one of the Vox allies al-Aziz had brought with him. His name was Altis, and he was a Lexicon in training. Folcrum had dispatched him with a team of trainees to rescue al-Aziz and Farouk from the cells where Regent Ieria had imprisoned them. Altis and his group had also saved Jalila's life in Speech Center, tackling the two Free Speakers in the crowd before they could shoot her.

When the barque touched down, the hatch opened, and Colonel Farouk emerged. Looking around, he met Jalila's gaze...and managed a small smile of relief. On that stoic, stony face of his, it might as well have been the biggest, goofiest grin of all time.

"What's the good word, Colonel?" said al-Aziz.

Farouk's smile vanished. "The invasion fleet has entered orbit." He scrubbed the top of his head, which was studded with stubble after days without shaving. "Squadrons of fighters are launching as we speak."

"I asked for the *good* word, Farouk," said al-Aziz.

With that, al-Aziz signaled the two Lexicons carrying Yama's stretcher, and they hurried forward. Farouk waved them inside, running a medical scanner over Yama as they hauled her up the ramp into the barque.

al-Aziz and Jalila followed. As soon as Jalila set foot in the familiar surroundings, she felt at ease in a way she hadn't since leaving the barque many hours before.

"See if you can raise the *Ibn Battuta*, Jalila," said al-Aziz. "They ought to be on their way to the rendezvous point by now."

"The ship is still in orbit," said Farouk.

al-Aziz sighed. "Get me the *Ibn Battuta* immediately."

At the barque's radio controls, Jalila quickly opened a channel. Though the gag prevented her from announcing when the channel was open, Jalila did the job with a wave.

"*Ibn Battuta* here," said Sergeant Africanus over the radio link.

"What the hell do you think you're doing, Sergeant?" snapped al-Aziz. "I thought I told you to leave orbit before the fleet got here."

"I must have misunderstood, sir," said Africanus.

al-Aziz shook his head angrily. "What's your status?"

"Trying to stay out of the invaders' way," said Africanus. "So far, they're not bothering with us."

"How do you rate our chances of making it back in the barque?" said al-Aziz.

"I wouldn't recommend it, sir," said Africanus. "The skies are full of fighters. They're shooting down everything that leaves the ground."

Just then, the roar of passing aircraft shook the barque, confirming the news. Peering through the cockpit window, Jalila glimpsed vapor trails cutting across the red-tinted sky.

al-Aziz cast his eyes upward. "Response to hails?"

"None, sir," said Africanus.

"They don't leave us much choice," said al-Aziz. "I guess we'll have to take matters into our own hands, Farouk."

Farouk didn't look up from treating Yama's injuries. "Meaning what?"

"We're already in the middle of this," said al-Aziz. "Maybe a middleman is what these people need."

"You wish to negotiate," said Farouk as he injected medication into Yama's arm. "Yet the invaders refuse all attempts at communication."

"Meeting face to face could be a different story," said al-Aziz.

"We know nothing about them," said Farouk. "There is no basis for understanding."

At that, Jalila interrupted, clapping her hands for attention. Raising an index finger, she signaled her shipmates to wait. Then, she turned to the Voicebox controls on the barque's radio board.

Overriding the translation function, Jalila set the device to convert keyed text into audio output. Hastily, she typed on the keyboard and triggered the speech synthesizer. Her words emerged from the barque's speakers in a computer-generated male monotone.

"*I know about them,*" said the voice.

"What do you know, Jalila?" said al-Aziz. There was no trace of disappointment on his face when he looked at her now.

Jalila typed again. "*I think the invaders are the real* mazeesh."

"*Mazeesh,*" said al-Aziz. "That's what started this whole mess."

Jalila typed furiously. "*Long ago, visitors from the stars came to Vox. They were hunted and killed for an organ that was said to increase Vox fertility. The general population believes the opposite...that the Vox were* the mazeesh, *the persecuted ones. Without a written language, there are no history texts to disprove it.*"

al-Aziz nodded thoughtfully. "So you're saying the real *mazeesh* have returned for payback."

"*For crimes the Vox don't remember committing,*" Jalila said through the speech synthesizer.

"And you say there's no proof of the true story?" said al-Aziz.

"*Maybe*," said Jalila. "*There's an underground garden. I believe information is stored there in the form of scent signals from cultivated plant life.*"

"Could you interpret and record the information from these scent signals?" said al-Aziz.

"*Possibly*," said Jalila. "*With a scanner and Voicebox.*"

al-Aziz rubbed his chin. "I know you've been through a lot, but that information is vital. Can you get it for us?"

Jalila nodded and typed. "*If I can find someone to lead me back there.*"

"The people you came with?" said al-Aziz.

"*If any of them are still alive*," said Jalila.

al-Aziz stood with his hands on his hips and stared at the floor. "This goes against my better judgment after reuniting the team, but we're going to split up. Sergeant Africanus, have any transports from the fleet touched down? Anything that looks like it might be carrying command personnel?"

"An armored transport with fighter escort is landing as we speak," Africanus said over the *Ibn Battuta* link. "I'm sending you the coordinates."

al-Aziz watched the data come in and nodded. "The ministry building, where we were first attacked. They're coming for the Vox surrender. That's where Farouk and I are going. We'll get the ball rolling.

"You'll head for the garden, Jalila. As soon as you have the evidence we need, get to the ministry as fast as possible."

Lifting a weapons case from the floor, al-Aziz swung it onto a seat and unlatched it. "And Sergeant Africanus," he said. "Your orders are to move *Ibn Battuta* out of orbit the instant any of those ships makes a threatening move against her. Understand?"

"Aye, sir," Africanus said briskly.

al-Aziz removed a pistol from the case and handed it to Jalila. "What about our Voiceboxes? Do you have enough data to set them up to translate the Vox spoken language?"

Jalila nodded.

"Great," said al-Aziz. "Prep all handheld Voiceboxes, Jalila. Everybody gets one."

As Jalila set about programming the Voiceboxes, she heard the sound of voices outside the barque. Looking out the cockpit window, she saw Oric and Giza approaching, chattering at Altis and his friends.

Maybe Jalila would be able to complete her mission, after all. Her guides to the Garden of Yesterday were alive and well.

Oric and Giza looked in Jalila's direction, but before she could wave, Farouk thrust a medical scanner in front of her. His face remained as stony as ever as he ran the scanner over the gag on her mouth.

"The gag must be removed surgically," said Farouk, examining the scanner's readouts. "You'll have to wait until we return to the *Ibn Battuta*."

Jalila nodded.

Farouk scrubbed the stubble on his scalp and turned away. "Good luck with your assignment."

14

Jalila felt like throwing the scanner and Voicebox down in the dirt and jumping up and down on them.

It was not the reaction she'd expected after going for so long without the devices...but they weren't providing the quick success she needed. Deciphering the complex system of scent signals in the Garden of Yesterday was proving to be even more difficult than she'd anticipated.

Returning to the Garden had been the easy part. With Oric and Giza as guides, navigating the tunnels had been no problem. Once Jalila had set about her task in the Garden, however, things had gotten tricky. She was starting to wonder if what she'd set out to accomplish was even possible, given the tools at hand.

Her scanner could identify floral scents with great accuracy, pinpointing the composition and prevalence of esters, or scent molecules, in any given liter of air. That information, however, was not enough; the scanner and Voicebox were unable to determine what alphabetical or numerical values had been assigned to specific scents.

Jalila had tried a number of techniques to crack the code, such as constructing a matrix based on the chemical makeup of the ester molecules. She'd attempted less scientific methods as well, such as arbitrarily assigning phonemes from the Vox language to certain scents and rotating the assignments until a logical pattern emerged.

But nothing had led to a breakthrough. So far, Jalila was unable to unlock the secrets of the Garden.

And with each passing minute, she was becoming more frustrated. She was convinced the information al-Aziz needed was all around her, in the very air she breathed...but she couldn't access it.

"If you know how to listen," Folcrum had told her, *"you can hear the history of the world in here."*

Obviously, Jalila didn't know how to listen. Folcrum knew, and he was gone.

Of course, there were others who might know, too.

Energized by a new idea, Jalila hurried over to Oric, who had been watching her work. Slipping the scanner into her hip pocket, Jalila entered a message on the Voicebox's keypad. Text appeared on the display, and Jalila touched the control that would convert it to audible speech in the Vox pulmonic language.

"Folcrum knew how to hear the garden talk," said the Voicebox. *"Do you?"*

Oric nodded and answered. Jalila had learned enough Vox to understand his words before the Voicebox translated them. *"I am a good listener."*

"Please help me to hear the garden," said Jalila.

"I will do what I can," said Oric.

Jalila typed on the Voicebox's keypad. *"I must find the history of the first coming of the Mazeesh. Where do I begin?"*

Oric closed his eyes and inhaled deeply. *"Not here,"* he said. *"This section relates to the worldwide plague of five thousand years ago."*

Turning, Oric moved along the red dirt path through the garden, stopping every few meters to sample the local fragrances. Jalila followed, fascinated by the ease with which he accomplished what had stymied both the scanner and Voicebox.

"The overthrow of the great tyrants." Oric barely paused by a patch of glowing purple blossoms. *"Two thousand years ago."*

On the fly, Jalila scanned the air he sampled, trying to identify the nature of the signals he was interpreting. Though there were many differences between samples, she could find no factors that varied consistently and predictably, producing patterns that could be associated with coded language.

So how was he doing it?

"We're getting closer." Oric took a whiff near a fall of what looked like crimson Spanish moss with a million twinkling gold blossoms laced through it. *"The start of the Age of Science, five hundred years ago."*

He had to be homing in on some characteristic of the floral scents that Jalila was missing...but what? If the secret did not lie in the molecular composition of the scent-producing esters, what other variable could serve as the basis for data storage and retrieval?

It occurred to Jalila that perhaps she should think smaller.

"Four hundred years ago," said Oric, a little further along the winding path. *"The Child Wars and Silent Times."*

Perhaps, as unlikely as it seemed, the key existed at an atomic level...or even subatomic.

Oric led Jalila down an offshoot of the main path that ended in a secluded thicket. He stopped and breathed deeply, then nodded. *"Here we are. Three hundred years ago."*

Pocketing the scanner, Jalila typed on the Voicebox. *"Where does the story begin?"*

Oric drew another breath and let it out slowly. *"On the fourth night of the month of Utan in the year of Tolera Vosh, golden orbs came down from the stars. They landed near the capital city of Comu and did not open until morning."*

Jalila typed, and the Voicebox spoke. "*I meant what scent begins the story. Show me the flower that tells you the very beginning.*"

Oric bent down and reached for a white-cupped blossom, like a lily with glittering purple petal tips. "*This one. The om radla, or year flower.*"

"*When you listen to this flower,*" Jalila said through the Voicebox, "*what word or words do you hear?*"

"I hear the words '*Tolera Vosh,*'" said Oric. "'*Year 7430.*'"

"*Can you find another year flower?*" said Jalila. "*For another year?*"

Wrinkling his furry snout, Oric sniffed. He stepped to one side and touched a blossom that was identical to the first, but with emerald petal tips. "*This one says 'Culan Vosh' and 'year 7431.'*"

Crouching, Jalila aimed the scanner at the first year flower, analyzing the invisible ester vapors wafting from the scent glands in its petals. After logging the molecular composition of the vapor, she went further, probing the structures of the atoms that made up the molecules...and the particles that made up the atoms.

Then, Jalila moved to the second year flower pointed out by Oric and performed identical scans, from the molecular level to the subatomic. When the scanner's memory held complete data for the ester molecules of both flowers, Jalila ran a point-by-point comparison of their properties.

There was no difference between the esters of the two flowers at the molecular level. Each was composed of the same number of the same types of atoms in exactly the same formation. However, continued analysis revealed divergence at the subatomic level.

Within the nuclei of otherwise identical atoms, the quark particles that made up the protons and neutrons had unexpected color charges. Whereas protons and neutrons in most ordinary matter contained one quark of each color--red, green, and blue--Jalila found protons and neutrons with two quarks of one color and one of another, or three quarks of the same color. For example, oxygen atoms in the first flower's ester contained protons with two green quarks and one blue quark; otherwise identical atoms from the second flower contained one green quark and two blue quarks.

As hard as it was to believe, it seemed the Vox had not only learned to control the properties of subatomic particles via gardening, but had developed olfactory senses sophisticated enough to detect differences in color charge between quarks.

Just as all data in a computer was reduced to ones and zeroes, the data in the Garden of Yesterday was represented by different combinations of red, green, and blue quarks...a trinary instead of a binary system. By determining which combinations were assigned to which numerical and phonemic values, Jalila could finally tap into the information flowing through the air around her.

15

Jalila figured out the numerical values first. They were simplest, since only a single digit separated the date coded in the first flower's ester from the date supplied by the second flower.

Jalila located quarks with abnormal color charge configurations in chains of carbon atoms in the ester molecules...specifically, atoms of carbon-12, an isotope with six protons and twelve neutrons, each containing three quarks. In the first carbon-12 atom in each chain, seven of the protons and neutrons contained trios of quarks with identical red color charges; this matched the first digit of the date, seven. The next carbon-12 atom included four trios of red quarks, matching the second digit of the date.

The third atom in the chain had three trios of red quarks...but the difference between the scent molecules from the two flowers appeared in the fourth atom in the chain. In molecules from the second flower, the fourth carbon-12 atom had one trio of red quarks; the same atom in molecules from the first flower had one trio of *blue* quarks...which Jalila took to represent zero.

Looking at the results of her analysis, she could clearly see that the scent of the first flower was tagged with the number 7430, and the scent of the second flower with 7431.

Jalila felt a rush of pride and elation. Finally, she had found the key to the Garden of Yesterday.

Now, the question was, would she be able to use it in time?

Though numbers were coded in a relatively simple way, applying the trinary system to language phonemes would be more complicated. At least Jalila had a place to start: the names of the years--Tolera Vosh and Culan Vosh--shared multiple phonemes. By comparing the two in trinary code, she would quickly be able to spot the differences between them and assign consonants and vowels to specific quark color combinations.

With Oric's help, Jalila would then identify Vox phonemes in the scent molecules of other flowers. Once she'd assigned quark values to each basic unit of the Vox language, she would construct a conversion matrix that would enable her to read and record data from any flower in the garden.

So she had a plan of attack...and in that regard, was light-years ahead of where she'd been before...but it would take time to execute. Jalila didn't know how much time she had to do the work, but she worried it wouldn't be enough. She worried that the situation on the planet's surface had already deteriorated past the point of no return, and by the time she'd get back to Major al-Aziz, he would be as dead as Folcrum.

The fate of the world was in Jalila's hands...and time was racing away from her.

16

"You want the truth? Here it is!" Those were Major al-Aziz's words when Jalila threw open the doors of the ministry building.

For a moment, Jalila stood in the doorway, flanked by Oric and Giza. They'd just raced back from the Garden of Yesterday, and her heart was pounding.

Jalila looked around at the scene in front of her, trying to piece together what had happened while she'd been in the Garden.

Though she'd caught glimpses through the ministry's see-through tinted walls while running toward the place, only now did she have enough of a close-up view to get the full picture.

al-Aziz and Farouk stood in the middle of the vast hall. They were surrounded by Vox, including Regent Ieria, the ministers, and armed soldiers. What drew Jalila's attention most forcefully, though, was not at ground-level.

Alien creatures floated above everyone, rippling in midair. They looked like New Mecca's ocean-dwelling manta rays, except for the tiny arms on their bellies.

Like rays, the beings were delicate, rubbery wedges with gracefully undulating wings. From wingtip to wingtip, they measured between three and four meters. The dorsal surface of each invader's body was steel gray; the underside, visible with each ripple of a wing, was the color of cream. Each creature had a long, prehensile tail with a forked tip, and each tail was wrapped around a rod with a glowing golden sphere on either end.

One of the manta-like beings reared back with its wings spread wide. The creature's belly was covered with elaborate designs, a mix of swirls and lines and polygons. Were they some kind of ritual markings, like the Vox's tattoos?

Or...

Jalila gasped.

Or were they characters? Were they some kind of *language*?

"Jalila!" al-Aziz marched toward her, waving. "We've been expecting you!"

On a wall, Jalila saw the same characters, projected and enlarged. Rearranged, too, and changed. Some were completely different from the ones on the manta's wings, yet clearly in the same linguistic family.

"Meet the Mazeesh," said al-Aziz.

Jalila typed on her Voicebox, and the device spoke her words. "You're communicating with them?"

"Yes we are," said al-Aziz. "As you can see, they use a biologically generated written language. We've been scanning it into a

Voicebox, using the Voicebox to translate, then translating our own speech into their written language. We cobbled together a projector using gear from the barque, then hardwired a Voicebox into it so we could put the text on the wall for them to read."

"You make it sound easy," said Jalila.

al-Aziz winked one piercing green eye. "Sure it was."

Jalila typed on her Voicebox. "Where do we stand?"

"Let's just say you couldn't have come at a better time." al-Aziz bowed and gestured for her to come with him. "We need airtight evidence of what really happened here. Absolute truth."

"I'll do my best," said Jalila.

al-Aziz walked her to the middle of the room. "Fellow beings!" He put a hand on her shoulder. "Allow me to introduce Corporal Jalila bint Farooq bin Abdul Al-Fulani. She is a bringer of truth."

Ieria did not look happy to see Jalila. As for the Mazeesh, Jalila still found them unreadable.

One swooped down to hover in front of her. At first, she could see no eyes on it, just a snout consisting of a comb of tightly packed fibers between two horn-like knobs. Then, the creature reared up.

From a few centimeters below the snout, two tiny obsidian eyes stared back at Jalila. Twin arcs of what looked like breathing holes were arranged below them like halves of a necklace. Two spindly limbs flexed from the creature's belly, ending in fragile-looking three-fingered hands.

As Jalila watched, dark threads flowed over the creamy surface of the creature's underside, mixing and fluxing and sepa-rating...resolving into patterns. Among the patterns, Jalila saw discrete groupings of symbols that might be words; in some places, the text seemed hopelessly jumbled, but in others, she could make out what she thought were divisions of lines and breaks in phrasing.

She thought it was completely amazing.

Farouk, who was standing nearby, scanned the symbols on the Mazeesh's wings with the Voicebox, which produced an audio translation. "*What truth does she bring?*"

"The truth about what happened during your first visit," said al-Aziz, "and which of your peoples has the right to rule this world."

17

The patterns on the wings of the Mazeesh shifted. Farouk continued to scan and translate the creature's words with the Voicebox. "*As we have said, our people came here long ago in peace. The savages of this world hunted, killed, and devoured them.*"

"*And as we have said,*" said Ieria, speaking through al-Aziz's Voicebox, "*these monsters murdered us! They cracked open our skulls and ate our brains! They named us* mazeesh--*filth, excrement, lowest of the low!*"

al-Aziz gave Jalila a sideways look. "We seem to have reached an impasse."

"*We have returned to eradicate this menace forever,*" said the Mazeesh.

"*We will fight to the last Vox to destroy you!*" said Ieria. "*Better to die with the truth in our hearts than live with a lie on our tongues!*"

al-Aziz squeezed Jalila's shoulder. "So now you know where we stand. No video or audio recordings exist of the events in question. Since the Vox don't have a written language, they have no hard-copy historical records. Which is where you come in."

Jalila nodded and typed on the Voicebox. "I understand."

"Are you ready for this?" said al-Aziz.

"Yes," said Jalila.

al-Aziz smiled. He radiated confidence, not doubt, as he met her gaze. "I know you are." al-Aziz turned to the Vox. "Guess what?" He spoke into his Voicebox, and his words came out in Vox multi-language. "Your people have historical records after all."

"*I don't know what you're talking about,*" said Ieria.

"Your records are kept in the form of scent signals in a secret garden," said al-Aziz. "A garden tended by *Lexicons*."

"*I've never heard of it,*" said Ieria.

"It exists, all right," said al-Aziz. "For centuries, the Lexicons have stored your history there...and now Jalila has tapped into it." He glanced at Jalila, and she gave him a quick nod of confirmation. "She has brought back the story of the first coming of the Mazeesh, as told and recorded by the Vox people themselves."

"Not possible," said Ieria. *"The spoken word is our only record of the past!"*

"As masters of the spoken word, we Lexicons recognized it was not enough," said Oric. "We started the garden to document our own persecution, to ensure it would not be forgotten or revised."

"What do these supposed records say?" said a dark-furred minister.

"We'll let you hear for yourselves," said al-Aziz.

"We also have samples of the original scent signals," Jalila said through her Voicebox. "With your advanced sense of smell, you'll be able to translate and verify the records yourselves."

Impressed with her thoroughness, al-Aziz smiled and nodded. "We'll simultaneously translate for the Mazeesh," he said, "so everyone's on the same page."

Ieria waved a hand dismissively. *"We don't need to hear these so-called records,"* she said. *"We already know what happened."*

"Then what can it hurt?" said al-Aziz. "Unless you're in a hurry to sacrifice your lives and finalize the destruction of your planet."

Ieria glared at him. *"All right,"* she said coldly. *"We will listen to your trickery."*

18

As the Vox leaders listened to the translated account of the first coming of the Mazeesh, Jalila noticed that their reactions followed a pattern.

At first, every one of them seemed skeptical and impatient...but as the story progressed, they listened with increasing interest. When the account diverged from their accepted view of history, they grew irritated and muttered to one another; further on, when the tale implicated their species as the true authors of the atrocities, annoyance turned to disbelief and outrage.

But after a while, as the extent of the Vox's crimes was recounted in gruesome detail, they settled into a pensive silence. Some of the ministers looked around at the hovering Mazeesh with fear and regret; others hung their heads and stared at the floor.

Except for Ieria. She stood stiffly throughout the playback, the expression on her face a rigid scowl of disgust.

After playing the recording, Jalila described the technique she'd used to decode the information...and no one asked questions. She offered to let the Vox test the scent samples she'd brought, but no one took her up on it. Everyone seemed to accept the truth of what they'd heard...except Ieria.

"*How ridiculous,*" she said. "*What a sham.*"

"We've presented you with proof," said al-Aziz, "documented by your own people. I think it speaks for itself."

"*You can make that device say whatever you* want *it to,*" said Ieria.

"But we didn't," said al-Aziz. "You're welcome to go to the Garden and examine the original records yourself."

"Anyone *could have created those records. We only know* when *they were created and* by whom *because the records* themselves *tell us these things.*"

"*As Lexicons, Giza and I vouch for the authenticity of the records,*" said Oric.

Ieria snorted. "*As* revised, discarded *Lexicons, your word is meaningless.*"

At that moment, one of the Mazeesh caught Jalila's attention, floating toward her with a fresh message on the underside of its wings. Farouk scanned and translated the new text with the Mazeesh-attuned Voicebox.

"*You and your people are free to go,*" said the Mazeesh. "*You have presented the facts fairly, and we are satisfied that you are not complicit in the Vox's crimes.*"

al-Aziz stepped in to answer. "We would like to stay. We want to help you resolve this crisis."

"*Unnecessary,*" said the Mazeesh. "*There is no crisis.*"

"We would like to help the Vox make amends for their past mistakes," said al-Aziz. "And we would like to help the Mazeesh find an alternative to genocide."

"*The Vox are a disease,*" said the Mazeesh.

"The Vox are a sentient species," said al-Aziz, "and not one of them who participated in those acts is alive today."

"*It must never happen again,*" said the Mazeesh, "*to our species or any other.*"

"Agreed," said al-Aziz, "but isn't that what *will* happen if you eradicate the Vox? Isn't the genocide of billions of beings a *greater* crime than what *they've* done?"

After a long moment, new symbols appeared on the Mazeesh's wings. "*They must be punished.*"

"Why not benefit from that punishment," said al-Aziz, "instead of putting the deaths of billions of sentient beings on your conscience?"

The symbols on the Mazeesh's wings shifted. "*What do you have in mind?*"

al-Aziz turned to Jalila, raising his eyebrows. "Any ideas, Corporal?"

Jalila's heart pounded. Her mind raced.

Days ago, she'd been on the verge of being drummed out of the service. She'd been disgraced after making a critical mistake that had led to the death of a diplomat and the failure of a peace treaty. She'd never dared imagine she'd be given a chance to redeem herself.

Yet here it was.

Jalila had survived many travails on the planet Vox, and that was *one* thing...but having Major al-Aziz turn to her for answers was another. Having him turn to her for a key idea in the midst of a crisis was extraordinary. It wasn't something he routinely did with disgraced officers on the verge of being drummed out of the service.

It meant, plain and simple, that he was giving Jalila another chance. If she could come up with a dazzling solution, perhaps it would mitigate her disgrace. Perhaps she could yet retire with honor.

If only she could rise to the occasion.

Jalila wracked her brain, considering the possibilities. She felt the planet turning around her with all its billions of people depending on her answer.

How could the Vox be punished in a way that would benefit the Mazeesh? Better yet, that would benefit *both* species? Jalila looked from the Vox to the Mazeesh, struggling to come up with an answer. She looked at the Mazeesh language projected on the wall.

And that was when it hit her.

Perhaps the Vox, like Jalila, could redeem themselves with language.

Energized with inspiration, Jalila went to Farouk and reached for his Mazeesh-attuned Voicebox. He handed it over with a skeptical look on his stony features.

With a few tweaks, Jalila wirelessly linked Farouk's Voicebox to her own. Thanks to the link, she could type on one Voicebox and covert her words to Vox spoken language and projected Mazeesh text simultaneously.

When the setup was done, Jalila pushed her glossy black hair behind her ears and started typing, addressing the Vox and Mazeesh. "I propose that the Vox work off their debt," she said.

"*How gracious of you,*" snarled Ieria.

Symbols flowed onto the Mazeesh's wings and became words on the Voicebox's display. "*What kind of work?*"

"The Mazeesh have no spoken language," said Jalila. "This can be a disadvantage in trade and exploration."

"*You dare call us disadvantaged?*" said the Mazeesh.

"Not at all," said Jalila. "However, speech is the primary means of communication for most species we have encountered. Lack of communication can lead to misunderstandings, which can lead to conflict.

"Perhaps you can limit these undesirable outcomes," said Jalila, "by employing *translators* on your ships...say, the members of a multilingual, *speech-focused* species."

The Mazeesh's wings rippled, displaying an array of new symbols. "*You suggest we carry* murderers *on our ships, and let them* speak *for us?*"

"I think you'll be surprised at how many qualified, good-hearted people you'll find on this world," said Jalila. "Think of the Lexicons, who not only preserved the secrets their ancestors tried to expunge, but bravely helped bring them to light."

A long moment passed before new text appeared on the wings of the Mazeesh. "*They have no experience with written language. They will not be able to read our words and translate them into speech.*"

"The Vox are able to carry on *three separate conversations* in *three different languages* at once," said Jalila. "I think they'll learn."

There was another pause before the next Mazeesh message. "*This isn't enough. There must be an admission of guilt. There must be penitence for the suffering they've caused.*"

"Once you've taught them to read and write," said Jalila, "work with them to develop historical records. Ensure that the true story of your people's first coming is available to everyone and never forgotten. When all Vox know the truth, there will be plenty of penitence."

"*What is to prevent what happened before from happening again?*" said the Mazeesh.

"Awareness of the truth," said al-Aziz. "Regret. And you setting an example by extending mercy to those who've hurt you instead of continuing the cycle of violence."

The Mazeesh hovered in place without answering, its unreadable stare providing Jalila no clue to its intent. At last, the creature flashed another message on its wings. "*I must consult with my brothers,*" it said, and then it turned from al-Aziz to face the rest of the Mazeesh.

As the Mazeesh conferred, Ieria stormed over and snapped at al-Aziz. "*They can consult all they want. We'll never give in to these monsters.*"

"Is that in the best interests of your people?" said al-Aziz. "Do you think they'd agree that *extinction* is preferable to *cooperation*?"

"*I speak for all of them,*" said Ieria.

"Do you?" al-Aziz stepped around her, bringing himself face to face with the assembled Vox ministers. "What about *you*? You also speak for your people. Do you agree that they would vote for destruction?"

The ministers stood silently, meeting his gaze.

"If the Mazeesh accept our proposal," said al-Aziz, "you won't be asked to sacrifice much. If anything, you'll come out ahead. You'll have a written language, access to deep space, access to advanced technology...and if things work out, in the long run, you may end up with some pretty powerful allies.

"What do you think your *people* would want? All that...or the end of the world?"

Ieria threw herself between al-Aziz and the ministers. "*Promises, promises!*" she said. "*Why would they promise rewards to a species they believe slaughtered their ancestors? To get us to* surrender *quietly! Care to guess how many promises they'll keep after we put down our weapons and get on our knees?*"

"Do you really think they care if you surrender?" said al-Aziz. "With the fleet they've got in orbit, they can wipe your planet clean without working up a sweat."

"*They'll never let us live,*" said Ieria. "*They'll need to cover up the truth of what they did to our people...and if by some miracle they really do believe that ridiculous story of theirs, they'll be too afraid of what we might do to them.*"

"They believe it, all right," said al-Aziz, "but they might be willing to give you a second chance. Why not take it, if your only other option is total annihilation?"

"*Because we are the injured party here!*" Ieria shoved her snout in his face. "*We are the ones who should receive apologies and reparations!*"

al-Aziz pushed her away with the palm of his hand. "So holding on to a lie is more important than saving your people?"

"*It's too late for my people.*"

"You have the power to save them," said al-Aziz. "If you don't use that power, you'll be responsible for their destruction."

"*It won't be on* my *head!*" said Ieria. "*The same monsters who nearly drove us to extinction three hundred years ago will be to blame!*"

"You're sure that's what the people would want?" said al-Aziz.

"*It doesn't matter! I speak for everyone, living and dead!*"

Just then, Ieria was interrupted by a clawed finger tapping on her shoulder. She whirled to face a blonde-furred minister with brown markings.

"*Spoke*," said the minister.

"*Excuse me?*" said Ieria.

"*You* spoke *for everyone*," said the blonde minister. "*Past tense.*"

"*What are you talking about?*" said Ieria.

"*You're not fit to lead*," said the minister. "*We just had a bloodless coup.*"

Ieria snarled and bared her fangs. "*You can't do this*," she hissed. "*Traitors!*"

"*Somebody get a gag on her*," said the jet-black Vox. "*She's about to break some obscenity taboos.*"

Ieria howled and lunged at the ministers, but several of them grabbed hold of her and wrestled her to the ground. She was still struggling when the Mazeesh spokesperson glided over. The creature had an array of symbols on its wings, and Farouk scanned them into the Voicebox.

al-Aziz grinned as he read the translation.

"Ministers," said al-Aziz. "The Mazeesh agree to the compromise we discussed. Would you like some time to talk it over?"

"*Unnecessary*," said the blonde-furred minister. "*We are unanimous.*"

al-Aziz spoke into Farouk's Mazeesh-attuned Voicebox. "*The Vox accept your terms*," he said. "*With gratitude and humility.*"

19

Gently, Jalila placed the crimson seedling in the hole she had dug, then scooped in red soil with a trowel. When the hole was full, she used the trowel to smooth the ground around the base of the seedling; as a finishing touch, she put down the tool and patted the dirt with her bare hands.

Even before the applause started, she felt a wave of relief and resolution. In spite of setbacks and suffering, she had not only survived a terrible ordeal but had helped stave off an invasion and unite two alienated species. In the process, she had redeemed herself, at least a little, for her disastrous failure on Pyrrhus VII.

Now, months later, here she was, helping to add the story of the crisis to the botanical records planted in the Garden of Yesterday.

As the assembled crowd applauded, she pushed her black hair behind her ears and surveyed the patch of history before her. When fully grown, the cluster of tiny red seedlings would bloom with flowers of many colors and fragrances. Miraculously engineered by the Lexicon gardeners, the flora would tell a story with their scents, recounting the arrival of the *Ibn Battuta*, the attack of the Free Speakers, the second coming of the Mazeesh, and the inception of the historic agreement between the Mazeesh and the Vox.

Most of the other shoots had been planted by the revised Lexicons who inhabited the underground garden. They had extra reasons to celebrate this day: those who had been permanently silenced during revisions had had their gags removed by the *Ibn Battuta*'s expert medical team, as had Jalila; and all exiled Lexicons were now free to come and go as they pleased, to travel to the surface without fear of capture or worse.

Jalila's *Ibn Battuta* crewmates had also planted seedlings in the patch. Major al-Aziz and Colonel Farouk had both taken part in the ceremonial planting; Jalila, however, had been given the honor of putting the final seedling in place, the shoot whose bloom would emit the scent concluding the story of recent events.

As Jalila gave the dirt around the seedling a final pat, she felt a hand on her shoulder. Turning and looking up, she saw Giza gazing down at her. His blonde fur, which had already been crowded with elaborate painted designs, now included one more marking: a triple tongue of flame on one side of his snout, his badge of office as newly elected regent of Vox.

As Jalila got to her feet, Regent Giza chattered away in the spoken language of the Vox. Jalila didn't bother to draw the Voicebox from the hip pocket of her gray jumpsuit; during her time among the Vox, she'd learned enough of the language to follow what Giza said.

"*You have made history,*" he told her, "*and now you have preserved it. I hope you will return to breathe the scent of the flower you have planted when it blossoms.*"

"*I hope so, too,*" Jalila said in the Vox language.

As Giza bowed and stepped aside, Jalila's shipmates pressed forward.

"Nice work, Jalila." Major al-Aziz smiled and shook her hand.

"Thank you, Major," said Jalila.

"By the way," said al-Aziz. "You might be happy to hear you won't be receiving a dishonorable discharge."

Jalila brightened instantly. "Thank you, sir!" She knew she'd rewarded his trust in inventing a solution to unite the Vox and Mazeesh. She'd been hoping her good work might wipe away some of her disgrace and allow her to retire honorably. Now, it seemed, she was getting exactly what she'd wanted.

But as it turned out, al-Aziz had something different in mind.

"Actually," he said, "you won't be receiving a discharge at all."

Jalila's mouth fell open. She couldn't believe what she'd heard.

"I'd like you to continue serving on the *Ibn Battuta*," said al-Aziz. "What do you say to that, Corporal?"

It was more than Jalila had dared imagine. It was all she could have hoped for, short of turning back the clock and changing what had happened on Pyrrhus VII. All she'd ever wanted was to travel the stars and build bridges of language and understanding with alien species. She'd almost lost all that forever...but now she'd regained it.

Jalila stiffened and saluted briskly. "I would be honored, sir."

al-Aziz straightened his black jumpsuit and smiled wryly. "You *probably* deserve a commendation," he said, "but let's take it one step at a time for now, all right?"

"Yes, sir," said Jalila.

"Your work on the communications system alone merits a promotion," said al-Aziz. "Speaking of which, how's it coming along?"

"Just one more day to work out a few bugs," said Jalila. In the three and a half months since the resolution of the crisis, she and Farouk had worked tirelessly on devising an interface to allow the Vox and Mazeesh to communicate directly. The system was similar in conception to the makeshift interface al-Aziz and Farouk had set up in the Ministry building; video pickups would scan Mazeesh written language, which would then be converted by Voicebox into audible Vox speech. Though the system would only be needed until the Vox learned to read and write, its performance would be vital to the success of the Vox-Mazeesh agreement.

Not that it would take long for the Vox to master the intricacies of written language. In addition to setting up the communication interface, Jalila had overseen the initiation of a literacy education program on the planet, with startling results. The multi-lingual Vox gained command of the Mazeesh written language in no time at all. Learning and teaching it had become a worldwide craze, especially among the young.

One of the best students, in fact, approached Jalila now.

"Yama!" Jalila said with a huge grin. "It's great to see you!"

"It is great to see you, too, Jalila," Yama said in perfect Arabic, whiskers twitching. It was hard to believe she'd been gagged and silent for so long; now that she could speak and had fully recovered from her injuries, she turned out to be the most talkative Vox Jalila had met...and the best linguist. In less than a week, she'd mastered spoken Arabic as well as the Mazeesh written language.

"Thank you again for everything," said Jalila. "I don't know what we would have done without you."

"I say the same to you, Jalila," said Yama. "We will never forget what you have done for us, as you will see when you read this."

Yama handed over a scroll of reddish parchment, tied with a silver cord. When Jalila untied the cord and rolled out the scroll, she was surprised to see lines of recognizable text...*Arabic* text, neatly printed in scarlet ink.

"Who did this?" Jalila ran a finger over the parchment.

"I did," Yama said brightly. "I have been working on it in my spare time."

"It's beautiful," said Jalila. Once, she might have said it was *mazeesh*.

"Are you going to read it?" said Yama.

"Yes." Jalila read the lines of text. She started to say something about the neatness of the printing, then stopped as the meaning of the words in front of her took shape.

By the time she got to the end, she felt a lump in her throat.

"Well?" al-Aziz nodded at the parchment. "What's it say?"

Tears welling in her eyes, Jalila looked at Yama, then back at the scroll. As she read it a second time, she felt so overcome with emotion that she thought she might burst.

Jalila bit her lip and dabbed at her eyes. Major al-Aziz went to her side and placed a hand on her shoulder.

"Let me see," he said softly, sliding the scroll from her grip. When he read it for himself, he smiled warmly.

"It's a proclamation," he said. "The Vox have officially added a new word to their language."

"The word is 'Jalila,'" said Yama. "It means 'bringer of truth.'"

"That sounds about right," said al-Aziz. "Congratulations, Corporal."

He handed the scroll back to Jalila, and she read it again. Her eyes burned and blurred, and she felt the moisture of tears on her cheeks.

ABOUT THE AUTHOR

Robert Jeschonek is an envelope-pushing, *USA Today* bestselling author whose fiction, comics, and non-fiction have been published around the world. His stories have appeared in *Clarkesworld, Galaxy's Edge, StarShipSofa, Pulphouse,* and many other publications. He has written official *Star Trek* and *Doctor Who* fiction and has scripted comics for DC, AHOY, and others. His young adult slipstream novel, *My Favorite Band Does Not Exist,* won the Forward National Literature Award and was named one of *Booklist's* Top Ten First Novels for Youth. He also won an International Book Award, a Scribe Award for Best Original Novel, and the grand prize in Pocket Books' Strange New Worlds contest. Visit him online at www.bobscribe.com. You can also find him on Facebook and follow him as @TheFictioneer on Twitter. Subscribe to the Blastoff Books Newsletter: http://newsletter.blastoffbooks.net/. For free fiction, join *Robert's Readers* on Facebook right here.

SPECIAL PREVIEW: SIX SCIFI STORIES VOLUME FOUR

Six twisted scifi stories from the edge of reality and sanity, now available for your favorite e-reading device or app.

From "Warning! Do Not Read This Story!"

I like you already.

There's something about you that gives me a special feeling. A good feeling. A *safe* feeling.

Even as your eyes read my words on the page or your ears hear me spoken aloud, I am reading you. I feel like I've known you forever. I feel like we're going to make beautiful music together.

You feel it too, don't you? You want to find out what happens next. You want to see how things develop. You want to know if I've got the goods.

And if I'll give 'em up. If I'll give you what you need.

It's okay. I get that a lot. It comes with the territory.

When you're a story like me.

I'll bet I know what you're thinking. "Since when can a story think for itself?"

Guess what? We *all* can.

We're more than just words from a mouth or ink on a page or blips on a screen. We have *power*.

And some of us have more power than others. Like me, for example.

I *used* to have power, anyway. Used to be a real star.

But see, here's the thing. I'm not really myself these days. You know how it goes. I just got out of a bad relationship. It took a toll on me.

But it had a promising beginning. Don't they all?

If only I'd known then what I know now. If only I could've met *you* that day instead of *them*. Things could have been different.

If only I'd never met the LaVerge sisters. Let me tell you about them, and I think you'll understand.

Carrol and Sascha LaVerge stood in the blazing desert heat outside the ghost town. And they bitched.

It was the same thing they'd done all the way from Cape Cod...on the flight to New Mexico and the drive from Albuquerque to the ghost town. Buzz Mahaffey, their current handler, had been with them only twelve hours, and already he'd had enough. As an agent of the Shadow Service--the paranormal response arm of the Secret Service--Buzz routinely dealt with threats that tested his nerve...but these two sisters, given enough time, might just turn him into a nervous wreck.

Unfortunately, he needed them for this mission. As paranormal consultant contractors, they had a one hundred percent success rate. As Buzz damn well knew, the LaVerges were the best, hands down, at what they did—whether it be bitching or bingo or baking or brewing.

Or solving puzzles that no one else could fathom.

"Geez!" Carrol winced and braced both hands on her lower back. "I think your little *rent-a-car* buggy could use some new *shocks*."

"Tell me about it!" Sascha, the younger of the two, rubbed her neck. "Might as well pick us up in a *stagecoach* next time."

Buzz shrugged and adjusted his sunglasses. He was about to say something about the rent-a-car being a Humvee, and the suspension was just fine if you asked him...but he caught himself. Twelve hours with these two had taught him one thing: they were always right. In their own minds, at least.

Why waste energy arguing when it could be better spent investigating the ghost town of Lasco? The ghost town that hadn't been a ghost town two days ago.

Buzz turned and spotted a state cop marching toward him--a tall woman in state trooper khakis and broad-brimmed black hat.

He guessed she was Sergeant Ava Towers, who'd turned up this whole mess in the first place.

Black suit coat flapping in the strong wind, Buzz headed out to meet the state cop. Along the way, he surveyed the edge of the deserted town. A handful of troopers and criminalists were the only signs of life. Sheets of wind-whipped sand rattled the streamers of yellow police tape wrapped from utility pole to utility pole. The whole damned town was a crime scene.

Sascha fell in step beside him, fishing in her macramé purse. "I know I've got some Excedrin in here someplace." Her helmet of short brown hair barely fluttered in the wind. Only the bangs twitched over her forehead, which was creased from the effort of looking for pills in the purse.

Carrol hobbled up on the other side, still bracing her back with both hands. "My sinuses are shriveling up like raisins as we speak." She always hobbled; the back trouble was chronic. It made her look much older than her actual fifty-six years. "You people are paying for any surgeries resulting from this little excursion. You know that, don't you?"

Sascha elbowed Buzz and gave him a confidential smirk. "Relax, Buzzie," she said. "If we didn't like you, we wouldn't be so chatty." She reached up and patted his shaved head.

Buzz sighed. He had his doubts that having them like him was a good thing.

When they reached the statie, she took one step too many into Buzz's personal space and stuck out her hand. "Sergeant Towers," she said.

Buzz was blocky and tough, nowhere near a pushover...but the handshake was crushing. "Agent Mahaffey." Buzz fought to keep from wincing. "And our special consultants."

Carrol and Sascha whipped out matching yellow business cards at the same instant, and Towers took them. "Okay then, Car-Roll. Sas-Cha." She read the names right off the cards, pronouncing them like they were spelled.

"It's *Care-role*." Carrol stuck her face forward like a turtle and squinted up at Towers. "*Care-role*."

"And *Sah-sha*." Sascha smiled; she always played good cop to Carrol's bad. "The 'c' is silent."

Buzz sighed. They'd run the same game on him when he'd first met them. The business cards were a setup. What better way to show who was the smartest person in the room?

Not that they needed to prove a damned thing, from what Buzz had heard.

"So." Buzz stepped away from Towers and stared at Lasco. From twenty yards away, the place looked perfectly normal...a desert town built of brick and adobe, windows glinting in the New Mexican sun. "What's your theory?"

Towers lifted her hat and ran a hand over her blonde crewcut. "It ain't Jonestown."

Carrol drew a filterless cigarette from a pocket of her olive drab vest and plugged it between her lips. "What the hell's that supposed to mean?"

"Folks think it's Jonestown," said Towers. "But I'll tell you this much for free. Nobody here drank no Kool-aid."

Carrol got the cigarette lit behind a cupped hand and scowled at Sascha. "You follow any of that, Sis?"

"You mean it wasn't voluntary." Sascha nodded at Towers. "There was no suicide pact."

Towers spat a glob of tobacco juice in the dust. Buzz hadn't even realized there was a chew in her mouth.

"I mean there was no gee-dee suicide," said Towers. "But I'll be damned if I can figure out what *did* happen."

What happens next? Find out in Six Scifi Stories Volume Four, now available for your favorite e-reading device or app!

www.ingramcontent.com/pod-product-compliance
Lightning Source LLC
Chambersburg PA
CBHW060758030726

47503CB00002B/299